outskirts press

The Watcher
All Rights Reserved.
Copyright © 2022 Jeffrey D. Barbieri
v1.0

This is a work of fiction. The events and characters described herein are imaginary and are not intended to refer to specific places or living persons. The opinions expressed in this manuscript are solely the opinions of the author and do not represent the opinions or thoughts of the publisher. The author has represented and warranted full ownership and/ or legal right to publish all the materials in this book.

This book may not be reproduced, transmitted, or stored in whole or in part by any means, including graphic, electronic, or mechanical without the express written consent of the publisher except in the case of brief quotations embodied in critical articles and reviews.

Outskirts Press, Inc.
http://www.outskirtspress.com

ISBN: 978-1-4787-7852-3

Cover Photo © 2022 fiverr. All rights reserved - used with permission.

Outskirts Press and the "OP" logo are trademarks belonging to Outskirts Press, Inc.

PRINTED IN THE UNITED STATES OF AMERICA

ONE

I'd been troubled for so long, my mind ached. I had tried to set up roots in a few different places, but nothing ever took. So I wandered. I popped in at home to visit my parents every now and then, but even those trips seemed to depress me more than help. I was lost and I had been for the most part of my life. It's a sad waste of life when soul goes awry. I had such potential, but I never found a way to use it. I was given bits of schooling and training here and there, but never enough in one given category to make the effort truly worth it. I was intelligent enough to get by, almost too smart for my own good. But I never let myself stay in one place long enough to settle or to really figure things out.

The brain is a funny thing. It can twist the truth and let you see things from a point of view that is completely different than that of the next guy or even the rest of the entire, free-thinking world. I liked to think of myself as a positive person, the whole glass was half full thing, but I knew I wasn't fooling anyone. I was born with a hatred that often reared its ugly head. I called it my beast, and if you saw this beast, it was most times followed by someone having their head handed to them. This anger and hatred had grown over the years and had, at some times, consumed me. I had become disgruntled with our country's government and its politics, and often times thought of various ways to overthrow the present establishment through massive death and destruction. In general, I believed this world to be a wicked pace, ruled by 2 idiots and fools. I could not understand why the cattle continued to follow the leaderships of our sovereign nation when the transparency of their selfish plans seemed too obvious.

Our elected officials no longer looked out for the benefit of the people or the country as a whole. They looked out for themselves and their cronies. Most recently, it seemed that oil companies and developers were running our government. Their unscrupulous greed had pointed our nation's entire economy toward a tailspin that we would be hard pressed to recover from. That was my present view of the world. It haunted and pulled at me to do something, but what, I had not a clue. There was precious little that someone like me could really do. So, I bit my tongue and simply tried not to think about it. I buried myself in my work, and booze and marijuana. I clouded my ever-vigilant brain the best I could and just went through the motions of living. But in the process, I had become a bitter middle-aged man without much hope of a future. I spent a good part of my day high on weed and when I clocked out of the job, I crawled inside a bottle of Bud Light. I tried to make my living and just not think about the world that surrounded me and the evil tyrants that ruled its every corner. My opinion meant nothing, and I had precious little hope for anything good to come of my small pathetic life. I had even entertained the idea of suicide from time to time, but just never could give it my all. Something inside of me told me that the price that I would pay for an act such as that was far greater than I could presently grasp. So I just went on and squashed my delusions of grandeur that I had of one day being able to actually help to fix things.

I would try to enjoy the company of my friends and just allow things to fall where they fell. This day, in particular, I was driving three friends out into the desert. It was an already warm Saturday morning. We had left our apartment complex early to avoid the heat the afternoon sun would bring. Along the coastline, it generally stayed between seventy and eighty degrees, but the desert heated up over to a hundred on most summer days. We wanted to get there and back before it got too hot, though I would have loved to have gotten just one more hour of sleep. We had talked about this too many times to blow it off simply because I was tired. I had driven for about an hour and the sun was starting to blaze.

The desert air was dry and hot, but we all sat in the comfort of my car's air conditioning. The little Mitsubishi got good gas mileage and the AC blew very cold. It wasn't the roomiest of vehicles, but it was reliable.

"How much farther?" I asked, knowing full well that we had at least another half an hour or so to drive.

We had decided, rather the group had voted, not to smoke any weed, drink or have any other recreational drugs fresh in our system when we arrived at our destination. This as a long time coming and none of us wanted to ruin it. Needless to say, the lack of sleep and marijuana made for a long, cumbersome drive, and no one answered me. We finally arrived in the area just west of El Centro, California. It was a real gem of a place and couldn't imagine anyone ever really wanted to live here. This was shear desolation as far as the eye could see, nothing but rocks, sand, and the occasional bits of desert grass. I had gotten off of interstate eight and made all of the turns that were dictated to me from the girls in the back seat. We drove another couple of miles and came to an area that just did not seem like it belonged out here in the middle of the vast wasteland. I turned the car onto a long driveway, and we were surrounded on either side by lush greenery. It was as if someone had plucked an entire farm from somewhere completely different and transplanted it here in the middle of the great nothingness.

As we continued, the driveway eventually ended at the large parking area that was surrounded by rows upon rows of crops and several outbuildings.

There were a couple of barns, some old silos and what I imagined were some pump houses or old garages. In the middle of it all was a beautiful, old-style craftsman house. It looked so nice and inviting, like it must have looked the day they finished construction some seventy or eighty years ago. The barns were red with white trim and the house and long picket fence that surrounded the property were bright white. The main structure had all of the cookie cutter accompaniment and spindles on all the corners, a wraparound porch, and window's peak.

It looked like a picture. Though I was extremely anxious to get out of the car and stretch my legs, I had to be wary not to stir up too much dust. This was quite an arid environment, and I could see the cloud of dust I created when I first turned on to the gravel road behind us in the rear-view mirror. I pulled into the clearly marked visitor's parking area and we got out. It felt so good to get out from behind that wheel. My butt was starting to get numb, and my legs were stiff. It didn't feel nearly as hot as I thought it would, though the sun was shining very brightly down upon us now.

"Are we ready to do this or what?" Mark asked as he brushed his hair out of his face and straightened out his shirt.

"Oh yeah! We are so ready," Kimi told him as she straightened her top out as well. It had been a long, boring ride and we had all gotten a bit disheveled.

"Let's do it," she shouted. She as my wild and

crazy next-door neighbor. I loved her because she was so much fun but couldn't hang out with her very much for that same reason. She took things to the extreme and lived what I called an "over-the-top" lifestyle. I will always remember that sweet smell that permeated the air around us. I couldn't really relate the scent to anything, well maybe honeysuckle. It was a little strange, but nice. We walked up onto the long-wooded porch. The paint was cracked and peeling, but it seemed structurally sound. There was an old swing hanging from the ceiling to the right and in front of us was a sort of old, but very ornate doors. Karen walked over to knock, but the old cherry wood door on the right opened just before her hand made contact with it. An old women stood there and looked at us, then offered for us to enter. Karen went in followed by her husband Mark, then Kimi, and finally me. A strange feeling went through me like a wave that flowed from head to toe and back again.

For a brief moment, I wanted to run and leave, but I didn't. I resisted the urge. We had waited too long for this, and I wasn't going to be scared away by a funny feeling. That was before I noticed that the old women was staring at me. I tried not to stare back, but she was a fairly strange looking person. Her gray hair was tied up into a beehive type of style and it looked like it was almost purple in color, and her dress was a silky black. She pointed toward a doorway to the right and we all went in. She continued to look me over as I walked past her. She could have burned holes in me with her eyes, and I felt a tad bit uncomfortable, but I continued to follow my friends. The smell of the air was very different from outside. It was a musty, stale, as though the windows had not been opened for years. There were big bulky antique pieces of furniture in very corner of the room and the shades were pulled so that only a minimal amount of light entered the room. It seemed so lifeless, almost giving off the feeling of death. It was kind of creepy. There were two doors on either side of the little hallway. Both of them were closed except for the one at the far end of the corridor. The floor creaked as we walked across it and I thought our accumulated weight might be enough to send us through it, into the basement below.

The walls were dark blue or gray and ornate wood panels with intricate trim covered the bottom three feet. The carpet runner, which ran from the door we entered to the open door, was old, tattered, and very thin. The next room we walked into was completely different in look and style from the hallway.

We had been talking about going to a "past life regressionist" for quite some time, but it seemed that something always came up to throw us off the path. Kimi and Karen had been here before, and each had a great little story to tell about their trip, so of course Mark and I had been enthralled. This trip wasn't without its drama either. We were supposed to take Kimi's car out here, but it didn't start. I knew the problem was probably easily fixed, but we were not going to mess with it until we had gotten home. If we had to cancel the appointment again, we probably would never have made it, ever. As it stood, we were going to take Kimi's car because Karen's car broke down just prior to our last attempt, and Mark joked that he did not want to get jinxed by planning to use their car again. It almost made me feel like someone or something just did not want us to go. A large chandelier that had probably a few hundred twinkling gems hanging from it brightly lit the room and a red fabric, silk or satin material that reflected some of that light covered the walls. These shimmering curtains ran from floor to ceiling and gave the entire room a reddish tint. There were five chairs surrounding a table that was covered by a cloth similar in material to the wall curtains, but black. The old women asked us to be seated and we took the four chairs closest to us while she took the one on the opposite side of the table. The chairs were old and solid. They were meticulously handcrafted hardwood with very soft paisley cushion on the seats and back. They were surprisingly comfortable, almost conforming themselves to the curves of my body. I felt almost like my chair was sucking me in, like a cushiony mattress. I had been looking forward to this moment for almost a year now. I was enthralled with the stories the two girls had told us about being hypnotized and sent back in time to remember past their lives. Neither of them had spoken in a different language or anything like that, but both had been able to recall strange events and places that neither could remember prior to the hypnosis. Karen had made mention of being on a farm on a lush, green countryside, and Kimi remembered some things about life that involved a castle in medieval times. Neither had anything concrete, but both had vowed to come back here one day to try to dig a little deeper.

"I do not remember you," the old women said looking Mark right in the face.

"You have not been here before." Then she looked over at the girls.

"Both of you have been here before I remember you." Her voice was gruff, kind of hoarse, like she was a lifelong smoker. "I understand why you have come here. You want to be reminded of another life, another time. I can help you." She was stern, but polite. Then she turned her gaze on me and almost seemed to scowl a bit. "Why are you here? Who sent you?" she asked, giving me the stink eye. She was now staring at me with an almost disgusted look on her face. My mouth just hung open. I had no idea what to say. I didn't know if she was joking or is she was mistaking me for someone else. "No one sent me," I told her calmly, but with a hint of a smile. I looked over to my three friends on my left and they each gave a "what the heck" look. Again, I wanted to run and leave, but I did not. I wanted to go, but my feet seemed frozen to the ground and my butt to the chair, and I just sat there. "I came for the same reasons that my friends did, to see if I could remember a past life." My words did not faze her. She continued to glare at me. "I just thought it would be fun," I told her. "Do not toy with my young man.

What we are going to do here is not a joke." There was no hint of sarcasm or joy in her voice now. She was being serious, not maybe just pussyfooting around. The problem was, I still had no clue what the heck she was talking about or why she seemed to be picking directly on me.

"Look maam, I'm sorry. I didn't mean to be rude or disrespectful. I apologize. I thought you were kidding. I can assure you that I have never been here before, nor have I ever done anything like this."

She seemed to not even hear me, just continuing her hard gaze. I grasped for something, anything to say. "Honestly, if I have offended you, then I would be more than happy to go outside and wait so at least my friends here can benefit from this trip. "I was earnest. I was indeed willing to get up and walk out. I didn't know why she had singled me out, but we had worked too hard to get there just to turn empty-handed. If she didn't like me, there was nothing I could do, but I was not going to let my friends down just because this old bird had a bug up her butt about me. My kind words seemed to get to her.

"I also apologize then. Perhaps I was mistaken." Her voice was now slow and measured, calm, the bitterness gone. "I thought that you had been sent here to test me." She still held an even stare borderline on a glare, but it had softened very slightly. And though she did apologize, I was reasonable sure that she didn't fully mean it. She turned the dial on the table and the lights dimmed noticeably.

Quickly enough, the room seemed to fade around us. The bright twinkle of the curtains that surrounded the room disappeared to the sparkle here and there. I was slightly mesmerized by it and have to say that it was a nice effect.

"I would like to start with you, then," she said referring to Karen.

"Please place your hands palm up, flat on the table. I want you to take a long deep breath and let it out.

Relax and listen to my words." She placed her open hands, palms down into Karen's.

"You are going to get very sleepy."

Her words were soothing, very calming, and even I started to feel tired. I had never really been sure whether or not I could be hypnotized, so perhaps in a way, I was testing the old broad. I watched the proceedings with a good deal of skepticism. I didn't have too much faith that this process would even work, let alone show us something from another time and place. I listened intently to her words, and she really didn't seem to be saying anything extraordinary. But soon enough, Karen was out. She kind of slumped a little bit and then seemed noticeably asleep. The old women's voice was so mellow and even.

She asked her what her name was and where she had lived. Karen mumbled some things, but nothing coherent. Then she asked her what she had done and what her surroundings looked like. Again, all of the questions were met with a slurry, undefined response. When she finished, she called for her to awaken before continuing on to her husband. Karen woke up but seemed very groggy. She sat there quietly as the women followed the same routine with her husband before moving on to Kimi. Each of my friends seemed to experience the same aftereffects. It was as if they had all been in a deep sleep that they were having a hard time waking up from. I looked at them and could feel the nervousness growing in my stomach. I wasn't scared, but well, let's just say I was very unsure. She seemed to have such a chip on her shoulder for me, still holding that hard stare when she looked upon me, but she proceeded, nonetheless. I sat there with hands on the table, palms up, just like my predecessors. She put her delicate, wrinkled hands into mine and I could immediately feel a tingle. It was like some kind of energy passing between us. She shook her head slightly and flinched a tiny. Bit. I thought that she might want to stop, to pull her hands away from mine but she didn't.

"Close your eyes and relax. Tune out everything around you and listen to my voice," she started.

"Let it take you in and embrace you, surround you." Her words seemed too comforting.

"You are feeling sleepy. Your eyelids are heavy." As I listened, I could actually feel my eyelids getting heavier. She continued to speak, ever so softly, even and calm. Eventually those comforting words seemed to blend into a long drone, almost like a buzz in my ears. I felt myself starting to slump in my chair, but I could not move to pull myself up. I wasn't really sure that I even wanted to, but I did not want to fall onto the floor either. Waves of energy ran through my hands, up and down my body, draining me, pulling at me. It was almost euphoric, but then it started to change. The pulling feeling started to grow, first at my feet, then it worked its way up into my stomach and lungs. I was having a hard time catching my breath and I started to gasp. It was pulling at my stomach, almost to the point of pain. It was the strangest feeling, both of pleasure and agony. I wanted to call out, to scream for it to stop. It was too much. I couldn't take it. The pulling got so intense I thought I was going to be ripped in half. I could not breathe. I wanted to beg for it to stop, but I couldn't. I couldn't open my mouth. My entire body was unresponsive. I got scared and started to panic. I thought that I was going to be pulled in two, then suddenly, just like that, it stopped, and the most wonderfully relaxed feeling encompassed my body. I suddenly felt better than I think I ever had before, so powerful so strong, almost like I could fly. It was incredible.

I sat there waiting for her to say something, but she didn't. I did, however, sense that something had change. The musty smell of the house was gone, and I could almost feel a breeze, like someone had just opened all the windows. It was so clean and so fresh. I decided to open my eyes. I was expecting to see the old women sitting across the table with solemn look, maybe even a smile. A few months back I had been knocked out by an acupuncturist and when I woke up and the fuzz cleared from my mind and eyes, the girl who had stuck all of the needles in me, was sitting in front of me smiling. She had done a good job and she knew it. She was just waiting to hear how happy and relaxed I had become. This was similar feeling, and what I was expecting here. But instead of seeing the lady seated across from me, I saw something totally unexpected and absolutely amazing. I was no longer in the old house out in the desert, but instead I was out in the open, way open. I seemed to be high up on a mountainside, just above the clouds. It was a great rocky field. It looked like I could be on the moon or inside of a dormant volcano. It was desolate. There were other mountaintops around me in the distance. They too were shrouded in a mist, which lightly covered the immense rock on which I stood.

The air was crisp, and I could see traces of my breath. I had the same clothes on, shorts, t-shirt, and sandals, but I wasn't cold. Yet all around me there was snow here and there on all of the other mountains as well. This was too weird. I pinched myself on the arm, but nothing happened. So, I pinched real hard, to the point of bringing a tear to my eye, and again nothing. Then I remembered. This was what I had wanted, the reason I had gone to see the old bird. I must have been a goat herder or a mountaineer. This was awesome. I could not have dreamed that my visions would be so vivid. I looked around for my climbing gear or my rod and staff. I looked for a clue that would show me what I was doing there. Then someone stepped out from behind a rock outcropping in front of me that made me question the whole thing. I rubbed my eyes to make sure that I was not seeing things. This should not be, I thought to myself. How could it be? But it was. I looked real hard at the person standing before me.

His hair was long and straight and he was dressed in what looked like a one-piece black tunic. He wore round-rimmed sunglasses with blue tinted lenses and seemed to have at least one ring for every finger.

He shuffled out from the rocks using a black cane with a fancy silver top. He looked at me, straightened his clothes and himself and walked toward me.

"Lovely," he said, "just lovely." He continued to walk and shuffle toward me.

"Do you know what you've done here, son?" he asked in a slurry British accent. I did not answer immediately. I just stood there with my mouth hanging open. It was strange enough to see this person standing here in front of me, but to have him actually speak directly to me was over the top.

"Hey son," he said, "my name's Chalmers, I'm here to help."

I thought about things for a moment and wanted to laugh. So, this was supposed to be my past, I thought. It made no sense. This was when I realized that it was just all a dream, figment of my crazy brain. Chalmers didn't take too kindly to the smirk that must have fallen across my face.

"I asked you a bloody question," he said with a very abrupt tone. He moved right up to me and got up into my face. I didn't know what to do, what to think.

Was this some sort of bad trip, like the time I ate some bad acid and thought I was going to lose my mind? I didn't have the cramping and the vomiting I did that night, but the simi-nauseous waves running through my body and the strange visuals did seem familiar. I opened my mouth to speak, but no words came out.

"No boy, this isn't a bad trip or even a hallucination," Chalmers told me, as if he were reading my mind.

"This is something you asked for; something you should have left alone." He took a half step back and looked me over. "We may both be in for it now," he said with a bit of a scowl. I did not laugh out loud this time. I was being scolded. How comical. This was not what I expected, but I was still quite amazed.

"What are you talking about?" I asked him with a smile. I joked because I didn't care. It didn't matter what happened here. I was going to wake up any second in the old women's room with a crazy story to tell, and my friends and I were all going to share a laugh over it. He hauled off and whacked me with his cane. "Does seem real enough to you?" he asked angrily. "I don't know the extent of the damage you did, and I don't know how much time we have together, so shut up and listen." He had my undivided attention now. He had cracked me pretty hard on the left upper arm, and it stung.

"I'm sorry sir, forgive me, but I don't have any idea what you are talking about." I gritted my teeth and tensed the sore spot.

"But rest assured, I am listening to you," I told him as I rubbed my arm a bit. "Don't placate me. I can hear what you're thinking. I need you just to shut up and pay attention." He ran a hand down the side of his tunic to straighten it, then pushed some of his hair back out of his face and over his shoulder.

"You have opened a door that may or may not close at any moment. We have precious little time to talk." He stopped and looked over each shoulder as though he was afraid that someone might walk up behind him. "I'm going to be blunt here, boy, so bear with me. Do you know why you are here?" "Well, that's pretty much the question that has stymied all of mankind for its entire existence," I started off, but was cut off. "I'm not talking about the human race, you mook. I'm talking about you and your punishment.

Do you remember anything about it?"

Now that was strange thing for him to say. Something in the back of my head clicked. I had always felt that I was under some kind of punishment. I don't know why I thought that way; I just did. It seemed that no matter how hard I tried, I just couldn't get ahead. I felt as though I was being punished and I didn't know why. It had, until now, been just a weird thought that came and went in my mind. So many things ran through my mind, that I didn't know what to say. He stood there for a moment, waiting for an answer. Then he finally spoke. "Well do you remember those?" he asked, nodding toward me. I figured that he was referring to something behind me, and I was honestly a bit afraid to look. I turned slowly, not sure what to expect. I've always had a pretty vivid imagination and often remember some of the crazy dreams that I had. If Chalmers was here, then who would know what other creature might be back there. I had some pretty wicked nightmares in my lifetime and was preparing myself to see some crazy monster. But was I completely unprepared for what I saw. Attached to my back were two very large, fluffy, white wings. They were big. Then as if by sheer instinct, I moved my chest and the wings moved up and out a bit. I flexed my shoulders and back and they expanded out to at least a ten- or ten-and-a-half-foot span. I then tightened my chest muscles in, then out and was able to move them up and then down. I was beginning to remember, and the more I played with them, the easier it became to make them move. I was really working them, feeling the burn in my chest, when Chalmers shouted at me.

"Bullocks! Enough of that! You can play later. We have some serious business to attend to." He looked over his right shoulder, then his left. "I don't know how much time we have." He got close to me. "How much do you remember?" I was still playing with the wings. It was so strange. It was like I had them along. I even contemplated trying to fly, but had Chalmers interrupted me. "Remember?" About what?"

I asked. "About why you are here, about your punishment." I was miffed. I shook my head, not knowing what to say, but before the words came out of my mouth, I knew what he was talking about. I seemed to drift from one dream to another, from the cool relaxed mountaintop to the middle of a ware zone. It was absolute chaos. My senses were all rushing to catch up and I suddenly couldn't believe the craziness that surrounded me. The smell was horrific and there seemed to be fire falling out of the sky in every direction. There were angels and demons waging battle in the air and on the ground. It was insanity. I hurried to hide myself behind an outcropping of rocks to watch from a relatively safe spot. It was absolute carnage. There were angels, or what looked like angels, all dressed in gold and silver armor on the ground and in the skies. They had shields and swords and there seemed to be rays of light and ball of fire impacting the ground around me. I pulled myself up tight against the rocks and tried to see what the angels were fighting but saw nothing but dark spots here and there. Then I realized that the little black shadows were what they were attacking, and the darks things were fighting back. I looked in awe as the things launched their counterattack. They shot great balls of nothingness up into the skies. The giant black globs leapt out of cannons up into the fiery bright sky and exploded in the midst of the oncoming angels. The blackness and streaks of blue and purple light stretched out of the explosions, reaching out for their enemies. The blackness spread out about a hundred yards in all directions then imploded in on itself. I watched as the angels hacked and slashed at the shadowy demons. It was surrealistic, but no more than seeing Chalmers on the mountainside. My gaze jumped from skirmish to skirmish. I had to duck out of the way a couple of times but could not look away from the battle. As I watched, something deep inside me told me that I had been here before. I watched the dark beings seem to grow out of the ground. It was as if the shadows that had been cast by the fading sunlight had come to life and were attacking the angels as they flew out of the sky toward them. The angels just sliced through them or shined a light on them causing them to fall back into the nothingness from which they came. This was a battle of light and dark, and it seemed that the light was winning. It also seemed oddly familiar. This was a desolate place, barren. Rock formations jutted up through the cracked, dry ground, reaching up into the heavens. The brown colored terrain gave way to black chary spots here and there were explosions had burned the ground. The twin suns were rising, creating shadows at the base of the rocky mounds.

This it seemed, was the breeding point for the black monsters. They flowed like a river from the darkness, quickly breaking off into individual creatures. Each piece that broke off took on a life of its own and immediately went to work attacking the angels. The angels, themselves, were magnificent.

They were clad in silver and gold armor, like knights with wings. They carried broadswords and shields, which glistened in the suns' light. Their shiny round shields seemed to form a force field of blue light, which propelled the attackers, blocking them, blasting them to bit. The swords not only cleaved through the shadows, but they also emitted a fierce blue stream of light energy, which engulfed and destroyed every beast it touched. They wore helmets with nasty looking face shields. Their arms and legs were protected by chains, and they all wore similar bright, silver breastplates. Explosions burst all around me and I used my arm to shield my face. "What are you hiding from?" a voice that sounded like it came from inside my head asked. "You cannot be harmed here." It was Chalmers. He appeared around a hundred feet in front of me, walking toward me, through the chaos. He did not duck or move out of the way as fire and streaks of black and blue fire erupted all around him. "Do you remember this?" he asked nonchalantly. I looked at him in awe for a moment, then up at the corps of angels that were descending upon us. And then it was as if a veil had been lifted from me and I remembered. I had once been an angel of the corps that now battled tooth and nail in front of me. Not only had I been one of them, I was a leader, a general. And thought things did not presently look to promising, I knew that my soldiers were about to clean house. We had never lost a skirmish such as this, at least not under my watch. I turned and looked at Chalmers. "Punishments over I take it?" I asked, puffing out my chest, preparing myself to enter the fracas. I could feel the blood pumping through my veins, the power in my hands. I had waited a long time for this, and I was going to take out my angst on the shadow demons. "There in lies the problem, my boy. Your punishment is not over. This is something completely different." He walked right up to me and stopped. Then he reached out and waved his hand in front of my face and we were suddenly back on the mountain. I still had the juices flowing through my body and I wanted to fight.

"Why did you do that? My troops need me," I told him angrily. "If you only knew how true that statement was," he affirmed, looking away. He stepped back and started to pace around, the mountain mist shrouding his feet. “I need to go back,” I demanded. “I’m afraid that’s not possible,” Chalmers told me. “What we have here is a bit of bloody head game.” He grasped his right hand with his left behind his back and looked hard at the ground as he continued to walk in a small oblong circle. “You see, you are not supposed to be here yet. I know it sounds strange, but it is not your time. Your punishment isn’t over. You opened a door to a different dimension, and now we are here together.” He took a long breath and let it out, then smiled slightly. “I shouldn’t even be here, talking to you like this. It shouldn’t be possible.” My blood slowed from a boil to a simmer, but I was still worked up. “I don’t thing I understand. My punishment isn’t over, yet here I am.” The smell and the taste of the battle still tickled my senses. He got closer and looked me dead in the eye. “I know this is going to be hard to understand, but you do have go back.” I had an idea of what he meant, and I so did not like the sound of it. “Go back to what?” I asked. My head swam now. I was calming, but I was still quite agitated. I prayed that he was not talking about sending me back into that earthly shell when my men needed me so badly. “What exactly is going on here?” I rubbed the back of my head. Chalmers took a step backward, but still held an even gaze. “You, in your infinite wisdom, decided to be a hypnotize. That process opened a door that may or may not fully close again.” “And that means?” I interrupted. "That, my boy, means that we have a problem. It means that you are going to have some aspects of this old life of yours creeping through into your human life." I continued to give him a look like I still did not fully understand. I was here now.

This was no dream and my troops needed me. What else could there be? "This life of yours as a general in the corps of angels isn't over. It has merely been put on hold until you've been deemed worthy to return to it. You must continue on a mortal human being until you learn your lesson. Unfortunately, parts of your true identity will undoubtedly bleed through," he said in as plain terms as he knew possible. I let his words sink in. I did not throw any more questions at him, I just thought about what he was saying. I was beginning to understand now, but I wasn't happy with it.

All of this did explain my delusions of grandeur that I had since I could remember. I had always thought I was meant for bigger and badder things, but I couldn't have fathomed anything on this level. "I can't go back to that life of misery. I can't. I don't belong there. I've learned my lesson. I need to go home.

Please," I begged, knowing full well what Chalmers was going to say. It was not up to him. There were far greater powers dictating my destiny. "I am sorry, but you must go back. You must find a way to curb that violent streak of yours that got you into trouble in the first place. You have to find some semblance of self-control." Then he seemed to think that someone was behind him, quickly turning and looked over his right shoulder. "I'm afraid I don't have much time here. To be honest with you, I'm not really sure how or why we were permitted this brief moment together, other than the fact that the corps so desperately needs you." "Ok," I concluded calmly. "What do I have to do to be able to go home?" "If it were that easy, I would have dropped you a hint some time ago. Unfortunately, I don't bloody well know." He looked around for a minute before continuing. "I really have no idea. The best advise I can give you is to contain that wicked mean streak of yours. You know, try not to kill anyone. I think if you can do this, your punishment might be rescinded." Sounded easy enough. "Well, I'm sure as hell not going to kill anyone. That much is sure," I told him. I did have quite a temper, and I have had my share of fights along the way, but I was trying to think differently now. I was trying to relax and go with the flow. Granted, there were sometimes when I could have killed someone with my bare hands, but I was trying to put that behind me. I was working hard to respect karma and live a better life. It was a recent epiphany, one that was long overdue. "I hear you talking, but remember, I have been watching you for a few thousand years. I've watched you make the same mistakes over and over, never seeming to learn a bloody thing. Now you are going to act like some kind of a saint. I'm sorry, I just know you too well." He almost sounded a bit disgusted, condescending. "Come on," I started, but Chalmers cut me of.

He gave me the open palm, the "talk to the hand" gesture. "Hey man, I was there when you cracked that guy over the head with the whiskey bottle a few years back. Do you remember that? You were all jealous and pissy, got drunk and clobbered the guy. You easily could have killed him." "But I didn't," I told him with a smirk. I remembered what he was talking about. There had been an incident where I had thrown a party and several uninvited guests had decided to show up well after an entire bottle of Jack Daniels had been consumed. A girl I had been seeing had brought some guys to the party to show off.

Well, I ended up showing them what was what. I had asked them to leave and when they refused, I blasted the one closest to me with an empty bottle. Glass shards flew everywhere and the next thing you know, everyone was brawling. "And what about the bloke in the McDonald's parking lot back in Pennsylvania? You actually tried to kill him." Again, I knew exactly what he was talking about. I was sitting in my car with a friend. I was in the passenger seat. My buddy was talking to a mutual friend, or someone that I thought was a friend out of the driver's side window. Some "he said, she said" was being tossed around, and the next thing I knew, the guy came around to my side of the car and punched me hard in the face. I never saw it coming, nor did I remember getting out of the car, but I do remember beating the piss out of the dude. I cracked his head off the asphalt hard enough that he had to wear a bandage around his head to school for a couple of weeks. I had snapped and had the best intentions of choking him to death, and had it not been for my buddy pulling me off the guy, I most likely would have.

"And the bloke up in Allentown? The fellow you hit so hard that he flew off the porch and over the hedge? You remember him, right? Did you know that you fractured his jaw?" I remember that incident too. I had gone up to Allentown to surprise my girlfriend by bringing her out for a night on the town with the rowdy boys. I had gone up onto her porch to knock on the door and could see that she was quite surprised to see me when she answered. She was already dressed to go out, but it wasn't with me that she had gotten dolled up for. The look in her eye told me that something was drastically wrong, and a minute later her date pulled up. I told myself not to hit him. Repeated that thought over and over again in my mind, but when he walked right up to me and smiled, I just decked him, sent him clear up and over the bushes. I didn't even fully remember doing it. I just saw my fist and his feet up in the air in front of me. "You are lucky that she loved you like she did. The kind of money that the guy had was hard for anyone to ignore. She loved you but was enthralled with the lifestyle that he offered her. She did keep you out of jail and out of court, but it meant that she would never be able to see you again." That struck a chord with me. It was a pearl of wisdom that was previously unbeknownst to me. "I never did see her again," I told him solemnly. I had always thought that she just didn't care that much about me. Now I learn that she really did, but even more than I ever could have imagined. She really was one of the good ones that had gotten away. He could see that I was having a moment but knew that he had precious little time to bestow his wisdom upon me. "I'm sure that this is hard for you to hear, but this kind of behavior is what got you punished in the first place. You have to learn to control yourself. You have to holster the anger." He looked down at the ground and then back up at me. He then straightened out his sunglasses and ran a hand through his long hair. "Look, I'm not sure what you are going to remember when you wake up from this but try to make an effort to keep your head. There is never a need to kill or fight. There is always an option. Just walk away. You will have to try to..." he started to say but did not finish. Everything around me quickly seemed to fade to black. "Remember." His words echoed in my head. I wanted to reach out for him. I needed to anchor myself to that world, that dimension, but I couldn't. I was being pulled away. The strange feeling that I had in my stomach when all of this had started had returned, but this was much more powerful. It pulled at me, and I doubled over in pain.

Then I woke up on the tattered paisley carpet of

the old women's house. "Joey, are you alright? Kimi asked as she jumped out of her chair and knelt down to check on me. I was groggy and my muscles hurt.

I wanted to jump up, but I really couldn't move at first. It felt to me like I had been asleep for days, and during that entire time, I had been clenching hard, my whole body, tight like a knot. It was like the time I ran the jackhammer for about four hours straight and when I was done, I couldn't let go of it. The action and vibration and the fact that I had held it so tight for so long had me locked to it. My boss had to come over and pry my fingers from the handles. That was how I felt, but this feeling ran throughout my entire body. I was literally as stiff as a board. Eventually I stirred and opened my eyes. "I'm okay," I finally managed, but I wasn't really positive that I truly was okay. Slowly but surely, I started to move my appendages, wiggling each finger and toe back to reality. "Oh man Joey, you were out," she said as she put her palm on my forehead to check on me. As I started to come around, and began to pull myself up, I wondered to myself if any of what I had witnessed could possibly be true. Even now it seemed so real. I felt like I truly belonged up in the orange, purple skies with the other angels. The words, "kill them all echoed inside of my mind. The blood lust of the death of demons and shadows still pulled at me. I wondered why I knew that sunrise was the best time to attack a shadow armada because it was then that they were in their weakest state. It was the time that they were exposed by the rising sun. Why, did I know this? Why should I know that? I pulled myself up first to my knees, then back up onto the chair. I was groggy. “How long was I out for?” I asked Kimi, blinking my eyes, I was still not fully able to see through the fog that filled my mind. “About twenty seconds. You went under, slumped down and then fell out of your chair. Do you remember anything” she asked as she ran her hand through my hair and down onto my neck then gently rubbed it for a few seconds. My vision started to clear, but my head still swam a bit. I looked at my wiggling fingers and at my left forearm which was still partially asleep. I tried to shake out the whole pins and needles feeling and that’s when I saw it. Out of the corner of my eye, I saw it. I allowed my gaze to linger for a brief moment so that my mind could catch up and comprehend what I was seeing. I rubbed my eyes, but it was still there. I looked back over my other shoulder and saw a similar sight. I still had the wings, big white fluffy wings. How was this possible, and why had no one else mentioned it? You would think someone would have said something, anything. But no one said a word about it. I sat there with my mouth hanging open for a minute, not sure quite what to say. “I can’t really remember anything,” I lied. It just rolled out of my mouth. I even tried to make it sound like I was disappointed. “I pretty much feel like I just took a long nap.” I hated lying to my friends, or lying in general, but I didn’t feel I had much of a choice. If they weren't going to say anything about the wings, then neither was I. I was just handed a whole lot of I wasn't sure what to think about any of it just yet.

But when glanced across the table, I could see the old women staring at me. Her eyes were a bit wider than they were before, and I swear that she didn't blink a few minutes. She did not take her gaze from me, but she did not speak either. It was kind of freaky. What was I really gonna tell them? I mean, I could still smell the remnants of the battle that I witnessed in my nose. It was the scent of sulfur and death. I had a bit of a headache, and I could feel that my head must have bounced off of the floor pretty hard. I was slightly rattled, still trying to figure out what I had just seen. "No, I can't remember anything," I said, shaking my head. The women still hadn't blinked, but instead of the hard stare she had been throwing my way earlier, her eyes seemed wide with amazement. I sat there for a couple seconds to catch my bearings, shaking off the grogginess. "Wow," I said, "I was really out. Did I say anything?"

"You didn't say anything that we heard," Mark told, laughing a little. "Dude, we all went through the same thing, but you just passed out and went down like a rock. "How's your head?" he half chuckled.

Kimi rubbed the back of my head and found the spot that had made contact with the floor. "Ouch!" I winced, pulling my eyes from the lady's. "I'm sorry," she said kindly. Hey, do you know what I saw?"

she asked from behind me. I was sort of nestled up against her. "I was a concubine in the harem in ancient Egypt," Kimi told me with a smile. This made perfect sense. She was pretty wild and fun, so it seemed quite apropos. "And I was a princess with a castle and servants," Karen added. "And Mark here was a shepherd on a hillside," she continued, with a smile. "Dude, just what I expected. I was a shepherd in charge of goats. Get it? I was in charge of goats, all lonely and out in the hills. Explains a lot, doesn't it?"

He was so funny. Mark and Karen were the perfect couple. They had married out of convenience, but all of their friends knew they would be together forever. They complimented each other perfectly. Karen and Kimi had been roommates before she and Mark were married. Now only Kimi lived next door to me in our little "Melrose" style apartment complex. Melrose Place was a television show in the late 80's, early 90's about a group of people that lived in a place similar to mine. All of the doors pointed inward, towards the center, in our case the pool. Everybody knew everyone else's business. And just like in the show, people from one apartment hooked up with people in another from time to time. Every so often we would get to see a neighbor come out of one door and go into their own, first thing in the morning.

We called this the walk of shame. It was always comical to catch someone creeping around the place with motely hair and wrinkled clothes, especially if you knew both partied involved. Mark glanced at the old women across the table from us and realized that she was staring at me. “Uh, how much do we owe you?” he asked trying to snap her out of the semi-trance she seemed to have fallen into. He pulled his wallet from his back pocket, and when she didn’t respond, he waved it in front of her. She finally pulled her gaze from me and told us there would be no charge. Well of course that brought a twinkle to Kimi’s eyes. We were always all so broke that any little bit helped. “Okay, that was fun. Let’s go” she said as she got out of her chair, in a hurry to leave before the women changed her mind. “Are you sure?” Karen asked as she returned her wallet to her little purse. She gave the lady a smile and also hurried to get up and get out of the house. I made the same effort but moved a great deal slower. Mark almost had to help me stand up, but I finally managed. I was still pretty slow and more than a bit stiff, and I had to be very careful not to knock anything over on the way out, especially with my wings. I had pulled them in as tight as I could, trying not to look like I was holding them in. I probably looked a bit awkward, but what was I gonna do?

The sun seemed a whole lot brighter when we got outside. We all donned our sunglasses and I wondered how I was going to get into the car with my wings as I walked toward the light. There was no way I was going to be able to do it without looking like a fool. The old women had followed us to the door and was still giving me the hard stare. I knew she could see the wings; I knew it. I wanted to stop and ask her, but I also just wanted to get into the car and go home and figure this out. But it was her earlier words that still rang out in my head. She thought I was there to test her, and I guess, in the end, I really was. I kept wanted to stop and go back. I had a couple of questions I needed answers to. Her expression had given way to my idea that she knew something about what had just happened, and I needed to speak to her alone. I had to know what she had been staring at, whether or not she saw them. We all walked toward the car, but Karen stopped us. “Wait,” she said. “We have to give her something. Come on, her house smelled like moth-balls.” She was correct. It was the right thing to do.

So, we kicked in twenty bucks apiece and when she turned to walk back toward the house, I took that as my opportunity. I decided to go with her. I had to ask the lady if she could help me or knew what was going on. “Maam,” I asked after Karen almost had to force the money on her. “Can you tell me if you saw anything that I might need to know about?” Now I didn’t mean to, but I think I scared her a little.

Karen and I both sensed that, and then even she gave me a look. The poor, frail women simply stepped back and slammed the door real hard. That was that. So I figured I had no choice now. We just turned and headed to the car.

"What was that all about?" Karen asked me.

"I have no idea. The whole thing has me weirded out. Did this sort of thing happen the last time you guys came here?" "Ah, no," she said sarcastically. "I would have definitely warned you in advance if I thought there was a chance you might fall and have your head cracked open." We got to the car, and I thought about how I was going to get into the driver's seat. It was a little car, an oldie but a goody. It was roomy, but not that roomy. Karen noticed my trepidation.

"I'll drive," she insisted. "Roll the window down and relax." "Come on Joey. Snap out of it. We have some drinking to do when we get home. Sit in the front and roll us up a couple of joints for the ride,"

Mark clowned. "Yeah Joey," Kimi called from the seat behind Mark, "roll em up. Get to twistin." Karen then jumped in the driver's seat, and I gently, ever so gingerly sat down behind her. I eased my way back into the seat, not knowing if it would hurt to lean like that against the wings. Like an old timer, I leaned back super slowly, but the crunch I braced for never came. My back made contact with the upright part of the chair, and I didn't feel a thing. There was no crackles or pops, no nothing. I took a quick glance back over my left shoulder and was completely amazed to see that my wing had passed through and seemed embedded into the seat itself.

"Are you okay?" Kimi asked, with a look of concern. I looked up and saw her looking at me checking out my wings. "Yeah, I'm good, just a little stiff, that's all," I told her with a smile. I had gotten mesmerized by the sight of my wings sticking through the seat and got caught.

"You guys have something to roll on up there?" Karen handed me a magazine and Mark reached into his pants pocket and handed me a plastic zip lock bag that contained about three or four grams of some good California green leaf. She started the car and I started to roll. I had a little weed myself, so I mixed the two in a nice pile on the magazine, then spun a perfect joint. I flipped it over to Kimi, "Lady's first," I said with a smile "That's what I'm talking about," she joked, pulling out her lighter. I took one last look over my shoulder at the strange old house in the middle of the desert. I thought, for a second, that I could see the old women peeking out through the lacey curtains at me, but I wasn't sure. I also wasn't sure whether or not this whole trip might have been the beginning of the greatest adventure of my life or the biggest mistake I had ever made.

TWO

The drive home through the desert was long and my mind reeled the whole way. I was so deep in thought that I didn't even realize that we had parked sitting outside my apartment complex. Kimi was already out of the car and headed in through the front gate before she looked to see that I wasn't behind her. "Come on Joey, Wake up. Let's party." Then she hurried up the stairs to her apartment. "You okay?" Karen asked as she opened the door. Karen and Mark had moved to the other side of town a few months ago, and they had planned to go home and shower before their night of drinking would commence. "Yep, just spacing out. What a weird day," I commented as I got out of the car. I was still a little stiff, and I swear my joints creaked when I managed to straighten myself out. I peeked over my shoulder to watch the wings slip out of the cloth material that covered the back seat. "I'll see you guy later, right?" The bright white wings left the gray seat cover and even passed the metallic door jam.

They went through the metal just like they went through the cloth. It was kind of amazing, yet scary.

"Oh yeah," they both said with a smile. Then they went over to their car, waved good-bye and drove off. I headed up to the stairs to my place. I lived right at the top of the steps and Kimi lived in the apartment next door. "Later," I yelled over to her, but got no reply. I assumed that she hears me and went into my place. The door was locked so I knew my roommate wasn't home. Dan worked in the retail industry and had a strange schedule, so we often missed each other, and that was fine with us. It wasn't that we didn't like each other, but rather it almost felt like I had the place to myself a lot and so did he. I walked in and went to the bathroom. This was the first time I was able to look in the mirror and see what the wings looked like. It was the weirdest thing. I moved the muscles in my chest and back and they moved accordingly. It didn't take me long to figure out what muscles controlled what. I must have stood there for fifteen minutes playing before I heard Kimi yelling in my door. "Joey, let's do a shot!" I never even thought to close the door when I was home. I had been in such a hurry to look in the mirror, I just spaced out. It didn't matter though, as a few of us liked to all share the open-door policy. She was already in the living room when I peeked out of the bathroom. I was down for a shot right now. I could really use something to try to settle my restless mind, and a little booze did sound good right about now.

"I'll be right there," I told her. I wanted to try one

more time to move something, my toothbrush, the shower curtain, anything with my wings before hitting the sauce. I was enthralled and I was going to have a difficult time not playing with them all day and night. I spread them out and turned back and forth. It was so strange. I could touch them with my hand. I could even feel the touch through the wing itself. I squeezed a part of the right one. It was sort of boney along the top edge, perhaps made a cartilage. They came out of my back and seemed to be partially attached to my shoulder blades as well as the big muscles of my torso. That joining allowed for me to control the boney mast. I called it a mast because the feathery part attached to it was like a sail. It was like a sheet stretched from the shoulder blade to the tip of the joined mast. They looked heavy, but they were pretty much weightless, and I had total control over them. I could move the tip of each wing like I could my finger. How did it work? How did the mind move the toes? I willed the muscles and the tendons to move, and they did. The wings worked the same way. They were, as solid feeling as my arms and legs, but they passed through everything else. Even water ran right through them. I wondered how I would keep them clean, and then, would they even get dirty? It was all so strange. I could have played for hours, but I had a guest, and it did appear that these things were not going away any time soon. "What are we having?" I asked as I came out of the bathroom with a big smile on my face. Dan and I shared a two-bedroom apartment that sat about three blocks from the Pacific Ocean. It was cozy, sometimes too cozy, but we made do. We had mutual respect for each other, and we were friends, so it made things fairly easy. Our complex was a simple concrete style box that surrounded the pool. It was no Four Seasons, but it was nice enough.

There were about twenty-six units, and the two-story structure protected the interior from the wind. So on those days where the wind as strong to sit at the bench without getting sand blasted, it made for a nice warm environment. It also gave the ladies a nice sheltered place to lay out and tan. "Oh baby, I scored a bottle of Don Julio," she said as she headed into the kitchen. She opened the refrigerator and grabbed a lemon and sliced it into little wedges. Now I felt Don Julio was so good and smooth that I didn't need the salt and lemon, but since the work had already been done, I thought I would oblige my guest. One shot down then two, and then three. We chased them all with some Bud Lights that were nearly frozen. This was what I needed right about now. My apartment was on the second floor on the street side of the large building, and it had a great view down the road almost all the way to the ocean. I got to see a lot of pretty girls walking by on their way to the beach every weekend through those windows. That spot was truly a bonus and was always appreciative for having it. Kimi and I sat at the kitchen table and watched as the sun got lower and lower, getting ever closer to the edge of the horizon. This was always my favorite time of the day when things got so bright and colorful. "What time does Dan come home?" Kimi asked as we sat and finished our beers. "I don't know. His schedule is a mystery. Want another beer? I asked, getting up to get myself a fresh one. I grabbed two and cracked them open, then handed her one. I put the bottle to my mouth and let the cold liquid just pour down my throat. It was both tasty and refreshing and felt so good to relax I set my beer on the table and admired the setting sun. The sky was a mix of red, orange, blue and purple. It was another magnificent San Diego sunset. I had a bit of a buzz and felt almost inspired. That was right before I heard the sound of explosions echoing from behind me. I turned to look at what had made the noise and suddenly I was back on the battlefield. I was back in the midst of the shadow war. My little apartment had been replaced by destruction and chaos. The sky was filled with thousands of angels and there were explosions and fires all around me. The smell of death filled my nostrils and I had to bob and weave to avoid being crushed by the fiery brimstone that fell from the sky. This was insanity. I looked for Chalmers, for my support, but he was nowhere to be seen. I was naked in the middle of Armageddon.

Then I saw him, no me. I saw myself all dressed for battle, laying waste to the shadows. I was mesmerized. I looked at my mirror image flying in and out of the smoke-filled skies. Clouds of blackness shot out of odd-looking cannons up into the sky in my direction. I watched as I simply flew around them, marveling at how fast and graceful I was. Then suddenly I was no longer on the ground watching myself fly, I was that angel. I became him. I was the one now flying through the air. The cool air in my face felt good as I soared down from the heavens. On the ground below I could see shadows everywhere. They looked like regular old shadows cast by rocks or trees, but these were different. Every so often one would rise up from its two-dimensional form into what appeared to be a creature with height and girth.

Then it would instantly move to join its fellow shadows in attacking us. They were vile, smelly creatures whose sole intent was to dispatch us and claim entire worlds for themselves. They weren't as fast as us, but they were relentless. You could hack through fifty and fifty more would spring up, and every so often several of them would merge to form a big more menacing being. They tried everything and anything to beat us back, but we had never lost a battle such as this under my command. I glided down through the sky with my sword in hand. A blue fire covered my hand and extended to the long sharp blade, and my golden breastplate twinkled in the now dimming sunlight. This was what I lived for, what I had been created for. This was my life, and I loved what I did. I hacked and cleaved through a dozen shadow demons in the blink of an eye. I felt so strong, so alive.

I could have killed them all. Then Kimi touched my shoulder and jarred me back to reality. "Joey are you okay?" she asked. She looked at me, knowing that she had just made me jump.

"What the hell's going on?"

"I don't know," was all I could say as I regained my balance. I was dizzy. Kimi was my good pal, and I didn't want to lie, but I had to. I have always been a quiet, keep to myself kind of person, and I had to figure this out before I told even my closest friends. As crazy as she was, she would have thought I had lost my mind if I told her what was going on. And, of course, there was always that chance that I really had lost it. This was truly stranger than fiction, and I needed to figure things out before I talked about it to anyone. "I just have a lot of stuff going on in my head lately. I haven't been sleeping very well because of it and I keep spacing out."

She smiled. "I space out a lot without a bunch of stuff on my shoulders." She slid the chair back and stood up. "Are you going out tonight or are you just gonna hang?" she asked. She knew me too well. She knew that I could just be as happy sitting home, whereas she needed to get out and play often. I rubbed my hand through my ever-thinning hair and in the process, bumped my wing with my forearm. "I think I'm gonna take it easy for a while. I might catch up with you guys later." I knew she was meeting Karen and Mark, and that it would have been fun to rehash the day, but I had bigger fish to fry, and I was already a bit loopy. "Okay, I'll make sure to have a couple of good-looking girls hanging out with me in case you show up." She gave me a little hug and smiled, then she turned and left. I was alone again.

Time to play with my wings. I had half a buzz now and was finally able to relax a bit and see what I could do. Then it occurred to me that if I could see and touch the wings, well then, I should also be able to talk with Chalmers. It even sounded weird to think of such things, but I felt I had to give it a try. I closed and locked the door and drew all of the vertical curtains shut. "Chalmers, are you there?" I asked out loud, quietly at first. I stood there and moved my wings up and about. I had them pass through the table and the couch and then reached over to the point where they made contact. Both the wing and the couch felt real and substantial, yet the wing moved through it. I saw it with my own eyes and touched it with my hands, but to see one thing move through another still looked unreal.

"Chalmers!" I called out again.

"Come on man. I feel like I'm losing my mind here." Of course, I got no reply. Why? Because these was no Chalmers. There was no Chalmers, and these wings were some residual figments of my hypnotized imagination. I was getting frustrated, so I decided to go for a walk. It was still quite warm outside, so I threw on my sandals and headed down to street to the cliffs. I went there often enough to go and listen to the music created by the Pacific Ocean crashing against the rocks. It was my happy place. I was still feeling pretty good from the tequila and beer, and I tried to push my frustrations aside. I tried to concentrate on the good things in my life like friends and family and the fact that I lived walking distance from the ocean. I thought of how nice the weather was year-round and I thought about playing basketball outside in shorts on Christmas Day. I always reveled in that, being from the northeast and all.

Happy thoughts in my happy place were what my weary mind needed right now. I stood there on the sandstone ledge that ran the length of the shoreline looking out at the ocean. Waves crashed a couple of feet in front of me and occasionally I got a little bit of the spray on my face. It was nice. I held my arms out straight just above my head and looked out over the water. I opened my wings as far as they would spread and then just soaked it all in. I didn't quite know what to think, but I did know that everything happened for a reason, and this would eventually add up to something big. I looked up at the pier, which ran about a quarter mile out into the ocean. It was connected to the end of the street on the next block over. Normally it was well lit by orange tinted streetlights, but a recent summer storm had beaten it up pretty badly. The lights were mostly out, with some of the railing was missing here and there. It had been closed to the public for almost a month now. I would be alone out there, I thought, out there in the dark. I felt like something was drawing me out into the darkness. I learned that when a thing called to me like that, it was best that I listened to it. I stood there for another moment or two and a couple people walked past me. This was a common place for bums, hippies and people that just wanted to get up close to the ocean much like myself. I wanted privacy to play with my wings. If I had them then I should be able to use them. I looked again at the end of the pier. It was dark and lonely, the perfect place to try things out. I walked back up the stairs that had brought me down to the water's edge so many times. The pier was on the next block over, but the large metal gates, that were almost always open, were locked. The city workers had closed it to prevent people from using it until it could be repaired. As the most government, city or state-run projects, it seemed that the work might never get done. There was a fair amount of light on the gate, so sneaking around it would not be as easy as it appeared. Had I known how to use my wings, I would simply fly over it but if I knew how to use them, I wouldn't be going out onto the pier this night. I wondered if I tried to use them right here, right now, would I draw too much attention? It was the same attention that I wanted to go out into the darkness to avoid. Another quandary, I thought. In the end, I carefully climbed around the gate and hurried out to the end of the long concrete structure. I imagined that the pier must have really been swamped by the storm, as there were dried bits of seaweed everywhere. I had seen waves come up over the railing a few times since I lived here but had not seen damage of this proportion before. Most of the lights close to the shore had been burned out, but there were still a few of them lit further out here and there.

Normally the pier was fairly well lit, but lately it looked dark compared to the brightness of the surrounding area. There was a lot of ambient light from the bars and businesses on the next block over.

Newport Avenue was the main drag of Ocean Beach, the suburb of San Diego where I lived. A lot of cars cruised up and down the three-block span from Sunset Cliffs Boulevard to the ocean as the main drinking establishments of our community were located here. I hurried in and out of the darkness, looking to be sure that one had seen me, all the way down to the end. The moon was coming up over the hills behind me that drew border between Ocean Beach and Point Loma, another, more affluent, suburb. Occasionally a jet would fly over my head on the way out of town. I liked to come out here and see the planes come and go. Sometimes there were several lined up in the skies east of the city waiting to land. The airport was just over the hill, and it was a known fact that pilots really had to get their planes up in the air quick to avoid the hills that lay between the runway and the pier on which I now stood. The limited streetlights and moonlight reflected in the ocean, and I watched it rise and sink as I hurried by. When I reached the end of the pier, I stood out there, sure that no one could see me, and spread my wings as far as they would go. The full span had to be twelve or fourteen feet. It was awesome. I flapped them like a bird would, but I could not catch any air. Apparently, the air passed through it just like everything else. But the feeling of them and the thoughts of myself as a warrior made my chest heave with pride. I felt like I could honestly take on the world. I was feeling the rush. I looked back at the long shoreline and wondered what people would think if they knew what I was truly capable of. In this place I had always felt like a small fish in a big sea, but now I was learning that I wasn't the fish at all. I was the shark. I was the predator that devoured the evil around me, and I would soon be recognized for what I truly was. I was a hero, a savior and I wanted what was due me.

"Is that what you think?" a familiar voice asked me. "Do you think you are some kind of bloody superstar?" Chalmers asked from darkness behind me. I had been caught, and I must have looked like a total idiot. "Uh, no," I stammered. "Well, I mean yeah, I guess." I coiled my wings back behind me. "I'm not really sure what to think really." "Good answer. You shouldn't know what to think. I don't bloody well know what to think."

He had gotten close enough for me to see him. He was dressed exactly the same as he had been earlier in the day, and he still worn his sunglasses. "I do know one thing. You need to stop playing with those things," he said, pointing the tip of his cane at my back. "Those things will get you into trouble." I didn't like the sound of that, but what trouble could I get into here, I thought. I was all alone out here. "You do understand that I can pretty much hear everything you think in that feeble mind of yours, right?" he asked, sounding a bit condescending. "And if you knew what was really at stake here, you would listen."

His words sounded foreboding. He stepped forward and looked at the shoreline. "You are shining like a beacon for all of the evil things of this world to see. The more you mess with those wings, the brighter you shine." That was strange thing for him to say. "What do you mean?" I asked, pretty much without thinking. "I came out here to be alone in the dark." I must have sounded sheepish, like a child looking for answers. "Look boy, whatever door you opened today has stayed ajar. The fact that you can still see and touch the wings is a testament to that. The more you investigate this opening, the more things on the other side will see you." He paused and looked for his next words, trying to explain this happening in "easy to understand" terminology. "it's like you wedged your foot in the door and now you can't take it back out, even if you wanted to. Each time you think of your past lives, each time you try to use your wings to fly, you are shining like a giant spotlight for all to see." I did not like the way this conversation was headed. "What are you saying?" I asked nervously. I thought of the shadow creatures and the strange beings that my angelic other self-had just been battling in my visions. But in those visions, I was safe. I could walk right through the battle unscathed.

"Are you telling me that there are monsters coming after me...here?" "Monsters," he quipped, "that's rich. But yes, in a way, I guess there are monsters looking for you." He must have sensed the panic brewing inside of me. "What I mean to say is that they aren't actually looking for you, but if you advertise the fact that you are here, well that's another story. They have always been here, just like you.

You've walked past them numerous times, neither knowing the other's true identity. But now you have the wings. You can no longer hide in plainsight." He shuffled around a bit, looking at the shore and all of the lights. "This world is a strange place.

There are beings from both sides of the battle of light and darkness here. Most don't have a clue what they truly are or why they are here. Many of them, such as you, are here as a form of punishment."

There was the word that stuck in my head the whole ride home through the desert. The idea of me being punished haunted me, pulled at me. I had always felt like I was being punished, thought that way my whole life. I don't know why I did, I just always had, and now I was learning that I really was. "So, what did I do that was so bad to warrant this punishment?" I asked, hoping to be enlightened. I sucked the wings into my back and sides as tightly as I could get them. “You’ll know soon enough,” he said, sounding a bit anxious. “Look, I don’t know how many people are aware of your presence here, but I do know that the more we talk and the more you wave your wings around, the more you will be noticed.” I quickly spun around looking around for prying eyes. I wondered if by having the two of us together, might we be seen from the not so distant shore? If one of the baddies happened to look in that direction, would we warrant further investigation? “So just by you being here, talking with me, you may be exposing me to the bad guys? I asked, starting to feel nervous and a bit anxious. “What happens if one of those things actually does find me? What do they want with me?” I was getting seriously freaked out. “Are they going to kill me?” Chalmers looked down, then back up at me and nodded. “Or worse,” he added with a solemn tone. “You aren’t prepared to face the things that will be looking for you, should you keep up this course of action. Believe me, son, just let well enough be. You don’t want to know what’s really out there.” Okay this was not sounding good at all. “Hold up,” I cut in. Is there some way for me to close this door. And what could be worse than having one of these things grab me and kill me? I paused to catch my fleeting breath, not really sure I wanted to hear the answer to that question.

Well, you could be drug down into the darkness where you will be tortured relentlessly for eons until you die or could be eventually converted to fight for the dark side. Does that sound scary enough? He paused to see that what he was saying was sinking in. It was. "Look, you won't be able to use those wings, not here anyway, so get that out of your melon leave them be. You will not be able to fly no matter how bloody hard you try." He seemed both annoyed and a bit paranoid. He kept taking little glances or peeks over his shoulders and past me. He was making me even more nervous than I already was. I wanted to ask him what he was looking for, but I didn't want to turn the subject away from me just yet. "So, you're saying that these creatures, the things that I saw fighting the angels in my visions, want to drag me into the depths of hell and either torture me or convert me into a demon?" Panic was beginning to well up inside me. "Or both" he added. Most likely I would say both. But yes, that is what I am saying, he finished. He seemed quite nonchalant about it.

"What the hell?" I asked angrily, out of frustration. "I didn't ask for this," I yelled, my blood boiling. I didn't mean to yell or get loud. It wasn't like anyone would hear us this far from the shoreline, but I did not want to bite the hand that was feeding me. I needed this man, or thing rather, right now. I needed his guidance and any information that he could offer. "The hell you didn't. No one twisted your arm to go to that hypnotist today. You bloody well did that on your own." He pointed his cane right into my face. "I know that no one on this planet seems to want to be held accountable for their own actions, but you did this, no one else. So, deal with it." He was heated. "You, yourself have bitched about that time and time again. Everybody wants to have someone else to blame when they do something wrong, when they have an accident or other mishaps. Isn't this the exact same thing you were complaining about the other night? Isn't this why you have been thinking that there are so many frivolous lawsuits going on today?" He paused and looked me in the eye. He knew that I knew what he was talking about. He didn't have to read my mind.

He could see it in my eyes. I had just had a conversation with Dan about this very topic two nights ago.

We were talking about lawsuits for people who had died from lung cancer and their families were suing the tobacco companies. This conversation then morphed into one about people suing just to sue, and people trying to find fault for their actions and mistakes with everyone and anyone around them except themselves. "How the hell do you know so much about me anyway?" I snapped. It distressed me that he even knew what I was thinking. "Are you some kind of glorified babysitter?" I didn't mean for my words to sound so harsh, but they just slipped out. I must have sounded a bit condescending myself now because I could see the expression on his face change. "Yes, I'm your bloody babysitter.

I was sent to watch over you centuries ago, and to be quite honest with you, I'm over it. It's always the same old thing with you. You have been given chance after chance after chance and you just keep messing up. I tell you, I'm tired of it, just plain tired of it." He sounded a bit angry now. He stopped looking around and stepped right up to me. "Would you please just get over yourself, you egotistical lunatic? Honestly, this is getting old. And by the way, I'm a Watcher, not a bloody babysitter. Bullocks! I was sent to watch over your butt when you were cast out and I've been doing it ever since. Now, if you don't want me to advise, and you think you can handle all of this yourself, then be my guest."

"Sir, please, I didn't mean anything disrespectful. I'm sorry if I came off that way. I completely respect you and I really need your help.

Please sir, tell me what to do," I pleaded. He took a step back and took a long deep breath.

"First of all, I am a Watcher, sent to report on your progress, like a probation officer. Unfortunately for both you and I however, you just can't seem to learn your lesson." He brushed some hair out of his face.

It was a little breezy and his long, straight hair blew around a bit. "As for what you are supposed to do, well I don't know. I honestly don't know how you are to overcome this punishment and be set free. My best piece of wisdom to lay upon you is that you are supposed to live. Just live and let others live. It's not for you to be the judge, jury and executioner. I've heard you say it time and time again, but you need to live your life that way. You have to control that temper of yours. Try to make it through on bloody lifetime without killing anyone." It was my turn now to pace back and forth a little. I had been working for years to control the beast that lived inside of me. I feared no man because I knew what I was capable of. There is always someone bigger and tougher out there, but I just never allowed myself to think that way. I always just thought of myself as this bad ass, and to be honest most people that knew me or had ever seen me fight, felt the same way. Now I learn that this rage comes from my long distant past life, and that in that other life I was famous for it. Chalmers had said it. I wasn't the judge, jury and executioner, but in that lifetime, I was.

No wonder it took me so many years to break such bad habits. I used to be so mean that when someone wronged me, I would pay them back tenfold. That was the way I worked, but I was working on trying to change that mindset. I had learned the karma was good enough executioner, and that it didn't need my help. I walked around a spot on the concrete decking, wondering what I should do. "Do you think that knowing all of this, I can go back to being the man that I was? Do you think that I can ignore these freakin wings? I'm sorry that I messed up and went to see that crazy old women in the desert, but how was I supposed to know something like this

would have asked me what kind of superpower I would want if I could have any, it would be to fly. I had so many dreams of flying that often times when I awoke from those dreams, I would feel depressed because I would quickly realize that I couldn't.

"Can you handle this?" Chalmers asked sarcastically. He knew that I was deep in thought. And he was right. All of that was going to take some extra effort.

"Let me ask you this," he started. But then he was gone. He didn't finish his sentence. He didn't even say good-bye. "What the heck?" I asked out loud, but quietly at first. I looked around to see where he went, but he just wasn't there. I spun around on the slick, damp concrete looking for him.

"What the heck," I yelled this time. I looked around to see if anyone was coming out onto the pier.

Perhaps I had been spotted. Maybe the cops were on their way out to get me. I looked, but there wasn't anyone coming that I could see. Chalmers was just gone. That was that. I looked at the lights and thought about all of the people out having fun. It was Saturday night.

Kimi, Mark, Karen and whole bunch of my friends were at the local bars drinking, having a good time. A part of me wanted to join them, but another part of me just wanted to go home and chill. I stood there for a minute or two, then decided to sit down on one of the benches and just relax. Maybe Chalmers would come back, I thought. The moon reflected off of the ocean and I sat there and marveled at the

way that image rode the waves up and then down over the crest of each one. The seat was moist from the wet air, but I didn't care. I had much more important things on my mind. I sat there for another fifteen minutes or so and listened to the ocean crash upon the beach and the rocks off in the distance. It was a very soothing sound. I let it creep in and wrap around my brain. I was completely alone out here now, and the odds of anyone heading my way were very slim. So, I pulled my feet up and laid back on the damp cold stone bench. The stars and moon lit up the sky pretty good. I took long even breaths and let them out slowly. I closed my eyes and allowed myself to completely relax. After everything that had gone on today, this felt really good. I laid there for a while. I couldn't even tell you how long I was there.

But finally, I came to the conclusion that this all must have been a dream, that I would wake up and all of this would soon be over. I must have eaten something funky that caused my imagination to get the best of me. I turned things over in my mind's eye. Everything that has happened could and most likely will have come from my own crazy brain. The effects of the pot and the booze were wearing thin. It was time to either go home or go to the bars. I leaned over the side of the bench and took a deep breath.

How nice would it be to look back and not see

the wings? It would be so wonderful to know that this nightmare had come to an end. I closed my eyes and leaned over to look, then opened them ever so slowly. Unfortunately, the wings were still there, sticking deep into the concrete. I didn't let myself get frustrated, I just got up and went home. I got to the locked gate at the end of the pier and climbed around it like I had before. It was a little difficult to do because I was thinking about the other things that what was at hand. I slipped a little on the damp metal bars but recovered quickly. It was a long way down to the sidewalk below, and I had to get my head into what I was doing. I finally managed to get past the gate and then rolled on down the back alley toward my complex. I went through the back gate and down a small, open-air corridor, emerging quickly by the side of the pool.

"Joey D," a voice called out loudly from behind me. I knew exactly who it was. That was one of the many joys of having a roommate. Alone time was very, very limited. The thing was, he knew me like a brother.

I might be able to sneak things past him here and there, but he was going to know that something was amiss with me.

Like I said, I didn't like lying or liars in general, but I was going to have to dodge any issues that came up with all of this nonsense, which now filled my mind.

"What are you two fags up to tonight?" I asked spinning around to face Dan and Rob. Those two always seemed to be together I didn't even have to see Rob to know he was there. It did help that they were standing outside of Rob's apartment smoking, as usual. His place was on the ground floor, right next to the pool. That spot was a bonus on sunny days as it often held views of the ladies sunning themselves on the pool's decking.

"I just got off of work" he told me, taking a drag from his cigarette. "Where were you? Are you wet?" he asked looking at me funny. Dan was a big guy, not tall, big. We got along pretty good. He was happy or joking pretty much all the time, and he was fairly neat and tidy. I'm not saying he did a whole of cleaning, but he didn't make a mess either. Rob, on the other hand, was scrawny and his hair seemed to turn gray overnight. His apartment in comparison, was always a mess, like a tornado had gone through it. He looked pretty drunk already. I couldn't have looked much better myself I took the bottle from Rob and slammed a big shot. It gave me a bit of a chill that I shook off.

"I was down by the water chilling, thinking about some things and I must have sat down in a puddle."

"Smooth," Dan commented followed by his usual laugh. "What are you two up to?" I asked, as I swilled down another big shot. "Nothing," Rob said. "It's late. Dan worked a little overtime tonight," he started.

"And you sat home and waited for your boyfriend? How quaint. I'm sorry I spoiled your little moment," I chided. This banter was commonplace. Rob's nickname was the Gimp because he was always hurt, gimping around.

He was like a fragile piece of glass that broke easily. Since I knew him, he had broken his hand at work, his leg at a party, had almost got knocked unconscious playing two hand football on the beach, and had pretty much been declared insane by his place of employment. "You did," Dan said between puffs on his cigarette. "We were about to go to get something to eat. You wanna go" I knew that I probably should eat, but I didn't want to go with them. They were on a different schedule from the rest of the world.

They would be hanging until dawn or later, well, at least till Rob passed out.

"No thanks, but if you get burritos, grab me one, would you?" "Carne Asada? Dan asked me, knowing that was my favorite. "Yeah, I'm going to chill," I told them, which was like saying good night. These two were my good buddies. We hung out together often enough to know each other pretty well. I knew, walking up to the stairs of our apartment, that even if they didn't get Mexican, they would stop and bring me a burrito anyway. I was done in. It had been a long even-filled day and I welcomed the warmth of my bed. As I lay down, I felt as though I could sleep for a week. I said a little prayer that I would wake up from this dream and I turned out the light. I begged for help quietly in my mind, pleading for this to be just a dream, then I faded off to sleep.

THREE

As I slept, my mind wandered. I drifted off to far way worlds, places with orange, purple and blue skies. I saw the battlefields, and the orchestrated chaos that seemed to be everywhere. It was magnificent.

There were entire solar systems in the midst of a war. It was an epic fight between good and evil on an interplanetary scale. I was drifting through space gliding along what appeared to be a line of battle between two factions that involved countless worlds. I was being pulled or pushed toward one planet in particular. It had similar landmasses to earth, but the colors were all wrong. It was grey and brown and engulfed in a haze of smoke. It was a dying world in the midst of a great conflict. I had seen this kind of thing in my visions before, but as this particular battle waged, I began to see more and more angels crash to the ground. I knew this was not supposed to be happening, but it was. The angels were actually losing to these lizard-like creatures that called this world their home. The reptilian beasts were lashing out with spears and machines that shot larger projectiles into the sky. There were thousands of these machines and many of the angel corps never even got close to them before they were dropped. The irony of the situation was not lost on me as I realized that sticks and stones were felling some of the most powerful creatures ever created. The number of the beasts was incredible and even though they outnumbered the angels fifteen or twenty to one, they still should have been on the losing side of the battle. That's just the way it happened. We came up with a game plan according to the strengths and abilities of the adversaries we were pitted against and attacked in very uniform group. And we never lost. We never experienced anything like what was happening here in front of me, not this as long as I could remember. I surveyed the scene from above, and then drifted slowly down to the ground. My feet touched the hard surface of the planet, and for a moment, I feared that I would be killed. But I realized quickly enough that no one or thing could see me. It was either that, or they just didn't care. These were massive creatures, probably twelve or fifteen feet tall and heaped with muscles. They were much taller and a great deal thicker than me, very fierce looking and they smelled horrific. They grunted and hissed at each other. I could see how excited they were. They were slaying the mythological angels that had come to put an end to the reign on this world. It had been foretold for eons in their ancient scripts that one day an armada of angels would come. When their rule reached its pinnacle of success, they would be struck down. They knew this day would come, but instead of their demise, they were dispatching the warriors of the light, unending their mythology. Strange, I thought. I knew about these beasts. I had read a report about them. I knew their history, the way they fought, their weaknesses. They presented little to no challenge. This war should have been over before it had even started. I had developed an easy to follow battle strategy for this place. Apparently, no one read it. I remember doing it, but that was another life, another time. Perhaps, I thought as I surveyed the scene, it never happened. There were fallen angels scattered around me, and some were being brutally beaten by the sinewy creatures. I could smell burning flesh and I wanted to get sick, but I didn't. I just continued to feel the swirling feeling in the bottom of my stomach. I didn't know if the smell had gotten to me or if it was the guilt of not being there to lead my men. I milled about, looking at the carnage, feeling nauseous and helpless, excruciatingly helpless. Finally, I came across an angel that lie broken and bleeding on the gray colored ground. I was captivated by the way he was sprawled about, hypnotized by his dying eyes. Then he spoke. I looked around to see whom else he could be speaking to, but there was no one else around. He was definitely talking to me, reaching for me, for my help. I got scared and looked to see if anyone or anything else could see me, but no one else seemed to notice or care. I looked back down at the fallen, broken angel and he spoke to me again.

"Why have you forsaken us?" he pleaded. Though I stood before him in common street-clothes, shorts and a t-shirt, he recognized me. "We need you Joseph." He sputtered, gasping for air. Liquid seeped from his ears and his nostrils. "This," he groped for his breath, "shouldn't be happening. We should..."

He tightened up, fell limp and then he died. How was it possible for an angel to die, I wondered. None had ever died under my command. This was something I had not witnessed before. I put my hand on him and he felt cool and almost damp to the touch. The ground around him was saturated with a blood-like substance, though it wasn't red. It looked more opaque like water. I looked at the dead being and knelt down close to it, and my heart began to ache. It was like a vale of incredible sadness fell across me.

I looked over the poor dead being. It had been so strong, so powerful. His hair was blonde and long and I would have to say he was a relatively good-looking guy. His armor was silver with gold accompaniments.

His breastplate reflected the light around us except for a huge slice right through the center of it where he had been cleaved wide open. I wanted to, but I could not pull my eyes away from him. I looked him over thoroughly. I knew I didn't know this person, but a part of me felt like I did. He was like a distant member of the family or circle of friends, known, but not known. An unbelievably sadness filled me. I felt like I did when my brother died. And I started to cry. His words echoed in my head. "Why have you forsaken us?" he has asked me. The words burned into my brain. "Why have you forsaken us? Why have you forsaken us?" Thunder cracked loudly all around me and lightening filled the sky above. Smoke billowed from behind me as the lizard creatures set fire to a pile of corpses, both angels and their own.

They were grunting and making an evil laughing kind of sound and I was disgusted. I wanted to kill them all. I unfurled my wings in a show of force and tried to rise up from the kneeling position that I had assumed over the dead angel. My hands had curled into tight fists, and I wanted to tear their faces off. I wanted to kill them all. I would kill them all. But when I stood, my knees buckled, and I fell. When I tried to pick myself up again, I realized that I was not the battlefield anymore. I was in my bedroom, on the floor, all tangled up in my sheets. My hands were clenched so tightly that I could barely open them. It had all been a dream. I jumped up real quick and looked in the mirror, hoping beyond hope that the wings would not be there, but they were. "Crap, I thought as I ran my hands through my hair to my face.

I rubbed my cheeks and forehead. "How can this be?" I asked out loud. I almost wanted to cry. I had been so wound up. Was this how it was going to be every day, every night? It seems so real, that I was having a hard time snapping back into reality. I could still smell the death of the battlefield in my nostrils I needed to do something, anything, so I threw on some sweatpants and hurried out of my room. Dan's bedroom door was shut, which meant he was either sleeping or at work. There was a Carne Asada burrito on the table for me that he had gotten me sometime during the night. I put it into the fridge and then I looked out of the big kitchen window at the coming morning. I was still pretty wound up from that dream, so I tried to bang out some sit ups and push-ups. I just couldn't stop thinking about the way those lizard men were laughing. They were killing my people and laughing as they did it. My heart ached and I wanted to choke someone because of it. I didn't know what to do. I did know that if I lingered around in that apartment any longer, I would surely lose my mind. So, I threw on some shorts, a t-shirt and my sneakers, grabbed the MP3 player on the way out and I went for a long jog. I was absolutely spoiled to live so close to one of the coolest places that I could imagine. The ocean pounded against the cliffs that I jogged along a path that ran right along the edge of Sunset Cliffs. It was a magnificent place. I was going to get some exercise and clean out my ruffled brain in one fail swoop. On most days, I got to see several pretty girls jogging by, but I doubted that would happen so early on a Sunday morning. I always found that little bit of energy to turn up the speed whenever I saw a hottie, so in a way I was motivated to work even harder than I had been. I found a good song to listen to and got to running. I had this feeling so many times before. I always dreamed that if I could run fast enough, I could just launch myself up into the air and glide. But now things were different. I actually had the wings, and contrary to what Chalmers told me, I really did feel like I could use them. I ran and ran and just did not seem to be getting tired. I was completely wired because my vision. I wondered if it from my past or it was something that was yet to come. I thought about the angels face and blood coming out of his ear, spilling into his hair and onto the white metal that shielded his shoulder and neck. I started to have a hard time breathing, but I kept running, faster and faster. I tried to free myself of the anger and sadness, and in a moment of weakness, I unfurled my wings. I just felt like I could fly. I wanted to soar up into the heavens and return to my rightful place. I felt needed, like I had to be there. I ran hard and fast and then I just sort of dove. My arms were outstretched to guide me up into the sky. And for a moment or two, I was flying. Then my chin made hard contact with the ground. The cliffs were made mostly of compressed sandstone and there were spots of sand and some of grassy vegetation and ice plants. I didn't hit any of those. I landed abruptly on one of the harder places. My MP3 player went flying and whole body was jarred from the impact. I laid there for moment before picking myself up to my knees.

"Lovely," I said aloud, as I looked all around to see if anyone had seen me. "What an idiot," I thought.

There were a couple of cars cruising down Sunset Cliffs Boulevard, but I didn't think anyone saw me and I didn't care if they did. I pulled myself up and brushed my dirty self-off. I went over and picked up my MP3 player. It still worked. I then checked myself over and saw that I was good other than a couple of scrapes on my palms and on my knees. "Crap" I thought to myself. I felt like such a fool. It was time to go back home. By the time I got to my door, the lingering dirt and dust had mixed with sweat on my stomach and arms. The t-shirt I started out with was a mess and so was I. I walked into my bedroom and looked in the mirror to see if I had cut my chin. I hadn't but I was pretty dirty. The funny thig was, my wings were still clean and bright white. I extended them out and admired them. I moved them up and out and then I saw Dan walk by and look at me. "You need the bathroom?" he groggily asked on his way past. It didn't matter if what I said, he was going in. If I really had to go, it would be after he was done, and then I wouldn't want to go. That's how it was around here.

We had a great understanding of each other.

While he got ready for work, I decided to go and jump in the pool. It was still pretty early, but the water was warm enough. The little cuts on my hands and knees stung when the water touched them though. I rubbed them up good to get the dirt and rocks out, then I swam a couple of laps. I looked up in time to see Dan head out to work. He waved, then made a hand gesture like he was shooting himself in the head. Then he was out. I did a couple more laps and even tried to use my wings a little to push me along, but it didn't work. I couldn't even feel any difference between the air and the water. I got out of the water and dried myself off. The water either never touched the wings or it had just rolled off, but they were dry right away. So, I touched my right wing with my wet right hand, and it did get wet. I could feel the wing with my hand, and I could feel my hand through the wing. I moved the muscles in my side and back and shook the beads of water that I had just left there off of the wing. The water drops fell onto the deck of the pool, and I walked back upstairs. It made little sense to me and though I was trying not to freak out, it was getting harder and harder. As I dried myself, I began to feel very much alone. This was going to be some burden to have to deal for the rest of my life. It wasn't just the wings. I was still haunted by the face of that dead angel. I felt that it was time for a drink. I rarely ever drank before noon, never at this hour, but today I was saying to bad. I knew of a bar on Voltaire St. that was open at 6am.

There were two bartenders there that I found to

be very attractive. One had blonde hair and the other was a sweet little red head that I thought was absolutely gorgeous. Beside their stunning good looks, both made great bloody marys. I cracked open a Bud Light for a long walk and headed out the door. I walked several blocks and soon enough I was on the corner just across from Lucy's bar. It was open but looked pretty empty. I went in an sat the bar by myself. Unfortunately, neither of the two bartenders I was hoping to see was there. It was weird to be there at this time of day for me, the sun still shining and all. I ordered a bloody mary and sipped at it. Then I surveyed the scene. There were a couple of people seated by the back of the bar that paid no attention to me. The rest of the place was vacant. The morning news was playing on the television and the three pool tables were empty. I liked to sit by the window to watch the world go by, though not much was happening at this time of day. I had slowly become captivated by the vodka display at the end of the long rack of booze. It was an advertisement for various flavors of vodka. It must be so weird to order a pepper flavored vodka in my drink. Then I realized that I was drinking a bloody mary that might well have some of that peppered vodka in it. I looked past the vodka display to the mirror that covered the wall behind the booze. I slammed down the first one, and then ordered another. I looked at the old man that had wandered in and now sat down at the bar to my left and then the bartender to my right. Neither was paying attention to me. No one else could see my wings. I was just another patron to them. I flicked my wings outwardly for a brief moment, like stretching in a yawn. I glanced around for a reaction, but nobody saw me. I could see my entire wingspan from tip to tip. I had not been able to see the full span before, and it was pretty impressive. It was also a tad bit disturbing. They served a good reminder that my life was never going to be the same again. I was starting to feel the alcohol. My thoughts were deep. The sun was bright outside, and I wasn't quite sure why I was sitting in a bar at this time of the morning. It didn't stop me from ordering another drink though. The ever-present feeling that I was losing my mind haunted me. It was such a strange feeling, a feeling that I did not want; so today I drank it away as much as I could. I saw fuzzy images in my head of my mom and dad and little brother. These were real people. My life was real. I had memories, pictures to back them up. But I also had visions of battlefields in my mind that stretched out as far as the eye could see. I had no physical proof of these things. So I had to try to think about what was real and what wasn't. I had hoped that when I woke up this morning the wings and such would have just ended up being a bad dream. Sadly, this didn't happen, so here I sat. I had purposely left my cell phone at home so that I could be alone to think today. As it was, the odds were that none of my friends

were even awake yet. It was Sunday morning.

Sunday morning, I thought. Maybe I should go to church and ask someone about what was going on, but I didn't much believe in organized religion. I wondered whom I would even talk to. Who would have a clue as to what has happened to me? I would be laughed out of any church around here, I imagined. There were a lot of Latinos in the area, hence a lot of Catholic Churches. I think that just about all denominations were accounted for here in San Diego, but I couldn't imagine finding one that would want to listen to my story. It wouldn't jibe with any belief system that I was aware of. I contemplated this thought as I swilled my drink and watched the news on the television in front of me. They were discussing the soon to be passed alcohol ban on the beaches.

Another law to punish the masses for the crimes of the few. It was ridiculous. I would become a criminal for having a beer while we played volleyball on the beach. We played twice a week, on Wednesdays and Sundays. I was in no shape to play today, but it was all in fun. I would be missed, but there were always enough people for the games to go on.

"The needs of the few or the one outweighs the needs of many."

The words just slipped out of my mouth. I wasn't talking to anyone in particular, but the bartender responded with an "amen to that brother" while he cleaned and straightened things up behind the bar.

It was disgusting, and we were all sickened by it. One more law to have to abide by, one more rule set forth by our out-of-touch-government. Instead of properly punishing the idiots that caused trouble, we all got punished, but wasn't that the new way of things? I ordered another drink and left a healthy tip. I wanted to be sure that my glass never got completely empty. I was getting drunk today and I didn't care.

I must have been on my third or fourth, and feeling no pain, when a fairly raggedy looking fellow strolled in. He must have had a chip on his shoulder or something because I caught him looking at me in the mirror as he walked past. Now I'm originally from the east coast, so that kind of crap doesn't fair well with me. He was giving me the eyeball, but when I turned to look at him, he looked away. At first, I just shrugged him off. What was I going to do? He was a scrawny little thing, no match for me, especially after I had had a couple of drinks, but there was no way I was going to start a fight over a lingering stare either. Not anymore. Even if I hadn't talked to Chalmers about the fighting, I was not going to fight anymore. So I just ignored the guy. That was before I realized how bad he smelled. Now there are few things that I hate more than body odor, and this guy smelled like absolute crap. I looked up from my half-empty glass to the bartender, and took a quick peek in the mirror, and if that roach wasn't still checking me out. It made me uncomfortable and a bit angry. He was close to my height with long, greasy hair creeping out from under his filthy trucker hat. Both the hat and the hair covered his eyes, and his scruffy beard covered the rest of his face. His skin was a deep brown color from the constant, daily exposure to the sun and his clothes were wrinkly, torn and extremely disheveled. And by the wickedly pungent odor that emanated from him, I could tell that neither he nor his clothing had been cleaned in quite some time. I wanted to say something to him, but I kept my mouth shut. I hadn't spent too much time in that bar before. I think I may have been there only three, maybe five times, and I sure as hell hadn't been there this early in the day, so I wasn't sure if this was the norm. The close proximity to the beach and year-round summertime weather brought an abundance of bums to this area. Every now and then I got to see one escorted out of a bar, but for the most part, they were a part of the local environment. It wasn't up to me to throw the guy out, but his odor was getting to me. I don't know if it was because of the booze and the empty stomach, but his smell made me want to puke. And I had pretty much had all I wanted to have of a smelly bum eyeballing me, so I finished my drink and got up to leave. I had been sitting there for about two hours, give or take, and I didn't realize how wobbly my legs had gotten.

"Whoa, there buddy. Need a cab?" the bartender asked, smiling. He saw that I was thinking about turning him down.

"Seriously, there's a cab depot right there," he said, pointing to the lot full of cabs across the street.

At first, I thought that there was no way I was going to call a cab to go seven or eight blocks, but after a couple of feet, I turned and nodded to him.

Two minutes later a cab was sitting outside. As I walked over to the blue taxi, I noticed, in the reflection of the car's passenger side window, that the bum had followed me outside. I didn't care by now; I just wanted to go home. I paid him no mind. I climbed in the backseat of the cab and had him drop me off outside my complex. I stumbled up the stairs, opened the door, and curled up on the futon. I was exhausted from the morning exercise and the booze as well as all the craziness that had haunted me. I wanted to crash out hard, but I was a little fearful. My mind was awash with all of the crap I had seen and done. As it was, my wings were embedded deeply into the black mattress. Too weird, I thought.

Sleepiness was tugging at me, and I did want to fall out, but I had little choice. I started to fade but caught myself. I didn't want to fall asleep, not now, not anytime soon.

So I pried myself from the warmth of the black cushiony mattress and headed for the door. I'm not saying that I was so much afraid falling asleep, I just wasn't all that excited about it right now. I decided to go back to the happy place and watch the people walk by the waves crash on the rocks. I packed my marijuana pipe with some of California's finest green bud and tucked it in my pocket just in case. It was like an emergency first aid package for my brain. I didn't smoke any just yet, because I was already half in the bag, I just carried it with me in case I needed to mellow out. The back alley behind my complex led directly to the ocean. It ended in a raggedy three-tier set of stairs right next to an apartment complex that was as weathered and beat down by time and by the salty air as the dilapidated staircase. I walked down the creaky steps and headed out across the rocks and sandstone that made up that part of the shoreline. I stepped over the cracks which the ocean water swirled below and found myself a nice place to sit down and watch the waves. I made some calls to several friends, but no one answered. They were, most likely, still asleep, or just too busy. I was bummed, so I just sat back and watched the water and a few people that walked by. Depression started to fill head and I wondered what I would do to keep myself occupied for the rest of the day and pretty much every day thereafter. I hated going to the bar by myself and I knew that Dan wouldn't want to go out because he had gotten up so early this morning. I had already spent about two hours in the bar today, but I would have relished more just to occupy my mind. My friends would be playing volleyball down the beach later, but that was still a few hours away. I was quite literally bored to tears, buzzed, and I was feeling hopelessly lost. I interlocked my fingers behind my head and leaned back against the rock wall. I could just relax and think of something to do with myself, so I closed my eyes and listened to the soothing sound the ocean made. I could feel my eyelids growing heavy, and though I did not want to fall asleep there, it was nice to relax a bit. Then someone put their hand on my shoulder and startled me. Now, all of the roommates that I've ever had and most of my friends know full well that when I get startled, I jump up, fists clenched, ready to swing.

So I snapped to and was fully prepared to bust someone in the lip. I opened my eyes to see a face that I had never seen before, yet something called out to me from the back of my mind. He was somehow oddly familiar. I had my fist poised ready to deal out a crushing blow, but I paused allowing my brain a few seconds to try to process the image. Then it all fell into place.

"Careful Bastion, didn't they warn you not to creep up on me?" The words just came out of my mouth, and suddenly things were different.

"Didn't mean to startle you, general. I just wanted to tell you that that creature is dead. They're all dead.

We've killed them all." Bastion was referring to the head of a beast that lie dead in my hand. I had just bludgeoned it thoroughly and then, to add insult to injury, I had torn its head from its neck. I was an act of defiance and disgust.

"Are you planning on using that thing?" he asked nodding at my raised hand that was still poised to strike him. I looked, but instead of a clenched fist, I saw a flaming sword firmly clenched in my hand.

I had a firm grip on the hilt and though the flames danced up and down the shiny, blood-stained blade up over my hand, it did not burn me. I slowly lowered the sword and slid its gold trimmed black leather sheath, which was attached to me near the hip. I looked around and realized that I was no longer on the rocky shoreline of Ocean Beach; instead, I was in the middle of the field of death and destruction. There were bodies everywhere, and the ground was drenched in the bluish-green fluid that had previously pumped through the veins of the dead race. The air smelled pungent and the twin suns of the world on which I stood were setting turning orange sky to a deep crimson color. I looked down at the body that lie at my feet and saw that I had not only ripped the head from the body, but I had hacked up the remains pretty good.

"Report," I commanded.

"Complete and total victory. We lost no one, but we completely annihilated the enemy."

Bastion had snapped to attention to make the report, but then started to relax. He was a strong soldier.

His body armor and long hair were covered in the blueish-green blood that had flowed through the veins of the creature we had just destroyed.

"Just like you ordered, Joseph, we killed them all," he told me with a devilish smile. He did enjoy his job immensely.

"When you are on the field of battle, you will

address me as sir," I scowled. I could feel the churning in my stomach.

"This was too easy." I stepped over the carcass and walked around to look at some of the other dead.

"This was no challenge at all." Bastion's inflated chest sunk a bit, and the twinkle in his green eyes dimmed. He knew where this conversation was going. He watched me step over the lifeless carcasses, occasionally prodding a body with a foot.

"Sir, we totally kicked ass. No offense, but why can't you just be happy with that?" He knew he was asking dangerous questions, but he was more than just my wingman and number one officer, he was confidant and a friend. And we had had this conversation before.

"Why can't I be happy with that?" I asked angrily. I bent over and picked up the lifeless body of one of the felled aliens, held it up with my left hand, and punched the thing in the middle of its chest with all of my might. My fist not only punctured the body, but it actually blasted through the other side. I let go of the thing with my left hand and held its full weight with my right wrist, which was firmly implanted in the thing's midsection.

"This is why," I told him as I raised the thing up slightly then flung my arm down and out, hurling the body off my arm back onto the ground hard. I then kicked the pile of flesh out of my way.

"I'm sick to death of this. I want a real fight. I

want a fight to the death, an all-out brawl, where we have a distinct possibility of losing." Bastion looked down at the ground, then back up at me. He just wanted to revel in our victory, but I was taking that away from him.

"I just will not understand that way of thinking. We've talked about this before. We're supposed to win every battle. We're the best of the best. When the powers that be calls us in, we kick it. That's our job, our destiny. Why can't you be happy with that?"

"Because I want a challenge. That's why. Why can't you understand that Bastion?" I asked him in fury. I knew my friend could not understand this, and neither would my superiors. I had been chastised for this way of thinking, but it haunted me, and I could not shake it.

"Let's go," I told him, and fully expanded my wings. I leapt up into the crimson sky and surveyed the carnage below. There were literally thousands of bodies scattered across the landscape. The other angels also jumped up into the sky as well and we all fell into formation. I allowed myself a brief moment to relish the victory at hand as I looked over the multitude of the dead. We had overcome incredible odds to achieve a victory here. We had a fair amount of troops on our side, but the number of bodies was nearly beyond imagination. Now I led my troops through the skies and let the comforting winds blow across my face and through my long brown hair, helping me to relax, then something splashed my face. The tide had started to come in and the place that I had chosen to sit was now being it by the ocean's spray. I jumped up out of the way of the next big splash and realized that my hands had gone to sleep. I had been using them as pillows and must have fallen asleep for a moment or two. I had to shake the sleepiness out of my head, and when I did, I had this weird feeling of having long hair. I could almost feel it on my shoulders and neck. This was a strange feeling because although I had long hair many years ago, I currently kept my haircut very short. I touched the back of my neck and then rubbed my head and felt nothing but normal bumps on my lumpy melon. But it did feel like my hair was long and swinging all about when I shook my head again.

It had gotten pretty dark, so I wondered how long I might have been asleep. As it was, this was not the best of places to take a nap. There were a lot of bums and some troublemakers that hovered around this area. I had come down here in the early afternoon and now it was near dark. I looked to my right, which was the direction from which I come and realized that I would not be able to go that way without getting wet. The tide had come in enough to cut off my route home. I would now have to take a bit of a walk to the next place that I could get back up to the top of the cliffs. I turned to go that way, but something caught my eye in the direction. I thought I saw someone standing on the other side of the water looking at me. It was pretty dark, so I couldn't be sure. But it did look like a person. I continued to stare at it, checking it out, and then it moved. I watched it move further away into the darkness, and then it was gone. I turned and walked in the other direction but stopped to take another peek over my shoulder at the place where the person had been. And damned if I didn't think I saw the head of someone peeking at me from behind an outcropping of rocks. It creeped me out. I still had the pins and needles feeling in my hands, so I shook them hard trying to get the blood circulating. I hurried myself along, but I had to be careful and mind my footing. It was slippery and dark, and I sure I did not want to go swimming tonight. I stepped across a good-sized fissure, then took another quick look back. The head that I thought I saw was gone. This caused a bit of curiosity and nervousness. Now, I'm not afraid of any man, however, I really wasn't looking to fight tonight. So, when I got an area that I could climb up onto the streets above, I did so. My senses were screaming to me. Though I saw no one, I knew something was amiss. I had learned, a long time ago, that when I had these feelings, it was my best interest to pay attention. I quickly moved myself into the shadows, to keep the odds even. I wasn't about to have someone creep up on me. That just wasn't going to happen. I was smarter than that. I decided to take a long roundabout route to get back to my pad, just in case I was being followed. I knew it sounded totally paranoid, but so much has happened to me as of late, that I had to be extra careful. Chalmers had warned me about things seeking me out, and though I was most likely imagining this nonsense, I thought to side with caution. I walked up the street, being careful to avoid bright places as much as possible. I got about a half block from the area that I had climbed up the bank, and something in the back of my head told me to stop. I ducked behind a parked car and peered back to the place where I had climbed up the steep bank, and damned if someone didn't creep up onto the street from that very same spot. The person was carefully looking around, peeking over the edge of the cliff to the walking area down below and then up and down the street. It almost looked like he was sniffing the air, like a dog following a scent. It freaked me out big time. Part of me wanted to go over there and confront the guy, but I kept hearing Chalmers words of warning in my head. He told me I wasn't ready for such things.

Right now, my head and my heart told me to hide out and let whoever or whatever it was pass. So I stayed out of sight and just watched the figure search the cliff side. It had paused for a moment and looked up the street past me, and when it did, my heart near jumped up into my throat. I laid down flat on the asphalt and I mean flat. I tried to look under the cars at the figure, but there were tires blocking my view and it was too dark from that angle. "Crap," I thought as I found the courage to take a peek, only to find that he was gone. Now I was really freaked out. "Am I just paranoid or am I being messed with royally?" I thought as I sat there for about a minute. Then I said to hell with it, and got up, brushed myself off and just walked down the sidewalk, back to my apartment. I did, however, pull a handful of flowers out of the little garden that I was standing next to. We had a lot of those in OB. Everyone planted flowers outside their apartment complex or their home. They pretty much bloomed year-round.

Anyway, I figured if someone were tracking me, maybe this would throw him off the scent. I was really feeling stupid by the time I got home. I'm supposed to be this big east coast tough guy, and I'm hiding from in the shadows from no one.

"Where you been?" Dan asked. He was out on the walkway having a cigarette when I came in through the front gate. "Just went for a walk. What are you up to?"

"My co-worker called, and he wanted to go down to Bullfrog's for a game or two of pool and some beers.

You down?" he finished his smoke, and we went inside. "Oh yeah, I'm down." I finally had something to do.

"Sounds like a good reason for a magic shot, eh?" "Maybe three?" Dan quipped back. "Oh yeah." I got out into the kitchen and grabbed the Absente and the wormwood and whooped up a batch of old school Absinthe, aka: magic shot.

Absinthe was still illegal in the United States, but you could purchase the liqueur called Absente. You then buy the wormwood extract from the herb shop. Mix the two together with some water and fair amount of sugar and you get Joe's home-made Absinthe. I would put my stuff up against that European stuff any day. "Me like," I thought out loud, as I loaded up the glasses and handed one to Dan. We clinked them together and slammed the down. Then we both winced at the strong licorice taste.

"Good stuff," Dan sputtered. It had a wicked light green color to it and a very bitey taste when it was made properly. "I think that's enough of that." He smiled a big smile and got himself ready to go out. We both knew the Absinthe should kick in by the time we got to the bar, giving us an edge at the pool table.

It was slightly different kind of buzz than normal alcohol or marijuana and it seemed to kick in rather quickly. We knocked fists with a smile and headed out. The night air was brisk, but we were both from the east coast, Dan being from Boston and me from Jersey so neither of us really felt the cold. Plus, Dan had a good bit of insulation. He is a heavy guy, and his heart was as big as his gut. He was a great roommate, and I had a pretty good deal of respect for him. He was also fairly agile for his size. We had wrestled on several occasions, and though I was quite the toughie, I usually ended up with the brush burns and sore ribs. I always knew that if I could stall long enough, he would get winded in a minute or two and I would have him, or if I got rough enough I would have him, but he usually got the best of me in the short run. We walked down through the alley, rounded the corner, and then headed down the street. It was a cool, dark evening and there was a fair amount of people out. We got down to the bar and snagged a pool table and a pitcher of beer. This place was my definition of a dive bar. It was a bit of a hole, with ten pool tables, and heavy metal music playing through the speakers. It generally drew a slightly raucous crowd, which I liked and was usually packed on Friday and Saturday nights. One of the pool tables were located just inside of an open window right off the main drag. It was the best spot in the house, as you could not only have a beer and play pool, but you could watch all of the pretty girls walking by on their way to the beach. I racked, Dan broke, and the game was on. I lost the first game before the Absinthe and the beer kicked in and bounded back rather quickly on the second. We were about to start the third when Dan's buddy walked in, so I decided to let him play. I sat back on one of the stools that were next to the table where I had set down my beer and I tried to watch them play. I was distracted by my reflection in the big mirrors, which surrounded the room. I was starting to feel the buzz and started playing with my wings. I quickly caught myself playing, contorting my chest and shoulder muscles back and forth, up and around. It did look pretty cool, as my full wingspan was quite large. I used my wings to pretend to move the balls around the table, but as usual, they just passed through everything. I wiggled and moved a bit more, and again saw how stupid I must have looked in the mirror. So rather than have the other two guys think I was crazy, I stopped and just sat back on my stool. But as I sat back, my left wing brushed our little round cocktail table just enough to topple an empty beer bottle. It clanked off the carpeted floor, but did not break, amazingly. Dan and his buddy Jake both turned to look, smiled, but said nothing. I had to have had that drunken startled look in my eyes. But this was much more than me being clumsy. This was a true moment. I had to look to be sure that I hadn't bumped the table with my stool or my leg, but I hadn't. I was a good three feet away from it. I picked up the bottle and set it back on the table. No harm, no foul. I then tried to move it with my wing, but it just passed through the glass container and the table as before. I tried it again, and again the wing just glided through everything. My excitement dwindled a bit. I finally figured that I must have bumped the table without knowing it. That was the logical conclusion. It was a mistake to think that I could have moved the bottle with the wingtip. I had a decent buzz and I had allowed my imagination to get the best of me. I had to just shrug it off. I watched Dan beat Jake and it was my turn again. I hurried some beer down my neck and racked the balls. Jake went to refill the pitcher while Dan broke, and I watched two striped balls go down. He sank one more ball before it was my turn. I was really buzzed now, and we all started giggling at something stupid that someone at the next table said. It was just some random stupid thing, but when Dan started to laugh, it was usually contagious. I tried to line up a shot, but the beer and the Absinthe had kicked in and I just couldn't stop laughing. I tried to take a quick sip of beer to help me stop for a second, but I started to laugh again and it near came out of my nose. I turned toward the wall to spit out the little bit of beer that was in my mouth, and I felt the weirdest thing. I could feel my wing touch something.

"What the heck." Dan asked. "Did that ball just move by itself or did you kick the table?" I looked at the table and one of the balls was still moving slowly across the tattered felt. It took a half a second to register it, but I wasn't even close enough to the table to have been able to bump it. I had to have moved the ball with my wing. I had to have. I was ecstatic but could not show it. I was pretty lit, and I did not want to look like an idiot. What could I tell them, that it was me, that I hit the ball with my invisible wing?

"I think I bumped the table when my beer almost shot out of my nose," I told him with a smile.

The ball was one of his and it stopped right in front of the side pocket. "Sorry," I said with a slight shrug.

I knew he wouldn't complain because the roll benefited him.

"I'm not going to complain," he told me with a smile. His face was still red from laughing. And the rolling ball had blocked my only shot. I really wanted to try to move something else with my wings, but like I said, I didn't want to look like an idiot. I tried to take a shot, but the buzz that I needed to play properly had left me. I had gotten all excited and lost that happy little buzzy relaxed feeling. I had to try to concentrate instead of going with the flow, and it only took me about five minutes to lose the game. As it was my heart just wasn't into it anymore.

"I'm going outside to have a smoke," I told them, as they got ready for another game. I still had the full pipe load of pot in my pocket and the bar was mere feet from the beach. I no longer had the paranoid thoughts of strangers following me, especially here and now. Besides that, I was quite a formidable foe when I had couple of drinks in my system. I thought about the dream or vision, I had earlier, the one in which I was a general or something like that in the corps of angels. I must have strutted my way through the overcrowded bar.

"Hold up, I'm coming with you," Dan told me, following me. "I'll be back to kick your butt in two minutes," he told Jake. "Crap," I thought. I just wanted to go outside to play around with my wings, but I wouldn't be able to do that with him standing there. We walked together past a few more pool tables where people were playing, so I opened my wings wide to see if I could move other balls on other tables on our way out. My wings passed through people, tables, and drinks, and they also sailed through all of the balls on the tables without moving a single one. I didn't let it bring me down though. I was giddy at the fact that I had actually felt something through my wing. It was freaky.

As we smoked, I opened my wingspan and let my wings pass through the walls, and the various people that passed by, but I felt nothing. I didn't even walk to the beach to smoke. I had smoked pot since I was eighteen and had become pretty slick about it. I could sneak a puff right there in front of a hundred people and though everyone would smell it, no one would ever even guess it was me that was smoking.

Dan smoked his cigarette, and I stole a hit here and there. As it was, this was considered a hippy town, a throwback. No one even gave two looks when they smelled marijuana. There were a lot of people out for a Sunday night, and I decided to stand right out in the middle of the busy sidewalk with my wings fully expanded. One older lady walked right through the middle of my left wing, and she sneezed, I chalked it up to coincidence, but it would have been funny to find out if she was allergic to feathers or something like that. I tried to be cool, but Dan saw me and punched me hard in the arm.

"Ready to get your butt kicked again?" "If you

can beat Jake, then I'll take the table from you," I told him with a nod.

As I walked in, I twisted my wing all up in the doorman's face. The guy didn't budge, but I thought it was funny. "How about a shot? Dan asked as we headed back into the bar. "I wish," I laughed. "I gotta work tomorrow." I did appreciate the offer, but I was already half in the bag. I did figure, however, that I had just had a long nap on the rocks earlier, so I could justify another beer or two.

We played a few more games, drank more beers, and had fun. After a little while of trying to move things discreetly with my wings, I just stopped. It wasn't going to happen again, and I needed to keep my game face on. There was no way I was going to lose every game. We must have played seven or eight more games before finally heading home. It was late, far later then I should have been out. The rest of the night was uneventful, and my half drunken stupidity drew very a little attention, as there were bigger idiots out and about than me that night. I waived my wings in people's faces as I passed them.

They wouldn't see or feel them, so it was like an inside joke to me. I wasn't hurting anybody, but it was fun to flick a snooty girl or a muscle head in the face every here and there. It was kind of like flipping them off without anyone knowing about it. It was harmless. At least I thought it was. Had I really known how dangerous that was, I surely would not have done it. As it was, there may have been several pairs of eyes upon me, just like Chalmers had said. He knew I would be drawing attention to myself, but his words never really sank in or perhaps I was just working extra hard to ignore them. I didn't really have much of a worry or much of a care anyway at this point. I was stumbling and bumbling up the street and to my place. By the time I reached the apartment I was ready for bed. I made sure that I had gotten pretty drunk to avoid the absolute fear I started to have about going to sleep. I feared that I was going to have one of those crazy visions again, and I was determined not to be sober enough to deal with it or remember it. I hit the sheets and I was out.

FOUR

The alarm clock seemed to go off way to early. I knew I had to get up for work, but my head just wasn't in it. I hated calling in sick, because I always felt guilty. As it was, there were only three of us in the whole company. The other two were related to each other and never seemed to get very sick. I, on the other hand, got sick every six months or so because of my allergies or the slight change of seasons and missed a day here and there. I also felt the need for a mental holiday every now and then. Today was most likely going to be one of those days.

As I stirred, I felt the effects of the beers and magic shots I had mere hours prior. I knew better than to try to keep up with Dan, especially on a work night. I was contemplating on why I had stayed up so late when I realized that I had made it through a whole night without the nightmares or visions. I sat there for a moment and thought about it. No, there was nothing that I could recall. All of the other dreams seemed to linger on after I woke up, but this morning I was free of those things. I pulled my lazy butt out of bed and went to make some coffee. As

I did this, I thought about what I would say to my boss. The sun was just creeping up over the city and would soon be climbing up over the hill behind my apartment. I looked out of the kitchen window at the world and wondered what this day would bring and it wasn't long before I knew.

"That was a pretty good show you put on last night," Chalmers commended.

He had pretty much scared the crap out of me, and I jumped to the ready, hands balled into fists.

"Good morning to you too," I said with a sarcastic tone. "What happened to you last night?" I asked as I poured water into the coffee maker. "You just disappeared." He turned to look out the window and spoke with his back to me.

"I'm not even supposed to be here," he told me before turning to look at me.

"I'm just a Watcher. If my little pearls of wisdom are not appreciated, I can leave and never return. I will always be watching you, but you will never know it. I am here now to help out if I can, and I do so at peril, remember that." That caused me to stop. "What kind of peril?" I asked. "Great peril son," was his cryptic reply.

"I'm a Watcher, not a bloody babysitter. I don't know if anyone else is watching you and I sure as hell don't have a clue if anyone is watching me. That's just the way it is. It's the way it has always been.

You live your pathetic little life and I sit and

watch. And then, every once in a while, I go and report your progress, or lack thereof, to my superiors."

"Like a guardian angel?" I asked. "No, not a guardian. I don't get to guard you. I've never gotten a say in anything you do, until now, and I don't know how long this will even last." He ran his ringed finger through his long hair, pushing it out of his eyes. I felt a chill run up my spine.

"What do you mean?" "I mean that I'm not supposed to be here. I'm not supposed to be able to talk to you and I'm not sure how my superiors would respond to it should I be caught." He turned back to look out of the window, and I wasn't sure, but he appeared to be looking for something. I really did not like what he was saying. It scared me a bit.

"Who are your superiors and what might they do?" I asked. I was also wondering what they might do to me. "Hey, you let me worry about that, okay? He continued to look out the window.

You'd better get ready for work," he told me. "I thought I would call in sick today," I started, but was cut off. "Yes, I know. Bad idea. You go to work, and I have yourself a normal day. No need to draw attention, like you did last night."

"Honestly, what are you talking about?"

He turned and looked me right in the eye. "From my position, you were lucky you didn't bring the entire evil armada down on yourself." He was both angry and terribly disappointed.

"We have a chance here to make things right

and you act like an idiot." He turned back toward the window.

"Look, I'm sorry, but you gotta understand, I've dreamed of flying forever," I started.

"That's because it's what you used to do. It's what you will do again if you can solve your bloody puzzle.

That is the prize at the end of your long journey." He spun to look at me again.

"Do not forget that I have always been there. I watched you being born, growing up. When you think you are all alone, you aren't.

I'm always there. I've always been there."

"My God," I thought. I slide down into one of the chairs at the small round kitchen table and let my head rest in my hands. It was all beginning to sink in. This is how it was going to be. It wasn't going to go away. I thought back to all the times that I thought that I was alone, and there was a great deal of them.

I must have done some pretty embarrassing stuff. I thought of all the bad things, I had done as a child. I was such a devil when I was young. I have broken into people's houses, vandalized, stolen everything under the sun. I mean I did some really bad stuff. I slashed tires; I threw rocks off a railroad trestle down onto cars on the freeway below. I had even learned that if I wedged enough rocks into a switch on the railroad tracks, that I could make a speeding freight train come to a complete stop. "Oh my God", I thought.

"Ah, you see the light," Chalmers said with a semi-smile. Boy did I. I rubbed my face. "Why me?" I asked "Why am I here? What am I being punished for?" Chalmers looked over his shoulder, out of the window.

"I am limited as to what I can talk to you about right now. I don't want to raise any red flags. Remember this. I told you there are beings from both sides of the Great War are here on this world. There are creatures such as you here that only you will be able to see, hear, and smell. Be mindful of the things around you. There are things here that would do you great bodily harm." I wanted to ask him what to look for. How I could tell who was who, what was what? But he put a hand to silence me.

"You've always seen them. They are things you thought you saw out of the corner of your eye, but when you turned to look; nothing was there. They are the things you smelled, but no one else could smell. You know what I'm talking about. Well now you might really be able to see them, and rest assured, they will be able to see you. Be mindful. Be careful." Then he looked past me. "Your coffee is done," he commented. I turned to look, but when I looked back, he was gone. "Crap," I thought out loud. I took a peek outside to see if there was anything there. He seemed to be fairly preoccupied with something out there. I looked but saw nothing out of the ordinary. Perhaps he was looking for something that was beyond my range of vision. Perhaps there was something out there that he was just now warning me about. I decided to close the blinds and just get ready for work. A half an hour later, I was rolling out the door with my lunch box and my MP3 player. I have to say that I was a tad bit paranoid, but I made it to my car safely and was off. It normally took me about twenty minutes to the office. Today, though, it seemed like forever. I just couldn't shake that feeling that Chalmers had been watching me my entire life. I had spent a great deal of my life alone, or at least I thought I had. That was just the way I was. I had a lot of friends, but I cherished my alone time. I think that started or had been programmed into my head when I was young.

My father worked the night shift, so I barely got to see him. My mom had also worked part-time so when I got home from school, I had to keep myself occupied for a good part of the day. My brother never had a problem making friends and would be with them playing or studying, while I sat home alone. The television became my buddy later in life, right around my teens, when I put on a little weight.

I had been forced to become self-reliant, and eventually, I just kind of became a loner. A small part of me even thought I was better than most, above them because of my upbringing. I took care of myself while others relied on their parents for so much. Now I see where this idea may have come from. I always made a conscious effort to try to contain these thoughts. Now, I would have to try even harder.

I would have to be humble until I could figure out what I was being punished for and how to get it over with. I did long to be able to soar through the heavens once again, though. But for now, I would have to succumb to the idea that I was pretty much the low man on the totem pole of life, especially at my place of work.

As usual, my boss, Steve, was grumpy and gruff. He was an older guy, and he reminded me a lot of myself.

He was a prime example of what a mean old man I could become if I let myself go. He was shorter than me, so he felt he had to be a great deal louder than everyone else as to assert himself. In essence, he had short-man syndrome. Couple that with the fact that he had been quite spoiled as a child and it provided for the crotchety old man that presently stood before me. I had learned how to deal with it quickly enough though. I was good at that, it seemed. I absorbed his harsh words every day and just made the best of it. As it was, it wasn't me that he was angry with at all, it was his customers or vendors or even his nephews and nieces. I knew what to expect and how to deal with it. I just didn't let it get to me. I simply considered the source. I knew he was going to be a grump each and every morning, but the pay was decent, and I could handle the job. I was out of the office and on my way to the job site in no time flat. I drove to the house that I had been working on, unloaded some tools and went right to work.

Business had been booming and I was able to drive a spiffy new work van. The new vehicle was nice and it made us look successful. Today I was pre-wiring a home for speakers and surround sound and all that good stuff. I liked to work alone, even though I had most recently been enlightened to the fact that I never really was alone.

There were other people in the house working, such as electricians, and plumbers, and roughing it in their respective trade materials. The plumbers were running their pipes that would be hidden inside the walls and the electricians were running their wires. I was also running wires, but they were different in size and purpose. Nonetheless, the job consisted of drilling a hole in the joists, sticking the wire through the hole, climbing down the ladder, moving the ladder and doing everything again so that my wires could crisscross the house in an orderly fashion, without interfering with anyone else's space. I knew the building codes and I knew that my work was low on the priority list. Electricity, ductwork, and plumbing all took precedent in the structure. I had to work around that stuff. It was monotonous and I did it over and over and over. It was good exercise, but it was extremely boring. This was my job today and I did it the best I could. I was courteous to the other workers on the site and did what I had to do to get in and then out at the end of the day. But today, I realized, was going to be different. As I donned my work gloves, I couldn't help but feel more than just a bit paranoia and a tad bit of fear. There were a lot of different people of this particular job, and a good chunk of them were Mexican.

Now, I'm not saying that I personally, did not get along with them, but there was an underlying racial anxiety that we all pretty much shared. We did all work together as best we could though for the benefit of the job, the situation, and the fact that if any of us did anything stupid, that person would surely be fired. I went about my normal day, but I couldn't help but feel distracted, and my job was suffering because of it. My mind was elsewhere. I should have called in sick. What the heck was Chalmers thinking, I wondered. Had I known that the bum that had spotted me sitting at Lucy's was the same guy that had been following me the previous night down by the cliffs and that he had gotten dangerously close to my place of residence, I would have understood. He was protecting me without causing me to panic. But I didn't know this, I thought this was just more of something to keep me busy, to keep my mind off of things.

As it was, it wasn't working. I was moving slower, and my mind was not on my work. I continued through the day, listening to my music, drilling holes, and pulling on the variety of wires that seemed to constantly twist up on themselves all day. I was frustrating to have to constantly run back and forth to unsnarl knots that formed on the long runs of wire that went from one end of the house to the other.

By the time lunchtime rolled around; I had worked myself into a bit of a froth. I constantly looked over my shoulder to see who might be watching me. I was extremely paranoid, and my constant glances caused some of my co-workers to wonder about me. I couldn't tell if I had inadvertently started something with some of the guys or if they were eyeballing me for other reasons. Was it my glances at them that were provoking things or were they really looking at me, watching me work. I couldn't tell, but every time I stopped what I was doing and looked around, it seemed that someone was checking me out. Any of them could have been a demon. I climbed all through the wooden structure of two by fours, two by tens and whatnot. All morning long, the wings simply passed through everything. My mind was working overtime. I was over-thinking everything. I had to stop, catch myself and regroup a couple of times, but still my mind played tricks on me. It got old fast, so when the group of laborers got together and pulled out their hot plates and microwaves, I just walked over and sat down right next to them. I knew I wasn't welcome there and I knew they were probably cursing me out in Spanish, but I didn't care. If one of them had been sent to do my harm, I wanted to know about it. I looked them all, each and every one of them dead in the eye for a more few moments. After about ten or fifteen minutes though, it became pretty clear that my paranoia had gotten the best of me. And if I had no enemies before I invaded their lunch area, I was doing a good job at creating some now. Ii was quite evident in the way they were looking at me and talking amongst themselves. I finished my sandwich and went right back to work. I had to catch myself for fear of losing my mind, and for possibly getting myself into trouble with the job supervisor or Steve. I did my best to ignore the looks and glances that I caused with my lunchtime stare-down.

When the day started to come to a close, I worked it so as to be able to return my work truck and get in my car before the boss got back to the office. I didn't feel like making the 'end of the day' report. I skated in and out without notice. I needed some alone time. I had to figure this crap out before I really lost my mind or got myself hurt or fired. After all, this was just Monday. I had to come back to this same job site all week. I had to get my head right and get it done now. I had allowed myself to get pretty worked up by the time I got home, and the best way to fix that was first, a couple of tokes from the bong, and secondly with a workout. As I drew my second big hit from the tall glass water pipe, my mind ran through the events of the day, and I could not shake the memory of the laborers constantly peering at me. It made me mad, and I could get mad now because I was home. No one was going to get hurt. I thought the weed would have settled me down, but it didn't. I was angry now.

This was my country, after all and these were

a bunch of job-stealing illegal holes for the most part. They did shoddy work and brought down the pay scale and all the bleeding heart called us cruel for wanting to send them home. A part of me knew that I was probably imagining the whole thing, that no one was staring at me at all. For all I know, they could have been watching to make sure that they were out of my way, like I was doing for the plumbers and the HVAC guys. It could have been that simple, but my mind didn't work that way. I was a conspiracy theorist. I built mountains out of molehills. I dwelled on things that I shouldn't have. It was a problem I dealt with my entire life. I always over thought things. I dug into my closet and pulled out my heavy bag and hung it on the hook in the doorway. Then I threw some snaps and jabs at it. It was big, a seventy-pounder, heavy and thick. I was giving it a good working over, and it was hard on my knuckles. I needed this though. My mind was wondering back and forth between the then and now, and the next thing I knew I slammed my fist so hard into the side of the bag that I punctured it. Sand was running out of the broken canvas sack around my gloved fist and all over the floor.

"Crap," I said as I watched the sand continue to spill on the carpet. Then my mind finally registered what had just happened. I had punched through the dense, reinforced material. That was a pretty tough feat to do. I pulled my hand out of the bag, took off the protective leather gloves that I wore to save my knuckles, and brushed the sand off my hand. I looked at the hand, then the bag and then back to the hand. I had just pulled off quite a feat. As the sand leaked out onto the carpet, I wondered what else I might be capable of. I went over to the weight bench. Now I've had a bad back for some quite some time, and I was always leery of having to spend the next week in pain because I got crazy with the weights. But right then I felt like I was Superman. I was pounding weights, feeling quite powerful it was invigorating. I was able to do more reps on the bench press than I ever thought possible. Now I'm not saying that all of sudden I could pick up a car, but I did do thirty-two hard reps when my norm was around fifteen or twenty. I kept this up for about an hour, and then I decided to go for a good jog. That was always a good way to let off steam. I grabbed my MP3 player, stepped around the mess of sand in the small hall-way and headed out. I ran like Forest Gump, and soon out by the crashing waves of Sunset Cliffs. It was nice.

It was beginning to get close to sunset now and there was a bit of foggy haze rolling in, so I was surrounded by a warm glow. I was starting to get sweaty and was trying to breath in long drawn breaths. I passed one, then another pretty girl. That was always a bonus, but for as many pretty ones there was usually at least one idiot.

The path was thin in some spots and some parts were very close to the precipice, which dropped right into the Pacific Ocean. There were cliffs, and coves with the sea splashing onto the shoreline. I loved the sound, the smell and the colors. The path, itself, was essentially just a sandy trail that cut through the green ice plants. Some areas were wide and windy, and some were near treacherous with potential for deadly falls. I gave my usual quick glance and smiled at a pretty girl that passed me in the other direction, and looked up ahead to see a couple of jerks blocking the path where it narrowed. The lady looked right at me and didn't even try to give me some space. I had to jump up over the guardrail that separated the road from the jogging path.

"Dumbass," I muttered loud enough that she had to hear it. I jumped back over the guardrail, but I didn't look back at the two. I had to keep my eyes on the path ahead to watch out for other people that might be in front of me with their blinders on. This was always a big problem with me, and it always had potential to wind me up. It just seemed that people would have a clue to yield a little when someone was jogging by, or maybe just not stop and stand in the super narrow parts of the trail. What bugged me the most was when someone would look you straight in the eye and still step right out in front of you.

Man, that pissed me off every time. I've seen people get so mesmerized by the water that they would walk in front of a moving car. So even though it was nice to get out and try to get into the zone, I had to keep my eyes open, ready to bob and weave around these people. I even thought, from time to time, about giving some of these idiots a little nudge that would help them over the cliff's edge. It bothered me that I had those thoughts. I mean, I wouldn't want someone doing that to me. It's not like I would ever really do it, but I did think about it every so often. I came out for a jog to relax and ended up even more pissed off.

As I ran, I thought about the things I had seen the past couple of days. I thought about the man I really was and how having all of that crap cooped up inside my head might actually be a big enough reason as to why I was angry all the time. Very rarely did I find anyone that would match up to my tough standards, whether it was about work ethics or a relationship, and I was haunted by a desire to always be much more than I was. I knew I was destined for bigger and badder things, but I had no idea it would be something like this. I was thinking along the lines of public office, like a senator or something, not some avenging angel.

When I got home, I wiped the sweat from my face and smoke a little more weed.

After all, what better way to celebrate getting some good exercise besides smoking? I didn't smoke the little cigars I used to smoke anymore, but I could really have used one right now. Instead, I kind of moped around a little bit. Then I looked up and Chalmers was standing there.

"Want a toke?" I asked jokingly.

"No thank you," he replied with a smirk. He happened to glance at the mess of sand on the floor. "I see that you've let your emotions get the best of you again. Wonderful job, however, this isn't the reaction I was looking for." "I know," I told him as I emptied the cans and plastic bottles out of the recycling bucket into a plastic bag.

"I don't know what came over me." I kept myself busy as to avoid looking at him in the eye, and also because I didn't want Dan to come home to a mess of sand in the hallway. I used a cup to scoop the sand up into the bucket while I listened for another pearl of wisdom.

"It's really nothing new, is it? That's just the way it is and the way it has always been. Time and time again, it has been your undoing.

This rage of yours is what got you sent here in the first place."

"I heard you say that before, but I really don't know what you mean. I don't understand why I'm being punished. I've seen bit and pieces, but what did I do that was so bad?" I asked, scooping up more sand.

It was everywhere.

"I guess I have been a bit cryptic about things. I forget you don't fully remember everything. And though I can hear what you are thinking, I just can't dig into your brain." He walked over and sat down on the gray couch and watched me clean while he talked.

"We are all a part of a central consciousness that stretches across all of time and space. At one end there is nothing but darkness and hatred while at the other end is enlightenment and happiness. We, you and I are part of the side of light. You protect the souls that reside here, and I watch you do it, reporting back to my superiors every so often. These souls are members of the Great Joining and they can stay in this joining as long as they desire. On this plane of existence, they have eternal lives and live forever, together intertwined. But every so often, they all eventually choose to be assigned to a body on some distant, strange world where they will live out a short life and then return. Each time they die, they return to the plane to share its experience both good and bad, so that all could share, and all could learn. Every life is different and each one unique. It is how they live and learn, and how they grow. There will always be a small part of them left behind with the group consciousness, like a voice in the dark to call them home when that small life ends. That is the duality of the soul, a part is here on this world and a part remains with the Great Joining of Souls. It is a magical thing that few can understand. Think of each life like a big rubber band, stretched to be both here and there." He paused for a moment, as though deep in thought. Then he continued.

"So you see, you are a part of something bigger, something so wonderful that words cannot explain." It was almost funny to me to hear him talk this way.

"On this ethereal plane there lies a division, and the lines of this division are often times tested. On one side of things there is light and on the other side there is darkness. And in between there is chaos. The dark always wants to take over and extinguish the light, and light always wants to brighten the darkness.

This bloody line is in constant turmoil, and skirmishes small and great fill it from one end of time to the other. The dark side always wants to push that line further into the light. And the light side is content to hold the line in its place. For this reason, the light is able to be victorious on almost every front." I stopped scooping up sand. This was getting deep. This was some important crap and I wanted to pay attention. "This division between the light and the darkness is fuzzy yet defined. The Powers That Be are in constant battle to keep the line though both sides have a different agenda. While the dark side continues to push, the lighter side is happy just holding the line. And by trying to just keep the boundary where it lies, the light actually gains ground every so often because it doesn't exhaust its resources so quickly. This is the way things have been for a very long time. This has been the way that order has been kept. There had been, in the long distant past, times of extreme light and times of extreme darkness, but this present discipline has been able to hold up for eons." He leaned forward and put his hands on his knees.

"Then one day, you decided to challenge the whole bloody way of things. You decide to throw a monkey wrench into all of it. Bullocks!" He stood up and began to pace the living room while he continued.

"You know, long ago you were very instrumental in the war. You were a warrior, a great leader of angels. You protected all things light and good on more worlds than you could ever imagine, and you were spectacular at it. You were a true hero." He sounded almost melodramatic.

"But then one day you went too far. You got greedy and decided to try to push the line backward to force the light upon the dark. You did this without permission of God, and for that you had to be punished. For that, you would wander through time on different worlds in different lives and suffer. You would experience each lifetime as a normal being, just like everyone else, but you would know in the pit of your stomach that you had at one time, been greater than all of them. And this knowledge would eat at you and taunt you. You would know nothing of your past, but it would constantly and consistently call to you." He continued to pace around the little section of the living room.

"This revelation would be buried in a distant memory, but it would haunt you from life to death to life again. And unlike the souls that surround you, you would not report back to the Great Joining after each death. Instead, you would be reassigned immediately. You would jump right into another body and be born into a new world of torment. You would forever be teased by the fact that you know you could have and should have everything you could ever want or need, but instead, success, victory and fame would always be just out of your reach in these lives. You would be seen but not seen for what you were, and you would be overlooked time and time again. No one would ever know that you were once responsible for their very lives, that you and yours kept the alive and in the light. This would be the long

lasting punishment for your transgressions. You would live a million lifetimes on a thousand different worlds as a natural inhabitant of each, living among the other species of the planet. You would eat what they ate and drink what they drank, and you would be humbled. This is the judgement of the central consciousness that binds and guides us. This is the commandment and word of God." His voice seemed to echo through my mind. I got up and walked away from the mess and made my way over onto the futon where I sat and listened. This was all making such perfect sense to me. He was on a roll, so I allowed him to continue.

"You were one of the greatest warriors the corps had seen in a very long time. You even rivaled Lucifer in your power, might, and wisdom. Then you made the same mistake that he made and challenged the Throne. Your decision was not as fatal as his. He wanted to take over, while you simply wanted to push back the darkness. You had been an instrument of God on the side of light for eternity, and you did your job well, but you always aspired for more. You wanted to challenge the order of things with an unauthorized preemptive strike, and you decided to enter into darker territory to try to save a dying world. You almost succeeded, but the price would prove to be more than you could have ever imagined." He looked down and shook his head back and forth slightly.

"It had so irked you just to hold the line and stop there because you knew that your troops were capable of so much more. You had begged, pleaded just for a chance, one bloody shot at the prize. But the Powers That Be had their own agenda and time and time again you were forced to withdraw from a war that you knew you could win. It frustrated you to no end and eventually you put a plan together that would test the boundaries of the very fabric of the universe." That did not sound good, I thought. I was really not like where this story was going, but I allowed him to continue uninterrupted.

"Time and space mean nothing in this realm, but the edge of light and dark is the difference between life and death. The further that one traveled into the darkness, the more it reached into you and eventually it would take you, own you. And once that happened, everything you were, everything you knew would belong to it. You would not return to the light, but instead learn to hate it and eventually join with the darkness to fight against it. Once you were lost, there was little to no chance that you would ever find the way back home. Because of your stature, you had access to information that was privy to a chosen few. Included in this data was a tentative schedule of worlds that were falling. You chose one of those worlds and took the war into your own hands. This world was on the brink of destruction. Corruption had invaded every nook and cranny of its governments. Its industries had poisoned the air and water.

Plant and animal life were dwindling, and the shadows had begun to fall upon this place. There was a lot of good souls that would be lost if things were allowed to continue as they were, so this proved to be the best-case scenario for you to show your might. You had sized this place up for some time and knew that your time had come. There was a good chance that this world would be deemed unsalvageable, as often times happened to appease the bloody line between the light and the dark. Sometimes the decision to send in the troops came too late and the shadows would be allowed to consume everything.

No one liked this, but it was often times a necessary offering to keep the precious line in place. Neither side wanted an all out war, as neither wanted to gamble the share each held of the universe. But you were about to force everyone's hand."

I could tell through his intonation that he as a bit bitter about the whole situation. Perhaps he had even empathized with my plight. He said that he had been with me a very long time. Maybe he also thought that such a decision was long overdue. Or perhaps he was angry with me. Maybe he thought that my choice to do what I did was wrong. I could not tell which it was, so I allowed him to finish without interruption.

"You had one of your legion's finest soldiers stand-by as you entered the cold, cold darkness alone. Only your most trusted Lieutenants knew where you were going and what you had in mind, but you were still left on your own. You wanted it that way because that would be the only way the Powers That Be would listen to what you say. This way you would show them all that you and your legions were ready to take on the darkness. They would see through your lone actions that you were ready to push the line and finally give the darkness a good kick." He did a lot of talking with his hands. His rings glistened as they passed in and out of the rays of light that were shining through the windows. A part of me knew what he was talking about. It gave me the strangest feeling of both pride and guilt that didn't sit well in my stomach. He smiled at me, but it wasn't a funny, ha-ha smile. It was sarcastic.

"Here is something you didn't know." His look and tone seemed a bit condescending now.

"Your presence was detected long before you

arrived at your destination, and the shadows rallied. You should have seen this. You should have planned for it, but your desire to show everyone that you were right clouded your judgement." He chuckled.

"You could have easily dispatched every monster on that world, but you weren't just fighting them."

Now he was smiling.

"You know how I told you that you give off a light here when you play with your wings and the like?

Well, imagine the glow you give off in the heat of battle. You were deep into the darkness, far deeper than you should have gone, especially alone. As you took on the hordes of shadows, creatures from the depths of the blackness, emerged for the first time in eons. Once your identity had been discovered it became monumental to pull your knowledge and power into the dark forever. Alarms sounded on both sides of the line and as you fought so heroically, you accidentally started a war that still rages on and through today. One selfish, arrogant act provided the groundwork for an all-out push from the darkness to take advantage of the light's unwillingness to push back and for the first time in a very long time they started to lose ground." He folded his hands now and looked down at me. He could tell that I understood what he was talking about now. His words were sinking in, and I was starting to remember.

"While you fought through an onslaught of shadows and demons, far worse creatures approached your position. Reinforcements had been called in.

The funny thing is that you were actually very close to achieving our goal. You had taken quite a beating and near your last breath, but you fought on. This was going to be it. This was your one chance to show everyone that you were right, that it was time to push the line. If you did not succeed, then there would be no reason to return. You had based everything you had on this belief. You had moaned about this for centuries, and this was your one and only chance to shine or go out in a blaze of glory. You were finally putting your money where your mouth had been for a millennium. And with your dying breath you were about to prove them all wrong. You would have achieved your goal. You had cleansed the entire planet, but they just did not stop coming. Then the lights went out. It was as if a giant hand had reached out of the black and plucked the entire world out of the light, pulling it deep, deep into the abyss. And the world that you thought you could save was engulfed." His condescending tone changed and looked away.

"It's strangely sad to watch a world die. The poor bloody desperate fools scurry about trying to figure out what is happening. Usually, this sort of stuff doesn't happen until a world has beaten itself up pretty good, like wars and hate, violence and suffering running rampant. By then most of the good souls have long since gone and remains are left as a peace offering to the dark side. The Powers of Light give in and let go of the world and balance is kept. That's the give and take of the grand scheme of things. That's the ebb and flow of time and space and everything that ever was and ever will be rolled up in a nutshell.

The dark and the light are always pulling everything they can toward themselves, trying to suck in new life and young worlds. They are both part of the central consciousness, but at either ends of the spectrum, joined by the line that you once protected. And each is an important as the other. Each as the other. Without the one, there is no other." I knew what he was saying. There could be no sweet without the sour, no positive without the negative.

"Things don't usually happen quite so quickly. As a planet or solar system, or even a universe is pulled closer to the light or the dark, it changes. As a world draws closer to the blackness, its days are not as bright, and its inhabitants begin to loathe their own existence.

Wars break out, and evil starts to overwhelm every corner of every governing body. Things go from bad to worse, and eventually all is lost. Accordingly, as things drift toward the light, planets, and people prosper and grow and eventually attain enlightenment. But just because a planet or galaxy seems destined for enlightenment, things can happen to change that course. Believe it or not, karma does play a big part in the control of a world's path. Bad karma on a massive scale could cause it to slip into the abyss and into darkness forever. People and places slide in out of the dark all the time, but when it happens on a grandiose scale, the entire course of a world can change. This is the cause of the ever-fluctuating line between the light and the dark. You've lived countless lives on both sides of the line, always hidden from yourself and those around. You've been in some pretty bad places and suffered through tremendous pain during your punishment. All of the time though, your true identity had been concealed to you and your enemies. Now the door has been opened and you can see who and what you really are, but there are others that will be able to see who you are as well. The more you pry around into your true life, the more you show yourself to them." I just sat there with my mouth hanging open.

Really, what could I say to all of that? How could I have known that I was so important, or that I was really that arrogant?

"I'm so sorry," I told him. "I had no idea."

"I am sorry too. That is a lot to dump upon you, my boy, but I felt you had to know everything. This is your story, your legend. It is also the reason why I am sticking my neck out here for you now. I believe that you are worth the trouble that I may or may not get into should I be found talking to you." He looked down and then back up at me.

"This may be my one and only chance to truly help you, son. I need you to understand what is at stake, and I am willing to give up everything to help you." I didn't say anything. I couldn't. My mind was whirling with all of this new information. It all made sense. There was so much, but the more I thought about it, the more I did remember things. I remembered the tube.

"My God," I thought out loud. "This is insane." I remembered the staging point where we all gathered to attack. We would step up and go over our game plan and our objective. Then I would lead my troops into the swirl of light and color. I remember the feeling in my stomach when we entered the tunnel, the mix of adrenaline, anxiety, anticipation, and the tiny, ever so teeny bit of fear. The trickle of information became a flow. There was so much, almost too much to analyze, to comprehend. The images I saw were so vibrant, so colorful. I could feel the emotions flowing through me. I almost felt like I was in the tube, on my way into battle. In my mind, we all raced into the darkness, warriors ready for battle. We always had a pretty good idea what we were up against. Sometimes it was shadows, sometimes we fought monsters, lizard men, creatures that looked like giant mutated insects. The things we battled were in the process of dragging a world down into the darkness. They were residents of the domain that surrounded each world as it slid.

In essence, when they attacked, they spread fear, anger and misery. They fed off of it, as well as off of the flesh of the living. A world such as this might be invaded by gigantic insects or perhaps by swarms upon swarms of smaller ones. It made little difference. Each would install the terror and would eventually consume a planet's inhabitants and resources until all was lost. Nothing helped a planet fall faster than when its masses lost hope and lived in total fear. In all of my days, I had realized that there were few things more determined and more frightening than the shadows. When the shadows fell upon a world, it had little hope. Most of the time, those worlds were allowed to fall. It's not that we ever actually lost a battle, but sometimes we were just not deployed. There is a difference. I had been forced to see planets destroyed when I thought that we could save them. We were held back because in my opinion, because our higher ups were afraid to take a chance. They feared that should we lose, then the darkness would have the upper hand. So even though all of our battle were hard fought, we were supposed to win.

It was designed that way. That was the way we held the line. I had pleaded for a good fight for as long as I could remember, and I petitioned for our chance more times than I care to think about. I felt that my troops were ready to battle right up and through the very gates of hell itself.

Unfortunately, I was the only one that thought that way. So, when I went down the tube alone, I gave my superior's little choice. I would be forced to learn humility. I would live these lives as mortals, but where others would succeed, I would forever fall. I would not just be one of them, I would be forced to struggle in everything I tried. I would become the king of having the carpet yanked out from underneath me time and time again. I would be daunted by false hope and always, always just scrap by. There would be no Holy Grail for me. I wasn't sent to these worlds to prosper and enjoy myself. I had been sent there to learn my lesson and would be constantly haunted with pain and misery. The funny thing was that in the life, right here and now, I had experienced what I called a spiritual awakening. I was already trying to be humble, to be thankful. I was learning to ask what I wanted and be grateful when I got it. I was learning to live and let live and lend a hand to people that were less fortunate than me. I could well have been very close to ending my ongoing punishment. It was the best chance I had to fix things in a very very long time. Then all of this crap happened. And as this thought settled in, it took the wind out of my sail. Chalmers stood out near the kitchen, dining room area, which opened into the living room where I sat. He knew exactly what was going through my mind and watched me go from sitting straight and upright to slowly slumping. He shared his attention with a peak out of the kitchen window every now and then.

"I'm sorry," he said. "I was so sure that you were going to be forgiven and returned to your place of power." He looked down at the ground and then back up at me.

"I imagine that my disappointment was evident

the instant you saw me." I thought about the look disappointment Chalmers had showed me the instant I saw him. Now I understood.

"How do we rectify this?" I asked with a hopeful tone. That caused Chalmers to smile a bit. "I told you son, you have to go on and live out this life and just be humble and helpful. I don't know if that's enough, but it couldn't hurt." Then his smile broadened a bit. "I'm not saying that there weren't times in this lifetime that you weren't a complete and total jerk, it's just you seem to have been growing in the right direction. I had actually developed hope. I would love to see you back at your full potential. I am so bloody tired of seeing this miserable mopey side of you." He walked toward me a little. There was a hint of excitement on his face. "I'm just happy that we are now on the same page, that you now understand what is at stake here." He looked genuinely pleased, and I knew that he wanted to say something more, but he looked back over his left shoulder and must not have liked what he had seen. He was gone again, just like that. He just faded away into thin air. I knew that I would see him again soon, but for now I would just let all of this new knowledge sink in. For the first time in a very long time, I kind of felt pretty good about myself. I had hope and knowledge of my past and future lives. Today I was enlightened. Few people could ever hope to be so lucky. I knew it was going to be a challenge to get through all of this but at least I had something to look forward to. Had I known that my extended visit from Chalmers was like lighting a candle in the dark, I might not have been so happy. Though I had knowledge, I had also allowed certain factions to become aware that something was amiss on this world.

FIVE

I sat there for a moment or two waiting for Chalmers to return, but he didn't. I had little else to do, so I finished cleaning up the mess. Then I moseyed around the apartment and thought about what he had just said. I had to think about it for a moment, but there was a distinct possibility that I had just learned the meaning of life. "How weird would that be," I wondered to myself. I knew why I was here, why we were all here. This day had started off pretty miserable but ended on a great note. I wished Chalmers would have stayed a bit longer, but the more I thought about things the better I felt. I finally had it all laid out in front of me, and this knowledge was going to make it a whole lot easier to follow the rules that Chalmers had laid out. I watched the sunset out of my kitchen window and thought about my punishment. It all made perfect sense now. I was arrogant for a good chunk of this lifetime and I probably acted the same when I was an angel. It seemed so funny to hear it now that I understood everything. "I was an angel." I let the words roll off of my tongue and tickle my ears. I was an angel, and I would be again someday. I knew how to fix things now and there would be nothing to stop me from returning to my rightful place of power. I had always thought that I was capable of so much more and now I know that I truly was. I took a seat, interlaced my fingers behind my head and laid back on the futon. I closed my eyes and thought about how lucky I truly was. My mind twisted with all of the new information that I had just acquired, and then suddenly I was no longer on the black cushy mattress or even in my apartment. I was in a place that I had been to many times but was not really sure where I was at all.

And I felt so very strange. Then I saw a familiar face. "You can't just open the portal and go through it by yourself, you just can't," Gregor insisted. "It is dangerous, and it is against the rules."

"Shut up Gregor. I can do and I will," I told him. "All you need to do is open and close the hatch. That's it."

"Yeah, and then take responsibility for doing it when you are missed. I don't think so, Joseph." Gregor was a true warrior.

He was much taller than most of us, brutally strong, and chiseled, like he was cut from side of a mountain. His wingspan was one of the largest in the corps and when he set his sights on a target, he would delve in with all of his might. He would live and die by the commandment of the Almighty, but he would always be just a pawn. That was what I felt like as well, just a tool to be used in a game. I loved Gregor. He was not only my great friend, but one of my most trusted soldiers. We had fought together so many times, that in many cases he knew what I was going to do before I did.

"Look Gregor, this is our chance. I'm ready. When I do this, we will be able to show them that we are ready for a real challenge. There will be no way for them to deny us."

"No Joseph, you are ready for this. The rest of us are not. You want to prove yourself and walk all over the commandments in the process. Why can't you just let things be? Why do you always look for the challenge that might cost us so much? What if you get your big chance to conquer evil once and for all and you lose? Did you ever think about that? Did you ever weigh the consequences?" He had his long curly brown hair tied back, exposing his thick neck.

"We won't lose Gregor and you well know it." I was working up a head of steam and had the whole "fight or flee" feeling in my gut. "Now stop acting like a mamma's boy and open the door." I grabbed my sword and my shield and lowered the face guard in my helmet. I so love that faceplate. It was a golden three-dimensional impression of a gnarled, twisted face. It made me look so nasty. I know it was weird for an angel to want to look evil, but I felt that every little bit helped. Gregor just stared at me. If looks could kill, he would have slaughtered me with his steely gray eyes. We had had this talk many, many times, but never actually approached the portal. He knew there was no way I was just going to walk away from this, and he knew that even if I opened the tube and stepped into it by myself, someone would have to close it. If it were left open and unattended, who knows what would creep out of it?

"Look Gregor, the time for such discussion has long since passed. I am going through and you will close the door behind me. Do this as my friend. Do not make me order you to do it." I put emphasis on the word 'not'. There was nothing that he could do or say to stop me now. I had waited too long for this moment. "Remember that you will not have much time to reach your target. You should be mistaken for a group of us, as none have entered here alone before, ever. But once they realize that you are but one, they will try to overcome you with sheer numbers and brute strength. You must complete your mission and get back here as fast as possible." He looked at me in the eye and extended a hand for me to shake.

He was a comrade and a friend, and he knew that this was a moment when I would usher in a new era for our kind or quell this nonsense of mine forever. With that he turned the lock mechanism and the rods that held back the evil realm slide back in their slots and the thick metallic hatch opened slowly. I could feel the evil fill the room and reach to me, the cold dark feeling wrapping itself around me. I let it cover me, embrace me and then down the tube I went. The tube wasn't much of a tube at all. It was a cosmic portal that led to the center of the Great War, where entire worlds were being pulled into the darkness or toward the light. Lights and colors swirled all around me. It was mesmerizing. This was one of the very few times that I had programmed the portal. I had picked the target.

In most cases it was picked for me, already set up when I amassed my troopers. But this was all my doing, my little secret. I had picked a world that few would expect. It was my way of attempting a sneak attack. I left the tube after a relatively short journey and entered the worst place possible. The swirling tunnel ended in a flash of light, and I was dumped into total darkness. It was a wicked, horrid place where the vilest of every race that ever lived now dwelt. Worlds upon worlds, entire galaxies and universes were filled with these miserable rotten creatures that would never leave. They were all souls once, but they chose the darkest paths imaginable. They were the worst of their kind, given a chance for greatness that was squandered in evil deeds. I had argued this decision with my cohorts many, many times and they all agreed that this mission of mine was shear madness that I was also squandering a wonderous gift. But I could not hear their advice. It was negative to me. They all knew that eventually I would do what I wanted anyway. After all I was their leader, the best of the best, arrogant to the very core. I was going to be the one to have to show them all. I knew where I was going. I had this target marked for a long time. Something about this place called to me whenever I entered this realm. I'm not really sure what it was or why, but I knew that if I were going to prove myself this world of evil would be the one, I would try to save. And the evil beasts that lived there would suffer my wrath. They were all miserable wretches anyway and what would it matter? This one was a short list of places to be left to fall to the darkness anyway, so if I failed, then all would be as it was meant to be. But if I succeeded, well that was another story. I needed to show the Powers That Be that I was right, and that my troopers and I were ready for a real challenge. I would have a bargaining chip next time that I met with the Father. It would allow me to show him that we had the power to win the war, to shine a light deep into the darkness. I was easily seen coming through the dark skies, but again the reputation of my kind traveling in a group had them bamboozled. I knew that they would cower from my presence, thinking I was at the very least a legion or two descending upon them. This would give me a chance to take up my position, and then I would unleash the beast that waited so long to be freed. I went right for one of the biggest cities on the surface of the planet, hit the ground swinging and never stopped. This was a world just like any other with buildings, people, animals, and the like. I was in the midst of all of them, just on a different plain of existence, a separate dimension. I was on the other side of the mirror, so to speak, where the shadows and demons lived. And I was fighting like a superstar. I was quickly covered in blood and bits of flesh, and I was just getting started. Eventually, the evil minions figured out that I was on my own, and the hordes started ganging up on me. There seemed to be thousands of them and no matter how many I dispatched, they just kept coming. But I was out of my mind with rage. Nothing was going to stop me. The beings that surrounded me would feel a wrath that had been brewing inside of me for eons. I had no troops to command, no rules to follow, it was just me and my sword. And I was truly in my glory, finally free. I had killed so many of them that I couldn't count. There were bodies and limbs everywhere. My own body was getting sore, and my mind was growing weary. I had fought longer and harder than this before, but not alone. It was hard to mind so many angels, and I had received several blows to my head and body. A couple of sneaky ones had gotten around behind me and got me good, but it had cost them their heads. Still my sword swung fiercely.

On this world, in this battle, many of the shadows resembled the people they mirrored in the other dimension, the inhabitants that lived here. So they looked like gray or black bipeds. They swung their arms and dark sword-like appendages at me. I finally cleaved myself a space amongst the monsters as to have a brief second to catch my breath. I was standing on a sea of corpses, covered in blood, or what would represent it, from head to toe. There were bodies and piles of goo that had once been shadows as far as the eyes could see in all directions, but in the distant hills I could see them massing, getting ready to gang up on me again. I was winded, that much was sure. Some of the blood on the ground was my own. I was definitely feeling worse for the wear, but I was committed. I was not going home until I killed them all. Just the thought of the glory alone gave me a new energy. I bent down a bit, then launched myself up into the dark sky like a rocket. I flew like a screaming eagle into the massing hordes and slaughtered a hundred in my first pass. I could taste their blood in my mouth, and it also burned my eyes. I blasted through the whole pile of them and banked up or so before I touched the ground. I was so nimble on my feet and agile that I was almost on autopilot. But then I stopped thinking and got careless for half a second. And that brief moment was all it took. I slipped on a fleshly mess and fell whacking my head real hard on the rocky ground. I got back up to my feet quickly enough, but I was noticeably dazed. I looked around and everything seemed to spin very slightly, but I continued to fight on. I swung my sword with what were quickly becoming my last fading ounces of strength. I was feeling more and more light-headed, but I battled on. I just kept on fighting. I didn't have a choice. I could not retreat, and I couldn't fall back and wait for help to arrive.

Even though the blood on my face almost

completely obscured my vision, I still fought on. I was slowing, losing consciousness, and for a brief moment I wanted to get away to regroup and rest my mind, but I couldn't. And for a moment I thought there was a very good chance that I would be mortally wounded.

But I just kept going, swinging, and hacking until I passed out. That was all I remembered before waking up in my quarters, in a whole lot of pain.

"How'd I do?" I asked Gregor, managing a smile. But just that small movement hurt. I looked down at my body. I had bandages pretty much everywhere.

"Joseph, you almost died, and the first thing you ask is how did I do? Well, you've killed them all. They are all dead, every last inhabitant of the planet. That's the good news. The bad news is that your battle left you exposed to outer-worldly forces, things you hadn't counted on. Had we not come to get you, you would have been lost. You slaughtered the entire populous of that world, but marauders and shadows from a neighboring galaxy saw what was going on and set their minds on finishing you off. They waited until you were nearly done in and attacked.

Fortunately for you, we were already on the way to get you." My small grin quickly melted away.

"Who?" I started to ask.

"It was Bastion. He ordered the lot of us to go and get you" Bastion was my second in command. He as very powerful and all of the troops respected him. He was my right-hand man and my friend.

"Seriously general, we got there just in time, and it was a helluva fight to get you back to the tube." I had done it. I had beaten back the evil ones all by myself, but my victory turned out to be an empty one. I had to be rescued and I would soon see what my pride had cost me. And though I was surrounded by my closest friends, suddenly I felt quite alone. I could feel a bit of sadness welling up in my stomach. I had taken my one big shot and I had failed. It was both sad and embarrassing. I could not look at my men, so I rolled over onto my side to face the wall and in the process, almost fell off the futon and onto the floor.

I was startled and it took a moment to realize that I was in my own living room. These little visions were beginning to feel quite real, and I was more than a bit thrown by this one. I looked down and my hands were shaking. So, I loaded up my pipe, took a hit, and then put on my shoes. I needed to get some air. I took a couple long drags, filling my lungs deeply and let them out slowly. I instantly felt a little better, but my insides were still twisting. I grabbed the MP3 player and headed outside. The night air was cool on my face. I looked down to see if anyone was around, but my complex was dead. It was Monday night, and it was fairly late. I walked up to the liquor store up around the corner and got a forty of Bud Light and then went for a walk. I had been so tempted to buy some tasty, flavorful Honey Berry Backwoods Cigars on my way out of the store, but I didn't. I just wanted to walk and drink. I stayed on the less traveled streets of OB, without much of a destination in mind. I had done this so many times before. I headed toward the soothing sound of the ocean.

While I walked, I took occasional sips out of the brown bag that contained my beer. My head swam as I thought about how arrogant I had been, and how much it had cost me. This was monumental. I had always had a hard time accomplishing anything substantial in this life. I didn't really know what I wanted to be when I grew up and I was near forty years old, and I just never seemed to be able to catch a break.

Even when I did, it was often followed by the carpet being yanked out from under me almost instantaneously. That's just the way it was and always has been. I'm not saying that I was a loser, but if you looked at my life up to date, it may appear that I was, to the untrained eye.

Soon enough, I was down near the cliffs and the ocean below me crashed hard on the rocks. I walked over to the short railing that protected the steepest, most rugged parts of the precipice. The rest of the little coastline was nice and open. I had always appreciated that because I know that something like this would be completely blocked off by a fence topped in with razor wire if it were located in my home state of New Jersey. It seemed that no one sued the city when people slipped and fell around here. But back east, everyone was out for a quick buck. I hated the fact that no one took accountability for his own ignorant actions. It was eerily similar to my current situation. I was going to have to take ownership of my actions. I was going to have to find a way to make up for what I did.

I was sitting on the little fence, relaxing, listening to the waves crashing down below. I was too deep in my thoughts that I did not hear or see anyone come up behind me. This was odd because I always felt things like that. I had taken some karate lessons back in the day and part of schooling was to sense when people were nearby.

"You got a light?" a voice asked from behind me. I was startled, and I turned and jumped up quickly with my hands clenched hard into fists. It was pretty dark now and I wasn't in the safest of places. There was a decent cliff just a couple of steps behind me.

"Hey man, you got a light?" he asked a bit more determined. Now I have never been a huge fan of the general public as a whole. It just seemed there were more idiots out there than sensible people. All I wanted was a moment of solitude. I came down to the cliffs in the pitch black of the evening to have some peace and quiet, and this person has to creep up on me and ask for a light.

"No, I don't have a light," I told him with a taste of anger heavy on my tongue. It was at this point that I realized how bad he smelled. He was still a few feet away, but his stench was near unbearable. I wanted to gag. "You don't have to be jerk about it," he commented in a cocky manner. Then he seemed to look me over, checking me out. He may have been looking to see if I were wearing any jewelry or if I had my wallet.

"You don't have to be a jerk either," I told him. It was obvious that I was a bit irate. I looked at him looking at me, and something-something felt familiar about him. I just couldn't put my finger on it, though. It was really dark, and I had had a lot on my mind the past couple days. Maybe it was the orange glow of the streetlights or the haze from the midst of the ocean, but the situation almost felt dreamlike.

He made no effort to continue on his journey. He just stood there eyeballing me.

"What? What else do you need?" I asked stretching out my arms, open palms facing up. He continued to stare which gave me the time to look him over. My eyes were always real good at night, but this guy seemed darker that he should have, and I don't mean dark skinned. There just seemed to be a shadow over him even though there was a fair amount of ambient light around us. He was as tall as me, wearing dirty, ripped clothes in layers, in that typical beach bum fashion, and he had gotten within about ten feet of me.

"You need to step back," I told him. He just continued to look at me.

"I know what you are," he finally said. The words crept to my spine. His voice had sounded different, strange. It was deeper and it sounded like it had a small echo to it, like it had been through a modulator or processing board. It was just creepy.

"Yeah, and I know what you are, a bum, now shuffle," I told him with authority. I shook that crazy, somewhat frightened feeling in my gut and bucked up. I hadn't been confronted by anyone since moving here, but I was always ready. I would not under estimate this dude. He was a bum, but he was still a man and there was always a chance that he could kick my butt.

"I know who and what you are, fallen one," he said in the same creepy voice, then he took up a fighting posture.

"I think you drank too much today grasshopper. And I think that you're barking up the wrong tree." This situation was going from dreamlike to surreal. I wasn't going to fight this guy, but I was starting to think I might not have much of a choice. And what was the 'fallen one' stuff? He was definitely sizing me up, digging in. And I got that fight or flee shaking feeling in my stomach. I looked hard at the guy that was about to attack me and I thought the lessons I learned in karate class.

"Don't get angry, just think and block his blows. The rest will come easy," I thought. And it would. I hadn't been in a whole lot of fights in my life, but I had been in some biggies. Bottom line was, if this guy wanted to fight, I was going to give it to him. He had his chance to walk away, but he seemed to have violence on his mind. Maybe it was the booze I could smell on his breath or maybe he was on something heavier. I had to be wary he wasn't high on PCP or something that would give him super strength. I was breathing heavy and shaking inside, like I had just stolen something and was afraid I was going to get caught. I closed my hands into tight fists and got ready. And then he came right at me, just like that. He bum-rushed me, literally. Talk about being thrown into the fire. I didn't have time to think, not time to react, but I did. I stepped and bobbed the assault, and for a second, I felt like things were going in slow motion. I sidestepped him and blocked his punch and then I hammered him. I felt like I was punching the heavy bag, because he just took blow after blow. I was faster and more lucid than I thought I would be, and I was in full control. I had fought hard in a couple of previous fights, but I always felt like I was out of touch with what was happening, that I had left my body temporarily. I saw bits and pieces, a head whacking off of the pavement or a couple of good body blows. These were almost out of body experiences. Things just happened, but I really didn't know how. It was like everything just fell into place and I fought like a warrior. I just remembered small bits here and there, but I couldn't tell you how anything really happened. It was like I got hit, blacked out for a second, hit the other guy two or three times, blacked out again, and was sitting on his chest, cracking his head open on the pavement. That was the way I fought. It was strange, but it was like my fists just knew what to do and made perfect sense that this ability might well be directly connected to my visions, my life of old. This time was different though. I was in control, and it felt good. I slide out the way and slammed the guy hard in the jaw, then again on his left eye. I seemed to almost have a taste of super speed, which I further contribute to the crap that was happening to me. My breathing calmed and my heart rate slowed. I was in a zone. I had a counter for every move that he made. I was ducking under punches and blocking kicks.

It felt amazing and quite powerful. But as the fight continued for a few moments it did, I started to realize that this was no ordinary run of the mill bum. This guy had skills. He absorbed a lot of blows and kept coming, swinging, and throwing kicks here and there. Had I not been in the proper mind frame, there was a pretty good chance he would kick my butt. He took a swing at me, and I leaned back out of the way, grabbing his arm and flinging him onto the ground very near the cliff's edge. I thought about Chalmers telling me not to kill, and for a second, I thought that was going right out of the window. But he rolled to a stop a couple feet shy of the precipice. He was covered in dusty, sandy earth, and when he rose bits of dirt fell off his body. He patted off his sleeves and brushed off his chin and chest, quickly ready to lunge at me again.

"Look, I have no money or anything of value. I

don't want to hurt you," I told him calmly. My stance showed him that I was ready.

"I don't want your money, general. I want your soul," he grumbled at me with that odd sounding voice.

He faked like he was going to jump at me, then backed off, then faked it again. He was testing me. I didn't know what to say, what to do. It was obvious that what I was dealing with was no ordinary bum or even a man. This might well be one of the beings that Chalmers had warned me about. How else would he know that I was a general in my past life? I quickly decided to take things more seriously. We circled each other for a moment, jerking like we were both going to attack, and eventually my back was to the ocean. I was playing around too much and ended up pretty much cornered.

"Your soul would earn me a second chance," he told me as he leapt toward me. The quick flash of the orange light reflected on the blade of the knife he produced. He was intent on dispatching me with either it or the drop off behind me. But I was way faster than he, and as he moved, I moved quickly and stepped to the side of him. As he passed me, I put my shoe up under his armpit into his ribcage. It was like a reflex. I kicked him so hard that he spun a bit and lost his footing. The momentum of his lunge and my kick sent him reeling over the edge of the sandy, rocky cliff onto the rocks below, and then into the dark foamy water. And then he was gone. I just looked at the water, waiting to see a body splash up. I couldn't have turned away if I had wanted to. Part of my mind was in total disbelief, and the other part was just mesmerized at the foam of the ocean far below. That was without a doubt one of the weirdest things that had ever happened to me. I fully knew that if I had not had the extra bit of strength I had lately, it could have most probably been me down there in the water, instead of that bum.

"Your soul would earn me a second chance," his words rang out in my head.

"Your soul would give me a second chance." This crap was just too much. I stood there with my wings all unfurled, breathing heavy, looking at the dark waters below for what felt like hours. I kept thinking about the body I had found washed up in a little cove just a few hundred yards away a couple of months ago. My morning jog had been interrupted by the sight of what I originally thought was a mannequin laying half buried on the beach. It sure as hell didn't look like a person the way it was contorted about.

I'll never forget the whiteness of the white on that guy's shoes. And I'll never forget the way it was twisted so. It didn't look real. I had stopped for a moment to look at it as I slowly jogged by but wasn't sure what I was looking at. Hesitantly I continued on with my workout. But on the way back I could see the lifeguards and cops around the scene. One of San Diego's finest confirmed that this was indeed a person that met his demise at the bottom of the deep blue sea. I didn't want to stop and gawk, so I headed home. It wasn't until I got within a block or two of my place that the whole thing hit me. The image of the mangled body turned in my mind and I thought that I was going to puke. That's about how I felt right now. All that crap had happened so fast that I didn't have time to think, but there was a very distinct possibility that I may have just killed someone. I paced and looked and paced and looked but saw nothing. I ran my fingers across the top of my head. I was bugging out. There was no way, no way that I just killed somebody. I almost wanted to jump in after him, but that wouldn't have accomplished the desired goal.

"I wouldn't worry quite so much about it," Chalmers told me very calmly.

"He won't be missed." He was standing about fifteen feet to my left, looking over the ledge.

"Yeah, that one's a goner." He looked at the crashing waves.

"But you won't find any bloody body-not from the likes of that one anyway." Again, with the riddle-talk.

"Look, I know you're not supposed to disclose too much, but what just happened?" I walked over toward him.

"Was that some kind of test that I just failed or what? Did I just kill a perfect stranger?" He looked at me and adjusted his sunglasses.

"Well, you saw that man yesterday morning at

the bar, but you were obviously too messed up to remember him." He brushed off his sleeves and tugged on his tunic to straighten it.

"He was stalking you. That," He said pointing into the briny sea, "was a demon, and you dispatched it promptly." I must have looked funny standing there with my mouth hanging open. Was that good or bad? Did I just mess it all up and condemn myself to another turn or two of this punishment? I had no words.

"Sure, that was..." I didn't know if I were in trouble or not or what I was supposed to do.

"So you mean...I mean, am I in trouble?" Chalmers smile at me.

"No, no you are not in trouble. I told you earlier that you would be in danger of being stalked by things like this. I even thought there was a chance or two that something may have already sniffed you out, but I didn't want you looking over your shoulder all day." He stepped back and snapped his fingers and suddenly he had his wooden cane with a silver dragon-shaped handle. He used the cane and right up to the edge where he pointed into the ocean with it.

"That guy could have killed you, man. He bloody well could have taken you down into the darkness, so I guess you can say that you did the right thing." I looked at him, then at the ocean, then back to him again.

"I thought you said that I couldn't kill, yet there is a distinct possibility that I just killed that guy."

"Not a guy, a demon," Chalmers interrupted.

"There is a big difference. You kill a human, your punishment most likely continues on to the next cycle, you kill a demon, and you keep yourself out of the darkness for another day. Does that answer your question?" He smiled at me, then turned and started walking.

"Come on. I'm going to walk you home. I have some things that I want to talk to you about." I looked back at the black waters.

"But...what about..."

"Leave it. Come on." He stretched out his arm for me.

"Come on," he called again. I finally walked over next to him, and we started walking home. My knees were a bit shaky, and my stomach churned just enough to give me that nauseous feeling.

"I'm not sure that I really understand all of this," I finally said.

"I'm not sure what to believe right now. Angels and demons and punishments and these freakin' wings it's all so surreal. I don't know what to think. And to top it off, I'm confiding in Chalmers of all people. I must have sounded like a beaten man. I didn't care. My head was swimming.

"You will have to get used to it. You have no other choice now. The door has been opened and it does not look like it is going to close. Ah, but here is something that might interest you. I have been given permission to guide you to a certain extent, and that is a feat in itself." He got a little overzealous and gave me a small whack on the shin with his cane.

"You will appreciate that fact the more you learn to use whatever powers you might have." That stopped my stomach.

"What do you mean? What powers?" I was noticeably curious.

"Oh yeah, I asked you to listen to me about good and evil, right and wrong, and you shrug me off. But the instant I bring up something like supernatural powers, well then, you're all ears, right?"

"Well this is some important crap, right?"

"And keeping yourself out of the darkness, isn't it? You have to get your bloody priorities in order, mate.

Whether or not you want to believe it, you are a pivotal player in the grand scheme of things." He shuffled along, using the cane to just kind of help himself. He tapped it on the sidewalk, the trees we passed, and drug it along the wooden fence so that it clattered loudly.

His words turned in my head and I thought hard about what he had said. I always had a bit of superiority complex, but I never dreamed of something like this. We walked in silence, other than the tapping of his cane. I continued to think about what had just happened, and then I realized that I almost missed something very important. I had been so caught up in what had happened that I let the fact that Chalmers had somehow gotten approval to talk to me.

"So how did you get permission to be able to talk to me? Do you know how I can get out of this place and back to where I belong? Tell me what to do," I asked in a flurry. Chalmers paused a moment. He knew that I was trying. He knew that this whole thing was a great deal more than my feeble brain could ever truly be ready for, so he let me slide a bit.

"I have friends," he told me with a smile.

"Don't forget that this punishment of yours is a punishment for me too, I too had been a bit over-zealous as your watcher in previous times. I had bragged to my peers about the wonderous sights that I had seen. I told them of our achievements and the battles that I witnessed while they watched lesser beings on lesser plains of existence." He swung his cane up so that it rested on his shoulder.

"So it was decided that when you received your punishment, that of course I would continue to watch over you. I too would be humbled." He scratched his temple with the tip of the cane.

"I should have seen it coming." He looked noticeably disappointed.

"I saw it coming for you-saw it a long time back. You just couldn't settle, couldn't just be happy in your own skin." But I never thought of my own actions as being arrogant, "how about me?" I asked him. The feeling of guilt for what I had done, coupled with the sight of watching that bum fall over the cliff pulled at me. As of late, I had been trying hard to see the good side of things, to see the glass being half full, but that crap doesn't always come easy to me. I have always been a bit of a tortured soul. I can see why now, but this wasn't going to go away. It wasn't going to stop. I had to find a way to shake the feelings that had been haunting me lately.

"What about what I did? How do you make up for that?" I reached back behind me and grabbed a hold of my right wingtip. It was so soft and bent around easily enough. It didn't hurt to bend it, but I could feel it.

"What about this? Will ever be able to use these things?" I asked the question, but I almost secretly knew what he was going to say.

"I seriously doubt it, but I honestly don't know. I saw what you did the other night at the bar," he started. I wanted to interrupt him by asking if he had really been there, but I caught myself. He was always going to be there, he had told me, on more than one occasion.

"I have to say I did not expect that. The problem being, however, is that it helped that demon find you. I cannot over-emphasize how important it is for you to stay hidden here." He whacked me again with his cane.

"You see how some things are real here and some things are not, correct?" I nodded.

"Well, I do know a thing or two, but I am not privy to all of the information regarding these things. I am not omnipotent. I have limitations as to what I am permitted to see and to know. For instance, I have hoped that you would have listened to me when I told you not to play around with the wings. You did it anyway, and that lead to the demon being able to track you."

"Well, why didn't you warn me about that guy? How long did you know about him?"

"I knew the instant he saw you in the bar the other morning, but I wanted to see if you would be able to recognize him for what he was. Besides, at the point in time, I had to be very careful what I said to you.

If one of my higher ups saw me giving you pointers, I may have been punished myself." I didn't really like hearing that.

"So, you would have let that thing follow me home, rather than tell me about it for fear of being reprimanded?" I asked with a bit of an attitude.

"Don't get all righteous with my boy. Do not forget that my presence here with you benefit the both of us. Had I been found out before I had the permission I now have; I may have been forever removed from your presence. And that, my boy, could have proved to very, very bad."

"How so?" I asked. I still had a bit of a chip on my shoulder. My hands were still shaking a little from the incident and my knees still felt wobbly.

"How so?" he sounded a bit cheeky.

"Perhaps you do not comprehend all the facts. I am a Watcher, and I have been with you for an eternity.

In that time, I have developed a small attachment for you. I actually want you to succeed. Because of who and what I am, that behavior exceeds my purpose. Should I have been reassigned then you would have been given a replacement, someone new that would not have given a crap about you. A replacement Watcher would watch and report but do little else or even have a care about you. Do you understand that?" His question was not meant to be answered. He was genuinely perturbed.

"I know that you do not understand everything that is going on here, but you will one day. Until that day though, implore you to please, please keep out of sight. You need to try to extinguish the light that shines from you. Think of yourself as a candle in a dark room. The more you play and experiment with your talents, the more you glow. We need to keep the wick as small as possible so that every demon or shadow that passes you does not recognize you for who you are the instant, they see you."

"How is it that they can see me, but I cannot see them?" I butted in. He stopped walking and looked me in the eyes.

"Are you going to tell me that you did not see something different in that man? Think about that moment in the bar. Think about the feelings that you had and the impact on your senses." The first thing I remembered was the smell, but the more I thought about that moment, the more I did think that I might have felt something. I just wasn't sure if it was a true feeling or if I was forcing something.

"It will take time, but you will understand. That demon you dispatched had spent a whole lifetime knowing that it was not what it appeared to be. It, unlike you, pretty much had known that it had been cast out. Now I'm not saying that every demon or shadow will know how it got here, why it was sent here, or what it really is, but some will." He looked around, giving the entire general vicinity the once over.

"It's those buggers you got to keep an eye peeled for." He stopped and smiled at me.

"And hey, now I am free to help you see things for what they really are." I rolled this information over and over in my head as we walked. It was getting pretty late now, and it was a work night. My brain hurt as I tried to figure all of this out.

"What can I do? I mean, I knew there was something wrong with that guy when he was eyeballing me at the bar that day, but I just thought that he was deranged. How can I tell the difference between something like that and some old crazy person?"

"That is something that we will have to work on," he told me, tapping me on the back of my head with his cane.

"There are going to be times that these things will stand out like a sore thumb, others not so much. In this case, there was the smell, and though you did not notice it, that man cast a hazy reflection in the mirror." The words had barely left his mouth, when I realized they were true.

"Is that some kind of cloak or are they like vampires that don't case reflections?" I knew that last part sounded a bit outlandish, but that was how my mind worked.

"Was he even real?"

"He was real enough to you. When he hit you did you not feel it?" Chalmers looked down at the ground as he spoke, and we continued home.

"This whole thing, this whole experience, well, there is nothing set completely in stone. Some things may be seen by others, while some things can only be seen, touched, or even smelled by you and your kind. Realize that every person on the planet exudes some type of body odor, but it is normally hidden with sone sort of sent or another. What was different about the way this creature smelled than most? If you can figure that out, then there should be no problem differentiating between monster and man."

"So, I will have to hone my skills, is that what you're telling me?" I asked, though I had been hoping for something more substantial.

"That is exactly what I am saying, my boy. But you will have to do so in a manner that limits your exposure to the bad guys." I turned to him to ask just how exactly I was supposed to do that, but he was gone again, and I was alone again in the dark.

For some reason, when he told me that he would

be permitted to speak with me, I thought the disappearing act was going to come to an end. As it was though, I was only two blocks from my apartment. I was getting fairly close to the center of town and there were people walking on the streets around me. I was going to have to make a conscious effort to try to smell out the bad guys, though I hoped that I didn't come across anymore, at least not anytime soon. So, I tucked my wings up close and walked into my complex and up the stairs. I had so much to think about. It was late and I had to get up early the next morning for work. I had for the most part, calmed down enough to go to bed and I slept like rock.

The next day I got up and went about my business. I went to work like a good boy and didn't play around with my wings at all. This continued for about a week and a half or two weeks, and in that time, I don't think I saw Chalmers even once. I felt a little lost and alone, but those feelings had always been commonplace in my world. That's the way it was with me. I got up went to work, came home and did my exercises and jogging. I continued to smoke my weed every day but drank very little. I tried not to be paranoid, but I watched out to see who might be watching me. This was pretty much my routine, my life. I tried not to waver from it to much for fear of being discovered. Call that paranoia if you like, I just called it boring.

SIX

Something felt wrong; I just wasn't sure what it was. Everything looked fairly normal. I felt my arms and torso, the back of my neck and my head and stretched like I just woke up, but I wasn't in my bed. I was sitting under a mighty oak tree in a park with a bunch of other trees, shrubbery, and a couple of trails with little stone bridges and such. I picked myself off the ground and wiped off my butt, then I took a couple of steps toward one of the little bridges and something in the pit of my stomach churned. I felt sick and stopped, and for a half a second, I thought I saw something move in the shadows in front of me.

I leaned forward a bit and squinted, but I halted the urge to step closer. The bridge's bases were made of stone cobbled together with mortar and they had two steel girders connecting the two sides.

Wooden planks reached perpendicularly across the two girders, making up the walkway. But what I was looking at was dark space underneath it, the shadow. It almost looked like there was something there swirling about. It was somewhat mesmerizing, and it was difficult for me to look away. I took a step closer for a better look, unsure of exactly what I was looking at.

"What are you doing?" someone asked from behind me.

"Are you trying to get yourself killed or is this another one of your adrenaline junkie stunts? A 'see how close I can get without getting snagged' sort of thing, maybe? I looked and again I thought I saw something move, and it caused the hairs on the back of my neck to rise to attention. Then I took a couple of steps back and turned to see the girl that was looking at me. She was very pretty, reddish blonde hair, blue-green eyes, and those nice pouty lips. She was staring me down and motioning for me to come to her. She was absolutely gorgeous. I felt like I had just woken up, but apparently, I was either still dreaming or greatly mistaken. I had to think fast. I was in a park on sunny day and there was a girl in front of me that I felt like I knew, but how could I? It was hard to explain. I did know her though, and as my head cleared, I felt more like I belonged here. Her name was Lori, and I had known her for quite some time. I couldn't remember ever seeing her before, but I knew her like family. She was my lover, and my best friend rolled into one. I knew her favorite color, favorite food, and what upset her.

And I remembered the feel of her soft, tight little body in my arms, but it still felt kind of like this was just a dream. A big part of me still wondered where

I was. I did not belong here, yet I felt like I had been here my whole life.

"Hello? You wanna get away from the bridge before you get snatched." She gave me a condescending smile, but still seemed pretty adamant about it. So I walked over to her and she took my hand. She leaned up on her tippy toes and gave me a kiss on the lips. Then she gave me a little punch in the ribs.

She was stunningly beautiful, and I pulled in close for a big hug. Man, it felt nice to feel her body up close against mine.

"So, what was that all about?" she asked, though I wasn't really sure what she had meant. So I just looked at her.

"Why would you even play like that?"

"What?" I asked, but I did in a joking manner because I was trying to cover for not fully understanding. I just didn't want her to know that I didn't know what she was talking about.

"I love you baby, but I just don't care for that remember." Again, I just looked at her.

"I would rather have you go back to jumping out of planes and that kind of stuff then messing around like that."

"Yeah, that would be nice if it wasn't so expensive anymore." That was weird. The words just came out of my mouth. She poked me again.

"I'm sorry," she said with a smile.

"Hey, look what I found," she said producing two baseball-sized pieces of old, bruised fruit. At first glance I wanted to laugh at her, but then I realized how hungry I was, starving in fact, and I took the piece of fruit from her with a smile. I wanted to stuff the whole thing down my neck hole, but I didn't want to look like a pig in front of her. I never dreamed such a ratty looking apple could taste so good.

"Thanks," I told her with a huge smile. As we turned and started to walk away, I took a last glance back at the little rock bridge. There was something there, and that something scared me enough to send a chill down my spine. We walked through the brightly lit forest, and I held her hand in mine. This was nice, real nice. But something still was not quite right. The sun was shining down on us, and as we walked, I started to see the tops of some tall buildings. We weren't deep in the wilderness as I had thought. Instead, we were on the edge of a big city or in a park in the middle of one, like Central Park in New York City. As we got to the edge of the cityscape though, I could see that something was amiss.

There was no way this was New York. There were no people. The place was vacant. I looked up and down the street and saw no one. Then I glanced up at the tall buildings and realized how old and tattered they looked. Quite a few of them appeared to be falling apart. The streets were strewn with the large concrete portions of the structures and garbage. It was like a war zone. We left the woodsy area and walked through the empty, litter-strewn streets, and I caught a glimpse of a person or two, a small group of people every now and then. My head swam with thoughts of the holocaust that must have hit this city, but deep down I knew what had happened here. I had seen plenty of pictures and videos of this city when it was alive and bustled with life, but that was a long time ago, before the shadows came. We took a long round about route to get to our destination. I knew why too. It was so that we could stay in only the most brightly lit streets. The more we walked, the more I remembered things, and the more this felt less and less like a dream and more and more that this was real. I knew where I was and how I got here, and I remembered my whole life, I also remembered living in constant fear and always seeming to be on the run from the shadows. It didn't seem as bad back when I was a kid, but the memories might have been hazed over by time. Maybe things just got worse as their numbers seemed to grow and the food supply started to run out. I remembered stories that were told of me of people actually keeping animals as pets' way back in the day. Now there were no animals on the planet at all-none. The shadows had invaded every corner of the globe, and though no one really knew where they came from, their emergence onto our world could be followed back to when I was about four or five years old. That's when the animals started to disappear, and quickly before anyone knew what had happened, they were none left, not an animal on the planet, not fish, no birds, nothing. I was so young when it began that I really didn't understand what was happening. It had started with people's pets vanishing into the night and soon enough, reward posters covering entire neighborhoods. I remember seeing all of those pictures of dogs and cats that seemed to cover telephone poles, fences and filled the bulletin boards at the local malls. They were everywhere. There were reward posters for every type of pet, but mostly dogs and cats. Some were handmade and some looked quite professional, and I remember thinking about how much money one could acquire if they found these missing animals.

It was quickly being discovered that a great number of pets that were kept outside at night were just not there the next day. But then when people started to keep their pets inside after dark, things turned very scary. Locked doors did not seem to protect them, and panic swept the globe. Birds and hamsters and the like disappeared from their cages. Dogs, cats, cows, horses all seemed to vanish into the darkness of the night. These were not isolated incidents either. They happened in every corner of the globe. The media went nuts over the stories and it dominated the newspapers and television. Scientist from all over the planet grappled with the problem, but the reports continued to roll in. Zoos and circuses were easy targets, and it created quite a buzz when Philadelphia Zoo reported that their entire herd of elephants vanished in just one night.

Some people had tried to keep their animals close to them, under a watchful eye day and night, but eventually that did not protect anyone or anything. Accounts were televised of people seeing their beloved pet yelp out for help, and then disappear into the darkness, never to be seen again. Many held out for hope and held vigils that they would one day see their pet again, but it just never happened. I remember seeing people making elaborate contraptions to try to keep their animals safe. I also remember the massive amount of sorrow that permeated my days over those events. So many people had deep feelings of attachment for their pets, that when they went missing, it was like losing a family member. There were funerals and whatnot for the missing animals every day. Soon enough there were no dogs, cats, cows or even birds. They had all disappeared. Then even the fish in the sea eventually vanished. Scientists, law enforcement, and the military were baffled.

No one had answers. I grew up without ever tasking real meat, except for the chemical compounds that had mimicked the taste of beef, chicken, and fish. The world waited and wondered for some time as to see what had happened and the brightest scientists from every corner of the globe converged to tackle the problem. But they could find no answers. The only things each recorded incident had in common was the shadow that seemed to consume the animal, and that nearly every disappearance happened after dusk or during the night. Then isolated incidents of people disappearing shocked the world, All the warring and battling over gas and money quickly took a back seat as this new fear spread worldwide.

People, and in some cases entire families, simply vanished here and there. The world held its collective breath and waited for its finest minds to come up with ways to protect them, but no answers came. I remember the day news came from a small community in Italy. A man claimed to have survived what he considered to be an attack. He had apparently been engulfed in a small cloud of the darkness, or shadow, and was able to fight it, to break free of its grip. He told the world that he felt a pulling force that was dragging him away from the light, how cold he felt, and how powerful it was. At first, he was thought to be a fraud, an attention grabber. He was lauded in some papers and jeered in others, and few believed what he was saying was real. There were pictures on the TV and in the news magazines of the man showing off the claw marks on his legs. It almost looked as though he had been pulled from the toothy grip of a shark or alligator. His cuts were deep and wide, and he was very lucky to have survived.

Soon enough, several people came forward to back the claims of the Italian man with their own stories of escaping the pulling grasp of the darkness. And as the stories were compared, more and more pieces of the puzzle fell into place. The attacks had seemed to fall off for a while, due mostly to the fact that there were very few animals left on the planet. Then it seemed like the floodgates opened up and people started vanishing everywhere. No place was safe. It happened on every continent in every corner of the world. There were a lot of children and elderly at first, but the dark forces did not seem to discriminate. Almost every disappearance occurred at night or in the very dark place and it was becoming obvious that anyone or anything that had been consumed by the shadowy darkness was not returning, at least no one had as of yet. These shadows preyed on the weakest of any group if it seemed possible. The majority of the latest and fastest growing demographic to disappear in the night proved to be the sick, elderly and the youngest. Parents all over the world were crying out in anguish as they awoke to find empty cribs or to find that their baby had been snatched from right next to them, in their own beds as they slept. Horror gripped our entire world, and all other actions or skirmishes now took a back seat to these incredible forces. These were very tough times to live through. There seemed to be a funeral every day for someone I knew or loved. After a while, we just stopped going. So many people had disappeared, that sadly, such things were commonplace, and they stopped taking on some of the meaning that such events did in the past. It wasn't like there was a need for a coffin, procession, or burial plot anymore. These shadows didn't seem to care about financial status, nor did they care about how many doors you were locked behind. It seemed that the only thing that slowed them down was sunlight and very brightly lit rooms. And many years after the first known attack had happened, still no one had yet returned from the shadowy blackness. Many did, however, escape during the attack. Some pulled themselves back into the light and were able to break from its grip. Some even had friends or family members pull them literally from jaws of the darkness. Many of the escapees complained about unseen pain that lingered well past their attack, beyond the scaring. They all shared visions of claws ripping at them, into them. Each shared nightmares of gnashing teeth and a cold, cold darkness that pulled on them. There were various opinions as to what was happening. Some called it an invasion or perhaps a long sleeping darkness that had recently awakened from its slumber. Earthquakes and heat waves had ravaged the world. It was possible that something had been unearthed or defrosted, something from the earth's distant past. Others thought it could be some terrorist plot, and some, as you might have guessed, claimed it was an act of God, a punishment for our every-growing transgressions. No one could tell exactly, but everyone agreed that there was a clear and definite threat of life as we had come to know it. In a few short years, the population of the planet had dwindled from several billion to just over a million or so. Social services had suffered on the global scale and even the sun didn't seem to shine as bright as it once did. It was finally figured out that no one should enter the shadows or go out at night.

Everyone started to sleep with the lights on, as the entire populous had become afraid of the dark. But the fewer and fewer people left around to keep the power up and running, the governments of the world asked everyone to move to the bigger cities where things could be better regulated, such as energy, food and water. Occasional blackouts still happened every so often, and the outcome was usually horrific. Almost the entire populations of certain countries had been sequestered into a ten-mile square grid in order to protect them. These small developments or communities were prone to violence, and many felt that there were more of a prison than a salvation.

Backup generators had been installed everywhere, but even they were subject to malfunctions. Most of the world lived in total horror of nightfall. The few that didn't, found ways to use that fear against the masses with schemes and fraudulent claims of hope. No one could answer the questions or bring an end to the attacks, so they all put their energies into protecting the people that were left. We were rounded up, huddled in masses. We had lived like this for years. Food and water had been rationed and there was very little privacy since so many people had been crammed into such a small area. I remember being scared all the time back then. It was hard for any of us to admit it, but we had tumbled from the top of the food chain right to the bottom. We had become the fodder of this unseen force that fell across our planet, and everyday life had become a fight for survival. I went to bed scared almost every single night. So, this was what my life had become. Half rotten fruit was like gold to us now. The rationings and the crap they called food had gotten old fast. Luckily for me though, I had Lori. She was a lot like me. We were a bit bolder than most. We had no problem venturing out into the vast city scavenging. Every once in a while, we would get lucky and find an apartment with a kitchen full of canned soup or veggies. That was like gold. It was a tricky affair to stay in areas lit by the sun or by the old power grid that worked so sporadically in some of the run-down parts of the city. There were some real scary places out there. But hunger had its way of creating a boldness, even a bravado in us. We knew that things were tough and that our government, our entire world was struggling to feed its remaining inhabitants, but the supplements they were sending us were getting worse by the day. We had a place we called home in the tall skyscraper. It had once been an office building, but it had been converted as a tenement to conserve and concentrate power. There were separate bathrooms for men and women on each floor that everyone shared, but Lori and I had a pretty nice place of our own. One of the fringe benefits of being a good scavenger is that we were able to upgrade our living situation. Food had become more important than money. We needed to be able to do what had to be done to make it through each day. And when you have food to barter with, you tend to get things you want. But sadly, sometimes I just took what we needed. Lori didn't always agree with my strong-arm tactics, but she never complained about the cabinets full of canned goods or the view we had. We had a luxury condo. It was extravagant compared to the way most now lived. We had emergency backup power and solar panels up on the roof just above us. Our place was lit up like a Christmas tree every night, not a shadow in any corner. We were as safe as we could possibly be, given the situation, but just like everyone else, I still slept in fear of the darkness. Even in this building, accidents and small brownouts happened. It was considered one of the most secure buildings in the city, but lamps still got knocked over, light bulbs burned out, and fuses occasionally popped. We had stopped going to funerals a long time ago, but that did not mean that we did not care when something as simple as an overloaded extension cord cost someone their life. We had a lot of friends, but there were also a lot of people that were jealous of what we had. Most people just left us alone though. They knew that I took no crap from anyone. They knew that we were very well armed and how I had quickly dispatched anyone and everyone that threatened our little way of life. I had instilled both fear and a good deal of respect in my neighbors. I had let them know that I was not to be toyed with, that I cared more about what I had than I did about a stranger's life.

Then one bright, sunny day, a gang showed up at our building and started to harass people. They stole from some and threatened others. I didn't let them bother me too much. This happened from time to time. Wandering bands of marauder rolled into town every now and then. Our building was generally open to the public. Lori and I had our own quarters and so did a few other people, but many lived in a dormitory environment. They shared food, bathrooms. It was a communal living. There were twelve of them, ranging in age from twelve, maybe thirteen, up to a guy that looked to be about fifty-something.

They were pretty hardcore, rough around the edges, unshaven and disheveled. All of them were quite heavily armed and they had a tendency to wave their guns around. We all knew how scarce bullets had become, and though there was a good chance that some of the guns contained no ammunition, none of us wanted to find out the hard way. It was easy to distinguish the leader of the group. He had swagger to him. He rarely spoke, but gave his men messages through nods, winks, and shakes of his head. And he seemed to have endless supply of what looked like little hand-rolled cigars. His skin was darkened by the sun, and I couldn't tell if he was Latino or Caucasian or both. I paid him and his men little mind. They went about their business, and I went about mine. I ignored the stares and the chatter and pretty much considered them to be a minor nuisance. I walked in and out of their presence with my head held high. I was smarter, and way faster than of them, and knew in the back of my mind, that if push came to shove, I would happily kill them all. They went about their business, and I went about mine. It was what it was.

They were there and they might well be staying for a while, so I had to get used to that.

Then one day, one of the accosted Lori. He scared her more than anything, but he told her that she would be his one day soon, which in my eyes was an indirect threat on my life. They had seen us together, knew the situation. But when she laughed him off, he got in her face. He told her that he took what he wanted and that he wanted her. I knew which one she was talking about. He was a cockroach. I immediately wanted to squash him under my boot. She said that he got really close, started to put his hand on her lower back as to pull her closer. She had to shake him off, and as tough as I knew she was, she told me that he had really scared her. She may as well have stuck bamboo shoots up under my fingernails. I was furious. Prior to this day, I thought little of them, which was solely because I was an arrogant type of guy. I had learned to think of myself as bulletproof.

That was how I managed in this messed up

world. I blew my chest out and walked around like I owned the place. The presence of the gang changed little in my swagger, until today. When Lori and I returned from a good day of scavenging, I quickly realized that there were a few of them watching me. It was as though they were planning something and casing me and my security systems. They would never get into our condo, that much was certain. I had things rigged so that if someone tried to break in, all of the surrounding lights would go out. Trapping the would-be robber in total darkness. Needless to say, no one ever got past our front door. But that didn't stop anyone from stalking us on our way in or out.

And if they didn't follow us up, right to our front door.

"Whatchu have in there, man?" a grizzled looking man asked me as I approached our place.

"You should let us in to check things out. You might have something we need." The fact that Lori gave me a nudge simply confirmed that my feeling was correct. This was the same guy that had approached her earlier, and now he was snooping around by the front door.

"Hmmm, I didn't think so," was all I said. With a half second, I had the barrel of my gun pointed in the man's face. Lori had the drop on his friend. He didn't have time to reach for his gun. She had him dead to rights and though she was small in stature, she was a formidable adversary when she was armed.

"Maybe we should look at your place and see if

there is anything there that we might need." I had emphasized the word 'we' just to be a smartass. I could see that he had a bit of a crazy look in his eye. I wanted to tell him that we needed to get along, to live together in peace, what was mine was mine and that I didn't care what he and his friends did to anyone else in the building. But all of that went right out the window when he stopped looking me in the eyes and looked toward Lori. It was so strange. I could almost hear what this piece of crap was thinking. I was a man, after all. I knew the wicked sexually desires that filled our heads. I knew that having a women like her by your side was absolutely priceless these days. So, when the small grin fell upon his face, it was quickly followed from a bullet of my gun. I didn't care. I shot him right through his freaking teeth. I knew that he would not let her alone. Sooner or later, he was going to hurt her, or me, or both. I had seen too many movies where mercy was rewarded with pain. This was a monumental moment for me. We had put up with them long enough. I was making a stand. And before the man's body hit the floor in front of me, I had spun and dropped two bullets into the guy that Lori had in front of her. I was so smooth, so fast and accurate that I almost amazed myself.

"What?" Lori asked, pulling me from my self-admiration.

"Why did you do that?" She knelt down to check on one guy and then the other.

"He wasn't going to leave us alone I could see it

in his eyes. This crap was going to end today." I didn't need to explain myself, but I did. I reached down and grabbed their guns and then I took Lori by her arm and led her inside. The rest was easy. I just locked the door and turned out the lights in the hallway.

There would be no bodies, no evidence, except for a little blood, when the lights came back on.

The Shadows would take the still warm bodies. That much was sure. Lori shook her head, got a glass of water and went to bed. She hated this sort of thing. I also grabbed some water and went over and looked out at the empty city below. I had stepped over the line and we both knew it. It was, however, a necessary step. But now I was all in. There was no turning back. This is what I believe that Lori feared the most. She had seen dead bodies before, and she had even seen me kill a few people. What she laid in her bed and now worried about was what was going to happen next. I had started a war. There were two down and ten to go. These thugs were no longer going to harass us. I would kill enough of them so that the rest would leave and if they didn't, then I would simply kill them all. I quicky cooked up a plan.

Things had to happen fast before the two men were missed. I needed to catch the rest off guard and in a group if possible. I didn't want any of my friends or neighbors getting hurt. They made it so easy. One of them always lingered around to keep an eye on their space and all of their belongings. They had taken over an apartment on the second floor. It was fairly large, with a waiting area. I was told that it had once been the office of a very prestigious law firm. The need for lawyers left in our world some time ago and most of the ill-prepared office worker types didn't last long when the crap hit the fan. The entire unit had been converted into a dormitory, but when the marauders came, they took for it themselves and kicked everyone else out. I had a couple of people watch out for me as I walked over to their spot. I knew it well. I had been in there a hundred times. I knocked on the front door of the little vestibule. At first, I thought no one was there and that my job might be a whole lot easier, then someone opened the door a crack and peeked through. I didn't give him time to react. I stuck my gun in his face and pushed the door wide open. He was forced backward and had little balance. He was easily disarmed. Then I simply put him in an arm bar, walked him out into the hall. Prior to knocking on the door, I had opened a small broom closet that sat right across the hallway from their place. I also removed only the light bulb in the little room. So, when the door slammed shut behind him, he was alone in the dark. Not a good place to be. He panicked, pounding violently against the door, and screaming, kicking, and trying to get out. The commotion only lasted a few moments, then the little closet was silent again. Like his two friends upstairs, the shadows had found him. He would bother us no more. I could see it in their faces.

One or two of the people that I had recruited to watch my back were not real happy with what I had just done, but they didn't say anything. They all lived in fear of the invaders. And though they would all be happy to see them go; none would make a move against them. They were too old or frightened. Most were unarmed. They would soon reap the rewards of my deeds, whether they agreed with my tactics or not. I made my next move without haste. I walked into their place with a ladder and some wire. I quickly popped open the ceiling tile and went to work. All of the switches in the building had been removed to prevent anyone from accidently turning off the lights and killing everyone. The entire structure was lit up inside and out a few hours before dusk and stayed that way til well past dawn. Many of the interior lights stayed on all of the time. A government agency would arrive and change the bulbs every now and then plus I always had a secret stash of them to barter with. Light bulbs were as valuable as food and water. I added a jumper to the circuit that lit their big room. I needed all of the lights to go out at once, so I ran the wire along the drop ceiling and out into the hallway. I draped the wire down behind a plant and tied a switch into the circuit. The plant had a big round pot and huge green leaves everywhere. It hid the switch well. I would simply have to walk up the hall, reach into the plant and flick the switch. And the beasts that I had learned to loathe over the years would do my dirty work, just like they had done with their friends. I then went back up to my apartment and waited.

Lori and I went about our business in abnormal silence, which lasted long into the day. I sat watching the monitors, waiting for all of them to go to into their place at once, but it didn't seem like that was going to happen anytime soon. There were several surveillance cameras in the main lobby and in many of the hallways on various floors. I had access to every working one of them. And though I did not have a direct view of the interior of their suite, I could see the corridor outside. They seemed to be in and out. They were obviously worked up over the fact some of their gang members were missing.

"Alright, what did you do?" she finally asked with her hands on her hips in a demanding tone.

"I took care of things Sweetie," I retuned with a hint of sarcasm.

"Please don't play dumb with me or talk to me like that. It's insulting."

I loved Lori and couldn't imagine my life without her. There were a few places to meet members of the opposite sex, and very little to do on a date, unless you think climbing through drainage tunnels, or scavenging through an old building to be fun. I needed her and wanted her to be happy. She was smart, and it was hard to sneak anything past her. And I'm a sneaky one, that's for sure. I got up and sauntered over to her and slid into the big chair behind her. Then I rubbed her stomach and then I moved up to massage her neck and head. She loved when I ran my fingers through her long hair. I think she liked the slight tug that I gave her when I did it.

"I remember being so afraid of everything when I was a child," I reminisced.

"When people started disappearing from their own homes, and we didn't know why, I was scared twenty-four seven. I just thought that was the way it was." I continued to massage her head.

"Then one day, when I was around nine or ten, I asked for a little love from above. I asked for some help."

"Then it was as if someone turned on a light. You can call it an epiphany if you like, but I was enlightened. I'm not saying I wasn't afraid anymore; I'm saying that I looked at life a little differently."

I kissed her neck at bit, and she shivered.

"From that day to this, I learned to appreciate what I had, and to protect it at all costs. Those guys were going to make things difficult for us and I am dealing with them. Nothing will happen to me, and I guarantee that nothing will happen to you." She pulled away from me.

"How do you know that? How do you know they won't come after us looking for revenge?"

"Because I'm going to kill them all." I didn't mean to say that so nonchalantly, I really didn't. I knew she hated when I acted so careless about the death of another person. I just didn't give a crap like she did. I knew the exact second, I saw them that they were going to be nothing but trouble. They were the bottom of the barrel and right now we were at the top. I was making a pre-emptive strike. My instincts told me that if I didn't, that I would surely regret it. Lori turned away from me in disgust. She hated this side of me, and I knew it, but it was a part of me, a big part. I wasn't sure if I had been born with it, or if it was something that I learned, but I sure could be a mean son of a gun when I wanted or needed to be.

These fools were to be no exceptions to that mindset.

"I don't like it one bit. They haven't..." her words were cut off by a knock on the door. I jumped up out of my chair and hurried over to the bank of monitors. There were several of them, all trained on various locations. I watched the people scurrying to and fro on the little screens. There was no sound, just video.

I flicked at the switch on the computer console and saw old man McGee at our door. I tapped a nob, to pan the camera up and back to see that he was alone, that this was not a setup. I saw no one so I opened the door and walked out into the hallway to see what he wanted. I didn't like anyone seeing all of my possessions for fear of them talking too much and starting trouble by shear accident.

"You've started some trouble downstairs." He was winded from the long climb up to our place. I met him in the corridor with a nice tall, cool glass of water and he continued.

"Apparently, one of the missing men was the leader's baby cousin, and he feels that the man was a victim of foul play. He has ordered that all tenants attend a meeting this evening so that his questions will be answered." He looked down at the floor then back at me. McGee was short and squat. He was one of the first residents of this building and he had some great stories of the days before the shadows arrived. He told us about how he used to have pets, animals that he kept inside of his home. The concept seemed so strange. I considered him a friend and I always made sure he and his wife had enough to eat and enough water.

"He said he would start killing people if he did not like what he heard." He was noticeably nervous, which was not good. Too many people had seen what I had done earlier, and I felt a pit well up in my throat. I looked up at the camera because I knew Lori was watching. I mouth the words 'I'm so sorry'because I truly was. I wish I hadn't done what I had done, but it was too late to take that back now. I had to come up with some sort of game plan. There was no way I could take on all of those guys with all of those guns singlehandedly. And there was little chance I would be supported by my neighbors other than maybe having them lie for me. I came and went as I pleased, and other than making sure that a large percentage of the building's populous had food, I still wasn't liked by all. And though I was a protector and provider, it would not be the first time that such a person was quickly voted off a Survivor Island. There were many people that thought I was arrogant and that would be happy to see me dead. I also had a lot of crap to divvy up, should something ever happen to me. I told McGee to wait, and I went back inside to talk to Lori.

"I'm so sorry," I told her, giving her a big hug.

"I have to go down there."

"I know baby," she comforted me.

"I'm sorry. I didn't want this to happen." She let go of me and stepped back, then went over to a cabinet and pulled out a gun. She yanked the clip and checked it and replaced it, then stuffed the gun back in the back of her pants. Then she pulled out a smaller one, repeated the process and the stuffed that one in her shoe. She saw me looking at her.

"You didn't think I would let you go through this alone, did you?" Then she gave me a little smile.

"Everyone's allowed to make a mistake. Let's just hope this one isn't too painful. What?" she asked. I knew enough not to try to answer.

That we learn our lesson, right?" I just nodded. Then I looked her dead in the eye.

"How about you waiting here and letting me take care of business." I asked, knowing full well that when Lori made up her mind, it was difficult to change it.

"Yeah, like that would really happen?" she scoffed.

Like I said, when her mind was made up, it was

made up. So, I loaded up with some weaponry of my own, including a couple of grenades and we went down the long winding staircase with Mr. McGee.

McGee was slow, but his lack of energy gave us time to strategize. We knew that there was going to be a crowd, so we had to be careful. We didn't want to kill any of our neighbors, but there was no way, no matter what it cost, that I was gonna let Lori get hurt. There were a few people that saw what I had done, and I wasn't even sure that McGee wasn't leading me into a trap. So Lori was to linger behind a floor above us. She would listen in on the radio, and back me up should I need it. As we got close to the main floor, I tried to study McGee. I couldn't tell if he was nervous or exhausted, but he was definitely winded. I walked down the last set of stairs and found a couple of men with their guns pointed at me.

"Where is your women?" one asked stepping close to me and looking up the stairs behind me.

"She's sick," I told him with a cocky attitude.

"What does it matter? I'm here." You were both required to attend this meeting," he told me as he pointed the barrel of his rifle toward my face.

"First of all, this is my home. You people are our guests. You may request a meeting with me, but rest assured I am here because I want to see what is going on, not because you demanded it." He stepped closer to me, and I didn't even have to think. I took a big step forward and leaned in and popped the gun barrel hard with an open palm, then I spun and pulled two guns from behind my back where I had them tucked into my belt.

"That was easy," I thought. I had the drop of both of them and could have blown their heads off, but I didn't. I just smiled at them and winked. Then I put both guns away.

"Like I said, I am here by choice. I don't want any trouble." I showed them my open palms and continued to smile. I knew that I had embarrassed them a bit, but they had to know that I am not the kind that plays around.

These guys had come into our building, threatened everyone, and really just tried to take over the place.

They all knew that I would eventually be a problem, but they hadn't yet come up with a plan to deal with me. That might change today, but I wouldn't go down without a fight. So I walked on past the welcoming crew and headed over to the main lobby where a crowd had already formed. I saw that nods had been passed by members of the gang and looks they gave each other. These were not kids, well a couple of them had to be eighteen or twenty, while the rest were grown men. They were takers that lived off of the other people and had a lot of practice doing what they did. Fortunately for us, so did I. I was way slicker than these guys, and I saw everything. The instant I walked into the enormous lobby, I had seen every one of them, even the ones that thought they were hidden. I knew this room too well. I could see that they were watching me, and I was watching them. The room was full of people, most of them sitting around waiting for the show to begin. I slid to the rear of the big room and leaned my back against the wall. There would be no one sneaking up on me. I crossed my arms and waited. I didn't have to wait very long.

"Is everyone here?" a voice called out from in front of the crowd.

A man wearing a big hat to hide his dreadlock hair and carrying a semi-automatic rifle walked into the room from where I had come. He was one of the men that been waiting for McGee and I at the bottom of the stairs. He stopped and looked at me, obviously not very happy.

"All accounted for sir," he shouted, looked at me again and then turned and left. McGee, who had sat down near me with his wife, peeked at me over his shoulder. He was nervous, but he knew that I had his back. I gave him a wink. He was a smart old bird, smart enough to make sure he stayed close to me if it all hit the fan. He knew that I would do my best to protect the two of them, if I could. When the speaker started up again, he turned back to face him. The leader of this group was tall and beefy. I knew that he was probably the toughest of them all, hence the leadership role. I also knew that I really didn't want to fight him hand to hand. He had long greasy hair with darkly tanned and wrinkled skin. It looked like leather. He had obviously spent a lot of time in the sun, but who didn't nowadays? I had run into him a couple of times, and though our eyes met, I never even thought to speak to him. I never did appreciate being eyeballed, and these guys stared everyone down like it was their job. His name was Tall, probably because he was.

He jumped up onto some tables that had been setup like a stage. He was noticeably wound up and he seemed very edgy. He walked back and forth and stared into the crowd, looking at all of our faces. He saw me and looked around the area that surrounded me. I knew he was looking for Lori. I just returned the stare and gave him an 'I don't know what to tell you' I gestured with my hands and head.

"I want to know what happened to our men," he demanded. He continued to pace and stare down his audience.

"Do not play games with me. Something happened and one of you saw it. Now I want to know what happened!" He slowed his pace a bit, but he continued to walk.

"We can sit here all night." That last statement held some weight. The main lobby was pretty big, and it wasn't the most well-lit room in the building. Not too many of use cared to venture here after night fell without extra lights.

"I'm not kidding. We will sit here until someone speaks." He raised his gun and aimed at the ceiling high above and shot out one of the lighting fixtures. The action received the murmurs Tall was looking for. He then reached down and pulled a chair up onto the makeshift stage. He turned it around and sat down on it backwards, facing us.

"When the sun sets, I will shoot out the lights above your head until I get answers." Then he aimed and shot out another light. I could feel the tension in the air. The sun was sliding below the horizon and the shadows were growing longer. McGee looked like was going to crap himself. I had to say something.

"So, what are we going to do? I asked, stepping forward, but not too far to give away my cover.

"We obviously don't know what happened to your man."

"My cousin," Tall shouted. "That man was my baby cousin, and yes one of you knows what happened to him. We will sit!" he demanded. And then he shot out two more lights. I knew that it wasn't just McGee I had to worry about. There were a few others that had seen what I had done, and I knew that it was only a matter of time before I was found out.

"This is stupid," I shouted back.

"You are wrong, and you are endangering the lives of all these people. I'm done with this," I told him and turned to walk away. As I took my second step, I let a grenade fall from my sleeve into my palm. I saw that the guys in the back of the room were raising their guns to stop me, but I stopped myself, pulled the pin and turned and threw the grenade at Tall.

"Run!" I yelled at the seated people. And I hurried back to the cover of the concrete wall. The grenade exploded as it got within about two feet of Tall's face. He was done, but his crew started to fire their weapons recklessly. I looked for McGee. He was hurrying his wife through the side emergency exit door into the near dark outside. I had to move. Bullets were ricocheting all over the place. I had to try to get McGee back into the light, but I also had to think about Lori. I knew that she would be on the move, having heard all of the gunshot, and I had to mind where she was. I didn't want her getting cornered up there.

"Stay put," I yelled into my radio.

"Stay put." I couldn't tell if she had heard me or not because of the noise that echoed in the giant concrete room. It was loud, really loud.

The sound of gunfire all around me made my ears ring. I knew that the door through which Mr. and Mrs.

McGee had just exited would lock behind them, trapping them outside in the dark. I also knew that Lori would be making her way down the staircase to help me. I had no idea if she had heard me or not.

"Crap," I thought. Then I attached the little walkie-talking back onto my belt and pulled out my guns, I moved away from the wall to give myself a shot. There were people running and screaming and bullets flying everywhere. The room was getting dark fast. I had to get the McGee's back inside. I slid over behind the huge plastic potted plant. It gave me cover and allowed me to hurry over to the door. I looked around and saw that all of the bad guys were pretty well covered as well. It would be hard to pluck them from their hiding places. Then I realized that they were all still standing in the brightest spots of the room. Tall made sure not to shoot out any of the lights that had been shining down on his men. I needed a distraction, and this would be it. I took careful aim and let out my breath slow and even and squeezed the trigger twice taking out two lights. I then hurried over to the door and smacked down hard on the latch. It popped opened. I spun and held it open so that I could still point one gun in toward the lobby and point one outside. I didn't know what might be out there, so I wanted to be ready. But I almost puked at what I saw. Poor old Mr. McGee was holding his wife's hands as he tried to pull her from the shadow that had her by the feet and legs.

"Help!" he pleaded, just before both he and his wife were pulled into the nothingness. He didn't let go of her. Even when she was almost fully engulfed, and a goner for sure, he held on to her. And just like that, they were gone. It happened very quickly. I leaned back hard on the door, letting my arms and my guns fall to my side.

"What have I done?" I asked myself aloud. Then I thought of Lori and my mind snapped into action. I had to get to her before she got shot, or worse.

"Lori!" I yelled into the radio.

"Lori, get back upstairs." No answer.

"Lori!" I went into assault mode. All of this had been a preamble to what was about to happen. It was time to open the cage and let out the beast. I pulled both guns and started laying waste to all of their crew. It was like shooting ducks in a barrel. I was on fire. It was so easy for me now. I slide from coverage to coverage, shooting out the lights and shooting holes in people. I let it all out. The beast ran wild and the adrenaline flowed. I hit shots on the move that most couldn't hit if they sat still and aimed. I knew I owed it to the McGee's and to the other people that I accidentally got killed today to end this threat once and for all. Today I gambled and I lost, and I hate to lose. My mind drifted off to Lori, but my body just continued the onslaught. That was when I realized that I was backing them right toward the staircase that led up to Lori's position. Not good. I had to reel in the monster. My left hand tingled as it always did when the beast had control, but I had to slow it down. A couple of them ran up the stairs, and I held my breath. I didn't have to hold it long because a couple of pops and then both of their bodies slide back down the steps toward me.

"Good girl," I thought. I took a second to look around and listen.

There were still a couple more, but I couldn't see them. One bullet, then another shot past me as I tried to get to the stairs. I couldn't really tell where they were coming from, and hence I was pinned down. I tried the radio again.

"Where are you?" I asked, breathing heavily.

"I'm at the top of the stairs, but I think a couple of them are up here on this floor with me. They must have come up the back steps to try to flank you. What should I do?"

"Stay up there but stay out of sight. Let them get past you and I'll pick them off as they come down the main steps. If I can't get a clean shot, you can get them from behind. We'll trap them in the stairwell."

I had an open view of the bottom of the stairs. They thought they were going to surround me, but it would be us that would surround them.

"Click the radio twice once they pass your position," I told her since I knew she would not be able to speak aloud for fear of giving up her position. I looked for the one that had just fired at me, then another shot ricocheted next to my face. I knew where he was hiding now. So, I pulled a grenade from my pocket and hurled in that direction. The explosion was loud, but I could not tell if I got him or not. I decided that I would side with caution. I would try to make my way around to look to see what was left of him, then I heard my radio click twice.

"Crap!" I thought, turning to see that I was uncovered. I could see the shadows of the men coming down to the landing. They didn't know it, but if they hurried, they could have a clear, easy shot at me. I had to hurry, but I didn't want to walk over to where the grenade went off to find that that guy hadn't been killed. I quickly decided that I had better get back to a spot with a clear view of the stairs. This, however, would give the other guy a clean shot at me if I hadn't gotten to him. The grenade had thrashed a lot of the back entry of the building. Several lights had been knocked out and it was pretty dark back there.

There was always a chance that even if the explosion and shrapnel hadn't gotten him, then maybe the shadow creatures had. I had to take the chance. I made my move, hurrying across the open area and back behind cover, I crouched down behind one of the large marble statues that littered the lobby's floor and check my ammo. I was good. I looked and saw the legs of the first and then the second man up on the landing, just a half a flight from the lobby floor. I could just sit back and pick them off as soon as they got halfway down the stairs.

"This is going to be easy," I thought. Then I got shot in my right arm. I had been overconfident. The grenade hadn't done its job. I was hurt...bad. I couldn't even use my right hand-my shooting hand. The two on the landing slipped back around the corner, and I no longer had a shot at them.

"Crap, crap, crap," I thought. Another shot whizzed just past my face, and I had to tuck myself up close to the wall. I picked up my gun with my left hand and moved toward a corner. I peeked around it to see if I could see the guy that had been firing at me, and almost took one in the face. My arm was killing me, and I banged it when I jumped back. I thought about Lori and prayed she didn't try to take two of them on, but I didn't want to break radio silence and give up her position. I had to think fast. I took another peek around the corner and came up with a plan. It was dangerous, but it gave me a chance.

"Lori, bottom of the landing. Send em my way." I then pulled the pin from the grenade and let go of the handle.

"One thousand, one thousand two," I said to myself, then I shot off two rounds around the corner. I jumped out and threw the grenade up into the remaining lights that lit the far end of the room where the shooter hid and moved behind another wall. The grenade went off and plunged the entire west wing into darkness. The man yipped but did not fire again. The shadows got him. He was gone for sure this time. Then Lori started shooting into the stairwell. The two had no choice but to hurry down the stairs right into my sights. I had to be quick and careful, but my accuracy would be crap with my left hand.

One, then the other popped out into my view and I started firing. They turned and started firing at me before I hit the first one. He went down in a heap, but I had to take cover. That's when Lori turned the corning firing. She hit the remaining guy in the side twice, one in the arm and one in the leg. As he went down, he twisted and turned his attention back to the staircase. He fired a couple of shots at her just before I shot him square in the head. He was still shooting in Lori's direction as he fell, and that's when it happened. That's when my fire went out, and my world ended. As the man fell to the ground, his automatic weapon continued to fire. His finger had constricted, locking the trigger down. Bullets ricocheted all over the stairwell. I ran toward the man as he rolled down the stairs, but the damage had been done. One of the shots took out the lights and the whole stairwell went dark. I ran as hard as I could and slid across the marble floor just in time to see Lori's face as she was pulled into a shadow. Her smiled turned to dread. The look on her pretty face made my heart sink. She screamed, and then was gone. I just sat there looking at the darkness for a moment or two, then vomited.

"What had I done?" I thought aloud. My heart and stomach hurt, and I could barely breathe. I started to cry, then I looked up and saw the oddest thing I had ever seen. A man walked out of the darkness from the stairwell. I pulled my gun up to fire, then I realized who it was. It was Chalmers. I no longer held the gun and I was no longer in the huge foyer. Instead, I was in some sort of hazy place. The pain in my arm and gunshot would be gone, but the deep, dreadful pain in my heart and gut remained.

"What, who..." I tried to speak, but the words didn't come out.

"You see what your arrogance has cost you? Did you see what I have had to see time after bloody time?"

"I'm not really sure I understand," I told him as I rubbed the arm where I had been shot. It felt just fine, but it had hurt just seconds before.

"You lived for a year and a half after that, before you fell prey to the shadows yourself. You became a miserable mess that just moped about. You were such a mess that you thought you could do what you wanted, to kill indiscriminately. These are the exact reasons for your punishment, and you've proven time and time again, and time again that you have learned nothing." He walked right up to me.

"This is what I have seen over and over, and until you figure it all out, it will continue to happen. This circle must be broken." He walked right up to me so that we were face to face.

"Learn our lesson, boy. Take heed to all of this. Now wake up!"

I woke up in my bed. I was sweating like a slave and my heart still ached hard for Lori. Then my alarm went off and I had to get my butt to work. It was a difficult task, but I plowed through it, and all day long I was distracted. I could not stop thinking about her. I had to figure out how to fix things and fix them fast.

SEVEN

My head swam with thoughts of my dream, or maybe it was a vision. I pretty much just stumbled through the day. It was hard for me to get things done. I couldn't stop thinking about Lori or shake that feeling that I had just lost someone very near and dear to me. There were even points here and there that it got so bad that I actually teared up a little. It was weird, and it was hard to focus on my job. When I got home, I smoke a lot from out of my bag of pot. I just wanted my brain numbed, and numbed it got.

I finally started feeling a little more relaxed and decided to check my mail and all of my e-mails.

"Same old junk mail," I thought, looking through my inbox. Hey, I won another contest! Imagine that. I just got used to deleting that crap without even opening it. I hadn't entered any contests lately, so there was no prize waiting for me. With my recent fun of luck, I'd accidently unlock a virus that would ruin my new laptop. This computer was supposed to have the most up to date protection, but it required patches that could only be made after the virus was discovered and analyzed. That was how my last laptop died. Oh, Critterware was able to create a patch for the problem, but only after mine and several thousand other hard drives got fried. That's why I thought it was ironic that each of my three e-mail accounts contained several prize notifications from that very company. I just deleted them all and went about my business. I forced down a couple of beers, but just could not shake that melancholy feeling that continued to haunt me, so I just went to bed.

I awoke the next morning feeling a whole lot better. Actually, I felt like I could take on the world. I still had a tiny feeling of sadness in my heart, but as with most dreams, it had quickly faded from my memory. I still took a lesson from it, but the faces and feeling had started to fade quickly away. I ran through my same routine that I did every day. I made coffee, and showered, and if I had time, like I did today, I checked my e-mail. There was another notice from Critterware telling me that I had won their grand prize. I started to get a big angry at the thought of how much time some of these hackers put into it with complete stranger's computers. There were worms and viruses out there that completely ruined people's hard drives. In some cases, their work or their homework, or even unfinished novels and pictures were destroyed. Those hackers needed to be strung up. I'm not saying that I never did anything bad, but some of those hackers lived for this, and even bragged about how they could tap into the most secure systems such as banks, big business, and government.

There was always some kind of crap out there that lay in wait for you to open a simple letter such as this, and then wham your computer is toast. I took a couple long deep breaths and let them out just as slowly, then grabbed my lunch and rolled out for work. I had gotten myself calmed down and got halfway there before my phone rang. It was a number I didn't recognize, so I just ignored it. I got a call from my ma, which I did answer, and I talked with her the rest of the way to work. When I arrived at the office door, my boss met me with a smile.

"Well, well, well, I didn't even think you would have taken the time to call me, let alone show up," Steve said with a smile. Smoke poured from his lips as he spoke, and he had a devilish grin about him.

"What are you talking about?" I asked him. We had worked together every weekday for almost a year and a half now, so we could read each other pretty well. He looked at me and realized that I really didn't know what he was talking about. Just then my other co-worker James walked up.

"Big pimp in the house," he said with a smile.

"Yeah, I see. You get a couple of days off and paid vacation, the boss gets a truck load of new computer, and I get to work extra hard to make up for you not being here." I just looked at both of them and couldn't help but smile, but I had no idea what they were talking about.

"You don't know do you?" the old man said as he took a long drag on his cigarette.

"You won," he said with a smile.

"Are you kidding? How did you now know this? They called Steve at 6am. And of course, he had to call me at 6:15."

"Why would they call you guys?" I asked, still not fully believing what I was hearing. Steve squinted at me.

"Didn't they call you?" he asked while sucking some smoke into his lungs. I thought about it for a second. My phone had been on the charger all morning, but I would have heard it ring. I got the one call on my way to work. Maybe I should have checked that voicemail. I pulled out my phone but before I could dial up the message, the phone rang again. It was the same number. I hated answering numbers I didn't recognize, but I had no choice now. This was going to be something good, or I was going to end up the butt of someone's joke, either way, it was time to get it over with. So, I answered.

"Hello Mr. Dinan," a very feminine voice spoke to me.

"My name is Lori Stillwell and I represent Critterware operating systems. I would like to let you know that by purchasing your new laptop and registering it in a timely manner, you were entered into our contest. And Mr. Dinan, you are our grand prize winner." She paused, I guess waiting for me to holler in excitement, but I was still waiting to find out if this was a well-orchestrated ruse by my co-workers.

"Do you understand what that means?" she asked, still expecting me to get excited. I still said nothing.

"It means you won an all expense paid trip to our corporate office in Seattle and a private audience with our founder and president, Mr. Lucious Barnes." The excitement in her voice was quite evident.

"There was a private jet fueling at Lindbergh Field as we speak. You may leave within the next hour."

So, what was the worst thing that would have happen if this turned out to be some big prank, I thought.

I could maybe sneak out of a couple of hours of work at the very least.

"Well, I'll have to go home and pack," I told her, stalling. If these guys were setting me up, I was really gonna milk this out and get as close to a full day off as possible.

"That's not necessary. As part of our grand prize, we are going to provide you with a brand-new wardrobe."

"How do you know what size I wear?" I asked, holding back a smile. I could see James and Steve looking at me intently, waiting to hear what was going on.

"We have a detailed file on you Mr. Dinan. When all is said and done, with the flight and accommodations, the wardrobe, and cash, you're prize if valued at over one hundred and fifty thousand dollars. A car will arrive at your home within the next fifteen or twenty minutes to take you to the airport. We will see you soon Mr. Dinan. Do you have any questions for me?"

"No, not at this time," I said. She hung up, and I looked at the time.

"Your cool with this right?" I asked the boss.

"Uh, of course he's cool. They gave him a dual processor top of the line DVD burning laptops and a new desktop," Jimmy commented with a hint of a sarcastic smile.

"Yeah, I'm cool. Go ahead and go. Have fun, and we'll see ya in a couple of days." A couple of days off sounded nice right about now. I didn't waste any time. I hurried past them back to my car and headed home. A couple of extra bucks would be nice right now too, I thought. I couldn't help but get excited, I just didn't want to get too worked up to find out that this was still just a big joke. I got home and there was a limo waiting in the parking lot of my apartment complex, and I realized that this was starting to look less and less like a prank. The chauffer was dressed in a nice gray suit, and he stood holding the door, waiting for me. I almost jumped right in, but I had taken a second to glance up at my apartment and saw Chalmers standing there in the window. He motioned with his head for me to come up.

"Hey," I told the driver, "I'll be right back. I just

have to pee." He nodded and waited as I ran up the stairs and opened the door.

"What's all this?" he asked, looking from me to the window and then back at me.

"it's nice seeing you too," I told him sarcastically, though it was actually good to see him.

"I don't see you for what, two weeks, and you can't even say hi?"

"Hi," he said in the same sarcastic tone I used on him.

"Now can you tell me what all this is about?"

"I won a contest, I guess." He just gave me a quizzical kind of stare.

"I won the Critterware sweepstakes. Something like a hundred and fifty grand worth of prizes." He continued to stare for another moment or two before he spoke.

"No man, this isn't right. You're not to win such things. This is still your punishment."

"Hey don't hate," I told him almost smiling.

"You don't get it, mate. You don't win like this, at least not in this lifetime. It simply can't happen.

Something is wrong. We need to take a minute and figure this all out."

"I finally get some love, win some money to get me ahead of the game, and you're gonna rain on my parade? Real nice."

"You are not understanding me. These types of things aren't supposed to happen. You're supposed to live a miserable life so that you learn whatever lessons you are supposed to learn. You're supposed to suffer, to constantly have the carpet yanked out from under you. This isn't right. Something is wrong here." He started to pace a bit. The driver downstairs tooted his horn, and I decided it was time to go.

"Look, I'm not going to argue, I am going to go whether you like it or not."

"Then go with great caution," he conceded.

"I am sure we will soon see that there is a great price attached to this prize."

"Yeah, I'll keep my eyes peeled." I said that just to appease him as I hurried out the door. The limo was way sweet but the jet that waited for me on the tarmac at Lindbergh Field was epic. I was given preferential treatment straight through. I didn't have to stand in line or anything, and I had the hottest stewardess that I had ever seen show me to my seat. The pilot came in and shook my hand, and then almost immediately, we were in the air. As soon as we got cruising altitude, the stewardess asked me if I wanted a steak or some lobster, which I couldn't turn down. Even the chair in which I sat seemed to be the most comfortable piece of furniture my butt had ever touched. The inside of the jet was opulent to say the least. A couple of our clients owned or owned part of a jet like this, but I never thought I would be privy enough to ride on one. I ran my hand across the deep gloss that covered the wood grain finish of the window trim and the table in front of me. The white leather chair, in which I sat, seemed to meld itself to my frame. I was feeling quite relaxed. The smell of my steak cooking somewhere behind me filled my nostrils and my mouth salivated for it. I loved that smell, and I couldn't wait to sink my teeth into it. I didn't even care that it was still quite early in the day. I had had steak, eggs, lobster, and hash brown potatoes. I ate like a king, and when I was done the beautiful Miss Monica came and took away the dishes, tidied up and then showed me some of my new wardrobe. I'm not the most fashionable dresser. I never was quite sure what pants went with what shirt. So, when I saw all of those nice clothes, I was really stoked. And as if that wasn't enough, I was given a full body massage. I never really had a professional massage before. Having a beautiful women rub me down was near incredible. Then Monica shaved me (ok, this was a little weird), and picked out my clothes so that I would look my best to meet with Mr. Barnes.

This was truly the pimp treatment. She was pretty and nice, and I almost didn't want to get off of the plane when it landed, but I did. I will never forget how relaxed I felt when I walked down the stairs and onto the tarmac. There was another limo waiting for me, which took me to what I called the Critterware Compound. The place was huge, and there were people everywhere. Eventually we pulled up to a tall building and the driver hurried around and opened the door for me. Where, again, I was met by another beautiful women, a strawberry-blonde named Lori.

She seemed so oddly familiar, but I couldn't place her. The way she walked, talked and moved, all gave me that weird feeling of déjà vu. She escorted me up the Lucious Barnes's office. As soon as the elevator door opened, I knew that everything was the best of the best. This was truly the nicest place I had ever seen. Lori walked past the huge security guards into Barne's waiting room, it was incredible, to say the least. I've worked in the construction field for many years here and there, so I know what I'm looking at and what to look for. I won't be fooled by some faux paint and texture to cover up imperfections. Every corner and every butt joint were mitered perfectly. The fools I worked with in Rancho Sante Fe could only dream of such fine craftmanship. I always loved architecture, the amount of time and effort handmade accentuations make to a room, the way the crown molding on the edges of the ceiling seemed to have at least seven or eight layers of trim-work on them. Each piece blended effortlessly with the rest. The door casements and the base trim were similar character. They were all a deep cherry wood color. They offset the various color schemes and décor of each of the little rooms we passed through. I kept thinking how nice everything was and how good Lori smelled and waited to be awakened from my dream. But I did not wake up; instead, I walked right into the office of the man that created one of the biggest, most successful businesses on the planet. Critterware was the operating system that ran almost every computer in the United States and a good part of the entire world. Lucious Barne's inventions had pretty much changed the entire world, the way business and commerce were done, even the way mail got sent. I was old enough to remember the days before there was a Critter in every house, back in the days before ATMs, where if you didn't make it to the bank by Friday at 5pm, you were screwed for cash for the weekend. Now I could do my banking on-line at 2am if I wanted to. Critterware had revolutionized banking, communications, everything, and I was about to meet the man responsible for it all. I was super stoked.

As Lori and I approached, the doors opened toward us, and they blew her scent into my face. She smelled so good and something in the back of my head called out to me.

"Thank you, Lori. You may go." The voice was very familiar to me. It came from a chair with its back to us. As she turned and left, I was again wafted by her wonderful smell. It reached out to me, pulled at me. I tried not to watch her leave, but I had to. I turned my head just enough to watch her for another half a second, out of the corner of my eye. Lucious Barnes was everywhere it seemed. He did commercials for his product, and he had cameo appearances on several different TV shows and movies, let alone the many hours of interview and press conferences he held every time his company came out with another ground-breaking, earth-changing innovation. It was almost like I knew him, but when he turned his face to me, I got nervous.

"Ah, Mr. Dinan, please have a seat. Make yourself comfortable." I did so.

"May I call you Joe or Joseph?"

"Mr. Barnes, you can call me whatever you like sir," I said jokingly. I was so nervous.

"This has been one of the best days of my life, I already feel like a king." Barnes looked genuinely happy.

"Good Joseph, I'm truly glad you're enjoying your time with us. That is our objective, and you can call me Lucious, please." I felt giddy.

"Okay," trickled out of my mouth, but then my mind kinda went blank. There was so much I wanted to ask him, but Instead I sat there with my mouth hanging open. I was never big on hero worship, but this was truly one of the most interestingly remarkable people of my time. Barnes smiled at me.

"Relax son, I want you to feel at ease. There is a great deal for us to talk about. Did you enjoy your trip?"

"Yes. It was awesome. Thank you."

"And I see that the clothes fit," he said with a smile. I had seen this man's face a thousand times. He had been on the news, in newspapers and magazines, and countless documentaries. He was everywhere.

But here, in person, he looked so different, so real. I had always thought him to be abrasive, but here, now he seemed quite cordial to me. He still held the air of royalty, but he didn't seem so stuffy "So, what can I do for you son?"

"You can spot me about 3 mil for a few weeks," I told him with a smile.

"Hold on, let me get my checkbook," he quipped back, reaching into his desk drawer.

"Psyche." We shared a bit of a giggle.

"That's funny. Most people are too intimidated to joke when they first meet me. It's all business and seriousness."

"You know what sir? I don't even know why I'm here. I'm just enjoying all of this and soaking it up," I told him with a smile. He looked me dead in the eye and seemed to be giving me the once over.

"You want to see something that I share with almost no one?" What kind of question was that?

"Absolutely," I told him with a smile.

"Come with me" he told me, rising up from behind his large black desk. He turned and walked toward the giant window behind him.

"This is my view." He presented to me like he was truly proud of it.

"I like to sit here, have a drink, and marvel at the world." He sat down and I followed suit.

"No one ever gets to share my view like this," he told me, honoring me. I had no words. The chair was amazingly comfortable, and the view was forever. I could see the entire Critterware complex, every building. In front of me, beyond the immediate compound was a little wooded area and past that, I could see the blue water of the Pacific Ocean, which ran right up to the horizon. To the north, I could see the edge of a city.

"When your name came up as the winner of my contest, I looked you up. I looked through your Facebook and Twitter pages, checked out all of your friends lists. I looked at some of the things you wrote and I looked at whom you would call a friend. I read through some of the files that various companies held on you and even glanced through an old half written novel you had buried in your computer." That caught me a bit off guard, but I allowed the man to continue.

"I just wanted to make sure I wasn't granting an audience to some idiot or deranged lunatic, you know?"

And I kinda know, so I just nodded my head in slight agreement.

"I'm just saying I like what I read. It's hard to find an honest and true person, when you have so many messed up people surrounding you."

"Sir?" I asked, not quite sure what he was saying. I knew I was receiving a compliment, but I really wasn't sure how to respond.

"These messed up people that fall all over the place to please me. They aren't genuine people. They fear me, and instead of thinking for themselves, they say and do what they think I would like. Do you know what I'm saying?"

"Yeah, I know what you're saying." I knew he was looking to converse, but I was still feeling so intimidated that words were hard to come by.

"I just never thought of things that way. I assumed that you would only be surrounded by only the best of the best, the brightest minds of our society."

"Don't get me wrong son, I am, but they're automatons, for the most part. They no longer think outside the box for fear of upsetting me. The whole 'corporate America' thing is stifling us."

I had had a couple factory jobs here and there, and so I understood what he was saying. Those who kept their mouth shut and did what they were told got promoted. Those who asked too many questions or asked for better training or equipment got shunned. Middle management didn't need anyone stepping on their toes or questioning their decisions and I felt this line of thinking was stifling our nation's growth as a whole.

"Then if I may sir, perhaps you have become a victim of your own larger than life persona." I wanted to be honest, but I didn't want to offend the man that had just given me so many gifts.

"I mean to people like me, and please don't take offense; you seem to have gotten pretty hard over the past several years." I looked down at the floor and back up to him.

"They're probably scared to death to offend you and end up losing their jobs." I could see that touched a nerve. He steepled his fingers together and thought inwardly.

"Hard, huh?" You really don't know me," he finally said, with the tiniest hint of anger. Then there was this bit of uncomfortable silence before he continued.

"But I can see where you might get that idea." He trailed off deep in self-inspection. Thankfully Lori interrupted the moment with two drinks. She slid in and out of that office like a whisper. One moment she was there and the next, she was gone.

"Thank you, Lori" Mr. Barnes told her. Then he noticed me staring at her as she handed my drink.

"That will be all," he told her bluntly, and she turned and left. The instant the door closed; he turned his attention back to me. He looked me in the eye for a moment and I felt he was looking into my soul.

"You pretty much speak your mind, don't you?"

"It's not always the best approach, but I do have tendency to tell it like it is." I took a slip of my drink, which tasted quite good. I had to take another sip to try to identify it.

"I get myself in trouble sometimes," I told him as I tried to guess the ingredients that made up the concoction that was in my glass.

"You won't ever figure out what it is," he told me with a hint of pride.

"it's my own special blend, sort of like your Absinthe, but different." He took a big swallow and turned back toward the window.

"What do you think?" he asked.

"I think it's pretty tasty," I told him as I tried to smell the bright green liquid that filled my glass.

"Not about your drink, I knew you'd like that. I'm talking about that," he said nodding toward the big window.

"Your view? It's awesome." It was awesome. The windows themselves were fifteen or twenty feet tall and encompassed most of what I figured to be the western wall. We were pretty high up and the sight before me was truly awesome.

First, I wondered if this was his office, how big must his house be? Then I guessed that I could probably see for ten miles in each direction.

"Not the view son. What do you see out there?" I really didn't know what he was asking me, but I could feel the drink working on me a bit. I had that weird fuzzy feeling in my stomach.

"What do you mean? Seattle? The entire Pacific coastline? I don't know?"

"Well let me tell you what I see, and we'll go from there," he said without getting frustrated.

"I see apathy, neglect, and pretty much a gross disrespect for the planet we live on." Then he paused and looked for a reaction from me. I sure wasn't expecting that, but it wasn't like I was going to sit there with my mouth hanging open. Funny thing is that that was exactly how I had been feeling lately; well not just lately, but for a very long time. So instead of gawking, I kinda nodded with a bit of a smiley smirk.

"I can see that."

What a strange and awkward situation this was. I had to process this scene because of the alarm clock was starting to ring at me. When the alarm goes off, I know something is afoot. Sometimes I can see why I heard the warning; sometimes I have to look around a bit. If it happens before leaving for work, I know to check for my phone, keys or a belt, something that I am forgetting or missing. If it happens when I first meet someone new, it usually means I need to avoid that person, and not make him or her my friend. Sometimes it happens at work, and I know that I did something wrong, crossed a wire or pushed a wrong button. Okay, so I wasn't trying not to look like an idiot in front of one of the most powerful men in the world, but I had to find out why the warning whistle just went off in my head. I had no time to think, but this moment would be analyzed later. It just seemed like an odd sort of conversation. I looked down at the floor and then back at him, took a deep breath and let it out. Then I smiled at him.

"Might as well let it all hang our right? Look Mr. Barnes, if you really wanna know what I think, then I'll tell you." He had left the bait to lay there, so I had to bite. I had to. He nodded and smiled...thank God.

"I think this country is messed up royally. I think we let the government run rampant for decades and now we are pretty much screwed. We were the big dogs, the bully on the block, and we let that crap give us all delusions of grandeur. We've become pompous pigs that overeat, watch too much TV, and in general, take advantage of the people and things around us to better ourselves. We're arrogant, overconfident, and we waste resources on an epidemic scale. And at times, I loathe the fact that my kind is going to destroy this planet one day." I stopped and took a breath, and then looked at Mr.

Barnes. He was smiling; his eyes looked like dime slots. And he motioned for me with his fingers to continue my rant, so I did.

"Where overpopulated, sucking this planet dry. We send our children to die in a war over oil, when if used in a different manner, those kids and the money spent could have improved our lives in a variety of ways. We live in a closed-minded world whose freedoms are shrinking. Our criminal justice system is a joke and there is no way to fix it other than destroy it down to its very roots and start from scratch.

Criminals should be put to work for us, to learn something and to better society rather than sitting, watching TV, rotting in a hole. They're the ones that should be on the front lines. If they wanna kill and destroy things, we should let them. They serve in the military for a few years, learn some skills and some discipline and they merge back into a better life." He was still smiling at me and seemed enthralled. So I just kept ranting. I didn't know how much he got out or what he did for fun, so I just indulged him.

Besides, who else could say that they laid out a rant on Lucious Barnes a mile long?

"I mean, as your common everyday hardworking guy, I'm kinda bummed. I don't know what goes on in your life, but I see a lot of decadence every day in my job. I don't make a lot of money, don't have much saved, and just like a lot of my friends, I have very little hope for the bright financial future. I don't know what I want to be when I grow up and I'm forty. I don't like the way things are run, but it could be worse. So I grin and bare it. I go to work, and I try to enjoy life the best I can. I have some good friends that keep a smile on my face, but none of us are truly happy." I paused and took a deep breath.

"That's pretty much what I think Mr. Barnes," I told him with a smile and a shrug.

"You asked." He sat there for a minute or two without really moving, and it seemed like time had stopped.

"So, what are you going to do about it?" he asked me in a nonchalant tone. That kinda caught me off guard, so I must have just stood there staring with my mouth hanging open long enough to make him think I didn't hear him. Mr. Barnes then stood up and turned his back to me for a brief moment as he walked over to his window. He asked the question again without really looking at me.

"What do you plan to do about it, Joseph?"

"Well, not much," I mustered.

"I have limited resources and pretty much no say in much of anything. I'm the low man on the totem pole at work. I don't have a college degree and I have no money. So, I'm content just to sit here and moan about it." I looked at his back, then up at the ceiling.

"That's pretty much it." I felt almost sheepish. Barnes turned toward me with a look of disgust.

"Very typical Joseph, and very sad. You would tell me of all of these tragedies and then follow up by saying that you would do nothing about it. You are content to let someone else rule over you and run this country, this world into darkness. You and people like you are exactly the reason that these types of things happen and continue to happen." Now he was adamant, and I really didn't like where it was going.

"Hey, you asked," I cut in. I was a little pissed off. If I had known I had been invited there to be belittled, I wouldn't have gone.

"I'm sorry that I don't have the resources that you do. Maybe you should do something about it." He looked at me with a smirky smile but didn't say anything for another uncomfortable moment or two.

Then he came back over to the enormous desk behind which I spun to face. He slid onto his side of the desk and looked at me with a big smile.

"Maybe I just need some help putting my resources into the proper hands to get things done." And just like that his face morphed. He suddenly looked quite a bit more relaxed.

"Most people wouldn't dream of talking to me in the tone that you just used. A lot of my people will secretly harbor feelings of anger and even hatred, but a few ever express it, and no one raises their voice at me like you just did." I didn't know what to say.

"What are you saying? Are you offering me a job?" I asked, because that was what it sounded like to me.

I asked with a smile, yet inquisitive expression.

"Let's don't get too carried away, son," he told me with a twinkle in his eye.

"I like the way that you think, but you would have to show a little more restraint if you wanted to come and work for me." He then stood back up and straightened out his jacket. So, it was a job offer, kinda, but there seemed to be a hitch.

"Is this the real prize of the contest that I won? Does the winner get an interview for a job?"

"You can say that." He clasped his hands together behind his back and started to pace a small circle on his side of the mahogany desk.

"I'm looking for someone to learn from me and eventually stand behind me."

I wanted to cut in, but he unclasped his hands and motioned for me to stop.

"As you know, I have no children, and hence no real heirs. Oh, I have those that feel they have earned the rights to help me run this conglomerate, but none have truly proven their worth. Come over here boy," he reached out his hand. I got up and walked over to the enormous desk. He put his hand on my shoulder and guided me right up to the window. We were pretty high up and right next to the glass that ran from ceiling to floor. It reminded me of my eighth-grade trip to the top of the World Trade Center, but this was nowhere near as high.

"This is my world. I created all of this with just an idea, and it grew from there. I never expected it to get this big, and I think that I've done a pretty good job managing it for what it is. I've put good people in positions to help me run this monstrosity, and they've all made a lot of money, but some of them have become complacent. I fear that we as a people are on the brink of a great changing, and I feel that I may need some help here." He walked over to a large telescope and looked through the eyepiece. Then he looked out the window to where the device had been pointed and then motioned for me to look through it. I did. I looked back at Barnes, then through the scope again.

"That is McVeigh. He is a senior vice president, and he has a propensity to get himself into trouble with his secretaries." He ran his hand through his salt and pepper hair. Lucious Barnes was about fifty-five or sixty but young looking. He wasn't frail, nor was he stout, but he held himself well. His suit was nice and steely gray color that matched his eyes. He stood about five feet, nine or ten inches tall, and weighed approximately two hundred pounds.

"I hand picked him fifteen years ago and he has performed remarkably, but his behavior just won't stop.

What do I do, fire him? He helped move this company into the world market and made us all a household name on every continent." I looked at him while he looked like he was thinking about something, but I did not say anything.

"I'm not happy," he continued, "but in reality, this place is run in the same manner as the rest of big business and as this county as a whole." He looked genuinely disgusted.

"What do you do?"

McVeigh isn't a bad guy; he's just becoming complacent and often times uses his power the wrong way."

"Why are you telling me this?" I finally asked.

"Because I want you to understand why I brought you here. I need someone. I need someone to watch over the likes of McVeigh and the others. I have to bring an innocent, someone that has morals, someone that hasn't been corrupted by the power yet."

"And you think that you would find someone with a drawing from a pool of people that bought computers from you?" the words just felt weird when they came out of my mouth, like I almost knew what he was going to say. Lucious Barnes smiled broadly at me.

"Come now Joseph. Do you think we just picked your name out of a hat? You were chosen, and I think you know why."

Boom, that comment just hung there. So much had happened to me over the past few weeks that this would almost have to be connected with it all. But I wasn't going to say anything. So I just gave him a quizzical, kind of frozen stare.

"Your writing," he finally said with a smile.

"What did you think I was going to say?" he asked expectantly.

"My writing?" I asked not fully able to hide my surprise. Barnes squinted at me.

"Yes Joseph, you're writing. What did you think I was talking about? Do you have some other tricks up your sleeve? He placed his hands on his hips in a demanding pose. Crap I thought. I was caught.

"Nothing," squeaked out of my mouth.

"Nothing that would interest you." I told him with a slight smile. Barnes looked me hard, looked away, then looked hard at me again.

"Now you're hiding something." Again, there was an awkward silence.

"That's okay," he finally said.

"We each have our own little secrets, "he conceded. He gave me a last look and then explained what he meant.

"You post a lot of blogs, which," his voice trailed off a bit, "led me to look a bit deeper into your writing."

My writing? I thought.

"How could you look into my writing? All I have are my notebooks and my," now I trailed off a bit because I understood, "laptop." This was not good.

"You looked into my files!?

"Come on son, don't sound so alarmed. We look into everyone's computer. We reserve the right," he said with a smile.

"It's all there in the small print. You clicked on the agreement the day you brought your new computer home. Don't you remember?" He saw the look I gave him and continued.

"Well, you don't have to sign it; you could use another operating system." Now his smile was clearly sarcastic. Lovely, I thought.

"So you just went through my computer and looked at whatever you wanted to?" I thought about my journal, all of my notes, the quarter finished novels and the random paragraphs.

"How must of my stuff did you read?" I asked, not really wanting to know. Crap, I had a feeling I was about to be embarrassed.

"You have a very active imagination Joseph," Barnes chided.

"I especially like the drama of the angels and demons." Yep, there it was. The drama of angels and demons were my journal. Oh my God, I thought. I had written a couple of pages here and there, but nothing major. Maybe he must have thought it was a novel I was working on. I didn't care. I was going to play dumb.

"Why my computer?" I asked pretending to feel like a fool.

"If it's any consolation to you, you can be assured that only my eyes saw what you wrote." That was supposed to be a consolation. Please. Up until now, everything seemed pretty hunky-dory, almost too good to be true, now here was the hitch.

"You looked through my writing?" I asked with a sad, but slightly angry tone.

"Well, if I hadn't, you wouldn't be standing here right now."

"But still, it's just weird. That's all," my voice trickled off. Wanted him to know how disappointed I was.

In reality though, I wanted to ask him what he thought, if he knew an editor or an agent that might be willing to help me out.

"That stuff is kind of private."

"Let me assure you, Joseph, that the end will indeed justify the means," he told me with a big smile again. He looked out the window, then back at me.

"I can see that you're not too happy. How about I show you around and you can see what I have to offer you?"

"Why not," I thought. What would it hurt? My stomach churned a bit, which was usually the sign that something was amiss, or that I ate something gassy. In this case, I felt it wise to keep my guard up. It seemed awful funny that he made mention of my journals over and above everything else that I wrote. I was fairly sure now that this trip and those events were directly connected. I just had to find the link.

Everything that we passed in Lucious Barnes'

building seemed too high-end, the best of the best. I couldn't even feel the elevator move, but it did, and it did rather quickly. Almost as soon as the doors closed behind us on the tenth floor, they opened in front of us on the ground level. I hadn't paid so much attention to the lobby on the way in because I was so nervous and anxious. But now I got to take a good look around. The ceiling was three stories above and there were fountains and fancy drapes and everyone that passed us seemed to bow or least nod genuinely in their small attempt to bow while they walked. That seemed a bit odd, but I just kept walking and looking. There was obviously a large amount of work going on throughout the building, but the top several floors were reserved for Barnes'penthouse and office suite. I felt like I was walking next to royalty, and in a sense, I was. This man had created all of this. He was responsible for each and every one of these people having their highly paid salaries. It made me look real good standing next to him, let alone be vying for a possible chance to work with him directly. This was turning out to be the second weirdest day that I've ever had. The place was huge and there seemed to be people everywhere. I was dumbstruck.

"So what do you think? Could you get used to working here?" he asked as we walked through the lush green courtyard that had to be nearly a football field in length and width. There were big trees and a lot of bright colored flowers, and there seemed to be pretty women all over the place. Now I know that they weren't smiling at me, but it was nice to see each of them that passed us smile and nod.

"I think I can," I told him with a smile. Then I thought about McVeigh. This crap must drive him crazy.

No wonder he takes advantage of the situation. I would have to work real hard on that, being the sucker for a pretty face that I am.

"But I'm real curious. Are you really going to tell me that you brought me her for my writings?"

"I'll ask you again, what other reason would there be? Do you have something more exciting to present to me? Because now would be a good time. I do have other individuals to interview." I had felt so special until that moment.

"And you picked them because of their writing too?" I asked with half a smile. I was quickly changing the subject. Barnes continued to walk and smile as everyone passed us and gave that same slight bow gesture.

"No," he said with a bit of a laugh.

"You are my great experiment." He continued to walk at a fair pace right up to the side of the building. A door then slid open electronically so that we did not have to slow the pace we walked.

"The others are the elite of the elite, people actually trained for this sort of thing." Oh was that a dig?

"I just don't understand why I was even offered

a chance here. Am I some sort of guniea pig?" We stopped at the edge of the great dining hall. Barnes grabbed a tray and nodded for me to do the same.

Then he walked around in the large common area.

"Do you want sushi, Italian or Mexican?" He looked me up and down.

"Sushi." We made our way over to the sushi counter and grabbed a rainbow roll, and some things I had never seen before.

Then we went back to a nice table away from the main area.

"When your file first came to my attention, I was intrigued. Our mainframe had been setup with several search patterns and logarithms to find very specific things. I looked at your original paperwork, which got me to looking deeper into your writings. You have a lot of potential, son. What are you doing with your life? You ruin it by smoking dope, with not much hope of a future. I've read your stories. I've read your superhero draft as well as the vampire and space travel stuff." I gulped. There was a lot of crazy stuff in there, and I didn't know whether to feel angry that my privacy had been invaded or elated because my writing might well be giving me this one chance to shine.

"But it was the political stuff that grabbed my attention," Barnes continued as he dipped some of the roll into his wasabi and soy sauce, then ate it.

"You have some pretty good ideas. They're what

caught my attention." He neglected to even mention the whole angel thing, which helped put me at ease.

"My favorite is your commitment to the magnetic train and the ingenious recycling program that you came up with. I love it." He stuffed another piece of sushi into his mouth and swallowed it. This was near surreal. I was sitting, having lunch with the world-renowned icon and he was talking about my ideas.

How bizarre could my life get?

"I really like the way you cover every detail. And after reading the piece, I thought long and hard how much someone might weigh the thought of a lifetime of hard labor in the garbage mines of Miramar when they thought about committing a crime. I love it." He was referring to a piece I had written in which prisoners were sent to recycle garbage as part of their sentence. Miramar was a landfill in San Diego County and I had laid out plans on putting a couple of fences around it and making jailbirds sort through the garbage. It was a good piece, I thought. He ate some of the weirder things on the plate and motioned for me to try them also. I did and I enjoyed them. I like the whole sweet and sour thing, as long as it wasn't too extreme. Barnes shook a finger at me.

"And your friends all have wonderful things to say about you." "Huh?" I tried to ask, but my mouth was full.

"Facebook, boy. Your friends really like you and can't say enough about you." He saw me looking at him oddly, trying to swallow my food.

"I had to ask around, check you out. You didn't think I'd spend the money and the time to bring you here just because I liked what you wrote. The writing just got me started." He leaned in a bit closer to me, and for the smallest fractions of a second, I thought he had this glowing red twinkle in his eyes.

"I know more about you than you could imagine," he told me with a devilish smile. We finished up lunch and strolled around the complex. It was sweet. We talked a bit more about the job that I was interviewing for and to be quite honest, it sounded too good to be true. Well, I know what happens when things sound too good to be true. There is usually a catch. It was hard to imagine that I could ever even be considered for such a job, especially considering the salary that was attached to it.

Man, that was a lot of money. It was gonna be hard to go back to work for the dinky little salary that I was earning now. I was making it work, but this was a whole different ballgame. This was a lot to process, almost like calculating the depth of space or how long eternity really was. There were so many plusses, but I knew that the minuses were there too, just hidden. My spider senses were warning me the whole time, and realistically, only an idiot would not see that there was more here than meets the

eye.There was no way that this intelligent, well spoken, superhero of a man would turn over part of the reigns of one of the biggest companies in the world to someone he did not even know. There was no way. Something was going on here. That much I was sure of by now. But I chose to set all of that aside for later and enjoy the moment. There would be a great deal of thought to be poured into this situation, but I also knew that the truth would soon present itself. I wondered what Chalmers and all of my friends would think about all of this. Mr. Barnes and I talked about business, politics, and friendship. It seemed that we enjoyed very similar interests, but it caused me to wonder why he thought the way he did about such things and seemed to do very little about them.

"It's all politics, son," he told me for probably the fourteenth time.

"I have employees and share-holders that are depending on me staying out of trouble. Look, I can speak my mind to you about such things, but I have to live and let live. You know what I mean?" I knew what he meant; I was just getting tired of hearing about it. I didn't like the way he kept skirting the issue.

"I see. The needs of the few, or the one, outweigh the needs of the many," I said jokingly.

"I would love to say no, but this is a business, a corporation that houses and feeds thousands of families.

We build parks and schools and give out scholarships, but I have to be careful what I say out in public.

Do I like the war...no, but what can I really do?

Do I like our criminal justice system...no, but again, what do I do? We both know that the entire system is messed up and the only real way to fix it is to scrap it completely and start over. At least that's what I think. Of course, being able to use the best lawyers that money can buy does have its advantages."

"So rather than fix it, you use the system to your advantage...but you're gonna tell me that you would really love to help if you could." I must have sounded very sarcastic, almost condescending, but I really didn't care. I could leave all of the contemplating about riches and fame until another day, and though I didn't want to offend my host, I had to let him know what I thought. My day, my little adventure was coming to a fast end, and no matter what was offered to me, I still had my morals to look after.

"That's rich." Barnes stopped walking abruptly.

"Do you take me for a clown, an idiot? Please, young man, do you think a fool could have built this empire?" He looked at me with that devilish look in his eye.

"I may be a liar, but I am no idiot." I wasn't sure what that meant, so I let him continue.

"I offer you a chance at the job of a lifetime, and in the final hour of our meeting, you insult me. Well, that's okay. There aren't many people qualified to stand next to me as you are." He looked at me up and down, and then looked behind me, at my back.

"Can't really use them, can you?"

"What?" was the only word that slipped out of my mouth. My heart jumped into my throat.

"You heard me, just give it a chance to sink in. I know that you've been wondering all day about the fact that I would bring you here, show you all of this, and offer you a job just because of some stories that you wrote? No wonder you feel that you can insult me to my face. You really must truly think me a fool."

He smiled broadly. He could see that nothing was coming out of my mouth, yet he spoke not a word until a vehicle pulled up next to us and came to a stop.

"Your ride is here." My mouth was still hanging open slightly as his assistant Lori climbed out from behind the steering wheel and opened the door for me.

"Alright Joseph, this completes our day." He motioned toward the open door. I looked at it and started to climb inside.

"Here, let me help you son," he said. Then the weirdest thing happened. He reached into the car and actually, touched my wing. I snapped my head around back and looked at him and saw him smile and nod as he closed the door behind me. I genuinely felt that. It sent a bit of a tingle down the wing to the muscles in my back. It felt so strange, so good. The car pulled away and the door lock snapped shut. I mean really, what would I say to the man if I could have even said anything at all?

"Hey you just touched my...what? Wing?" or

"Did you mean to just touch that wing of mine?" That would be idiotic, retarded. I had just worked for a few weeks to keep the wings off my mind and now I have to wonder how many people might know that they were there. Maybe he didn't mean to touch it.

Maybe it was just conflicting auras or energy fields bumping into each other. Whatever it was, it would give me much to think about. I knew that this job was mine to take or leave now. This had nothing to do with my writing. It was because of the wings on my back and because of what I really was.

I wondered, as the car left the enormous compound, if that touch was more than just a touch or if Lucious Barnes did something to me that I could not do by myself. Whatever it was, I was not going to try to play with my wings in the back of this car or even on the jet ride home. This would have to wait until I had a private moment. Then I would see is anything was different, and I would have to see why Chalmers never told me about any of this.

EIGHT

Either Lori or Lucious Barnes had set things up that I would have an extra day off at home to think things over once I got back and think it over, I did. I slept half my day away and when I finally got up, I walked down to the beach, stopping along the way to grab a six-pack. All of my friends, including Dan, were at work so, as usual, I was alone. I wasn't really alone though, there were a ton of people there enjoying the sun and the scenery. And let me tell you, the scenery was awesome. There always seemed to be plenty of beautiful women to look at here, so I just donned my MP3 player and sat and drank my beers in the warm California sun. I sat there and watched the beauty's walk by for four hours and thought about what had happened the day prior. I also wondered where my spiritual adviser had wandered off to. I mean, I know he was nearby, but why was he not around to help me figure out what had happened.

I thought that had I sat home alone, I might have been lucky enough to have an audience with him. But a sunny day off in the middle of the week was something that I did not want to waste sitting at home waiting for Chalmers to appear. I had greatly enjoyed this free day off, and I decided to follow it through with a few beers and a couple of shots at the bar on my way home. This was the first time in a long time that I actually felt good about myself and the future. I know what Chalmers had said about not being able to get ahead, but he also said he didn't know everything.

"I'm not omnipotent," he had told me. Since he had such little insight about my journey beforehand, I could only hope that he would better understand it afterward. I had a feeling, though, that he would try to squash my glee. I didn't act up with my wings. I had a very good buzz and a big smile. I must have been glowing. I had made eye contact with a couple of pretty girls and then something else caught my attention. For a half a second, I thought I saw Chalmers standing at the far end of the room watching me. I turned to look, but he wasn't there. I walked over to the place that I thought I had seen him but found nothing. I didn't know if my imagination was playing with me, or if I had genuinely seen him, but something told me to finish my beer and just go home. I gulped down the last bit of my golden beverage and squeezed my way back out of the crowd, out toward the door. It was late afternoon, early evening and a lot of people had showed up for happy hour. I saw one or two people that I knew, but I wasn't in the mood to talk. I had a strange feeling in my gut, not quite sure what to think or what to believe. No one seemed to be paying me much attention, and I liked it that way. The bar was set up to hold as many people as possible with a smoking area and a non-smoking section. As I passed into the smoking section, I smelled something. I was working my way toward the door, and as I left the somewhat smoke-free area, I had to pass through a packed in crowd of smokers. Normally, this was no big deal. I used to smoke myself, so the smoky smell didn't bother me too much. But this was something different than just smoke, and more than just someone with body odor. I knew what it was but didn't want to admit it. This is exactly what Chalmers had warned me about. I got out of there and did not look back. The attack from the bum on Sunset Cliffs still weighed heavy upon my mind. I was not about to deal with something like that again, not today. I was having a good day and I wasn't going to have it ruined by some idiot. I opened the apartment door and saw Dan crashed out hard on the futon. He was snoring like a freight train. He was a good guy, and he had created a kind of bowl effect on the mattress that fit around his body. I smiled as I walked by, and even thought about dropping something into his open mouth as a joke but didn't for fear of making him choke. I didn't mind him sleeping in the living room, as I did the same every now and then, plus the breeze kept things cool in that room. I went into my room and sent Lori a nice thank you letter on the computer and then laid back in my bed with my fingers intertwined behind my head. It was way to early to go to sleep, but I just wanted to lie there and reflect. I had hoped for some pearls of wisdom from my spiritual guide, but it just didn't happen. I was a little drunk and still a bit loopy, but I could not help but think about what he had said the previous day about me winning that prize. And the funny thing was that the more I thought about it, the more I got mad. Who was he to say that essentially, I would never amount to anything because of this punishment. Maybe my punishment was really over and this way my big chance to fix things. I liked the way Lucious Barnes, and I seemed to get along. I liked his opinion on things, and I looked forward to speaking with him again. I wasn't quite sure about it, but I had a strong feeling that he knew who and what I really was. The way he touched my wing made me think that he knew more than what he was saying. Perhaps he knew others like me. I also thought about Lori. Whew, she was beautiful, and seemed so familiar. I didn't know why I felt that way, but I felt like I had known her a very long time. I thought about the dream that I had had the other night.

I remember being scared, but I also remember being in love with someone, and being greatly saddened.

It was a bit hazy now, because of the booze and because it had been just a dream and as all dreams do, the memory of it faded.

As always, I remembered a lot of bit and pieces, but nothing solid. I do remember someone that reminded me so much of her. I just knew that there was something about her, so when I had seen that she wrote back, I was a bit excited. She wrote that she too was happy that we had met and that, out of all the interviewees, she really hoped that I got the job. She also said that she looked forward to seeing me again, and that she would call when she heard more about her boss's choice for the job. She concluded that she hoped to see me again. That was it, short and sweet. I rolled onto my side and looked at myself in the mirror closet doors. I looked at my face. It was the same face I had seen for nearly forty years. I didn't look any different. But then I looked at the wings that you could not miss.

They were huge, and that was when they were tucked in. I know I was drunk, but I just could not pull my gaze away. From the moment I had realized that they were now a part of me, my whole life had changed. I was such a miserable mess for so long that I could not remember otherwise. I didn't date much, nor did I have much of a social life.

Every cent I made just seemed to go toward keeping my head above water, and off the street. Suddenly, my world gets turned upside down and I learn that I might be handed the job of a lifetime. I knew that the two were directly connected. Drunk or not, I was no fool. I wasn't being offered that job because of my writing, that much was sure. It was just more bit of insanity to add to everything else that had happened over the past couple of weeks. I didn't know if I should be ecstatic or horrified. Then I rolled over and just fell asleep.

I woke up at six o'clock and lay there for a moment. I had the remnants of a hangover, but nothing I couldn't shake. It was hard to get up and get motivated after the two days I just had. I was basically offered a job with one of the biggest, most recognized company on the planet, so the mere idea of returning to my boring job that was not very exciting. I smacked the alarm and got up, had some coffee and got ready. As I drank my morning java and did my sit-ups and push-ups and generally went about my business, I couldn't help but daydream back to my visit with Lucious Barnes.

The glitz and glamour that would accompany such a job would be to die for, but today I would be crawling around an attic or pulling a wire through a wall. The ride to work was uneventful, but when I got to the office, my co-worker and my boss were right up in my face.

"What happened?" Steve asked me with a big smile on his face. He was a good guy. He had built his company from scratch and was doing pretty good. His nephew James also worked with us, and we made a pretty decent team. We installed the high-end audio and video equipment in the most expensive homes in San Diego County, and thought I had always felt that I was a bit of a jinx whenever I had been hired into a company, this one had prospered since my arrival. I looked at him and felt a little bad. I really didn't like working for the super-rich that we worked for, but it paid the bills. Some of our clients were nice people, but most were decadent beyond imagination. They had too much money and it showed. But I liked working with these two. We fed off of each other and I swear between us, there was no problem on the planet that couldn't be solved.

"I was offered a job," I said sheepishly. I didn't want to hurt Steve or James's feelings, but I wanted to be truthful.

"And?" he asked with anticipation.

"Nothing's been locked up just yet," I hold him sheepishly.

"But the odds are that I am probably to be leaving in the next few weeks." At first no one said anything, then my boss spoke.

"Well, I wish you luck with that. It kinda messes things up a bit here, but we'll manage." He looked a little bummed, then he smiled and looked at me.

"Might as well finish up with the Biggums," he said with a cocky smile. Crap, I thought. I hated those people, and he knew it. It was his bit of payback. I knew that he was jealous. He held himself in a pretty high regard and though he treated me well, he considered me a bit of a ne'er-do-well.

"I thought the only thing left was programming?"

"Yeah," he said with a devilish grin.

"And...do you mind taking your own car up

there? All you'll need is the computer." I looked over at James, then back at Steve.

"I'm taking James with me today. Call me when you're done."

Bang, bang, bang. Three shots fired across the bow. He knew I hated the Biggums. He knew I hated programming, just sitting there typing all day. I hated it. Now I could feel my bubble bursting. I was so happy three minutes, but now I felt miserable and angry. The last thing I wanted to do was to try to program the Biggums home automation system that seemed endless. There were so many items to control in that house that I could feel my stomach turn as I thought about it. I worked with James every freakin day. We did all of the hard stuff and Steve did the programming. I climbed the highest ladders and crawled through the tiny holes to get the wires where they needed to be. James and I did that, and we kinda came and went as we pleased. Today was going to be long and painful, and I was going to have to put in a full eight hours. That was the 'call me when you are done' dig. It was a long drive up there and traffic was sucking. I honestly, at that moment, thought that if I had known that I had the Critterware job, I would probably have quit this one and just went home. I was so happy just an hour prior, and now I was miserable. I got to the Biggum's mansion and went inside and got my laptop hooked up to their system. God there was a lot of data. Our main processor controlled the lights, and all of the complete home entertain system. It was sweet. You could control any light in the house and play different music in every room if you wanted to. Each room had an access panel or LCD display with all sorts of pictures and commands. The system was designed for ease of operation, but of course, this meant a great deal more programming. There was a full-scale movie theater in their home with a HD projector and DVD players that were hooked up to all of the televisions throughout the house. It was a dream come true to everyone that ever enjoyed electronic gismos. It was all top of the line, state of the art stuff. Three and a half frustrating hours passed. In that time, I think I mess up as must stuff as I fixed.

Tap, tap, then run around and look. Tap, tap, then run around and look to see if the proper lights lit with the correct commands. It was near maddening for someone like me. My boss should have been here doing this, but he was getting his revenge today. Forget the fact that he just got a, what, three-thousand-dollar computer or the fact he was about to have the ins with one of the biggest companies the world had ever seen. He just wanted to get my goat. He knew what he was doing by sending me here, which made things even worse. This was sucking big time, but at least it was quiet. I had to get as much done as I could before school was done. School got out at around 2:30 – 3:00pm, and the horde would then soon be upon me. It was the same thing every time I went there, and it was getting old.

I had had enough of the two older boys. They were so obnoxious that it sickened me. All five of them came home and walked all over their mother and treated her with such rudeness and disrespect that had they been my kids, they would have had their butts handed to them.

But they were not mine and for that I was glad. I was just done with them all, which was all the more reason to hate my present situation. I typed, and then typed some more. Then I loaded the program into the processing unit and crossed my fingers. I walked around the house to see what lights lit up with which individual wall switch. There were so many switches and so many lines of text that connected them all together. I did this all day, trying to get as much done as possible until I finally lost track of time.

I so wanted this job over. I wanted it done so that I would never have to see these people again. Today I was tired. The numbers dredged on and on, and there seemed to be no end. It was truly frustrating.

Then suddenly, without much of a preamble the orchestrated chaos began. I could hear doors opening and slamming shut all throughout the enormous house. Their voices echoed in my ear, and I felt the chill of their presence tingle my spine. I looked up and one of the demon children was standing in front of me, staring. I really didn't need a fat little one up in my face, but that was what I got.

"What are ya doin?" the boy asked, crowding

me. His name was Liam, but we referred to him as Lee-

Ham, like a fat little piece of pork.

"The same thing I was doing the other day when you got home. I'm programming." I had barely got the words out of my mouth when he blurted out the word, "huh?" it was always the same thing. He would ask a question, then not wait for an answer, and he just had that cocky air about him that truly disgusted me. This piece of crap child, that had no clue of the real world around him because his father made so much money, was about to bark up the wrong tree. I gave him a bit of a scowl and asked him to give me some space. He decided to push me as he often did to his mother in front of everyone. I actually think he got off on disrespecting her. But that would not work for me. I was sick and tired of being talked down to by some twelve-year-old.

"When are you gonna be done?" he asked, but before I could answer, he was speaking again.

"My dad says this had better work or he's gonna sue ya. He says he can't wait for you idiots to get done.

My mom says she wants all you cockroaches outta our house by next week." He laughed at me, right in my face.

"Ha, ha she called you cockroach." Some spittle got on me from his forced laugh. I wanted to hit him, but I couldn't. My hands clenched up into fists. I just couldn't help myself. I snapped the fist out at him to scare him a bit. I knew, in the back of my head, that I had gone too far, but I just didn't know how far I had really gone. I didn't come close to hitting him. I just wanted to scare him, but when my fist snapped out, I felt this surge of electricity jolt through my body. I was like static shock, but many times more powerful. Something amazing, yet horrific happened. A burst of blue energy leapt from my fist into the boy's face. The boy jumped and shook slightly, like he had just grab hold of a live electrical wire. He trembled for a couple of seconds, and then slumped hard into a pile on the floor. I didn't know what to do. I just stood there with my mouth hanging open watching the boy twitch.

"Well I didn't bloody well expect that," Chalmers told me as he suddenly appeared over to my right. He adjusted his glasses and looked at the boy. He looked at me, then behind and around me. Then he was gone again, but before I could even breathe, he appeared over my left shoulder, in the doorway.

"The coast is clear pick that boy up and put him in his room." I took a second to let his words sink in, but that was too much time for him to wait.

"Do it now or your finished," he commanded. I didn't think then, I just moved. The boy was still twitchy, but I picked his little body up rather easily. Chalmers took the lead and I followed him. I felt so bad, but there was no time now for remorse. I watched Chalmers peek around the corner of the huge home, and we quickly slipped from one hallway to another We reached the boy's room and he instructed me to leave the child in his private bathroom, I pretty much knew what to do then. I hit the test switch on the GFI (ground fault interrupt) electrical receptacle. This type of receptacle was a safety code requirement, which would shut off power to avoid electrical shock. Each and every receptacle that was located anywhere near water had to be of this type. I was going to make this look like an accident that this type of outlet was to prevent. I opened the valves on the bathroom sink and I splashed some water onto the floor on and around the boy. He still switched slightly. I surveyed the scene to be sure that everything was in place to make it look like the boy had gotten an electrical shock that had popped the GFI. I had gone from being scared stiff into full survival mode. And for the briefest of seconds, I thought that I probably should kill him to avoid my own discovery.

"Don't be silly," Chalmers told me.

"He will remember nothing...odds are that he will never see or talk again." Those words hit me kinda hard.

"No time for remorse now, boy," he told me.

"Get back to your computer and let's get outta here." I took one last look at the boy before I left. True, there was no time for remorse, but I was nonetheless filled with it. The kid was a real pain in the butt, but he didn't deserve that. I hurried back to my computer, downloaded my files into the system and started to pack things up.

I came and went at my convenience in this home, so I didn't need to tell anyone I was leaving. I just left.

I was shaking as I slid into the driver's seat of my car. Chalmers didn't have to get in, he just appeared in the passenger's seat next to me.

"Calm down," he told me.

"You will have to get ahold of yourself. There are greater things to worry about here than just one child." He seemed a bit callous about the whole thing.

"But what if he dies?"

"Then he dies. What do you want me to say? There is nothing we can do about it now." He was no nonchalant.

"You have to understand that I've seen you do such horrible things in so many lifetimes, that a little static discharge is nothing to me. Believe me, the kid will live."

"That's easy for you to say," I told him. I was beside myself with guilt and fear. I did not want the boy to die, and I sure was as fried chicken did not want to go to jail.

"It is easy for me to say. If I told you what I saw you do, you wouldn't believe it. As it was, your favorite saying when you were an angel heading to battle was 'kill them all!' Do you remember that? You screamed that command to your troops before every single battle. Oh yeah, that was right before you cleaved your way through and entire brigade of shadows and other horrors." He was being sarcastic.

"Kill them all." The words slid out of my mouth. They sounded so familiar. "Kill them all." I wanted to shout it our loud. My mind drifted back for the briefest of moments to a golden sky where my troops soared. We were headed into battle, and we were ready. We were very close to our enemies, and I could feel my blood pumping, the power rippling through my body. We had been through this a million times, but each time was different, and a fight to the death was still a fight to the death. A lot of lives were going to end this day and I wanted to be sure none of them would be my own or my troopers.

Form ranks. We hit em hard and we hit em fast. Take no prisoners. Kill them all!" I shouted above the noise of the wind that whipped against my body. I loved the adrenaline rush that surged through me right before a battle. I was so worked up that I knew nothing would stop me. And soon enough the slaughter began. They tried to put a fight, but we just hacked through them en masse. The fire burned in my veins and blood blurred my vision. This was a glorious day! The smell of death filled my nostrils as my soldiers battled on and everything seemed as it should. Then something happened. The beasties we were fighting and threw us a curve as they often did.

Darkness closed in around us and a shadow fell over my whole platoon. I felt a chill run down my spine as something, some sort of creature that looked like tar or molasses started to form in the shadows. It was freaky to say the least. Gregor didn't hesitate for a second (that was why I loved him so) He jumped into the air and slammed his fiery sword into the thing. It crackled and popped where the sword burned into its form, but it continued to grow and meld itself into something close to a gigantic humanoid.

Gregor's sword was stuck in the side of the thing, its blue energy rippled at the point of impact. It took a millisecond for three other troopers to come to his rescue. Shields slammed into the thing and swords burned and tore at its gooey surface. They were hacking and cleaving at the thing, and I was watching it, looking for its weaknesses, assessing the situation. Out of the corner of my eye I saw the darkness quickly closing in around us. It was a trap. The tar creature was meant to distract us. I jumped up into the sky and flew straight up til I reached the upper atmosphere of the golden orange world, then I came down like a missile. My sword blazed in a brilliant blue fire, brighter than it had in a long time. They had tried to flank us and now they would pay the price. I slammed into and through the black ooze with such energy and force that it splattered into a billion pieces. Then I turned to face the horde of shadows that now nearly surrounded us with a big, crazy looking smile on my face. I stood where the beast had been, completely surrounded and engulfed in the blue flames. I then pointed my sword out at the amassing shadows and released a blast of energy. It destroyed every shadow it touched. I spun slowly in a small circle so that I could extinguish every last one of them. It was a complete and total show of force. And it felt fantastic. It took about two seconds for my boys to see that I had everything under complete control, and they all just stepped back and watched. And in the midst of such death and madness they were able to share a smile. I, on the other hand, had lost my mind to rage. I was going to kill them all.

"Wake up, you idiot," Chalmers blasted me "You're driving here, you know." He was right. I was spacing out. I was about to pass through the exit gate of the little guarded community where the Biggums lived, and I looked as guilty as sin. I knew that I would be video taped leaving, so I bucked up and straightened myself out. And in a few seconds, I was out onto the city streets and headed home. I thought about Lee-ham. I didn't like the kid, but I didn't want to hurt or maim him.

"Stop worrying about that child," Chalmers scolded. It was so weird seeing him sitting next to me in my little old car.

"And don't act so holier than thou. I know that a part of you would have loved to choke him on more than once occasion. Let it be. There's nothing you can do about it now," He adjusted his sunglasses and looked me over.

"How were you able to do that anyway?" I took my gaze from the road and looked at him.

"Are you asking me? How should I know? You're the one that's supposed to know about this stuff, not me."

"I don't bloody well know what just happened. That was all you. Is there anything that we may need to worry about?" I thought about Barnes touching my wing and the feeling it gave me.

"You know I swear that I felt Lucious Barnes touched my wing the other day." Chalmers sat quiet for a brief moment.

"Interesting. That Lucious Barnes is a strange one. He is human, just like everyone else, but he has a haze around him that shields his movements from even my vision."

"Huh? What? What are you talking about?" I asked, cutting in. I didn't like hearing that too much at all. I knew it all sounded too good to be true. There was a lot of mess up stuff going on, and that was the icing on the cake. Chalmers looked at me and smiled.

"You are so impetuous. That is why this duty of mine has not been considered a complete chore to me.

Sometimes you are just fun to watch. And, incidentally, that is why your punishment has lasted so long."

He almost laughed at me.

"Yes, there have been some mess up things happening to you as of late, and yes there are connections, both of these things you already know, but I cannot comment on anything more than that."

"Because you choose not to or because you do not know?" I asked. We were still a long way from home, and I was still anticipating a phone call from the boss. My stomach churned and my heart thumped. I was so worked up that I didn't give Chalmers the chance to answer me.

"You are so predictable," he almost laughed.

"The one constant in the universe is truly you. No matter what happens, you've always have been the same mess up guy." He slapped his knee and laughed right in my face.

"I've stood by on the sidelines of your existence, watching you, sometimes root for you, cheering out loud for you, forever. I knew you would never hear me, but I still applauded you every now and then. I was in my place, and you were in yours. I could scream at you as loud as I wanted, and you would never hear me, but now things are different. We're both here. You see me and I see you. I hear you, but you still don't hear me. It's genius. Do you believe in karma and destiny and all of the like?" he asked. I wasn't sure if it was a hypothetical question. I nodded yes and he continued.

"Well, how funny is that I appear to you in such a manor? Would have listened to me more if I appeared as your new hero, Mr. Lucious Barnes or maybe some smoking hot model with beautiful eyes, like your new friend Lori?" He paused, and I reacted. He must have liked getting my goat.

"Oh yes, you know who I'm talking about," he continued.

"You mean Barnes' assistant?" I asked.

"Yes, I mean Barnes' assistant. You do recognize her, no?" He said with a smug look.

"Comic strands and karmatic irony. There were so many different life forms, different timelines and dimensions. What are the odds that two people would meet more than once on the same level and the same plane of existence? It does happen every now and then, though. Sometimes people are truly destined to be together because their strings had crossed in the past lives. Sometimes it happens once or twice and sometimes it happens often, like with you and this Lori person. I've seen her before, and so have you. You've met a few times, been lovers, even been responsible for each other's death in different lifetimes, believe it or not," he said laughing and seemed to trail off a bit. I thought about what he said in the silence that followed. We were getting closer to home, and I was starting to relax a bit. I don't know why it was like that, but I just felt safer there in my home turf. And after being able to calm down, I was able to think more about what Chalmers had just told me. I had such a strange feeling of déjà vu when I saw her, but I knew that I hadn't seen her before. I think I would have remembered, but then again, maybe I did remember her. That's why she seemed too familiar.

"Weird, isn't it?" when you know what to look for, it will mess with you. It's so chaotically random yet organized to such an exact science that it's creepy.

Strange that she appears here at this moment, amongst all of this recent craziness as Barnes' assistant, wouldn't you agree?" That one was rhetorical, he continued.

"That Barnes is an odd one as well. He's hiding something from both of us. So, be leery."

"What do you mean? Is he a bad guy? I knew that whole job thing was going to be too good to be true, I knew it" I took a deep breath and let it out.

"What should I do?" Chalmers didn't even look at me. It was like he was sitting there just enjoying the ride.

"I can't tell you what to do, I'm just a Watcher. I watch. I can advise here and there, but I must let things play out. This is your punishment, your destiny."

"You say that, but you told me what to do just thirty minutes ago in the Biggum's house. What kind of crap is that? I thought you had permission to help me."

"Son, I told you nothing that you wouldn't have thought of on your own. I just persuaded you to get it done and get your head in the game sooner than later. The rest was on you."

"Are you serious?" That's your story. You're gonna say that I would have figured all that out on my own, did what I did, and got out of there without freaking out in the process? Come on. Are you kidding me now? Are you going to help me or are you going to sit back and watch what happens?"

"You have to understand that there is going to be some things that happen to you that neither one of us will understand. This may level off, but I doubt it. I think things will most likely get worse and will definitely get more and more weird, and we will have to deal with them as they come. The fact that you say you could feel your wings, that Lori is here, and that the blue energy just burst from your hand dictate that strange, unexpected things are afoot." He leaned in close to me.

"You will have some big decisions to make in the very near future, and I can't give you all the answers because I do not know them myself. You will need to learn to calm your thoughts and see beyond that your earthly eyes show you. That is the kind of thing I can help you with."

"What do you mean? I pondered out loud.

"I have to figure things out pretty much on my own and then you come in after the fact and explain them? That sucks."

"Boy," he laughed now.

"You don't have a clue. You opened a door that is both wonderful and deadly. I only pray that you can make it benefit you and you can use it to propel you back where you belong. You are balancing on a fine line here. I know you want more from our time together, but this is all I can give you. I know that you were hoping for more, but in some, most cases, you will know as much as me." I pulled onto Sunset Cliffs Boulevard just as my phone rang. It was my boss. I was supposed to call him before I left, but in all of the craziness, I had blown it off. I apprehensively answered, expecting to be chided.

"How'd it go buddy?" he asked, sounding rather pleasant.

"I got a lot done, but it was painstakingly difficult. You know how it gets here towards the end of the day." I used the word here instead of there to imply that I was still in the area. He didn't really need to know what time I had left, but if he wanted to, he could look at the computer logs and see what time the computer had been used last.

"Well, we'll see tomorrow. I'm headed up there first thing. Can you get here by seven so I can have the laptop and head out?"

"Sure," I said, please to know that no one called him yet. I had fully expected to be grilled over what had happened to the boy, but he said nothing about it.

This means that the boy either has not yet been found or that Steve had just not been contacted about it. Once discovered, word of the accident would spread through the building industry like wildfire. It was a bit of a tight-knit group, the framers, electricians, and so on. We all seemed to work on a lot of jobs together, and they were gossipy as a group of old spinsters.

"Alright buddy, see you in the morning."

"Later," I replied while exhaling with relief. I flipped the phone shut and smiled.

"That went easier than I thought it would."

"You always expect the worst, spending all of your energy over thinking everything. Don't you get tired of it? I told you not to worry about it. Why don't you try listening to me once and see what happens?"

He looked at me hard.

"Let it go man. Just let it go, and see what happens, son." That sounded easy enough, so I made the decision right then and there to try to let things go more. I always tried to go with the flow, but with me, that was a very difficult thing and always had been, in this life and the last. I liked things done my way on my schedule, but the more I relaxed and really did go with the flow, the better things turned out, most of the time I realized that if I did not get what I wanted, it was for a reason. And the harder I worked to make something happen my way, the more it got me into trouble.

"Okay," I said simply. I was going to make a conscious effort to not even think about the boy or work or any of this stuff at all. I didn't know it at the time, but I really wasn't going to have much of a choice. I pulled into my spot and killed the engine, then I turned to look at Chalmers and he was gone. I grabbed the computer and my lunchbox and headed up to the stairs to my apartment.

Then as the door slid open, my jaw almost hit the floor. There in my living room sat Lucious Barnes' assistant Lori. She was pretty as the day is long, and there she was sitting on my old, dingy couch talking to my roommate.

"Hello." I said with a smile. What else could I do? I was as nervous a guy asking a girl to the prom for the first time.

"Hello, Mr. Dinan," she said as she got up. She extended a hand for me to shake which I quickly dropped my lunchbox and shook.

"You can call me Joe." I said with a smile.

She returned the smile and nodded slightly.

"And you can call me late for dinner," my roomy Dan said jokingly as he got off the futon. It was clear that she must have woken him up when she arrived because his hair was all askew. He pulled himself up, grabbed his smokes and went outside.

"Want something to drink?" I asked.

"No thank you. I would like to speak with you on the behalf of Mr. Lucious Barens though, if that is alright with you." She seemed so proper, so business like and stuff. My mind raced away, for a second, to that abysmal world of shadows in my dream. It was her alright, same form, same beautiful eyes, just a whole lot cleaner and not so raggedy. And best of all, we weren't presently scared out of our minds, hiding from the shadows, running for our lives. I wondered if she could remember any of it.

"Of course," I told her and gave her a big cheesy smile.

"Good news or bad news? I asked.

"Good news, I believe," she told me without much emotion.

"I am here to offer a job as assistant trainee to Mr. Barnes." Her voice was so soothing, and I realized how long it had been since I had really seen her. Not meaning two days ago, at Barnes' office, but back then. Back when we were lovers. I wondered if I would be able to have that again, or if this would be another let down. I had learned that the latter was pretty much the norm. Nonetheless, I wanted her. I almost needed her. I was already going to take whatever offer she made me. I had been so bored with my life for so long that any changes would be welcomed. It had been a while now since the discovery of my wings and such and if that was going to be my ticket to get my foot in the door, then so be it. I needed to step out onto a limb and see what happened. I was suckered in by this long, lost love of mine, but that was just the tip of the iceberg. I was not some naïve idiot, but I could let them all think I was, just as long as I remembered not to underestimate any of them. These people didn't get where they were in life by not paying attention to detail and minding things very closely. If they wanted me, then they must have known that I was special.

"Wow," that sounds pretty exciting. Would I have to move?" I asked jokingly.

"You know, I'd really hate to have to give up all of this." I waited for her to smile.

"It's not that bad of a place," she told me, taking a look around.

"Very nice, in fact; very clean. I like that," she told me with a bit of a twinkle in her eye.

"I try, I try." Then I leaned a little closer to her, looked down at the floor, then back up at her with a sultry look in my eye.

"How much does this job pay?" I asked trying to be funny.

"We'll start you off with a base salary of a hundred and twenty thousand, with a chance to increase that amount with incentives. You will have to move, but we will cover housing, and we will provide you with a brand-new Lexus. How does that sound?" I looked at her with a serious stare that wiped the smile from her face. She did not know what to say or do, and I just continued in my stare. Then after a few moments of the awkward silence, I spoke.

"Do you hear that," I asked still staring intently.

"No, hear what?" she asked, and I could tell that she was beginning to feel uncomfortable.

"The sound of the fireworks and marching band going off inside my head," I told her, jumping up from the couch. I moved my hands back and forth like a conductor conducting an orchestra and started humming aloud some old marching band type of song. Then I jumped around the coffee table, grabbed her by the hand and picked her up off the other couch and started dancing with her. I didn't get crazy, just did it long enough to get a chuckle from her and let her go.

"Can I take that as a, yes?" she asked, a bit sheepishly now. I didn't expect sheepishness from her at all.

Not this one.

"That's pretty much a yes," I told her without messing around. And then, there it was that smile with a little crook on the right side of her lips, same as I remembered. Weird though, she said she got that from getting kicked in the face during a foot riot when she was fifteen. That was a different person on a different world. How could she have that same little crooked smile? Whew, this was tricky.

"Do I need to sign something?"

"Yes, please read and sign these forms." She handed me a stack. I thumbed through them. Yep, there is was – the sexual harassment form. I took the pen she presented me and got ready to sign on all of the dotted lines. I stopped and looked up at her.

"So, if I sign all of these forms, then this goes into effect, and I really couldn't even ask you to go out and have a drink to celebrate with me, could I?" She gave me a quizzical look, then smiled.

"I'm afraid so." I set down the pen and looked into her pretty eyes.

"I think we should go out and at least get a fish taco and beer while we discuss this paperwork first Then." I received a bit of a snarled-up look, which again turned into a smile.

"I really have to be getting back" she started.

"With these papers signed, right?" I asked with a

smirk. She looked at me, then sat back down on the couch. Her smile was now cut in half.

"Fish tacos and a beer? I'll sign your papers. I would just like to hear a little about your company before I sign my life away. I'm not trying to be coy or anything, I just need to discuss a couple of things that may or may not be covered in this substantial stack."

"Ok, I would agree to a fish taco," she said politely.

"Two fish tacos, and one beer," I negotiated. She agreed with a bit of hesitation, and we headed out.

I lived about ten minutes' walk from a place that I wanted to take her, and our little journey would take us right down to the ocean. The more I looked at her and talked with her, the more I wanted her to be with me like she had been before. She had been the only bright spot in an otherwise horrific life. It wasn't very late, maybe five or five thirty, but there was a bit of a chill in the air. The shadows were long, and darkness of the evening was not far off. Walking down the street with this person made me trip back to darker days, when a trip like this to a bar or to the ocean would only exist in our dreams, we never dared venture far from home in that world, not at this hour anyways. I remember how much we hated the winters then, not so much because of the cold, but because of the shortened days. Sunlight was our friend. Very few ventured out into the darkness, but Lori and I had always been bolder than most.

The first time she went out into the night with me, I thought she would tear my arm off because she held onto me so tightly. When I was young, back when the crap started to hit the fan, back when there were food riots, I learned to become hard. I built a shell around me, not just a mental toughness, but also of muscle. I learned real quick to take first, ask questions later. I made sure my friends and family were taken care of, but when they were all gone, I got just plain crappy. How bad would it suck to come home and find your mother gone? A light bulb burst in the kitchen one night and poof she was no more. It happened a lot. It happened to every family. A mom or dad or a brother or sister would be there one second and gone the next. They might let out a shrill for help, but when the shadows fell upon them, it happened so quickly and only a handful ever escaped.

And just like that, your world is shattered again and again. Just when you were feeling like you could actually count on something, anything, you would wake up to come home and the house would be empty. It sucked big time. And by the time I was in my early teens, I was completely alone. I happened upon some guys that taught me how to survive, how to get my body and mind right. I was strong and smart, and they taught me how to be tough. They taught me the tricks of the dark and the light. After a while I took what I wanted. Human life didn't matter quite so much to me as my own happiness. I didn't give much of a crap if I had to kill to get what I wanted. I had become ruthless and evil. I had learned not to fear the shadows because if they got me, they got me. That was the attitude I had. That was my life. I had absolutely no fear of my fellow man. Most of the guns and ammunitions had been confiscated and destroyed in the years following the food riots. They had used people's ownership permits to track down most of the weaponry and put rewards in place to collect what they could.

Martial law ruled most of the land, and anyone caught with a gun was arrested immediately. The gun owners and groups like the NRA put up big stinks at first, but in the end, the authorities won out. There had been just too many guns related homicides when things started getting tough. That left hand-to-hand combat or improvised weaponry. Let me tell you the average man can't fight, and if anyone came at me with a knife or a sharp tool, I would take it from them and bury it in their chest. That was how it was. I was bad, bad, bad. Then Lori rolled into my life. I soon discovered that being around her gave me peace, and I truly wanted to be a better person. I still took what we needed, but I did it in a more civilized manor. I strove to impress her, and she did the same with me. I tried to get softer, and she toughened up. One night I decided to take her out on a recon mission. We would venture outside the boundaries set up by the authorities known as the safety zone. She questioned my judgement when day turned to dusk, and we were nowhere near a place of safety. I reminded her how much she had bothered me to come along on one of my journey's, and I let her know that we would be safe. She knew that I would watch over us, but that did not quiet all her fears. As soon as the sun went down, we got our stuff together so that when it did get dark, we would be safe. I zipped the tent shut and turned on all of the lights and checked all the connections to the backup battery systems. It was redundancy squared. I wasn't about to get caught out here in the dark, and I, sure as friend chicken, would not let anything happen to her. The shadows crawled all over the outside of the canvass canopy. They made their scary noises and chattered their unseen teeth. Lori was freakin scared she almost ripped my arm off. I knew that their two-dimensional nature would prevent them from doing anything to my little fortress, but as it once did with me, it would take her some getting used to. The first few nights were the worst, but as she learned to tune them out, and we ventured further and further away from our home base. We went on adventures that very few people could ever imagine, and we made it fun. It was so strange to be walking next to her again as I had so many times before. I knew she would remember none of it, and I dare not bring it up for sounding like a fool.

So I just walked and talked with her about Critterware and how she came to work directly for Lucious Barnes. Because as nice as it was to see her again, and boy was it nice, I had a very hard time believing that this was all a coincidence. I knew I was being played, but I decided that I would worry about that later and play along for now.

"Here it is," I said and held the door open of the restaurant for her. We quickly found a small table in the back and sat down. We decided on a pitcher of light beer, some calamari, and some fish tacos. I asked her when Critterware had hired her, and she told me that she had been there for almost five years. This, of course, blew the lid off my idea that she was hired and sent to get me because of who she was.

"Do I know you?" she asked me looking me over. I smiled in return, playing like she was hitting on me.

"I mean, not just from the other day. I'm not trying to be funny, but it's just that you seem so very familiar to me. Where did you grow up, here?" she asked.

I wondered if she was messing with me. There was a possibility that she knew everything about me, about our previous lives together, that she did have a secret agenda.

"I grew up in New Jersey, how bout you?"

"Wisconsin," she told me.

"I'm a farmer's daughter, believe it or not.

"You grew up on a farm, and now you're an assistant to one of the most powerful men in all of the world, hmm. That's quite an accomplishment. Your parents must be very proud." She noticeably blushed. She took a sip of beer and tried to stifle a smile. Our appetizers came and we ate some of the calamari. It was good, tasty.

"When was the last time you got to see them, your parents I mean?" I asked between the food and the beer.

"Those times are far and few in between, I'm sad to say. Mr. Barnes keeps me pretty busy."

"Traveling the world signing people up to the firm?" I asked jokingly.

"Exactly, and they almost always jump to grab the pen out of my hand to sign up, as you say. You, 'Mr.

Let's go have a beer and tacos', however, amuse me.

"Really," I smiled. "I amuse you?" I asked not sure if it meant to be funny or a serious dig.

"Look Joe I've read over your file, and I see that you haven't had a stable work history, or much in the way of savings. Your car is a decade old and at almost forty years of age, you pretty much make peanuts.

You, of all people should have jumped at me to sign up, but you didn't. So, I'm amused by you."

"Well, I know that I must appear quite destitute by your standards, but I can assure you that I'm doing quite okay. Yes, all of those things you said are absolutely true, but I do have good friends, and a loving family back east. I'm getting by okay. I could do a whole better, but I could do a whole lot worse too." I had felt a little bit slighted by her comments, but I didn't let it bother me too much. If only she knew how important I really was, what I was, she would think differently. If only she could just remember, even for the briefest of seconds, she would remember how much we had once meant to each other in a different place and time. She stopped chewing for a second.

"I didn't mean to insult you. I just thought it was pretty bold." She smiled at me.

"I know that you're going to sign, but just the fact that you would put it off so that I would have dinner with you was impressive. I feel a bit honored to tell you the truth."

Now it was me that got a bit choked up.

"Well thank you." I lifted my beer to her, and we clinked our glasses.

"Does it seem strange for you to be here?" I didn't think she fully understood what I was asking her by the look on her face.

"You know what I mean. If you read my life, you will see that I have no specific qualities that would put me into a position to even be offered this sort of a job." She swallowed her bit of taco and wiped her mouth.

"After Mr. Barnes personally hired me from that little diner back home, I learned not to question his judgement calls." She took a sip of her beer and wiped her mouth with her napkin. I thought about what she said, and I wondered what she had going for her to be hired in such a manner. It was similar situation to mine. Perhaps she was in the same boat as me.

Maybe she was different too. I, of course, had no way of asking her without looking like an idiot. There was no way I could prove anything even if I did tell her my whole tale. She'd think I was nuts.

"So, what are you saying, that you were waiting tables one day and the richest man in America just walked in and offered you a job?"

"That's pretty much my story." I gave her a look, and she knew what I was thinking.

"No no, nothing like that; there was nothing shady. I thought there might be at first, but he was a gentleman from minute one." She grabbed her purse and dug through it producing and old tattered folded up piece of paper.

"This is an open dated, first-class ticket home. He gave me this the day I was hired. Told me if I ever felt uncomfortable there, I could just go home." Its origination date was from five years ago. I gave it back to her and she continued.

"I actually think he put out the 'hands off' label on me, because no one in the company every approached me in such a manner. Good thing you snuck this dinner in under the wire."

"Yeah, I'm sneaky like that." I swilled some beer down my neck.

"You think that policy will apply to me if and when I sign my paperwork?"

"Definitely," she said with a big grin. "You want a

shot? I noticed that they have Don Julio behind the bar."

"Okay," I replied, not sure if she was kidding me or not about being able to see her. Our shots came soon enough, and we clinked the little glasses together and toasted my new job. Then we downed them.

Smooth. We continued to eat and chat, and then we had another shot or two. It was as if she didn't get out to party much and the more, she drank, the more relaxed she got. We finished eating and decided to head out. She laughed at me when I grabbed the check and paid it all, telling me I wasn't rich yet. I told her I would allow her that much if she permitted me to buy her more one more drink on the way home. But we didn't head home.

We went across the street to have a couple more drinks at a place that had a view of the ocean. Two hours after that, we were tanked. It was still early, but it was dark and chilly. We were actually only about four blocks from the house, but Lori decided that she wanted to walk on the beach before we headed back.

"It's nice to get out," she told me as we walked along the water line.

"I know I asked you this already, but are you sure we've never met before? It just seems so strange to me to be here with you right now. I feel like I know you. And for some reason I feel very, very safe here with you." She giggled and ran up the beach. Then she sat down in the cool, dry sand.

"Man, I'm messed up now," she told me.

"I'm not too far behind," I told her, sitting down next to her.

"What's the plan? You have a room somewhere?

"No, I was supposed to blow in, get the paperwork signed, and blow backout. You put the monkey wrench to that plan."

"You can stay at my place. I'll sleep on the couch." She didn't reply, so I just sat there next to her, and we listened to the waves crash just a few yards in front of us. Sometimes we could even feel the vibration through the ground beneath us.

"Did I say thanks?" she asked after a long moment of silence.

"Did I thank you for choosing to take me out for something that I have needed for a very long time rather than just jump at me to sign. That mean a lot to me because I know what this job means to you.

It was a pretty bold move on your behalf to put off the signings, and I really appreciate it." Then she leaned over and kissed me.

Man, that was nice. It felt like about fifteen seconds passed between that first kiss, but in reality, it was about twenty minutes of rolling around in the sand together and another twenty stumbling home. In a different time and a different place, I was practically married to this woman. We lived together for years. I knew what made her happy, and I quickly found out that the little tricks that we learned together worked wonders in the here and now.

I woke up and didn't even think about going

to work. I didn't give a crap about anything. I must have laid there for an hour. Eventually she stirred, then stretched out. She rolled over and hugged me and kissed me on my neck.

"Good morning," she said to me, and I returned courtesy.

"That was nice."

"Yes, it was." I ran my fingers over through her hair, and I could feel a quiver in her breath.

"So, what about those papers you brought me?" I could see the wheels turning.

"We'll have to be grand fathered in, like an amendment to the sexual harassment form."

"Nice." I jumped out the bed and threw my shorts on. Then I signed and dated every paper.

"Done."

"Welcome to the firm. Now kiss me." She said with a big smile. We laid there and made out. Chalmers had been right all along. I never gave another thought about Lima Biggums. When I listened and let go, good things happened. It was when I bucked the system, I found out, a long time ago, that I could pretty much mess up. I was on the threshold of big changes. I hadn't had someone in my life that I had feelings, in the way I did for this woman next to me, for a very long time. My job just squeaked me through, and I was so tired of just squeaking through. Now I was about to be somebody. I knew all of this would come with a price, but right now I didn't care. I turned off the cell phone and stretched out this moment as long as I could.

NINE

"What if I were to tell you that I couldn't careless?" Lucious Barnes asked me. "Would you believe me?" I thought about it, but there was no way this could be the truth. He was a prominent man in the field of philanthropy.

"I would not," I told him confidently. Then he gave me a devilish grin.

"That's what I like to hear, my boy. I'm glad you think that way. That's the way I want, no need to be portrayed to the general public, but in reality, I really just.... don't...care." The last few words just kind of hung there. I sat there looking at him for a moment, a tense moment, but then I cracked a smile and laughed.

"Yeah, okay," I said. Then I just looked at him.

"Why would you say such a thing?" What a strange conversation to have on practically my first real day on the job. I would never have imagined that this man would think this way, let alone say it out loud. We toured the compound, the facility and the surrounding city, went on a hike up in the mountains, and ate and drank together the entire time. I had decided to hold onto my share of the apartment in San Diego with Dan for now, after all, I could afford it. I was making bank and had little expenditures that I could see. Housing and food were included in my salary package and the closet and dresser in my apartment were full of the most stylish clothes. It was like my whole life had been caught up in a whirlwind and had been swept off to Oz. But just like Dorothy, on her first visit to the Wizard, I was being blanked by what I was hearing.

"Because it's true, son." He stood up straight and kinda puffed out his chest.

"Look at me. Do you honestly think I care about any of those people? It's all a ploy. I'm busy putting together an empire. I leave that stuff up to my people and show up for PR pictures every now and then."

He smiled.

"The look on your face tells me that they're doing an exceptional job." He walked out from behind his desk and put his arm around my shoulder, and then he walked over to the huge map of the world that covered one of the walls.

"Do you think I care about the people that live here or here?" he asked, pointing to some spots on different continents.

"They live to fight and murder and breed like rabbits. Don't you get tired of seeing all of the violence on TV and the papers?"

"So, what would you do if you don't want to help them?" I asked stopping there. In my mind, there were only really three things one could do about the whole situation, help, look the other way, or hurt. Me, personally, I'm all about a little bit of help with a strong push to look the other way. I couldn't imagine this man would even be saying such things to me, let alone think him capable of anything worse than that. He walked around his office as he spoke to me. I could imagine that he was to wound up to sit, as he seemed to be letting it all hang out. He walked up behind me and spun my chair so that we were facing each other.

"We could kill them all," he said with a wicked grin. He looked at my eyes for a reaction before he continued.

"Sound familiar general?" There it was. My stomach sank. I knew this moment was coming all along, I just didn't see it coming at this particular moment.

"Huh?" was I could get out.

"Isn't that what you used to do, Joseph?" He gave me a surly look.

"Wasn't that your job?" he asked, emphasizing the word 'job'.

"Come on, all along you knew why you were really here. You knew I didn't just pick your name out of a hat. Whether you wanted to believe it or not, you are here for a reason." I just looked at him with my mouth hanging open. He continued to look at me with a smirk, waiting for me to react. I didn't have to react or answer, my eyes had betrayed me.

"So let me tell you what I've really had in mind this whole time. See, I know what you are truly capable of. I know that you have powers beyond belief; powers that could squash any army of man, but you don't know how to unleash them. This is where I can help you. I know how to open the door that you peeked through. I can help you develop those powers." My mind was reeling. How did he know? How could he know? His words were swirling around me. I understood, yet it seemed so surreal. I had been found out. I had to shake that feeling, though, and get my head into the game. His idea sounded interesting, but why the deception, I wondered. Why did he wait so long to breach this subject? Why now?

"If you knew about me and what I could do all this time, why didn't you say something sooner?" His smirk turned to smile.

"I had to see if you were worthy son," he told me.

"You don't think I would have helped someone I didn't completely trust, do you? I had to get to know you, see what your convictions were, see where your loyalties lie. Do you think that I send my personal assistant to retrieve all of my new hires?" He waited for a reaction, but I gave him none, though I did have to now question if Lori's kindness had in fact been genuine. That bugged me more than Barnes playing his game did. I thought about the crap he was feeding me. He needed me because of who I was.

My convictions didn't matter to him.

“So, you lied to see if I was an honest man?” I asked. I knew that he needed what I had. I was the only person alive that possessed my abilities, but I was curious as to what he had in mind.

“Look, I can assure you that the ends will justify the means,” he told me through his gritted shiny teeth.

The hammer had been dropped. I was quite sure Chalmers was going to have a lot to say about all of this, and I was sure that I would see him when this meeting was adjourned.

“Though that may be true, it would cause me to question everything I had come to know here. I have to wonder what is true and what wasn’t. I mean, come on. You are right though. I did expect that something was amiss all along. It’s just that the charade was so good, I wanted to believe it. That’s why I’m a little miffed as to why you would bring this up to me now.”

I couldn’t stop thinking about Lori. I wondered if she reported back on everything we had talked about. I also wondered if she knew who and what I really was.

Lucious Barnes touched a button on his desk and an image appeared on the wall to our right. It was the national news channel projected onto the white wall. The picture was crisp and clear, and the sound seemed to surround me. The current article being spoken about was the war. The war had lingered on for years, but it seemed like forever. The bad guys just kept coming and they often times threatened the rest of the free world.

"We could, no you could end all of this," he told me, "And I can show you how." He referred to the carnage on the screen.

"Only you could put a stop to the threats that currently haunt our world." He walked over and stood next to the pictures of a war-torn land with soldiers running to and fro "This is your destiny. You are the person I have been waiting for, for so many years. You could end this war and bring harmony back to our world." That sounded pretty exciting, but it also set off a whole bunch of warning signals in the back of my head.

"How are you going to show me how to use my powers?" I asked with genuine curiosity.

"I have certain...techniques," he said. I waited for him to elaborate, but he didn't.

"Such as?" I finally asked. He smiled broadly.

"I have a comrade that is very familiar with your powers, and he will gladly show you how to use what God gave you." Just the way he said the word, God, gave me further concern for what this conversation was really about and where it was headed.

"I'm not really sure that you could help me?" I told him just to see the expression on his face. Of course, I wanted to know how to use my powers. I wanted to be able to stop the never-ending wars in the Middle East and around the rest of the world that we had just been talking about, but I wasn't sure about this whole situation. I just wanted to hear him out, but the whole sneaking around crap, had me very nervous.

"Do you think that I would have done all of this for nothing?" He acted like I had just insulted him.

"I have agents scattered across the globe looking for beings just like you. Of course, I won't disclose exactly how we came across you, but let's just say that there is something about you that alerted us directly." He gave me a strange look then.

"We wondered why we hadn't been alerted to your presence earlier. You're what, thirty-seven, thirty-

eight? We should have spotted you a long time ago. Did you recently bump your head or have some major life changing event that awakened you to the wings and these powers?" I didn't answer immediately. It might have proven to be dangerous to simply tell him the truth, so I shook my head.

"No, nothing like that. One day I woke up and looked in the mirror and I had wings. Weirdest thing ever." Barnes squinted at me. I could tell that he didn't believe that I was telling the complete truth, but he also did not want to accuse me or call me a liar, not just yet anyway.

"You just woke up and they were there?"

"Well, you gotta understand, sir, when I wake up, I'm groggy. I got up, got my coffee, shaved and showered, and then while I was getting ready, there they were." I smiled.

"I was an hour late for work that day and I seriously thought I had lost my mind. The days and nights that followed were hard to deal with. It was like a door had been opened and all of these visions flooded in. I had them in my sleep and sometimes even while I was awake." I had him. He was eating it up now.

"I saw the craziest things, angels and battles, planets with skies of every color. I seriously thought, for a few days, that I had lost my mind. I was beginning to have a difficult time distinguishing between reality and fantasy. I thought I was headed to the rubber room for sure." I paused for a moment to see if he was really listening.

"And?" he asked, waiting for more.

"Well, eventually, I just came to terms with it. I learned that this was simply not going away. Too many days had passed, and things didn't change. I had so hoped that since I seemed to just wake up with wings one day, that one day I would wake up and they would be gone. But the weeks passed, I just closed my eyes to them. I controlled my breathing with long, deep breaths and thought happy thoughts when those horrible things filled my head." Barnes gave me a quizzical look.

"You would turn your back on such a gift?" he asked, sounding a bit condescending.

"Come on, you make it seem like I knew what I was dealing with here," I told him with a condescending tone of my own.

“What did you expect me to do? These things didn’t come with an instruction manual. Don’t think I didn’t try to use them. I did and landed on my chin more than a few times.”

“But” Barnes started to cut in. I had to continue with my train of thought. So much of what I was telling him right now was totally made up and I didn’t want to lose hold of my idea.

“But what sir?” I asked trying to sound a bit irritated.

“What would you do? I thought that maybe I had died, and this was all just a dream, my last semblance of life. I’m still not sure that I’m not dead,” I told him with a wink and a smile.

“I mean come on, does all of this stuff really happen? Two months ago, I had a beer and went to bed.

Who would have ever thought I would end up here with you? Maybe I had the beer, fell out of bed, banged my head and died. Maybe that’s it.” I tried to round things off with a bit of a smile and some enthusiasm. Barnes smiled. If he didn’t believe what I was saying, I was sure that he would call me out on it.

“You seem so nonchalant about it. What if you are dead?”

“Well, if I were, then I might as well have good time, right? I mean what’s the worst that could happen if I really am dead? But hey, if I’m dead, then shouldn’t I be able to fly? Isn’t that what angels do?” He just looked at me, holding that same smile.

"That sounds reasonable. Why not go all out and test out your theory?" Now I smiled.

"What do you have in mind?"

"Well, first I want to say that you are not dead, nor have you lost your mind. But you were given a gift.

Whether you chose to believe that or not is completely up to you. What I would like to suggest to you is that you can make an everlasting impact on everyone and everything around you." He paused, looked out the window, then back to me. His eyes seemed to glisten.

"You, Joseph, can save them all." He folded his arms, looking quite confident.

"Your whole angelic life you've done nothing but lash out, kill and slaughter things. You've protected the light by killing the ambassadors of the darkness.

Well, I would like to present to you an option in which you do the same thing here on this world. But unlike it is on the astral plains, you actually get to save the people you love and care for." He paused for a moment and crossed his arms.

"What do you think?" Here it was. I don't care whether he believed me or not, he was about to give me my prize.

"Of course, it sounds good, but what could I do?" I asked with a sheepish tone. I didn't think it was possible, but I think that Barnes's smile grew wider.

"Son, you have the power and ability to fix everything and anything wrong with this world tucked inside you. You just need some help to bring it to the surface." In my mind's eye, I jumped for joy. This was just what I was hoping for. I was stoked, but I couldn't show it. We were negotiating now. I wanted to see how much he knew and how much I could get out of him before I would agree to anything.

"How?"

"I have a gentleman that is familiar with your extraordinary powers. He can teach you how things work; open doors to new possibilities." I smiled and nodded my head.

"Sweet," I commented with a crooked smile.

"But then what?" I asked trying to sound naïve.

"Then my boy, we fix things. With your powers and my abilities, we could conquer the world. We could end hunger, poverty, and stop the wars and battles everywhere." I didn't expect that. He was the most powerful men on the planet, and it sounded like he was talking, in a roundabout way, about taking over the world. Seemed a bit much, but the more I thought about it, the more it actually sounded possible.

The problem with me is that if things sound too good to be true, they usually are, and the sirens were wailing in my head that this was all wrong. So, I smiled a big smile and almost laughed.

"You're kidding right?" It became obvious very quickly that this was not the answer Barnes expect from me.

"No, I am not kidding. Do you think I would have

brought you here for anything less? Do you think I have time to throw around on you joking about such things?" I had insulted him a bit.

"I'm sorry. You gotta understand my point of view though. You give me this cushy, pretty much watch you job, with a huge salary, and then you tell me that you want to help me to help you take over the world? Look sir, I'm just a simple guy that must have bumped my head or something. This kind of thing doesn't happen to me. My whole life since meeting you has seemed so surreal that I have a hard time believing what I am seeing and hearing. I honestly have to believe that I am laid up in a hospital room somewhere and you are just a vision generated by my morphine drip. So please understand that I mean you absolutely no disrespect, but I just have a hard time believing that such things are possible and that you could be asking me to help you do it." The smile returned to his face, and he cupped his hands in front of him.

"You are right. I'm a bit passionate about this subject. It's hard to be one of the richest men in the world but have pretty much no power other than some lobbying here and there."

"You have no power?" I asked him.

"Please."

"I have no real power. I have political clout, but one man can't fix the world, not the way it is right now.

There are just too many governments, too many religions."

"Too many religions?" I asked.

"Which one do you believe in?" I didn't mean to cut him off, but he brought it up and I needed to know.

"The one with God and the angels and all" he told me with a wink.

"What did you think I was going to say, with an angel standing right in front of me? I actually have proof that my way is correct." Now I just stood there with my mouth hanging open for a second. Did he just say what I thought he said, cause this was the first time I've heard that kind of talk from anyone around here.

"You really think that I'm an angel?" I asked knowing how big that last comment was.

"You know I'm just amazed that you haven't been contacted about this before. I would have expected someone from the other side would have been in touch with you somewhere along the line." He told me with a puzzled look.

"Your discovery is pretty significant. When you started tinkering with those wings, you set off a bunch of bells and whistles that my people picked up." He leaned in close.

He made like he smiled the air in front of me.

"Once we were alerted to your presence, we sniffed you out." He then stepped around and past me. But as he stepped around, he blew on an exposed part of my wing. The chill ran right down to my spine. I spun to look at his smiling face.

"You have wings. You have the ability to destroy life on this planet if you so choose; yet you've done nothing to improve your own life or the lives around you. Today I am offering you a chance to change all of that." He walked over and looked out of the window.

"Aren't you tired of the way our government has handled things lately? Aren't you tired of the wars? We could end all of that. Remember when you were a kid and you could leave the door unlocked, or how about going to the playground without the fear of being abducted by some deviant. Those days could come back. We, you and I, could show them the way." I looked at him then down at the floor and shuffled my feet around a little before I looked back up at him.

"Why don't you just run for office? You have the money and the clout. Why not just run for president, or sponsor someone?"

"Even if I did run and became President of the United States, one man cannot fix what is wrong with this country. Our government is just too big. The Good Ole Boy Network would fight me tooth and nail. Too many people with deep pockets depend on things staying as they are. Our entire system needs a cleansing right down to its core. Do you understand what I am saying, what I am asking of you?" My head was spinning. This was truly a dream come true. I agreed with him on so many levels.

Our system was broken and there was little

chance of anyone fixing things, but I wasn't really sure I could trust him.

"I think I do, but I'm not sure I can do what you are asking?" I rubbed my head.

"It would be hard to believe that our government wouldn't appreciate a clear, fresh leader like you. Did you even try?" He looked at me again and the enthusiasm left his face. He turned to his desk and touched a command on it. The opposite wall held a 60-inch LCD TV surrounded by several smaller ones.

Each lit up and each displayed a different news channel. He touched another command and the volume of the big TV got louder. There was an Asian woman talking about a missing child. He flipped the channel and another women spoke about the amount of our troops that had been killed this week in one of the many wars that were happening. He changed it again and there were people protesting our President.

There was a replica of him on a stake on fire.

"It's not just our country, it's the world. Apathy rules this planet. Those with power abuse it on every level. Crime runs rampant throughout the world, and no one does a thing to stop it unless they, themselves, benefit from that act directly. Our Congress has the lowest approval rating ever and once again we will be forced to choose from the lesser of two evils to run our own country. Do you not think that there are forces beyond your knowledge controlling things? I haven't gotten where I am by guessing. I look at facts and I move where I know I will win. I cannot compete against incompetence that extends from the President and Supreme Court all the way down to the local magistrates. I ran the numbers, several times, and they always came up the same. I won't be able to win. Congress would levee huge penalties against my company, and I could lose all of it. Even if I won, the system of checks and balances would keep any major changed tied up in red tape for years. We need a fix, and we need it now." He changed the channel again and there was a man in handcuffs.

"That man there," he said pointing at the set, "is a repeat offender. He was already in jail for raping and killing a small child. How do you explain to parents of the little girl he just killed that the system failed them; that this man had been in and out of jail his whole life and that we have been unable to keep him locked up or reform him? What do you tell her brother and sisters? These people are the victims of a broken system. It happens every day. It happened to you, didn't it? That struck a bit of a low blow.

Twenty years ago, my brother had been killed by a couple of real pieces of dirt. He was driving his friend's home and his car got absolutely crushed. A couple of idiots had stolen a van and were driving it after dark with the headlights off to avoid being seen. They were driving way too fast for the street they were on, and when my brother pulled out into the intersection, he was creamed. He never saw it coming. The force of the impact lifted his car onto the top of another car parked on the street and it tore his aorta from his heart. Even though he received treatment on the scene, he could not be saved. And I will never forget the moment when the doctor walked into the room and told us that there was nothing he could do. Nothing he could do. That was the saddest day of my life. I chose not to answer him, and he continued.

"Our criminal system is pathetic. It needs to be thrown out and started fresh. Why is it that if you know you are guilty of a crime, but I do not turn you in, that I could be found guilty of adding and abetting or even conspiracy? But when a lawyer knows his client is guilty and goes as far as he can trying to deceive a jury, well that falls under attorney client privileges. In a sense, attorneys are allowed to lie to protect the guilty, and the better they are at lying and twisting the truth, the more money they make." He paced and his voice rose slightly.

"How would or could a politician fix such things? Rapist and pedophiles should have their parts removed. Do you not agree?" I just nodded and let him continue.

"But if I stood up and said that there would be a backlash of humanitarianism that would never allow such a thing to happen. When the eighty percent of the people of California voted that people over seventy years old should be given a driving safety test every couple of years, a senior citizens group threatened a lawsuit for discrimination and the bill was tossed. Do you see where I am going with this, son?" Again, I nodded.

"The needs of the many do not outweigh the needs of the few in this country. Instead, the needs of the few, or one, take precedent in most cases. There are too many people moaning and blaming everyone else. This once great country is becoming a laughingstock. Why aren't the bureaucrats doing anything about it? Because they are looking out for their own good, their own chosen few. We waste money on nonsense instead of improving from the inside out. We try to push our influence and way of life to every corner of the planet, yet we can't even provide healthcare to all of our own children."

I finally had to cut in. "I understand how bad this situation is, I really do, but how, even with my powers, do you plan to fix things? I mean, if the President can't get the ball rolling, what could we do?" He smiled and nodded, and his demeanor toned down dramatically.

"The President doesn't care about such things. He looks out for his cronies and doesn't want to rock the boat. I suggest you and I fix all of this ourselves and not give the rest of the world a chance to protest.

We don't ask, we just do," he said and then paused. I waited for a moment, but he just stood there with that weird look on his face.

"Really?" I asked, almost jokingly. His expression did not change.

"Yes, really," he chided.

"You have no idea what you are capable of do you?" He leaned in and stared at me hard in the eyes.

"You and I can and will change this world."

"I still don't understand how."

"Your training starts tomorrow morning at five-thirty. You might want to get some sleep tonight. You are going to need it." With that, he turned and went behind his desk.

"Do not take this training lightly boy. You are here for a reason. Let me help you discover your full potential. Do not disappoint me. You are dismissed." He then spun his chair to face the window and I left.

It was already getting dark. I hurried back to the condo where Lori was cooking dinner. It was nice to open the door to a delicious aroma. I hadn't had something like this since I was a kid or the occasional Monday night dinner party with my friends in San Diego.

"That smells awesome," I told her with a smile.

"How did your meeting with the old man go?" she asked as she flipped the pork chops.

"Old man, that's rich. He's like two years older than me."

"Well, you're my old man, aren't you?

"You are so funny," I told her as I walked over to her and gave her a hug. We spent almost every waking second together since she had come to get the paperwork signed a few days ago, and it actually pained me to let her out of my sight. I needed to be with her, to feel her touch. I knew things were happening rather quickly, but this was no stranger. We had a history, and not just any history. Ours went back for centuries.

"Watch the grease," she warned referring to the popping going on, on the stove.

"Go clean and pour some wine, would you?" She already had a bottle of red wine out and waiting. I reached past her and grabbed the opener out of the drawer. As I poured the wine, I talked about my meeting with Barnes. I didn't quite tell her everything, but just a generalization.

"Oh, I met your trainer. He's a little weird," she told me with a smile. She then handed me a wonderful plate of pork chops, mashed potatoes, corn and a bit of salad. It looked delicious.

"What do you mean?" I asked with a mouthful.

"You'll see. Now clean that plate so we can make out." I followed her orders and soon enough I had a belly full. We were lounging on the couch watching an old movie and I was playing with her hair. She smelled so good.

"You sleeping over tonight?" I asked with high hopes. Our little after dinner make out session left me a bit wound up.

"Now you know I can't. You're going to bed and wake up early and you're gonna be ready for your lessons. Otherwise, Mr. B will have my head." She wriggled her body around a little bit.

"I hope our trainer knows what he's doing because he looks like a whack job." She knew that she could be blunt with me.

"Oh, that's nice. Making fun of my new Jedi Master?" I tickled her and we shared a laugh. Then Lori got serious and turned around to look me in the eye.

"What are you training for? What's this all about anyway?" It genuinely stung me to have to tell her that I really couldn't tell her. I really liked her, you could say loved her, but if I told her the truth, things would definitely change between us.

"Yeah, and if Mr. B asks you what you know, you're going to lie to his face? No way. If I told you and he found out, he wouldn't trust me, or you. We're getting along pretty good right now and I don't want to mess that up." She got close so that her lips were right up next to my neck.

"You are such a good boy, aren't you?" She rubbed her hand down my leg.

"Well, I guess I'd better get going. You need to be all bright eyed and bushy tailed in the morning."

"I'd sleep a whole lot better if we had a little fun before you left." She continued to rub my leg and breathe in my ear and on my neck.

"We know that's not going to happen," she purred.

Five o'clock came early. I slipped out of bed and

got some coffee, shaved and showered. I was ready to go at five-thirty when my doorbell rang. I opened the door, expecting some creep, but instead there stood a guy in a suit.

"Come with me please, sir."

I got in the car and rode across the compound. This guy didn't look too bad, I thought.

Lori's words echoed in my mind about how creepy the guy that was going to teach me how to use my powers. This couldn't be the same guy she was talking about. That meant he was my driver.

Living in this compound and being treated the way I was, was going to take some getting used to. I got picked up for everything, and in a nice car, sometimes a Humvee, sometimes a Lincoln. And I got treated with a lot of respect. That didn't happen very often in my life. I turned the things that Barnes had told me around in my head. The more I thought about it, the more I knew he was right. There wouldn't be too much need of convincing me. I had never really been a fan of our system of government, so why not try to fix things, right? I hadn't seen or heard from Chalmers since I got here. Weird, he had said that he thought the way to end my punishment was not to kill, when in all reality, it appears it might well be just the opposite. I had to figure that if he was going to protest this course of action, then he should have already. I almost felt like he had abandoned me as of late. I know that I had precious little time alone, but he could have caught me in the shower or when I was putting on my shoes this morning.

The car wound around to a huge white building. I knew what this place was. It was a part of the research and development center. The driver got out and opened my door. I had learned to wait for the driver to open my door. I remembered the other day when Lori had to explain that to me. It was going to take some getting used to, as it did with her as well. She and I lived such similar lives, both changed by this job and our boss. How could you not respect the man? I thought almost out loud. I didn't want the driver to hear me talking to myself, so I just stopped thinking about it and hurried inside. There was no one to greet me, so I just walked in. The door was unlocked, and the hallway was lit up, so I just headed for the first open door I saw.

Man, it was early. My head started to throb a bit, and I had that strange fight or flee kind of feeling down in the pit of my gut. That was usually something I felt before I thought I was going to get into a fight...or when I was excruciatingly nervous like I was now. I needed to keep my eyes open to my surroundings and listen to everything very carefully. I was starting to like this situation less and less. I had to make sure my enthusiasm did not cloud my judgement. There was the corridor to the left was lit up, so that's where I went. Creepy place that it was. I pushed the door, which had opened a crack to a very big auditorium. It appeared to be the right place, but there was a terrible smell that reminded me of cigarette butts and body odor. I didn't like it one bit, but I couldn't tell if I was coming from a person or a room. It was kind of smoky in there. Most of the room was dark, except for the immediate area around this man. He was standing in a circle of light. I assumed was going to be my teacher. He was strange one all right. Lori was right. Where did they dig this guy up? He was willowy and pale, and he wore black glasses with a patch over one eye or lack thereof. He was a bit taller than me, but he looked frail. He stood next to a stool and a chair.

"Take a seat Joseph," he offered. I thought of John Travolta character in Pulp Fiction where Mr. Wolf comes to help him and Samuel L. Jackson out of the mess, they had gotten themselves into, and Travolta has to insult the guy by asking him to say please.

"A please would be nice." I so wanted to say it, but instead, I just sat. If this guy really did have some wisdom to enlighten me with, then I was gonna do what I was told, the first time. I just had to try to stop thinking about the smell.

"My name is Mr. Winston, or Winston, whichever you prefer. I have the most pleasurable task of enlightening you to your wonderful gift." He reeked of cigarettes to the point of nausea.

"I'm not going to ask you how you came to realize you had this gift, but I do not believe you simply woke up with it. Something caused your awakening, and now we have to see if we can push things a little more." That was a compliment with an insult wrapped inside. Not the best way to get things started with me, but as much as my senses were twitching right now, it was just icing on the cake. There was something definitely amiss here with this one, but I had to try to learn from him what I could. My head was cloudy because it was still too early, but I gave him a smile.

"I'm ready." You may not have such enthusiasm as your lesson progresses," he said sounding quite melodramatic. Enthusiasm, what enthusiasm? I was psyched, but I just wasn't awake yet.

"You can move the wings, yes?" he asked as he pulled from his pocket a pack of Winston cigarettes. I nodded.

"But you cannot fly." He lit the cigarette and inhaled deeply.

"Do you have the visions?" I nodded.

"And in them you fly?" Again, I nodded.

"Then you shall fly again soon enough." He stood upright and walked around me, studying me.

"You have a blue haze around you"

"Is that good?" I asked. He smiled a fake smile and told me yes, but I knew from the look in his eye, that he wasn't expecting that. He circled me a couple of times and looked me over good.

"Move your wings up and down." I did what he asked. As I did, I studied him. His veins almost seemed to be protruding through his thin, pale skin.

"Now let's see if you can make them work for real." He looked around.

"No one can see us here. I chose this room because of its size and because it is completely isolated."

What did I care if it were isolated or not? And who was this guy supposed to be that he was going to show me how to use my powers, I thought. I rubbed my chin as he circled me again.

"Look, Mr. Winston, I don't mean to sound disrespectful, but how exactly are you going to show me how to use my powers?" I look at him, at this stature, his build. He was old, frail, and extremely creepy.

"Were you also a part of the corps?" He had to know that I was going to ask him this, so why the face, I wondered. He looked like I had just insulted him. He turned and put out his cigarette, using his finger to snuff out the hot tip. Then he turned to me and unfurled his own wings. There were about as big as mine but nowhere near as nice.

Whereas mine were white, nice, plush, and feathery, his were gray colored and sinewy. It looked a lot more like old flesh pulled across a framework and some small rips and quite a few scars. There were small claws at the top of the frame where they were jointed. They looked just like him, just plain knarly.

I wondered if I pulled all of the feathers from my wings, would they look like that? He must have been able to see that I was somewhat impressed that he was similar to me, but he did not look as nearly as good.

As a matter of fact, he and his wings were fairly ugly. I wondered if he had been punished like me, or if maybe he might even be from the other side. How rich would that be?

"Not all that impressed, eh?" he asked as he lit another cigarette.

"No sir, I..." I started. I didn't mean to insult him.

"We'll see if you look this good after decades in the service of your country," he told me, taking a puff.

"This is an entirely different realm and I have been here for a very long time." He folded his wings back behind him and they just seemed to disappear.

"How did you do that?" I asked, truly wanting to know.

"You will learn all these things in time. Now, I want you to relax. Close your eyes. Take a long deep breath in through the nose and let it out slowly through the mouth." I did as he asked. I had done this a long time ago, back in karate class. We did it before each lesson. I also used the ten-second breathing exercises to calm myself down, every now and then when the situation called for it.

"Long, deep breaths," he repeated, sounding more and more calm. As it was, it was still way early and I was tired, so I must have drifted off to sleep. At least I thought I did. I had to have. I felt like I was floating. I tried to open my eyes, but I could not tell if they were closed or if Winston had darkened the room on me. I felt so disconnected. It seemed like it all happened so fast. I had no control of my body. I could not move. I could still hear Winston's voice telling me to relax, but it sounded so distorted, so drawn out. How much more relaxed did he think I was going to get? I really didn't like this. I was completely in the dark with no feeling in my body at all. I had always been a bit claustrophobic, and this had a similar feeling to it. I wanted to wiggle my fingers or my toes just so I would know that I was awake, or even alive. It felt like I had been like this for hours, but I knew it could not have been more than ten minutes. Then I saw the light, literally. It started as a pinpoint of whiteness so far away, then it got a whole lot closer, and it grew.

It seemed like I was in a tunnel and the light was an opening at the other end, far off in the distance.

Then suddenly, it was as if I rocketed toward the brightness, and it quickly swallowed me up so that I was inside of it. It was white and quite intense, but my eyes quickly adjusted. I was on a strange world, high above the ground. Below me hundreds, no thousands of angels floated in the sky at the ready. They were preparing for the onslaught that approached. It was quite a showing. I looked all around for the approaching enemy but saw nothing but darkness below. They had to have been preparing for someone or something, but I could see no one. Then a shadow fell over the entire scene, and I looked up just in time to see fire reign from the sky above. Fiery rocks and drops of what appeared to be something like molten lava seemed to fall all around me. I wanted to move, but I could not. I could feel my heart begin to race as I realized what was happening. My muscles tightened and my wings unfurled.

An entire legion of angels followed the balls of fire down out of the skies. There was distraction, then came the attack. The blackness that covered the land had actually been a sea of shadows. When the fiery rocks impacted upon their masses, they broke ranks and scattered. They were everywhere. Those that survived the fires would now face the sword. The shadow warriors danced and ran from the flaming debris that rained down. They tried to run but had no place to hide. First the red and yellow and orange sulfur flames pounded them, then the rest were sliced and diced by the blue fire of the angel's sword.

Each movement, each step choreographed since the beginning of time. Each lung and swing timed and precise. The shadow demons never stood a chance, and in no time flat they were dispatched. As I watched, my breathing grew heavy, and heart raced. I wanted to join in the battle. I had been born for this. I lived for it. I wanted to jump right into the fray, to lead my men to glory. The blood-rage filled me.

Then suddenly the lights went out, the fires were

extinguished, and I was in the dark. My breathing was still fast and heavy, and my heart still pounded in my chest.

"You may open your eyes," Winston told me.

It seemed so odd to hear his voice just now. If he had just hypnotized me, he had done a very good job. I felt like I had been in a different place. Its odor still lingered in my nostrils. I tried to regain my composure. I did what I was told and found myself back in the auditorium. I was all wound up, but a bit disoriented.

"Now guard yourself," Winston told me as he then lunged at me. I did not know what was happening, but my body and mind reacted instinctively. I moved out of the way and deflected his attack. This was surreal. And as I had so often in the past few months, I had to wonder if all of this was really happening or if I was dreaming. I had little time to think. Winston spun and came at me again. I was thrown to the floor. My own mind had distracted long enough for him to get a shot in. He hammered me good after that. I tried to regain my poise, my stance, but gave me a fairly hard kick in the ribs. I rolled out of his immediate reach and slipped back up onto my feet.

"Defend yourself," he commanded sternly. And lunged at me again. This time I tried a bit too hard and again, ended up back on the floor. He started to come at me again, but I jumped up out of the way.

"What the heck?" I asked.

"What is this?"

"This is your training boy," Winston scowled, and ran at me. He jumped toward me, but I deflected his surge. He crashed hard into the nearby wall, cracking the sheetrock.

"There you go," he purred. He was so disgusting, and he seemed to be enjoying his job a little too much.

The whole of him reeked of sweat and cigarettes. But his look was very deceiving. He was fast and quite agile. He took the hit on the wall in stride and bounced right back up. Then he was at me again. I was able to bob and weave some of the swings and kicks he sent my way, but I let myself get distracted again, and he whaled me a good one.

When I woke up, I was sitting in the chair again. My face and back hurt.

"What happened?" I asked, rubbing the back of my neck.

"You let yourself get distracted, and I clobbered you. Your lessons are complete for today. I will see you tomorrow morning at the same time." He lit another cigarette and paced in front of me.

"I want you to think about what you saw today. The more you think, see, and feel, the more it will all come back to you," he said, the stink of cigarettes spewing from his mouth.

"Think about it. Now go." That was rougher than I thought it was going to be. I must have looked like crap. I knew my eye was black. There was no doubt about that. My neck, back and ribs hurt. What was

Lori going to think. I wondered if she had known what I was in for. I also wondered if this was how it was going to be every day? I hobbled out of the building like an old man, all hunched over and beat up.

The sun was already past its crest. I pulled my phone out of my pocket and looked to see that it was almost five in the evening. Either I was unconscious for a great deal of the day or that took a whole lot longer than I thought it had. The car that brought me to the auditorium was there and it took me back to the condo. Lori was already there, but instead of greeting her with a big hug like I usually would, I hurried into the bathroom to see how bad my face looked. She heard me come in and called to me. I told her that I would be right there and hurried over to the mirror and braced myself for what I was about to see. If my training was going to be this bad and this rough, I was going to have a hard time showing my face in public. I took a peek, figuring on at least a black eye and some bruising and swelling, but saw nothing. My face wasn't' even red. There were no marks at all. I suddenly felt like a big wussy.

My back and neck still ached, but after seeing that there was absolutely no damage, even those pains just seemed to ease almost immediately. This was so weird. So, what was new, right? I stepped out of the bathroom and gave Lori a big hug.

"How was it?" she asked with big expectations and a twinkle in her eye. I had to wonder how much she really knew. She was Barnes's personal assistant. She had to have some idea what was going on. I wondered how much information she was privy to. Was I the first one that was put to these tests? Was this all a ruse to keep me here? I looked in her smiling eyes and had a hard time believing that everything she had said and done all been an act. It was a known fact that I was a sucker for a pretty face, though. And she was absolutely gorgeous. A couple of sips of wine, and bit of a massage, erased those thoughts of scandal and lies quickly enough.

The next day brought the same thing. I awoke early, met the car, and got with Winston. I needed to learn from him, but I greatly questioned his methods. I didn't like being wound up like that. And I definitely didn't like some chain-smoking old fool thinking he got the best of me because he put me to sleep and whooped me before I fully woke up. I could do without all that, but I felt like I had little choice.

I did what I was told. This continued for four days.

TEN

Day after day I reported to Winston, and day after day he smacked me around. I knew this was all part of my 'training', but also, I felt that he got off on it. I'm not stupid. I could tell. Three and half days of being what I would consider pretty much hypnotized, then beat up, and I was about over it.

Then midway through day number four something happened, and I never saw it coming. The day I arrived at the compound, Lori and I got off the plane into a nice shiny white Cadillac. It was so sleek, so comfortable. This would be the car that I would probably have bought myself if I could afford it, not white of course, but black or gray. The seats were like lounge chairs, and it felt as though we were floating down the road. I wondered if, sometime, I would be able to get one of my drivers to switch places with me and let me drive. Style wise, I would have got a Lexus, but the sheer comfort, nothing beat the Caddy. Lori must have been able to see that I was a bit nervous about everything. The morning after our fish taco date, I told her that I felt very privileged to have been offered the job, but this was big, corporate business. Most of the time, I couldn't even afford pizza night with the boys, let alone eat at fancy restaurants. I knew precious little about a life like that with a commensurate salary. In a sense, I wasn't going to know what to do with myself.

"You'll be fine," she told me with a smile. She pulled open her bag and produced a small package.

"A gift from Mr. Barnes," she said, handing it to me. I tore the wrapping and opened it and inside was a sweet shiny necklace. Now I don't normally wear jewelry, but this thing was nice. I put it on and hung just where it wouldn't get in the way but wasn't choking me either.

"Wow, thank you," I told her as she closed the clasp for me.

"You like it?" she asked.

"Oh yeah." It was titanium or silver, and it was thick, but not too thick to be gaudy.

"So you talked to him?" I asked.

"Yeah, and at first, he was quiet, but then he said that he trusted my judgement. As long as it didn't interfere with our working relationship he didn't care." Then her smile got a little bigger.

"I told him how you put off the final signing until after our dinner, and believe it or not, he was impressed." She was obviously talking about her conversation with her, and my now boss.

"Good," I said with a smile. She looked pretty in her business outfit with the little glasses and all.

"Say, how is it that someone like you is single anyway?" I don't know if that was proper form or not, but I was curious. To me, she was just so perfect.

"Oh, I don't know. I think I intimidate a lot of people with my position, and besides, I don't get out much.

I'm kind of married to my job." That then made me wonder about Barnes. I knew she wasn't interested in him, or she wouldn't be with me talking about spending time with me and making plans.

"What about Mr. B?" she made a bit of a face.

"I see him every day, and I travel with him all over the world. I am available to him twenty-four, seven, but I have no idea what he does when he isn't at work. I've worked with him for over five years, and aside from the occasional party or dinner, I never see him or have a clue what he does. I've seen him with some of the world's most beautiful women, but he has never been married and he has no children." Her smile returned.

"He does have a sweet home though," she told me.

"I stay there when he goes on his vacations." Then she gave me a sly look.

"If you're nice, I might bring you by for a look around. His personal bathtub is big enough to fit a fishing boat."

I thought about how much fun the two of us could have with that. But I also thought how weird it was that Barnes's life was so private, even from his personal assistant. That was something the tabloids had mentioned about him too, but who would have known that his need for privacy ran so deep?

We got to the compound, had a tour, the orientation, and all, and then Lori showed me my condo. It was nice, very posh, but nothing crazy. It looked and felt like a picture out of a Home and Garden type of magazine. The walls were tan and brownish colored. There was a nice little kitchen area with cherry wood cabinets, and granite tops and it had plenty of cooking space. The appliances were stainless steel and the lighting and plants placed here and there made it quite homey.

"You like?" Lori asked while she showed me the small dining room with the nice table and chairs. There were plants in this room too, and there was plenty of sunlight.

"I noticed all of the plant life in your apartment in San Diego, so I had them throw some greenery in here.

It's on you now to keep them all alive."

"I can't believe this is my home," I told her truthfully. There was a big L-shaped couch in the living room with a fireplace and a monstrous flat panel TV. There were two bedrooms, one setup for guests and one for me. The bed was huge. And the master bathroom was awesome. There was a separate shower and whirlpool tub. It was so sweet.

"Check this out," Lori told me as she adjusted some controls by the door. Music came out some speakers in the ceiling, a fire lit up in the small fireplace that was situated in the wall between the bath and the bed, and the big picture window that separated them fogged up.

"How's that for a romantic setting?" she asked.

"I think we should try it out and see. The rest of the tour can wait til tomorrow." I reached over into the tub and turned on the water, then I walked over to Lori and grabbed her gently, but firmly and started to kiss her neck. She was a bit shy about the whole situation at first, but she got over it and we enjoyed a nice long soak in the tub together. The grand tub was more than big enough for the two of us. That was how my visit here to this place got started.

Today, however, Winston was beating the absolute crap out of me again. I don't even think he waited for me to wake up, before he started to begin whaling on me. It had to be midway through day number four. I never really knew what time it was until the lesson was over. There were no windows, no skylights in this room; no way to see how bright it was outside.

"Nice necklace," Winston said, admiring the jewelry that Lori had given me, he had me in a hold with his right arm and he had pinned me against the wall. He had his body wedging me against the sheetrock and his shoulder up under my jaw. With his left hand, he had hold of my necklace and twisted it just enough to choke me a little, but not hard enough to break it.

"Today," he whispered up in my ear, "we are going to make a wager. You win, you keep this fine piece of jewelry, but if I beat you again today, then it's mine."

"No," I grunted. I didn't even hesitate. That wasn't gonna happen. His breath smelled rancid, but I could not avoid it.

"I'm not asking you; I'm telling you boy," he seethed in my ear. It was bad enough that this guy had beaten the crap out of me for three and a half days, and I mean quite literally beat the snot out of me, but now he was going to take my necklace? What the heck? I was learning no lessons here. He was teaching me nothing. Perhaps he thought he would have to break me before he could build me up. I had karate teachers like that. But I had always felt that I was already tough enough. Those methods never did much for me other than make me angry. Perhaps he was realizing this and decided to threaten me with something other than bodily harm. I know that Lori told me it was a gift from Barnes, but he had allowed her to help him pick it out, and she was very pleased that I put it on and left it on. It felt comfortable, looked good, and it made both her and I very happy.

"It ain't gonna happen," I told him calmly. This subject was not open for discussion. I didn't need to say anymore. I wasn't going to tell him that Barnes had given it to me, and I sure wasn't going to try to explain to anyone, including the boss, that his freak show took it from me. That wasn't going to happen.

Winston let go of the chain, then spun me around so that I fell down hard on the floor.

"You lose, it's mine. I'm not asking. I don't get paid enough to be here, golden boy." His crackling, smoker's voice had a bitter tone to it. I got up and looked at him and was about to tell him off, when he took a big swing at me. He was trying to knock me out. I leaned my shoulders way back and he missed.

Then he swung again with his other hand, and I moved to my right about a half a step. It was strange. I saw my spot before I moved, and then didn't hesitate. I brought my closed fist down hard on his left shoulder and neck, and when it hit, a blue spark leapt out of my hand. I had cracked him good. I didn't think then or hesitate; I followed through with a right-handed upper cut that lifted him clear off the ground. Again, the blue spark jumped out of my hand and into his face when it connected. I sent him up into the air. He landed pretty hard. He got up wincing and then laughed a little.

"That's a good start boy. Now you're getting the feel. But I'm still going to take that necklace home with me, and make you have to go back and tell your boss and your girlfriend that you lost it."

With that, he lunged at me. I stepped out of his path and punched him hard in his ribcage, up under the arm, and his whole body lit up with the blue crackle of light. I spun a bit on my heal and gave him a side thrust kick that sent him hard against the wall. He was slowed, but he shook it off and came at me hard and fast. I really wasn't thinking anymore, just reacting. He got a shot in every here and there, but today, now he was taking the brunt of it. The room lite up a blue fire every time I hit him and eventually, it was me that had him on the floor, up against the wall with my knee on his throat.

"Do I get to keep my necklace? I asked applying some pressure.

"Yes," he finally squeaked out. I let him up and he brushed himself and straightened himself. He stumbled a bit as he tried to walk.

"You did well today. You may go," he told me. Then he left me alone in the big room. I felt incredible, empowered, like I could take on the world.

After so many days of being beaten, I was allowed to unleash the beast for a brief moment, and that moment was wonderful. I wondered if Winston had beaten me as much for the joy of it, or if this was the reaction, he was looking for all along. I decided not to take the car back, but instead I jogged. I had a lot of extra energy running through my body, and I couldn't just go home and sit there. So, I ran. I ran way past my building and then back. I almost thought that I could run forever, but after I got home and sat down for a moment, the rush went away.

As I sat back and relaxed, I wondered why I hadn't seen or talked to Chalmers as of late. I had so many questions, even more after the events of today. I know that I hadn't really been alone in quite some time, with Lori, the drivers, the Boss, and Winston, but today, I went for a jog by myself and presently, I was all alone. I squashed the desire to call out for him. If he did not want to reveal himself, then he must have had a good reason. I did think about what he would say. I couldn't imagine that he wouldn't have wanted to make a comment about all that was going on here. He always seemed to have so much to say about everything else. Now would seem to be the worst time for him to disappear. It caused me to wonder if I really was alone. I might be under surveillance, for all I knew. Everything here was a part of the same package, and it would not be the first time that Barnes had employed subterfuge. And I still wondered about Lori. I wondered if she had ulterior motives. There was still that shadow of a doubt that haunted me. Everything fit into place so easily, almost like it was a set-up. So strange that I meet the women of my dreams, quite literally the exact person I dreamed about. Compound that with the idea that one of the most powerful men in the world has ways to access things that I alone could not. It was like my worlds were converging. The fantasy and the reality were becoming one. I went to the compound gymnasium and did a workout. I still felt better than I could ever remember. I was able to lift more than I ever lifted before, and I seemed not to tire. The scenery was nice too. There were a few pretty women doing their workouts and I shared a smile with a couple of them. That always worked as a motivator to me. I seemed to be able to jog a little faster, lift a bit more weight, or do an extra sit-up or two when I thought a pretty lady might be watching. I also knew that Chalmers was supposed to be there somewhere. I had to wonder if the cameras that seemed to be everywhere, might be monitoring my actions. Perhaps that was the reason he did not want to be seen with me. I decided it was time to venture off the compound for a bit, get out from under the ever-present watchful eye of Big Brother. I left the gym and headed to the motor pool. I was still a bit sweaty when I got there, I still had the same clothes on that I had left the house with this morning, so I could only imagine what the dispatcher must have thought when I walked through the door.

"I was wondering if I could borrow one of your Town cars or a Caddy?" I asked the man behind the counter. He was medium sized, a little chunky around the midsection and his thin, dark hair was a bit unkempt. There was a fairly good chance that he had been behind this wall of his for most of the day. He looked tired and bored. At first the dispatcher just looked at me. I was a bit of a mess.

"Do you have your employee identification card?" he asked, squinting at me. He seemed a bit put out, almost like I was asking for a personal favor. I presented it and waited to see what he had available.

"Where would you like to be driven to, sir?" he

asked as he entered my number into the computer. He almost seemed to jump to attention when the card scanner showed him who I was.

"I don't want to be driven anywhere. I want to see if I am authorized to use one of your vehicles for an hour or so." The dispatcher must not have been used to a request of this nature. I imagined that few people would want to drive a company vehicle when a chauffeur was at the ready.

"Weird," the dispatcher commented.

"Your name has no title next to it, but it says you have a level nine access." He reached down under the counter and produced a set of keys.

"The gray car is gassed up and ready sir. It was just detailed this morning. Check it out and if you don't like that one, we'll get another one cleaned up in ten minutes."

I took the keys from him with a smile. I expected a hassle but got the complete pimp treatment.

"I'm sure this one will be just fine. Thank you. I appreciate it," and I really did.

I rolled out onto the lot and hit the alarm key to be sure I was headed for the right car. I just wanted to get in and drive away from this place and think. Pretty much any car would do, but it was nice to be able to get behind the wheel of something like this. This is what we needed for those long drives through the desert from San Diego to Las Vegas, I thought. I was a long way from home. I missed the ocean, my happy place on the concrete wall at the end of my street. I wanted to see and feel the waves crashing onto the shore, so that was where I was headed. I needed to try to see if I could get Chalmers to come to me. I had so many questions, and I knew he would have the answers. He had to. I set the car's GPS to take me directly to the coastline, and I just followed the commands. It was a smooth ride with the windows open and the cool breeze blowing through my hair and across my face. It was about four thirty in the afternoon, and the scenery was spectacular. The compound was in a nice area surrounded by a lot of mountains, with trees and some nice places to go hiking. It was a nice drive that opened to a great view of the ocean. I was high up on a cliff, with the waves crashing far below. And I quickly found a small parking area to pull over and take in the scene. It was magnificent, just like you see in the movies, but bigger. I got out of the car and locked it and then looked for a place to chill. I missed the sound of the waves crashing, and I wondered if that was why I didn't sleep so great at night anymore. I had to figure, though, it was because I had another person in the bed with me. That hadn't happened in a while. I would never complain about it, but I wasn't sleeping as well or as much as I would if I were alone.

The smell of the ocean air reminded me of home. This place was wonderful and so much had happened to me, but I was almost missing my simple little life. I had always considered myself smarter than the average bear, and it was difficult to pull the wool over my eyes. Some things just didn't seem right. I knew that I had asked for something like this my entire life, but now it was all happening, it scared me. I always wanted to be the hero. I felt that if I died protecting my loved ones, I would die a happy man.

That's just always how I felt, and I know I had asked for a purpose, for a reason to get out of bed every morning, for a long time. Now I was receiving that wish, but it just didn't seem right. I stepped on some of the small gravel terrain beneath my shoes and looked around. This place was magnificent. It was essentially a big cove, almost like a private section of the coastline, tucked back from the rest of the western seaboard. It was ringed with a tree line, which was the edge of the wooded area through which I just drove. Behind the trees rose the purple mountain's majesty. Except for Barnes's tower, it would have appeared that I was deep in the wilderness. I made a mental note to come here more often. I would jog this trail every couple of days until I found that spot. I needed a place to be able to sit and chill and enjoy all of this. It was a little further away than my happy place in San Diego, but I would make it work. I needed a place to hide out with my thoughts, and I truly felt that this entire area was a gift for me from God. I stretched out my back and my leg and then I opened my wings wide. I could almost feel the light wind that blew up from the ocean. I felt it in my body, but the wind just blew the wings. I looked to my right and to my left and admired them. They were as majestic as the scene in which I stood. And for the first time in a while, my mind was beginning to feel at ease. There was so much stuff to think about over the past month or so that I needed this alone time.

I thought about calling my parents on the east coast, and I thought about calling Dan and Steve. I know they hooked him up good when I got offered this job, but I just hated to leave without giving him two weeks' notice. He was a good boss, and I respected him. But in the end, I decided to call no one. I just relished in my peace. I found a nice spot to relax and closed my eyes. This was what I needed. Thoughts of the battles and craziness started to creep in, but I shut them down and concentrated on the sound of the ocean. I wondered about Chalmers. I wondered where he was. There was no way anyone would see or hear him here. And though it was a good half an hour that passed, he did not appear to me. Then my phone rang.

It was Lori.

"Where are you?" she asked.

"I'm down at the coastline listening to the ocean." I told her.

"What are you up to?"

"I'm headed home. Are you okay? Mr. B told me that you and Winston had a breakthrough today."

"You can say that" I told her. It was a breakthrough, but I had mixed feelings about it. Don't ask me why I felt that way, I just did. I worked so long and hard in my life to control the beast, and now it was being provoked. And a lot of what has been happening here was in direct confliction to what Chalmers had said.

"Are you okay? Do you want company?" she asked.

"No, I'm good. I'll be home soon enough. Maybe I'll see you later?"

"Of course. Your morning workout with Winston has been put off for tomorrow. Mr. Barnes wants you in his office at nine."

"Ok, I'll see you in a bit." I hung up and went back to my meditation. I had to think about what I wanted, what was right. I asked for some help, some love from above. I needed some direction, some reassurance. I needed to know that I was on the right path. I did not know it at the time, but my meeting with Barnes the next morning would hold a great deal of answers for me. I got to sleep in the next morning, at least compared to the rest of the week. I didn't have to be in Barnes's office until nine. I had gotten to see Lori. We had fun and played a little, but she said something that caused me to want to get in bed early and get a good night's sleep. She mentioned that Barnes told her that he had some important business to discuss with me the next day. It was just the way she said it that made me nervous. I figured that it was important for me to be alert and receptive, so I crashed early. The sun was bright and the small office outside of Lucious Barnes's was aglow. I was dressed in a suit and tie and looked pretty good. I had gotten up early, did my sit-ups and push-ups and had gotten myself ready for the day. I was excited to hear what the boss had to say to me.

"Come in, my boy," Barnes offered.

"Please have a seat. Mr. Winston tells me that you two made some progress yesterday. Good. Today I want to discuss with you what I have planned for you and your powers." I had asked for answers just yesterday, so once again, it goes to prove what I asked, I usually received. I just didn't ask all of the time for fear of wearing out a good thing. But I made a mental note to start asking more, just out of shear principal.

"Do you remember this piece that you wrote?" he asked as he thumbed through a small stack of papers onto the top of his desk. He was seated across from me and the light shining in the big window behind him was beautiful. I looked at the papers. It was a small story entitled 'The World is Not Enough', and it was something that I was writing at one point, but kind of forgot about. It was a detailed story about how the future might be in a world where we had consumed all of our world's resources, and anarchy ruled.

"I remember this," I told him as I paged through it.

"And do you remember what the outcome of the story was? Do you remember what you had decided was the cause of the whole mess?" He placed both hands, palms flat on his desk and looked at me for the answer. I knew what the answer was well enough.

"There are too many people," I told him.

"Our planet could no longer sustain its populace. In the end, wars over food and water consumed the land and it was the people that thinned their own herd."

"Kind of like what is happening to our planet now?" he asked.

"Sort of. My story takes place in the not-too-distant future. Most of the world's greatest rainforests had been destroyed and global warming had changed the weather patterns so much that places that once were lush with plant life and vegetation were quickly being eroded away."

"And you do not think that is happening right now? That is why you wrote it?" he asked bringing his hands together so that his palms and fingers on his right had met those of his left. He almost looked like he was praying.

"I believe that unless there is a drastic change in the world, this is where it is headed, definitely. There are too many people in the world, and the planet's resources now are being stretched thin. If we don't figure out something soon, then this," I said grabbing the stack of papers, "Is going to be our destiny."

"In this story of yours, things get so bad that wars ravage the entire planet. Riots break out over food, and people start to run amok. Well, I don't believe that we are as far away from this future as you might think. The general populace is not privileged to the information that someone in my position is. I know how bad things are and how bad things will get over the next few years. We, and I mean humans, have destroyed huge portions of the forests that once covered our world. Why do you think China is having the worst winters they've had in over a hundred years? Remember the five-thousand-mile dust cloud that blew across their country two years ago? They turned a forest into a desert. What about Brazil, just hacking away at the rainforest there? We have to do something about it, do you agree?"

"I fully agree," I told him with full earnest.

"But what can we do?" Barnes pushed himself out from behind his desk and got up and walked over to the window.

"We've been throwing that idea around for about a decade now, and things have gotten worse and worse." He interlaced his fingers behind his back and took in his view.

"In the time we wasted to come up with a plan, the world has suffered as a whole." He walked back over to the desk and leaned against it and looked me in the eye.

"Time to be completely honest, my boy. I know what you are capable of, and I know that we can show you how to realize your full potential. We just have to discuss our goals once this is accomplished.

The fact that you were able to do what you did to Winston yesterday proves to me that we can open things up for you, but what would you do with these powers should you receive them? What's your game plan?" That was unexpected. I had been so caught up in all the craziness that I really hadn't thought about it too much. I had just allowed myself to get used to the fact that I never would be able to use such powers, at least until the incident with Lee-Ham anyway. And that little scene scared me to death. I never did hear anything more about the poor boy. Even yesterday, when I did let loose on Winston made me feel weird, and a bit nervous.

"I'm not really sure to be honest with you. I played with my wings and all but when I realized that I could not fly, I tried to hide them away. I mean, can you imagine if someone did see giant wings on my back, and asked me to fly? I would look and feel like an idiot. It drove me crazy at first. I tried and tried to make them work." I was talking without really thinking and I caught myself.

"Can I ask you, what exactly alerted you to my presence?" He smiled and rose to a standing position.

"Truth be known, you stand out like sore thumb to some people. Winston is someone who can relate, but we have agents in every corner of the globe gathering information for us. How do you think that we've been able to keep up with the changes in our software and technologies?"

"Why did he seem surprised when he told me I had a blue aura?"

"Ha, did you see this?" he asked, but he didn't give me time to answer.

"His aura looks like a smoky gray mist. Look, he's in a lot deeper than you are. He has nothing really to look forward to in this life or the next I don't know what you did or why you are here, but I know why he is. He overstepped his bounds and now he's being punished. He's been here for eons."

"He just seems so bitter," I commented, again without thinking. I had to pull my head together. I had so much going on in my brain, I couldn't focus.

"Yes, he is going to be a little bitter. And he is going to be more and more jealous of you as time goes along. You have what he lost, and he knows he won't be getting it back anytime soon. You're important and though he has his place, he can't do what you can," he finished with a smile.

"And what might that be?" I asked with a great deal of curiosity.

"You are going to save the world my boy." He spread his arms wide, his hands open, palms up.

"You are going to deliver us from evil" then he said something that sent a chill up my spine.

"You are going to fix this place and, in the end, save us all from the shadows." That comment hung there for a moment, and it felt like it sucked the oxygen from my lungs.

"The shadows are coming here?" I squeaked out. He began to pace again.

"I don't have a schedule for this planet's downfall, but we are close." His tone became quite serious now.

"The events unfolding in the Middle East, the constant warring and hording of fossil fuels, have us on a major downhill slide. We use up any and all of our resources faster than our planet can provide them.

We have a big government that seems to have no clue how to prepare for the future and we are losing ground in the world's global economy. What happens when we run out of oil? What do you think will happen then? Or better yet, what happens when we use up all our friends' oil, and only the bad guys have it? Then what?"

I didn't know if I was supposed to answer, my brain was still stuck on the shadows. It didn't matter, he continued his rant and I just soaked it up. I understood where he was going with this. If we split this world by war again, there would be battles all over the planet. There could be no defined lines in the sand; entire countries would be forced to choose sides in order to protect their interests. We would be easy prey for the shadows.

"We are on the brink son, and I kind of like this place. I'm not ready to turn it over to the shadows just yet. I've done pretty well here, and I want to protect my own interests. Our government seems not to care so much that we are no longer the dominant force in the world. We were the big dogs for so long I think they've gotten complacent. Our puppet President looks and acts like a fool and our image follows suit. And China is dying to take us out. Believe me, I know about their technology. My people have to keep our protocols one step ahead. They have soldiers that hide behind a terminal and try to crack our defense computers all day long and we can do nothing about it. We spent money, troops and resources into crap all over the world but fail to take care of any real business." He stopped pacing and looked out of the window for a moment. I still wasn't sure where I was going to help with things, but I let his rant continue.

"I know that you believe, as I, that our country lacks good, stern leadership, and that our world needs to lose some of its dead weight." He continued to stare out the window.

"The question still remains. What do we do about it?" I looked at him.

"I have some ideas, but nothing that would warrant anyone's approval," I told him.

"We're not trying to win anyone's approval here son. We're trying to save the planet."

"Well sir, you know, if you read my files, you'll see that I'm not the biggest fan of my fellow man. I think we need to find a way to get rid of some of the people or slow our growth. I know that big business depends on that growth and that our country has been leading the way, expanding by leaps and bounds, but we seem to draw the worst from all over the world. We grow, but at the expense of our heritage, and safety. I would love to see scum of the earth punished, in a lot of cases executed. We really need to take out the trash and erase some of the scumbag's DNA from the species, one and for all." He turned and looked at me.

"You're thinking on small term boy. We need to fix the world, eliminate the great chunk of people. We could end up with something similar AIDs spreading itself to the far corners of the world." He walked back over and put his hands flat on the desk in front of me again.

"Or we can find a way to use your talents to their utmost. I have a plan. You may not fully understand it, but I am confident it would work. First, we have to put a stop to this never-ending war over oil, while at the same time, sending a message to the entire world" He stepped away from the desk and moved to the wall behind me, which housed all of the televisions. He picked up his remote and activated a power point presentation. A big map of the Middle East popped up on the screen. He pulled a laser pointer out of his pocket and put the red dot on the country of Iran, located right next to Iraq, where all of our troops had been stationed for the past couples of years. He went on to explain that his people have been collecting data concerning this country's secret preparations to undermine the United States occupation in their region. This data was compiled for the express purpose of providing our troops and their leaders with information to prepare for an attack. But the President had rebuked this data in an effort to bolster a peace in the region. One never-ending battle had been enough for this man, who was about to leave office. He had reached the end of his term and did not want to entertain the idea of another front on the war on terror. But in all actuality, Barnes had later learned that we were just spread too thin. We didn't have the resources or the troops to mount a new attack, and the low approval of both the President and the war would make it impossible to acquire the needed funding for such an effort. In a sense, this collection of data was buried.

"I know that they want to destroy us, but they will not be acting alone. China has representatives that have offered to team up with Iran to help push our American forces out of the region." He stopped talking and walked back over to the desk and looked me in the eye.

"There is a secret base located under the sands of Iran that is currently housing over a hundred thousand Chinese soldiers. Sometime within the next month, they will launch an attack on Iran and its new government. Their goal is to pretty much capture the entire region and keep the oil for themselves." He was getting more and more intense.

"Our troops will be blindsided, and a good lot of them will probably be killed. This plan of theirs is designed to cripple us on several fronts. We lose access to all of the oil in the region, our troops will be killed or captured, and our economy will take a tremendous hit. We can't win an all-out conflict with the Chinese. Their army is a billion strong, and they are as technologically advanced as we are, in some cases they are ahead of us." This was a lot of information to process.

"Why would we not attack them before they attack us?" I asked. I wondered why I had heard nothing about this before.

"Do you think we would stand a chance against the Chinese? Look out the window. We are sitting at ground zero here. If we provoked them, they could send a few hundred thousand troops to our doorstep in less than a day. They could cut off our pipeline to the Alaskan oil fields and practically shut down our economy in a week." He was excited and animated.

"We could sustain ourselves with the oil fields in Texas and the Gulf of Mexico, but our allies would be forced to have to deal with China and Iran. It would be beyond our means to help them. Now, imagine if Venezuela and Korea decided to join the Chinese? We would go from being the world leaders to meaningless followers for the rest of them. Our way of life as we know it would be over." He stopped and took a breath. I sat and thought about everything he had just said. It all made sense. It seemed to me that when stock markets rise and fall as much as they had in the past year, that we already had a shaky economy. Oil prices had gone from around sixty-seven dollars a barrel to near one hundred in the that same time period. Our entire economy seemed to a layman like me, to be on the brink of collapse already. We couldn't handle a scenario such as that.

"Why had our government done nothing to prevent such a thing?" I asked generally concerned.

"And why have I not heard about this before?"

"The Cuban missile crisis," he said.

"You've heard of that right? Do you know what a scare that generated across the country? We learned that some things are better left in the hands of the government rather than scare the populace at large.

You are right. Our economy is riding a fine line. We are on the brink of not only a recession, but also a depression. The value of our dollar is based on the faith that it's worth something. It's backed up by gold hidden in vaults around our country, but the amount of dollars printed had far exceeded the value of our gold many years ago. Our government has a responsibility to keep its people safe, but they cannot disclose such information for fear of not looking bad in the eyes of the rest of the world, but of failing its people. What do you think would happen if gas prices rose to six, eight, or fourteen dollars a gallon over night because our currency was faltering? There would be chaos, pandemonium, anarchy." He stepped back away from the desk again and started to pace.

"Do you understand now what we are up against? Do you understand why it is important for you to take your training seriously?" Oh, I understood all right. This conversation actually scared me little. There were people I cared about in this world. I didn't want to lose them to war and definitely not the shadows. I could not, would not allow that to happen. I could count the amount of real, true friends I have on one hand. I really couldn't care less about the rest of the people in the world, but these few meant everything to me. I had often thought of various ways to thin the herd but could never really figure out how to do it without hurting these few people that I loved or their offspring. I had even, at one time, thought as Barnes did with the Sickle Cell Anemia scenario. I thought it would be a sure fired way to stop the chaos that seems to haunt Africa. Somehow the disease could be modified to infect the ground water or even be made into an airborne form. It would cover the land and reach into every being with a certain amount of melanin in their skin and destroy the oxygen carrying capabilities of their red blood cell. A person afflicted by this would literally suffocate in the open air. The over-population and hunger problems would end quickly enough. The rest of the mess would be up to whatever members of government survived, but their misery would be at an end once and for all. We just eliminate them. The problem with such things is that they rarely perform as predicted. A virus or disease like that could eventually take on a mind of its own and spread itself to the four corners of the globe. Granted, it could alleviate some of the world's starving people's and greatly thin the herd, but it would be considered genocide. Anyone responsible for such a plague would have their soul condemned to the darkness forever. And though I never before had the resources to commit such an atrocity, I knew that I would never truly be able to carry out such a horrific deed. So here was this dilemma that Barnes informed me about. It was intriguing to say the least. I had felt, for a long time now, that our world was nearing the brink of a great change. I could see the new weather patterns, temperatures rising and the glaciers receding.

Sooner or later, I thought, the planet would fight back on its own, but it just didn't seem to be working out that way. Eventually something had to be done, but that something was yet to be seen. Perhaps Barnes had a plan.

"I have some ideas how to fix things," Barnes started.

"But nothing concrete. I would like for you and Winston to up you're training another notch or two to see what you can come up with. I would like to find out if you are truly capable of the things that certain people claim." He stepped back and looked out of the large window again.

"The freedom of our country and perhaps the lives of every single person you know may be at risk. Show me what your capable of son, and I will show you how we are going to save the world." He was actually looking to me for answers. I thought he was going to show me, but instead, I was going to have to show him, or at least point him in the right direction.

"I'll see what I can do," I told him with as much courage as I could muster. This was some heavy stuff to have dumped upon me, and I had a lot of thinking to do.

"Will Winston be available tomorrow?" I asked, knowing that there was a chance he might have off on Saturdays.

"He will be available to you any time after today. Would you like to meet him at your regular time?"

Barnes asked, happy to see that I was anxious to get things started. I was anxious all right, but not for the same exact reasons that he would think. I nodded that five thirty would be acceptable and he moved his hand to show me that it was time for me to go. I thanked him, gave him a nod, and left.

As I exited the building, I found it a bit hard to breathe. I had just learned that I might well have the fate of the world on my shoulders. That's a lot to think about, especially for someone like me. I had always thought that if I had given a chance to save the world, that I wouldn't do it. I had felt that this world needed cleansing. There was just too much apathy and hatred floating around. Every single spot on the map was under someone's ownership, some government law that would want to inflict their own rule upon anyone that entered their borders. I would have been glad for a catastrophe. I reveled in the loss of life when it didn't affect me or anyone I cared about. I didn't care that a good chunk of the bottom of the barrel had lost everything in a hurricane or that entire communities had been washed away be a tsunami. I simply did not care. But I've been trying to change that way of thinking. I'm not talking about just in the time that I had acquired the wings, but for almost a full year prior to that. I could not seem to get ahead, no matter how hard I tried. I seemed to always take two steps backward for every one step forward, so I was working on doing something completely different. I was trying not just to think happy thoughts, but also think more of the things that I wanted. Instead of wasting my time and energy with nonsense and anger, I thought about having money and good friends around me. I thought about how I could help instead of how I could hurt. I visualized the things I wanted most and seemed to be finally turning my fortunes around. Now suddenly, I was saddled with the weight of the world. Greed, money, power and violence had brought us right up to the brink. My mind was muddled, and I was deep in thought, wondering why I hadn't seen or heard from Chalmers, when a horn beeped behind me. Then I saw Lori pop her head out of the back window of a car.

"Hey, jump in," she said with a smile.

"Lucious told me to take the rest of the day off and make sure you were taken care of."

"Taken care of?" I asked as I climbed into the back seat with her.

"Oh yes. We need to start with this," she said as she loosened my tie.

"And then a little of this," she continued while she ran her hands up into my hair and gave me a nice head massage. That did start to relax me. In no time flat we were out in front of her condominium complex.

"Let's go," she told me. She wasn't asking.

Her condo was laid out just like mine, but it was decorated with more of a women's touch. She brought me into her room and had my lie down on the cool sheets, then she started to rub my back. She knew right where to push. Then she put a little oil in her hand and rubbed it in hard and deep. She hit all the spots, even the muscles that connected my wings to my back. It was so nice, and I felt that I could melt.

She continued to this for about fifteen to twenty minutes, massaging me from my head right down to my ticklish toes, and when I thought she was done, she rolled me over. Then she massaged my leg and my arms and chest. I was so relaxed. I was in Heaven. Then we drifted off to sleep together.

ELEVEN

I awoke from my nap, and it was still early, not quite two thirty. I looked at Lori who was still sleeping soundly. I didn't want to wake her, but I needed to get up and do something. Her distractions had done my mind wonders, but now it was time to rise and shine. I threw down some push-ups and sit-ups to get the blood flowing to my limbs, then I slipped on my sneakers and headed out for a jog. My legs needed an extra little bit of stretching. So before I got too crazy, I stopped and stretched my body good. The sun was warm and bright. I found a good, rockin song on my MP3 player and headed out. I remembered the way I had gone to get to the ocean, so I made my way toward the coast and the cliffs down that long, windy road. It was just like home, just like Ocean Beach and Sunset Cliffs, but a whole lot higher. These cliffs here were monstrous. I could see the waves crashing on the rocks far below and I thought about how important it would be for me to figure out how to use my wings. I had to concentrate hard on the things I wanted, and I would let nothing else enter my mind. I had to break through the door that I had opened.

I needed to kick it in and take back the power that was once mine. Each morning, Winston started things the same way, with thoughts and visions of the past. His trances put me in the midst of battle, and when I woke, I brought a part of it with me. Unfortunately, it happened in very small doses. I needed something substantial. I needed to be able to fly. I needed my wings to work.

As I ran along the coastline, I opened them and begged to be able to feel the wind blow across them instead of through them.

“Please make them work,” I shouted out loud.

“Help me make them work!” Then as if it were a gift from God, the cliff opened and swallowed me. I had gotten too close to the edge, and I had let my mind slip into the false reality of the Great Wars for the briefest moment, but that was all I needed to lose my footing. I tumbled about a hundred or a hundred and fifty feet, before I was even able to reach out for something to grab ahold of. I reached and grabbed at the rocks and some old roots, but I kept falling. I had hit my knees and then my arm as I tumbled, and then I was airborne. I was tumbling free of the cliff side. I was no longer banging my arms and legs and my head, I was falling, and falling fast. The shoreline below seemed to be racing up to meet me very quickly. I threw out my arms and legs to make myself as long and wide as possible, and even spread my wings to their fullest in hopes of slowing myself. As I fell, I thought of my mom and dad. They would not understand what had happened to me. They had been so proud that I had gotten such a prestigious job.

Now, just a couple of weeks later, I would be another statistic of this precipice. I thought about Lori. I had spent the better part of this life alone, and it was only now, at the end, that I had finally found happiness with another.

My whole life flashed in front of me as I rocketed through the blue of the daylight toward the waters below. I pulled my hands to cover my face and closed my eyes. My body braced for the impact of the rocky coast, but it never came.

Finally, I pulled my hands away to see that I was gliding. My wings caught hold of the updraft and I was just kind of floating in place, drifting in the air.

"Wahoo!" I screamed out loud. I was so excited, but that quickly changed to nervousness. I warbled a little, and I thought I was going to lose my balance. I was drifting about a hundred feet or so above the rocks and water. It was awesome, but at the same time scary. At least I was still alive. I couldn't imagine having that crazy conversation with Barnes this morning, finding out how important I was, and then getting killed four or five hours later. That would have been a colossal mess on my behalf.

Whatever the case was, I had to be very careful. I could still end this day inside of a box if I didn't mind my crap right now. My wings were acting like a hang glider, but I was flying blind. I had no idea how to get myself up or down. I honestly did not want to move for fear of losing my hold on the wind. But I had to do something. The first thing I did was slow my breathing. I had to relax. I thought about the way I had flapped my wings up and down in the mirror, or when I had gone jogging. I just did what I had done then, and low and behold, I was now moving. I tried to stay in the updraft because I wasn't sure how much lift I would have. Slowly but surely, I was getting the hang of it. I zipped up and down, angling my body and the blades of my wings to point me in the direction I wanted to go. It was magnificent. Soon enough I was drifting through the breeze like a pro. Then Chalmers words rang out in my head. I hadn't thought about it too much while I was inside the hangar, training with Winston. I felt safe, protected there, but here I was out in the open, all alone. I was exposed to the people that would do me harm. As much as I was enjoying myself, it was time to try to land. I swooped down into the updraft and caught a breeze that pushed me up above the top of the cliff. Then I picked my spot and glided up and over the precipice onto the flat top near the spot where I had fallen earlier. I angled the wings almost perpendicular to my body and dropped easily onto my feet. I skid a couple of feet in the loose sandy gravel, but I did not fall. It was a perfect two-point landing, but as I gained my footing, I needed to use the tips of my wings to keep my balance. So all in all it was really a four-point landing. The funny thing was that I had dirt on the tips of my fluffy white wings. I shook first the right and then the left before it occurred to me that not only was I able to fly, but the wing did not simply pass through the ground as they had always done in the past. I had touched the ground, the dirt with them. What a miraculous day, I thought.

Then I wondered if they had also become visible to the human eye. I folded my wings tight against my back and hurried back home. The sun was starting to set, and the shadows were long as I neared the main gate of the Critterware compound. I passed through with no problem, no awkward stares or any hassle.

Soon enough I was home. I was tired and dirty, and when I looked in the mirror, I wanted to laugh. I had dirt all over my face and my hair was all over the place. I had passed a few people on the way to get to here and must have looked atrocious. Nonetheless, I was home and jumping in the shower. I had a good jog and was now ready to relax. I wanted to get cleaned up and go see Lori. But as I got ready to pull off my shirt, I grew nervous. I had put this shirt on before my wings had become usable, substantial and now I wondered how I would get it over them and off. So, I grabbed hold of the bottom of the shirt on both sides and began to pull it up, and then over my head, ever so slowly. But it just went right through them. Weird, I thought. I had gotten dirt on the tips of the wings, yet they passed right through the cloth of the shirt. I would have to show that to Winston to see what he thought of it. I also now wondered if they could be seen by the naked eye. I tried to be as inconspicuous as possible upon returning from my run, but I would have had a little luck hiding them from plain sight. As it stood, no one said or did anything to show that they had actually seen them. So, I put that thought into the back of my head and climbed into the shower.

The water was nice and warm. I looked to see if it passed through the wings or it if got them wet. I was again amazed to see each droplet pass right through. How odd, I thought. How was I going to get them clean? I looked at the dirty tip of my right wing for a moment, then reached down and picked it up. I cupped some water in my left hand and put it on the dirty spot, and it worked. I had been able to wash it off. The rest of the water then beaded up and trickled off. But only the tip that I placed the water directly on had gotten wet and when I let go of it, the water passed through it again.

So I did the same with the other tip to get it clean. Then I finished my shower and toweled off like I had always done. After that, I got ready and went back over to Lori's. I got to her house and knocked but got no answer. Perhaps she wasn't there, I thought. I checked my phone, but she hadn't called, so I used my key. I walked in and found her still dead asleep.

"Lori," I called to her gently.

"Baby, are you okay?" I put my hand on her shoulder and gently rubbed it to see if she would respond.

She finally stirred and then woke up, but very slowly.

"What time is it?" she asked as she rubbed her head and her face.

"It's five thirty in the afternoon," I told her as I sat down on the big soft bed next to her. I ran my hand down her shoulder and the back of her arm. I loved to touch her soft, smooth skin.

"Five thirty?" she whispered in kind of a startled murmur.

"How long was I out for?" I looked at her she tried to wake up and I marveled at how pretty she was. If I could ask for all of the physical attributes that I like in a woman, they would all be here. She was beautiful, even more in this disheveled state.

"Crap," she started.

"What did you do to me?" she asked as she slid her hand down under the covers. Her breath quivered again for a moment.

"I'm still tingly." She looked down.

"Whatever you did to me this morning," she started, "was fabulous," she finished with a smile.

"It was incredible. I'm not saying that I can handle that every day, but it was nice." She took my hand and kissed it. I looked at her and knew that I wanted to spend my whole life with her. She was my Queen, my Goddess. I hadn't had anyone in my life like this in a long, long time, if ever. I was so in love with her, but I wondered if she would love me if she knew what I really was. I wondered if she would feel the same about me if she really knew what I was capable of. So, I gently asked her.

"Baby, do you know why I'm here?"

"Because you love me," she said with a big smile. Then she rolled over in the big bed.

"No, I mean, do you know why I was brought here?"

She looked at me and smiled.

"I don't care why you're here, just that you are here." She wiggled around a little bit.

"It still almost feels like you are still inside me," she said through a big smile. It was hard for me not to smile with her, and I almost didn't ask her more, but I was changing. I was opening up to my full potential and I wasn't sure what was going to happen. I didn't know what I was going to become. And I wanted her to know and understand this. I wanted her on the same page with me.

"What did Barnes tell you about me?" He said that you were an important asset that we needed on our team. He also said that you had extraordinary powers, but that I was not allowed to ask you about them.

That was between he, you and that creepy old Winston. Why, is something wrong?" I wanted to tell her everything, but I didn't know how she would take it. What was I going to say, that I was an angel, or that I knew her in the past life. If someone dropped that kind of bomb on me, I would think they were crazy.

“I do know that Mr. B is very pleased, and he’s a tough guy to make happy.” She looked at me and knew that something was bothering me.

“Look, Lucious and I have traveled all over the globe since the time I was hired. At first, I thought he wanted me as some sort of concubine or something, but that didn’t happen. At the time, I think I would have done anything to get out of the rat town and crap job I had.” She looked away from me, toward the window.

“But he never laid a hand on me. I was small time in a small world, and he was the most powerful man I had ever met, so when he asked me to go with him, I jumped.” She pulled back the covers and slipped out of the bed as she continued talking.

“I had spent a limited amount of time in college. I just couldn’t afford to go to any big fancy school, but I did have a bachelor’s degree almost completed. One day I’m serving coffee and eggs and the next I’m in China organizing papers and answering the phone for Mr. Lucious Barnes, owner and found of the Critterware Software Development Corporation.” She walked around the bed and looked at me.

“From that point on, my life was as whirlwind of travel and adventure.” She was awake now, and as she talked; she began to remove the sheets from her bed. I helped, and she continued.

“All that was really ever asked of me was to work hard, and to mind my own business.” She grabbed up the dirty sheets and put them into the little laundry room and grabbed some fresh ones. I helped her put them on the bed and continued to listen to her.

"I've seen some strange things, and been to some very odd places, but I will never talk about it to anyone, not even you. I have a trust with Mr. Barnes that benefits the both of us, so if you are about to open yourself up as to why you are here, then please don't. What is said between the two of you and whatever you are doing with Mr. Winston is your business. Lucious agreed to be cool with us seeing each other as long as we didn't cross that line." She finished by tucking the blanket up under the pillows and then went over and threw the dirty sheets in the washing machine. Then she came over to me and gave me a big hug.

"Since the second I laid eyes on the photo in your file, something seemed very familiar about you." She stepped back and looked away.

"I'm a little embarrassed about this but, I brought your file home with me and just couldn't stop thinking about you. I did all of my research and planning for my trip to San Diego and with your photo staring at me. I actually looked forward to going there to sign you up. But when you delayed the signing of the documents to have dinner with me, I could have melted." She busied herself straightened things as she talked.

"I knew then that there was something more about you than meets the eye, and I fell pretty hard for you." Then she turned to face me and smiled.

"The funny thing is the more I get to know you, the more you seem to fit into the mold of the person I thought you would be. Does that sound odd to you? Wait," she said, holding up her hand.

"Don't answer that." She walked back over and wrapped her arms around me and looked me in the eye.

"I feel like I am falling in love with you, but I don't know if I should." She gave me a little kiss on the lips.

"I've gotten pretty hard over the past few years. I pretty much learned that along with the big salary and the perks, I also received the hands-off label. And that was a little hard to get used to." She bopped around, straightening and tidying again.

"So, it's been a long time since I've been with a man." She seemed a little embarrassed.

"Bottom line is, that I am so happy to have you here with me, right here and now. But a part of me knows that you have brought here for something bigger and much more important than me." Then she started to tear up a little.

"I don't know how long I am going to get to have you, but I want to enjoy every minute of it. I would love to know what kind of breakthrough you and Winston had, but I have to admit, I am terribly frightened by it." I grabbed hold of her and pulled her in tight.

"I know we haven't been together very long, and I won't spill any beans, but rest assured that I would be happy to spend the rest of my life with you. I knew that from the second I laid eyes on you. As far as I know, you'll have a hard time getting rid of me anytime soon." The words fell out my mouth, and I wanted them to have meaning, but both of us knew it was most likely a fantasy.

We got ready together and walked over to the commons. Then we sat and had some dinner together.

On the way out, I ordered some sushi to be brought to my condo and I grabbed a bottle of wine. I loved it. I didn't have to pay for a thing. I just flashed me employee card. Then we went to the campus movies where I grabbed some cups, and we shared the wine and some popcorn. We giggled as we walked back to my place. It was Friday night, and I knew Lori wanted to spend the weekend together, but she understood and respected the fact that I was going to work straight through it. That didn't stop me from trying to show my lady a nice night. We got home ten minutes before the sushi arrived. I poured some wine for her and water for me, but I did share one shot of sake. That was it for the drinking for me. I had to get up way too early, and I thought how lucky I was. I had almost forgotten that I had the world on my shoulders. Lori had done a magnificent job of easing my mind. After the sushi, I had gone to bed, and when I woke up, she was lying there next to me. It was well before the crack of dawn, and I did not want to get out of bed.

She smelled so nice. I pulled some of her hair

right up to my hose and breathed in heavily. I was going to hold onto that aroma and remember it when the going got tough today. I would be able to remember who and what I was really fighting for. Then I snuck out of bed, got ready, and left. A car was waiting for me, but I told the driver that I wanted to jog. I needed to get pumped up. I was stoked and I couldn't wait to show Winston that I could fly. I was wound up when I got to the auditorium, ready to rock.

Winston was not so enthused.

"Show me," he said. He was blunt and dry humored, and usually smelled like he had just eaten a crap sandwich for breakfast. I looked past him at the ashtray and wondered how long he must have been there. There were already four butts snuffed out and he was smoking on another. I wouldn't let this negativity bring me down though. I wouldn't let him get to me today. I opened my wings and took a couple of steps, brought my wings down hard and fast and dove into the air. I landed hard on my chin, chest and knees. That hurt.

"This is what you were so enthused about?" he asked as he took a long drag on his cigarette.

"I'm not impressed," he said, blowing the long stream of smoke in my direction. I looked up at him just in time to see him rub the back of his neck. He looked like he was hurt. I felt like a fool for trying to fly, but that little peek I got to steal more than made up for it. Ha, I must have stung him good the other day. I thought. He caught me looking at him and immediately stopped rubbing the spot.

"Enough of these games. Take your place boy," I don't know if it was the fact that I had whooped him or that we were here on a Saturday morning, but he seemed extra grumpy today.

As usual, our session started with some deep thoughts and reminiscing about my past life. Today, though, I slipped into my trance rather quickly. It was weird to wake up and get ready, then come here and be put to sleep. All of the other days, I was never truly awake when I got here. I'm so slow on waking up, it's nutty. But today, I was amped. I was ready to go.

Then just like that, I was out. I felt the same this morning as I had in each of the other mornings I had been here, but today, I kept my vision about me instead of just enjoying the ride. Each time this happened, there was a short transition phase that felt like I was going through a tunnel. It was like I was surrounded by swirling colors and streaks of light. The end of the tunnel was bright, and as I drew closer, I would be quickly pulled through into the midst of some battle. It reminded me of the Tube. And there was something here that I needed to find. Somehow, Winston was able to get me here; I just had to figure it out. I looked for the key but began to feel the tug of the end of the tunnel. Then just before I was sucked out into the light, I saw something I wasn't really looking for. For a half a click, I thought

I saw Chalmers. Weird, I thought. But then I didn't have time to think. I was thrust into the middle of a battle. I quickly spread my wings and jumped up into the air. I pulled out my sword and a blue flame leapt out of my hand and ran up its razor-sharp blade. In the other hand I held my shield, also re-enforced with a blue flame. And in an instant, I was in it up to my elbows. There were shadows and tar-like creatures everywhere, and they were nipping at my heals. I looked around for my platoon but didn't see them. I was alone. That was a strange thing in itself. We were not permitted to enter the dark realm alone. But then I quickly realized that I might not be alone, instead simply separated. In front and almost all around me was not the black of darkness, but that of a whole legion of shadows. I was being engulfed by them. I had no time to think. I just moved instinctively. I had to slice and dice my way out. I was whacking away when I felt something pull me down from behind. One of the tar things that usually accompanied the shadow armada had hold of my wings and was pulling me down into it. I didn't like that. I could feel it sliming up my wing, reaching its tentacles up toward my body and face. I didn't have much time to think. I still had shadows all around me. I didn't have a choice. I threw my shield into the large grouping of shadows so that its energy could reach out into the lot of them. It slowed them for a moment so that I could react. Then I grabbed the hilt of my sword with both hands and swung and spun into the tar thing, slicing into it and carving it into a million little pieces. It let go of me and slid back off of my wing into the puddle of muck from which it came. The instant it let go, I launched myself up into the sky. I beat my wings up and down hard to get up and out of everything's reach. I aimed my open hand toward my shield and called to it with my mind. The big metallic disc crackled with energy and then released itself from the horde of dark ones and leapt back upon my wrist and forearm. The mass was still closing in on me and I had to move. I pointed my sword straight out in front and took in a deep breath, then I blew the air out, along with a burst of energy that rocketed from the tip of the blade into the blackness. I could almost hear the shadows shriek as they loosened their connections and broke apart. It was so much easier to cleave through individual beasts, then the lot of them joined together.

Finally, I was free. I looked around at where I was. I saw no other angels of light. I shouldn't be here, I thought. This was a fallen world, one already turned over to the darkness. I glanced back over my shoulder to see the shear magnitude of the beast that nearly enveloped me. It was insane. Then out of the corner of my eye, I saw another and then another. The dingy gray land was spotted with them. I looked above me and saw the millions of shadows that drifted together and apart in a horrific chain that almost completely enshrouded everything. This was not good. I could feel the trembling of fear reaching into me, but I shut it down. This was no time to panic. I searched the ground and the skies for a way out, preferable the one that got me here, but I saw none. I flew onward and upward, then parallel to the surface of the planet. I was out of practice and in big trouble. If I had been at full strength, I would still have had a hard time breaking free of this place. And even if I did, where would I go? As it was, I had little time to figure things out. Soon enough, they were all going to recognize me for what I was. I knew that I was shining like a beacon on a dark, desolate world. The darkness and the shadows would soon rise up from below and reach down on me from above. I didn't want to panic, but I was nervous. Then, in an instant, they were upon me. The shadows had risen up from the surface and were reaching for me.

Many were joining together and combined to form another giant shadow monster. They were circling me from below, their numbers growing quickly. Others still, fell from the sky, surrounding me. I whipped my shied at the beast below. It blasted into it, shredding it. I was flying hard and swinging my sword mightily, hacking and cleaving. I felt the monsters nipping at my heels, and as I was about to call to my shield, I felt a great smack on the back of my head. Then, just like that, the shadows were gone. I was back in the enormous auditorium. My wings were working perfectly, and I still held the sword that was glowing in a blue fire. Winston held his shield and sword and had proceeded to attack me. It was the crackle of energy from the hilt of his weapon on the back of my head that had brought me back to this place. I barely had time to catch myself before he shot another bolt of power in my direction. The transition between these two worlds took a bit of a toll on me, and I felt a little disoriented. Winston used that to his advantage and swung hard at me. He meant to cleave me in two. I bobbed back out of the way and wondered why I had no shield. Then I remembered that I had hurled it at the shadows. I surveyed the floor below, looking for it, but saw nothing. I had the sword, but not the shield, and I could have used both right now. Winston came at me hard and fast. If I didn't know it, I would think that he truly meant to hurt me. I had stung him pretty good at our last meeting. Perhaps he would pay me back today. He had a wicked look in his eyes, crazy, like he was going to try to cut me. I bobbed and weaved and blocked his onslaught with my own sword, but I did not fight back.

"Why do you hesitate?" he asked.

"Fight, or I will slice you in two. Do not hold back," he commanded. I looked at him and wondered what more he wanted me to do. I did not want to hurt him. These were real swords, sharp enough to split a hair. He wasn't that fast, and I could have easily cleaved large amounts of flesh from him, shield or no shield. Then in my hesitation, he got me. He sliced me good. My caution was rewarded with pain.

"Crap," I yelled out. "I don't know what you want

from me Winston." The cut was shallow, like a paper cut. And like a paper cut, it burned and hurt deep.

"I want you to fight," he ordered from behind his shield. He knew what he had just done. He was provoking me.

"You want me to kill you? Do you want to die today, Winston?" I asked. Because I knew if I allowed the beast full reign, my 'teacher' would end up in pieces. Then I thought about who he was, what he was.

Maybe he wanted to die. I was thinking about telling him off when he lunged at me. I dodged him and blasted him in the side of the head with the hilt of my sword. It was a quick, hard crack of metal against bone. I knew I hurt him good. Then I spun to counterattack, and I sliced his shield in two. He was defenseless. I spun around and brought my blade very quickly right up to the side of his throat. I was so wound up and full of energy that I could have easily followed through by removing his head, but I didn't.

"I don't want to kill you," I told him. He was holding the right side of his head.

"I don't want you to kill me either," he told me. His eyes were as wide as paper plates.

"Then why did you do that?" I asked, still breathing heavy. My blood was blasting through my veins. The feeling of fear that I brought back with me from the shadow realm and the anger of the cut on the back of my forearm had me fired up. I still held the sword at the ready. But I could see that the fight was now over.

"I just had to keep you distracted, pull out of your fantasyland and keep you going." He let the piece of shield he still had strapped to his wrist drop and then he sheathed his sword. He slid the long blade into a leathery covering that was attached to his hip. When he let go of it, the sheathed weapon disappeared into thin air. Then he reached into his pocket and produced his pack of cigarettes. He pulled a fresh one from the pack and lit it.

"Distracted from what" I asked, still quite wound up. Then I realized where I was. At first my heart jumped a beat, but I quickly regained my composure. We were at least three stories above the hard concrete floor, and we were just drifting, hovering there. We had been flying the whole time, and I hadn't realized it. Winston smile that crooked smile of his, then he took a long drag on his cigarette and blew it out around him. It sort of blended into the little aura that he generated. He was so nasty, and his big ugly wings flapping behind him made his appearance even worse. I settled down and realized that I pretty much didn't feel the muscles in my chest, back and shoulders moving the wings. It was as though I had inadvertently discovered a wholly different set of hidden controls. They worked just like any other set of muscles, reacting to my thoughts. It was like I had been on autopilot. I thought to slowly lower myself to the ground and the wings angled and lowed. I looked around at them and marveled at the pitch they used when they went up and down, I then tucked them up and in and made a couple quick loops around the room. This was incredible. It was amazing. I was flying. I had looked down for the shield when Winston first attacked me and didn't even think about it. So strange, I thought. I had an excuse though; my mind had been preoccupied with the shadows.

"Holy Crap, the shadows," I shouted at Winston. I looked around the room to see that none of them had followed me. If even one of them escaped that realm and made it to the auditorium, it could prove disastrous. One shadow would eventually bring more, and this world wasn't ready for that.

"They did not follow you," Winston seethed. "I can assure you of that." I know he meant well, but he was just so nasty and greasy looking that when he tried to smile, it just made things worse.

"Even if they did, they would not be able to escape this room. It is special, re-enforced with an electromagnetic force field. No one knows what goes on in here that isn't authorized to know." He seemed pretty sure of himself.

"Besides, even if one of them got through, it would be no match for me," he seethed as his hand lit up in a red flame.

"You did not think that I would have really allowed you to kill me, do you? I still have a great deal more to teach you, boy" That Winston was the sly one. He suddenly looked a whole lot more formidable.

"Do not underestimate me. I can handle anything you can throw at me." He told me this with a confidence, sort of bravado. He flicked what was left of his cigarette right down and into the ashtray. It was nearly a perfect shot from thirty or thirty-five feet away. It rimmed around the tray and popped back out onto the floor, but he had hit the mark. He had smoked the thing all the way down to the filter, and before that one hit the ground; he was lighting another.

"Mind if I smoke?" he asked with a grin. I minded, but I wouldn't say anything to him. Besides, the smoke covered up his putrid odor. Chalmers had told me that I would know when I was in the presence of someone of my ilk. I likened the smell of Winston to that of the bum that I wrestled with back in Ocean Beach, on the cliffs, about a month or so ago. In his case though, it was the stench covered in smoke and it made my own clothes smell so bad that I had to put them right into the wash when I got home for fear of stinking up my whole apartment. I thought about the shadow world as I watched Winston glide down to the ground, and then fold his wings behind his back. He motioned for me to do the same, but I did not want to. I had longed for this moment for far too long, and I did not want to give it up. So I made a few more quick laps around the gigantic room and then tried to land right next to him.

I did a pretty good job, but I stumbled before I caught myself.

"How do you do that," I asked him.

"Do what?" he asked between puffs.

"How do you send me, in my mind, to a different world?" I asked with genuine curiosity. He looked at me.

"You do that to yourself. I am just a catalyst. I just help you along. You go to the places you need to go and see things that you need to see. I enable you to an extent, but you do the rest yourself." That was an odd answer. I wanted to ask him more, but he held his hand up to stop me.

"Only you truly know what you need. So, you pick the time and the place that best suits that need.

Today you needed to learn how to fly and how to find that sword of yours. I would love to tell you to practice your abilities after you go home, but in this case, I would recommend against it. You are safe from prying eyes here, but outside of this building, you are exposed to other forces that you may or may not understand. I am not at liberty to discuss too much about this type of thing with you, but rest assured you need to stay under wraps until our boss can come up with a plan. Now, I want you to try this," he said. He reached down with his right hand to his left hip and grabbed onto nothing. Then as suddenly as it had disappeared, his sheathed sword reappeared. He pulled out the sword and raised it up over his head. It was all aglow with the red fire.

He swung it down and around so that the blade was horizontal, parallel with the ground and kind of flicked it. A fiery red flame jumped from the blade out at the concrete block midway across the room. The energy of the flame impacted on the cement wall causing an explosion that split it in two.

I was amazed as I looked at what once was a two-foot thick, five foot by five foot, piece of reinforced concrete. It had been blown near to bits. It let out a loud crack then blew into pieces in a dusty cloud. I felt the force of the explosion ripple through my body.

"That was awesome," I said, unable and unwilling to control my enthusiasm. I wanted to try, but Winston shook his head.

"I want you to think about this tomorrow. Today I want you to end this session with some flying practice." I so loved the sound of that. Winston had me do some laps around the room, some big banking turns, and some quick stops. I did some movements that were similar to wind sprints, but in the air, flying. He had me hover in one place, then dive down, up and over and around the other concrete barriers that were scattered across the room. I flew up and down and occasionally, he would throw something at me so that I would have to dodge. It. I was getting pretty good, pretty fast. Winston called it a day and I dropped down into a perfect landing next to him. I must have flown around that building for hours, and I was barely winded. I fully expected my chest muscles or even my back to hurt, but that did not happen.

"You did very well today, boy. I think Mr. Barnes will be happy with our progress." He smiled at me through his yellow and brown teeth.

"We are not that much different, you and me, eh? But you are capable of so much more. Remember that. And remember what you saw today. We will continue this lesson in the morning. Good night."

He then lit another cigarette and walked out of the room. I was pretty proud of myself. I jumped up into the air for one last lap around the room. It felt nice. I would have preferred to be out in the open air, with the cool wind blowing off the ocean and across my face, but this would do. Believe me, this would do. I landed a little harder than I had wanted to and tweaked my ankle just a bit. I was glad that Winston hadn't seen that. I walked outside and saw that the sun was close to setting. That meant it had to be near seven o'clock at night. That couldn't be right. I pulled out my cell phone and confirmed it. Wow, I thought; a whole day had come and gone. I had been at it for around twelve or thirteen hours give or take, and I still felt great.

I got home and called Lori. She had already eaten, so I grabbed some of the leftovers out of my fridge and heated them up. Then I took a long, hot shower and thought about the day. As the warm water poured over my face and down my body, I let my mind drift. There were some things that I saw today that really caught my attention, one being what appeared to be Chalmers waving his arms at me just before I was pulled through the tunnel of light onto the shadow world. Here were two things that haunted me. One was my lack of contact with Chalmers and the other was the constant visions and exposure to the shadows. Chalmers had told me that I would never be able to use my wings, yet today I did just that. Perhaps he thought I would not be able to discover the hidden muscles that controlled them. Or maybe I didn't really have those abilities in the mortal form. Maybe they were something that had been pulled back through the rift, like the sword, something that existed in a different dimension that I was able to access. I had been able to glide the previous day, but my attempt to actually fly was a disaster, which I still felt in my chin. I was in own little world, deep in thought, lost in the warm refreshing water of the shower. Something touched my arm and I spun in the defensive posture; fists poised at the ready to fight. It was Lori.

"What are you doing here?" I asked her as I lowered my guard.

"I have a key," she said, as she slowly let her own guard down "I called you three times. I didn't think that I was going to surprise you." I knew this. I just didn't expect her or anyone else for that matter. I must have been in the shower a great deal longer than I had thought. She wasn't someone to hound me. She understood the concept of 'space'. She put her hand on my hand and ran it up my arm to slid into the warm water in front of me. Then she slid around behind me so that she could whisper in my ear.

"Are you okay baby?" She ran her hand up across my chest while she kissed my ear. The warm water poured on my chest and stomach and her warm body pushed up against my back.

"I'm good now," I told her, and I was. I turned around and we made out for a while, then I rubbed the warm soapy water all over her and she did the same to me. When we were done, I toweled her off. I scooped her up in a towel and carried her into my bedroom. Then we went from being clean and fresh to sweaty and messy. Afterward, we lay there. I wanted so badly to discuss with her the things I had been doing. I was pretty excited about the whole flying thing, but I would not be able to share that with her, not yet anyway.

After the conversation last night, I had decided tell Barnes that I wanted her to know everything, and I would tell him this at our next meeting. I snuggled up next to her and we watched TV until I fell asleep. I felt like I had slept for about an hour or two then something woke me. I quietly slipped out of bed and walked over to the window. I couldn't figure out what was bothering me, but I was drawn to the auditorium. I got dressed and walked across the quad to the place where all my training had been taking place. Something was calling to me, pulling me toward that place. The door was unlocked, but it was very dark inside. I had been here enough that I knew my way around, so I walked toward the giant room where I had my training. Both the exterior and the safety door were open, and I thought I heard voices.

My sense was telling me that there was something very wrong here, and I got that fight or flee shaky feeling. I had to sneak in and see what was going on. I slipped in and crept right up to the opening on the huge auditorium and peeked inside. I saw Winston inside the room. Barnes was there too. They were talking to each other, but there was someone else there that I could not see. I tried to angle myself so that I could see who it was. I slid along the wall and then snuck a peek and was not happy at all with what I saw.

There was a huge shadow that rose from the floor, up along the wall in front of the two. There was nothing in the room to cast the shadow, just the two men. It made my heart jump up into my throat.

This was no ordinary shadow. It was shadow creature, from the dark realm. But what was it doing here?

Winston said this place was protected from against their presence, but nonetheless, it was here. And it was conversing with Barnes and Winston. How? Why? I tried to listen to what they were saying but I got a little too close. The shadow saw me, and instantly the other two turned around. I had been caught and if I wasn't scared before, I was now. I was totally freaked out. I tried to run, but it was like I was moving in slow motion. The harder I tried, the less I could move, and the shadow quickly slipped right up behind me. It had a hold of my foot and quickly moved up my leg. I could feel its reach, its freezing cold touch. It actually hurt, both freezing and burning me. I tried to shake it off, but it was strong, and it had a hold of me good. Barnes and Winston hurried out of the big room and out into the hall where I was slowly being engulfed by the black tarry beast. My whole body was aching. I wanted to reach out for help, but the look on Barnes's face showed me that he was not going to save me. His was a look of both anger and disappointment.

"Mr. Barnes, help me!" I begged, reaching for him. But he did not move to help me. Instead, he just looked down at the floor in disgust and turned his back to me.

"Please!" I pleaded. The shadow was constricting my chest. It hurt to call out, hurt to breathe. It was sliding up my body toward my face. I was panicking. I didn't know what to do. I couldn't move my arms, my legs. I was helpless. My whole body was on fire. I wanted to call out again, but I couldn't. It had me and it was bent on taking my life, or worse. It was on my neck, moving ever so closer to my mouth. I could almost taste it.

Then I woke up. I was shaky, and covered in sweat, but it had all been a dream. I was still in the bed, next to Lori and I was both relieved and scared.

I didn't know if my mind was playing tricks on me or if this was one of my visions, a warning or something. I tried to go back to sleep, but I couldn't. I laid there for a while and thought about all the crazy stuff that had been happening. Finally, after an hour or two of rolling around, trying to get comfortable, I finally, finally fell asleep.

A couple of hours later, the alarm went off. I was so tired, but I forced myself to get up and get some coffee. Then I took a shower and prepared for a new day of training. I got about halfway to the training facility when I realized I hadn't even thought about the whole lightning bolt shooting out from my sword thingy until just then.

Basically, I hadn't done my homework. This, I dreadfully thought, was going to be one of those days.

TWELVE

Whether it was the fact that I was here on a Sunday, or that dream I just had a couple hours prior, I did not know, but my head just wasn't in the game. I just couldn't concentrate. I figured I'd be fine after the trancy thing that Winston did, but today of all days, he decided that we weren't doing that. He wanted to change things up. I had been looking forward to seeing if I could see Chalmers again on my way through the tunnel of light, but instead, Winston wanted to engage me with a swordplay.

"Draw your weapon," he commanded, as he pulled his sword from its sheathe. A red fire danced on its blade "Defend yourself."

I reached to where the sword should have been on my belt, but there was nothing there. The whole inter-dimensional thing took some getting used to. It had a great deal to do with concentration, and my head was so not into this today. But I had to plug through it. I had the weight of the world on my back, I thought to myself. It was partly serious, part joke. What a weird concept! I was having a hard time believing all of that this morning. Most of my training breakthroughs relied on me remembering what I did in the distant past and bringing it into this world. It was like waking a sleeping monster. Chalmers had told me that I had opened a door into a different time and place, and it had been left open a crack.

But he warmed me to leave it alone. Contrarily, Winston was trying to show me how to force it open the rest of the way. I wondered why the two contradicted each other as to what to do with my discovery.

Either way, it seemed that both wanted the impossible. Winston and Barnes wanted me to save the free world from the tyranny of its governments and Chalmers wanted me to turn a blind eye to all of it and just skate along unseen.

"I don't seem to have it," I told him with a bit of disappointment. He looked at me through the smoke that leaked out of his mouth.

"What do you mean, you do not have it?" He seemed a bit disgusted.

"You need to concentrate more boy. There is a part of you sliding between two worlds, and you need to keep track of things." He flicked his cigarette butt into the ashtray six feet away. It had a decent arc to it, and it landed dead in the tray. He rubbed his chin for a moment and started to walk around me.

"I know that you understand the gravity of the situation. My. Barnes assured me that you were up for this challenge, but it appears that you do not have your head, or your heart completely invested in this project." He walked right up to me.

"This is serious business. There is a great danger involved with what we do here. You lose your concentration, it could cost you your life, or your head. You get me?" He sounded pissed off. What could I say? He was right. I didn't have my head in the game. I was filled with doubt. I had that dream for a reason. There was something going on. I went from being alone without much of a social life to practically being shacked up with the exact women of my dreams. I went from being broke, living paycheck to paycheck, to having a fat bank account with money to burn. And I went from being told that I had to hide myself away, to finding out that I was now expected to help change the course of the entire planet.

"I'm sorry." I stumbled.

"My mind's been playing tricks on me."

"Then there is nothing we can do here today." He replaced his sword into its sheath and lit another cigarette. Then he got ready to leave. He appeared to be quite disgusted. I still hoped that he would put me into the trance that he put me into at the beginning of each of the other lessons. I knew it would not only relax me, but I would have a chance to see if I could see Chalmers again.

"Can't you hypnotize me like you do every other morning?" I asked. He took a long drag and blew it out.

"It is too dangerous. Your lack of mental discipline

has made that an impossibility today." He walked over and looked hard at me.

"Is it that women?" he asked with a serious look. "Has she bewitched you?"

When he got worked up, he took out his cigarettes. He huffed the one he had lit right down to the filter.

"I told Barnes I thought her constant presence was a bad idea," he started.

Whoa, I wasn't expecting that. Where did that come from, I wondered.

"No, it's not her," I cut in.

"I just have a lot on my mind. Why can't you just do the thing you do, and fix me?"

"Ha, he scoffed, "do you think it's that easy? You make it sound like I can just lull you to sleep with the snap of my fingers. Your lack of concentration put the both of us into a great deal of danger yesterday and you expect me to return you there?"

"What do you mean?"

"I told you yesterday, that I am just the catalyst. It is you that decides where you will go when you travel through the tunnel of light. Your mindset dictates when and where you will go for you, and when you don't think straight, you wander. Well yesterday you wandered into a very bad place. I can't control that, and I will not risk such things again until you get your head on straight. It's just not safe," he finished.

Then he walked over to his stool and sat down

and just smoked. I couldn't tell if he was disgusted or disappointed now.

"So, what do we do?" I asked, feeling like I had just let everyone down. I had been so confused lately, that I didn't know which way was up anymore. I just wanted to talk to Chalmers, at least see what he had to say about everything. Apparently, the something I was looking for in the tunnel of light was him.

It had to be. But if I looked for him, I allowed for the possibility that I could fall off course and be lost or end up deep inside the borders of the shadow realm. I took it for granted that Winston could just put me under, and then pull me out if I got into trouble.

Turns out, that wasn't really the case.

"You may practice your flying if you can still do that," he said.

If I can still do it, I thought, emphasizing the 'if'. That was a dig. Of course, I could do it. I didn't even give myself a chance to think about it. I just opened my wings and dove up into the air, and then landed hard on my chin.

"Ouch!" I yelled out loud, both because I was angry and because I was hurt. Winston did not even get off his chair. He just sat there.

"Go home. Straighten out your head. Remember that you are not just being trained here mentally and physically, but there is a link between the spiritual world here as well. You have to know that what you are trying to do is right. You have to fully believe in what we are doing here. You have to be one hundred percent committed. You have to chase away all doubt and all the distractions. Once you have done this, then you will be unstoppable, but until then, we can accomplish nothing. Tomorrow Mr. Barnes will sit in our lesson. Be here at nine with your head in order. You are dismissed," he told me with a wave of his hand. It was a very condescending wave. I wanted to say more, to try to explain, but I knew it was no use. I was useless. I couldn't think straight to save myself.

There was something wrong here and if I didn't figure it out, I would never be at peace. So, I walked out.

It was still very early, so I decided to go for a jog down to the cliffs. I just wanted the solitude of the ocean and the sound of the crashing waves in my ears. I really missed my happy place down by the shore in Ocean Beach. I missed my friends and my little Melrose Place apartment, but most of all, I missed my meaningless little existence. I didn't want to worry about saving the world. I didn't want to have to concern myself with such things as wings and angels and demons. I wanted it all to go away. But that was not going to happen. I was already dressed in sweats, so I jogged on through the compound and out past the front gate. I nodded to the guard on my way through and ran down the winding road through the wooded area. It was still very early on a Sunday morning and there seemed to be no one else out and about.

"Chalmers," I yelled.

"Where are you?" I didn't care who heard me now. I didn't. I ran a little harder and faster and when I got to the cliffs, I screamed out for him. I hollered out across the ocean for him five or six times, making sure

I stayed far enough away from the edge today. I would not risk anything crazy. I just ran until I came to a scenic spot that had an old, twisted tree with a bench under it. I decided to stretch my legs, placing a foot up on the armrest and trying to touch my toes. I followed with the other leg, then moved over and used the tree as support and stretched my leg back and up behind me. It felt good to be here.

"Chalmers," I said out loud into the morning fog which swirled up the cliff face and surrounded me.

"Please, help me. I need you." It was hard for me to ask for help. I had learned early on that I had to figure things out for myself. If I wanted something, I had to go out and get it myself. I didn't mind helping people, but I rarely asked for or felt I needed assistance from others, not enough to admit it out loud, anyway. Yet, here I was asking, essentially, a ghost for help. That's what he had become to me – a ghost. I hadn't seen him in almost a month, and I wondered if it was because of this place. Perhaps there was some kind of interference here. Winston said an electromagnetic field encompassed the auditorium in which we practiced. It kept us safe and hidden from prying eyes here and in different dimensions.

I did have reason to believe that maybe there was something similar to it working here. Maybe there was some kind of specific electronic frequency that blocked me from seeing or hearing him. That had to be it. This whole thing was based on energy, and dimensional barriers, what gets through and what doesn't get through. I had the power to cross the borders, but I had to concentrate, see what I wanted. I wanted to see Chalmers, but I didn't know how to make that happen. I decided to try one time on my own, and if I could not figure it out, I would have to ask Barnes to help me. I had no other choice. My sanity was at stake here. I stretched my arms up over my head, and then bent down to try to touch my toes. I had one chance to see if I was right before I would spill all my beans. I rubbed my hands together and took a deep breath and let it out slowly. One more deep breath and I ran right at the cliff's edge. I didn't even think about it. I just dove out into the wind. The cool updraft caught my wings and I drifted over the sea.

There was no doubt in my mind now. I had to find answers or ask for them. I wanted Chalmers my ace in the hole, but, as of late, that was proving to be too much of a distraction. I was going to find him or ask Barnes and Winston to help me find them.

The cool morning mist had enveloped me and though I could not see it, I could hear the ocean crashing against the rocks below. I didn't think, I just did. I drifted up into the sky and let the newfound muscles do their job. And I flew out through the light fog. I didn't care whether anyone saw me or not, but no one could and no one would. The cloudbank that settled on the coast was very thick. I flew out beyond it and upward.

"Chalmers," I yelled out.

"What the heck?" I continued up along the coastline. I could still hear the sound of the waves hitting the coastline.

"Chal-mers!" I yelled.

"Challllmers!" I flew onward and upward and continued to holler until my throat hurt. I was a few miles up the coast now and I saw the streetlights of the nearby town off in the distance. I didn't care if I had been seen, but I really didn't want to, so I turned to head back. I had gone far enough away that if it had been some phenomenon centralized at the compound, I would have to be outside of its range by now. I looked at my hands and my arms. I emptied my pockets. I had my cell phone, but nothing more. I looked at the phone. I carried it everywhere. If anyone wanted to track me or listen in on my life, they could easily do it with my phone.

It was small, but it could generate an electromagnetic field if properly configured. I thought about it, then I simply tossed it and flew out further toward the open ocean. I flew around for over an hour or so calling out to Chalmers, but never got a response. So, I finally headed toward home and called it a good try. I was bummed. Now, not only did

I lose my phone, but also my only hypothesis was proven wrong.

There had to be something more, something I missed. I was damp from flying through the clouds, so I went home and took a long hot shower. It was close to eight thirty now, and I could no longer wait to wake up Lori. I didn't care whether she wanted to hear it or not, she was going to know everything today. I was going to take the reins, and tell her the real story, not the one I had made up for Barnes. If I truly was going to help fix the world, then I needed to get things right with my head and heart. And it was going to start with her.

Flowers, coffee, and Danish still hadn't prepared Lori for what I told her. I had left out the part of feeling that I knew her and that we had a connection in the past life, but I told her everything else. I told her the complete and total truth, just like I was going to do with Barnes and Winston the next morning.

I caught her before she was fully awake and gave her little chance to mount a protest. I just spilled it all out. And her mouth just hung open. It was like we had gone from complete strangers to best friend, and then back to being strangers, all in less than a month and a half.

"Show me your wings," she asked of me, after a long period of silence.

"I want to see them."

"I can't do that," I told her sadly. I imagined that she must have thought I was insane or worse.

"I told you they are here, but in a different dimension. It's difficult to explain it all"

"And the flaming sword of yours? That's in a different dimension too? She asked with an edge of disbelief in her voice.

"Could you fly around the compound or show me anything that would back up this crazy story?" she asked with a bit of disdain.

"I could do that, but I won't. This isn't a joke, and it isn't a game. I'm sorry. If I am going to have you in my life, I need you to know everything about me. But that doesn't mean that I am willing to risk your safety. We could walk down to the auditorium later and I might be able to show you a few things." She took a sip of her coffee and got up from the small round table in the dining area of my condo. Then she walked over and looked out the window at the fog bank that still hovered over the not-too-distant coast.

"I don't know why you felt so obliged to tell me all of this. To be honest, I'm not sure exactly what to think here. I have a lot of questions. First of which, are you insane?"

"I can assure you that I'm not, well at least I don't think I am. Look, you don't have to believe me, but I had to tell you. I know it sounds unbelievable, but we just talked about the oddity of me being brought here." She looked out of the window, then turned to look at me.

"Seriously, I do think that you are nuts. You had

to know that I would find it hard to believe that you are some kind of avenging angel, sent here to save the world. That's just too weird. And besides that, it makes no sense. Why would you be here with us, at a software company? I've seen some serious stuff since I started working here, but this takes the cake. Why wouldn't you have told me any of this earlier."

She saw me get ready to protest.

"Don't connect this to the conversation we had the other night. This is a whole lot more involved than just work. We have been having sex, and now you come to me and tell me that you aren't quite human.

Look, if you wanted to stop seeing me, you should have just said something." She was getting pissed.

"Next thing you know, you are going to tell me that Mr. Barnes is sending you on some sort of angelic suicide mission that you won't return from."

"I wish you could believe me," I told her. I figured she would give me a hard time about all of this, but I didn't think she was going to freak out.

"But you won't show me your wings, or that you can fly. I'm just supposed to believe this craziness? She now asked with an angry tone. "That's exactly what I want. I would love to see this."

And within ten minutes, we were on our way to the auditorium. We walked there in silence. I couldn't tell if she was sad or disappointed or angry or what. When we got to the door, I held it open for her, but when I stepped in behind her, I was unprepared for what we saw. Winston and Barnes turned to face us.

Both were not expecting to see us, and the look on their faces showed it.

"Can I help you?" Barnes asked. We had been startled into silence. The situation just changed from a small lover's quarrel into something that could cost me the respect of both my boss and girlfriend all in the same moment.

"I was going to show Lori," I started, but Barnes cut me off. He held his hand out, palm facing me. It was a 'please stop' motion, coupled with a look of disgust on his face. Even Winston scowled a bit.

"Show her what? Miss Stillwell, I'm a bit disappointed to see you here this morning." His words were like a knife cutting into us.

"Since you're both up and having nothing better to do today, I would like to see you in my office in one hour," he said looking hard at Lori. She immediately turned and walked away. That left no one for Barnes to stare angrily at, but me.

"What were you going to show her?" he asked, knowing full well what the answer was going to be.

"I tell you that you have a chance to change the course of the world, and you decide to show off in front of your girlfriend? I would rather not have your abilities on the front page until we have our plans in motion." He paused and took a breath.

"This room hasn't presently been secured. Do

you know how to activate the electromagnetic field that surrounds this facility and protects you from being seen by some very bad people or maybe even some shadows?" His words belittled me.

"Why do you think Winston is always here before you? He knows how to secure things here. There is a great deal more going on here that you don't know about or see. I suggest you be a little more careful with your powers, son. You may end up showing yourself off to a lot more eyes than just that of Miss Stillwell."

I didn't know what to say. I felt like I had just gotten busted big time. I couldn't even look him in the eye.

We both stood there for a few uneasy moment before he finally spoke.

"You may go," he told me. I wanted to tell him that I was sorry. I also wanted to ask him if I had gotten Lori in trouble. But in the end, I just turned and walked away with my head down. I had just gotten my hand slapped, but it felt more like I got kicked in the head.

"Oh man," I thought to myself, when the thought of Lori being berated crossed my mind. She was going to realize her fate in an hour. I wanted to call her to apologize, tell her how much she meant to me and how much of my time was spent thinking about her, but I didn't do that either. I just went home. I didn't see Lori the rest of the day. I didn't have my phone, so I couldn't call her, and I sure did not want to go and just knock on her door. So I went about my day, hoping to hear from her, but I didn't. I went to the gym and then had lunch in the commons. Then I went to the movies by myself, went for a walk, had dinner at the commons, and then went home. During all of this I passed Lori's window about four times, but I never saw her, nor did I go to her door and knock. I sat and watched the TV until it was bedtime.

My mind was weary, but I found it hard to keep my eyes closed. All night long, I had a hard time sleeping, so I got out of bed and wrote a long letter to my mother and father explaining what I was doing. I, of course, left out the part about being an angel. Ma would not appreciate that or understand it. She was quite religious and would not take well to such talk. During my morning jog, I dropped it at the postal department. I didn't have to put a stamp on it. Everything in this compound was paid for by the company. I jogged by Lori's window, but hers was too high to look into from the street level. I couldn't even tell if she was there. I did about four hundred push-ups and a few hundred sit-ups. I tried to calm myself, but all of my efforts did little good. Finally, though, it was almost meeting time. I got dressed and headed over to the auditorium. I could feel my stomach knotting up. Winston was already there, as usual, and about two minutes after I got there, Barnes showed up. He walked in and tossed me a cell phone.

"Lori told me you lost your phone. I checked and its last known coordinates placed it about a mile and half off the coastline, out on the ocean. Did you know that your phone had a GPS feature? I could see your almost exact location. Were you boating yesterday or show boating? He looked disappointed.

"I am going to say this one more time. I would rather not explain to the world what is going on here because some child caught a picture of you on his cell phone." He locked his finger behind his back and paced around in an oval in front of me.

"Do you remember when you first came here? Do you even remember McVeigh? Do you remember what we talked about?" I nodded and he continued.

"I knew the whole thing with you and Stillwell was a mistake. I should have separated you two the minute you got here." My heart and my stomach dropped a little.

"I've sent her on assignment. Winston here tells me that you can't keep your head into training for an entire session. What's the problem?" He stopped pacing and looked at me.

"Do you want to do this? I mean, you know that you are not being held here against your will. You stand in my office and act like you are ready to help fix the world, and yet here you are dragging your feet. We have deadlines. There are timeframes coming up that we need to be ready for. I'm starting to feel that we may need to go in a different direction here." I started to say something, but he held up his hand.

"Look, I'm not saying you can't see Stillwell, but I need you to keep your head in the game. Can you do that? Can we make this happen?"

"Of course, we can make this happen. You don't understand how appreciative I am for what you've done for me. There have just been a couple of things that I've had on my mind that have been bothering me. First of all, I want to apologize for what happened yesterday. Lori told me that she didn't want to know what I was doing here, but I told her anyway, and look what happened." I paused for a moment, then I continued. It had been important to me for him to know that what happened was my fault, not hers.

"There is something else that has been bothering me that I would like to discuss with the both of you."

Then I proceeded to tell them everything. I told them about being hypnotized, about my discoveries, and all about Chalmers. I held back nothing. Today, I was cleaning out my closet. There would be no more skeletons holding me hostage. I was going to have a clean slate after today.

"I don't understand why you kept this information from me," Barnes finally said.

"I thought we were on the same team."

I thought about Lori and wondered where she went. Was she still in her condo or had she been shipped out of town? I hoped that she was not in any kind of trouble. I had conveniently left the part about knowing her from the shadow world out of this conversation. It wasn't that I was hiding anything I just felt that I might have caused her enough problems and drama.

Besides, it was small peanuts compared to spilling my beans about Chalmers.

"We are on the same team Mr. Barnes. I appreciate all that you've done for me here. I just had my doubt about things. You have to understand that." Barnes smiled at me.

"Of course, I understand." Then he started to pace again.

"So, this Chalmers character thinks that the only way for you to return to your place of glory among the angels is to live a good life and not kill another human being? Is that what he knows or what he thinks?"

I shrugged.

"Do you believe him?" I nodded.

"Well, I can tell you differently right here and right now. If you plan on making a positive change in this world, I'm afraid that some people will be killed. I never saw a way around that. You are going to have to make a choice. You can worry about solving this punishment puzzle that you just told me about, or you can fix things here and now." He stopped pacing and when I did not immediately answer him, he walked right up to me.

"Do you know without a doubt that the solution to your problem is do what this character suggests or is that a guess? Because I am offering you a chance to change the course of this world. I am willing to put my money and power where my mouth is. I would put every cent I have, every resource of this entire company at your disposal." He smiled and then put his arm around my shoulder.

"Even if you do feel like you are needed on some astral plane somewhere, you have to know that you are also needed here. If you truly believe in karma and believe that everything has happened for a reason, then can you question why you were sent to this particular world, a world on the brink? Look around you. We have a chance to change the course of history here and save the people that you love."

"But how?" I asked. I did want to try to fix things here. That had been my dream for a long, long time, but I never imagined I could actually have a say in things. Barnes slid from standing next to me, to standing in front of me holding me by both shoulders. His face was about a foot from mine.

"We can't formulate a plan until you show us what you are truly capable of." He let go of me and took a step backward.

"Today, son, you took a big step. I hope that you got the monkey off your back. I promise you that Stillwell is not in any trouble. I just want her out of your hair for a week or two until we can come up with a formidable plan. Do you not agree with me that her presence has added to your distraction?"

"I agree with you sir," I was so happy to hear that from him, but I still had no clue if she even would want to see me again.

"I promise to try my hardest." I told him this and meant it. It was true that I was no fan of my fellow-man, and there had even been a time when I believed that if I had a chance to save the world, that I wouldn't, that I would let it burn. But now when I was actually presented with the chance, I had to try. I had to at least make the effort.

"Remember son, we aren't just trying to save the world from the shadows here. We have a chance to fix it. We have a chance to change the system. The needs of the many will once again outweigh the needs of the few or the one. The bad guys get punished and the people who work hard will get the chance at the happiness they've earned. We can and will fix it all. You just have to show me the way.

Now, please, let's forget about all of this. Show me what you and Winston have worked on so far."

He stepped over to the door and lead into the training room and held it open for us. I walked in and Winston followed. We went right to work. Winston squared off and pulled his sword from his belt and nodded for me to do the same. I obliged. I just reached to where it should have been without thinking, and there it was. I pulled it out and the blue flame scurried up the long sharp blade. Winston's blade glowed a fiery red. We both dove up into the air. There was no thought about all of the nonsense that got me to this point. I just did it. Perhaps it was my talk with Barnes, or maybe it was his presence alone that inspired me to be able to attack Winston. But I beat him out of the air, and he landed hard in a pile.

"Very nice," Barnes said clapping.

"This is what I like to see. There seems to be no more problems then, eh?" he said with a smile. Then he looked at Winston.

"He seems to have improved. I will see you in my office after this day's training." Then he looked at me.

"I will be in touch. Keep up the good work." Then he turned and left the room, closing the heavy re-enforced door behind him. I walked over and helped Winston to his feet.

"That was a noticeable improvement, one that I was not quite expecting. I'm glad to see that we can now get onto the same page. Now, strike out your power at the large piece of concrete there," he said, brushing himself off.

I thought about what he had done the other day and I imagined myself doing the same. I saw it in my mind's eye, and like he had done, I flicked my sword and thought about what I wanted. A bit of blue light energy jumped from the tip of my sword and shot at the concrete. It impacted on the two-foot-thick rock and bounced off, taking a small piece of its stone surface with it. I did not have the same reaction as Winston had had, but it was a start. My teacher was unimpressed. We worked out for what seemed like hours. And we did the same thing the next day and the next one after that. Each day, I got strong and more focused. Each day I was able to blast harder and deeper into the concrete blocks. Every so often I would arrive at the facility to find new slabs of concrete bolted to the floor. Every so often, they got thicker. Winston accounted for my strength and continued to challenge me. We fought each other over and over. He seemed to know just how much pressure to apply, but it was growing more evident that I was surpassing all of his strengths. The concrete barriers were now about three to five feet thick, and I was able to blast them in half from a distance of fifteen to twenty feet. I was pretty proud of myself, but I still wondered what I might be getting myself into. Each night when I left and went home to my empty condo, I thought about Lori and wondered where she was, how she was doing, what she was doing. I missed her, and if I dwelled on the situation long enough, my heart hurt, and I would slip into my depression. But I would catch myself. I allowed visions from my past lives to flood my mind instead. I thought about the glory I once earned as a champion of light, and I prayed that I would have that feeling again soon. I didn't need the accolades; I just wanted the feeling of glory, of victory and of being in the presence of God again. Those memories built me up and gave me strength.

A week and a half passed by. My training continued to progress. Winston took it upon himself to bring an automatic weapon to class one morning and I spent a good part of the day dodging rubber bullets. I had gotten pretty quick, but he still managed to hit me a few times. Rubber bullets don't kill, but they stung like hell when they hit you.

"Not as fast as you thought you were," he laughed, as he took aim and fired. I had to think he took some bit of joy from hurting me every now and then. I didn't know why I felt that way, I just did. I had a pretty good ability to sense people and something about him rubbed me wrong from day one. He just reinforced that feeling every now and then. I figured that he was just mad because I was such a good-looking, fun, active guy and he was so disgusting. Or maybe it was because I was the golden boy, the chosen one and he was just one of Lucious Barnes's lackeys. Whatever the case might be, I knew that he would never really hurt me because Barnes would have his head. So I had fun with it.

Another few days passed, and the training continued. I moved on from rubber bullets to real ones, and for the occasional nick, I progressed quit well. We worked for eight, ten and even twelve hours a day.

Then one morning, Winston sat me down and told me that he was going to put me into a trance-like state again.

"I did not really feel safe sending you into the

rift, but I think you progressed enough for it to be okay.

There are some things you need and today is as good a day as ever. Relax now, you know the procedure," he told me.

"I want you to bring back your shield and suit of armor. Can you do that?"

I did know the procedure. I nodded, then closed my eyes and breathed in deeply and let it out slowly. He continued to feed me directions as I slipped into the trance. He told me that he would never truly be able to duplicate a battle on this world, like the ones on the other side of the dimensional rift. I needed to fight the monsters, the demons in a true fight to the death. He said that I needed this, and I would bring back with me a new appreciation for what I was presently learning. I thought about all of it and allowed him to proceed. I shook all of the craziness from my head, and he did his thing in no time flat, I drifted off to sleep. I felt the tug of being pulled through the tunnel of color and I allowed it to carry me through the rift. I didn't even look for Chalmers. I just kept my eyes closed and sailed through. I was over all of that now. I was on a mission and the faster I accomplished what was required of me, the faster I would get to see Lori again. I needed a chance to talk to her, to explain myself. I hoped she still wanted to see me. But I would also understand if she didn't. I had fully accepted my responsibility now. I had a duty, just like the days of old. I had given in to it, and as I did, I discovered things I never dreamed possible. I was like a superhero. Not only was I gonna save Lori, and my mom and dad, and Dan and Kimi, I had finally found a way to put my money where my mouth is. I was going to have a say in the restructuring of things. I was going to be able to stop talking and get to doing. Imagined a world where good people felt safe and happy, where rapist were castrated and murders were executed in a public forum, where repeat offenders were sent to the garbage mines of Miramar for a lifetime of hard labor sorting through trash, and where hard-working people actually got ahead of the game. This was my dream, my goal. I left the tunnel of light as I had in the past and was dumped into another war. This time I was well out of the foray, up high in the purple alien sky. A tremendous battle raged on far below. This place seemed strangely familiar. Perhaps I had been here before. I watched the battle and recognized the techniques the angels were using. It was a mode of attack that I had employed a thousand times before. I could see the angels falling upon their prey, all of their shields interlocked into a gigantic bowl of blue energy. It impacted the land like a gigantic battering ram, squashing and killing anything that fell beneath it.

Then the giant bowel broke open into a horde of four hundred angels. They flew out of the pile and hacked and cleaved everything in sight. It was magnificent. The blue energy and path of destruction spread out like a spoke on a wheel. I was so enthralled that I could not look away. Then something very odd happened. I felt that something wasn't quite right. This strategy was wrong for this particular battle.

I had to stop them, to warn them that they were all in danger. I angled my wings and descended toward the fracas, but it was too late. Explosions erupted from all around, and small projectiles shot up into the air encircling the entire scene. Each of the little missiles carried gigantic nets. They covered at least half an acre apiece. Two of the corners were attached to the ground, and the other two were attached to small rockets that shot them out and over a good many of the angels on or near the ground. The nets came down hard and fast, and what followed gave little time for escape. Explosions erupted all around, then there were three distinct sounds that made my ears ring: boom, boom, boom. They were followed shortly by a wave of hot air that almost knocked me from the sky. I saw three mushroom clouds climb up from the ground, and I wondered how many angels had been blown into bits and dust that made up those clouds. My heart sank. I looked to see if anything were left alive, praying for survivors, but before the smoke cleared the lizard inhabitants of this world were upon them. They hurled rocks and spears into the air. Most of my comrades had been extinguished in the atomic blast, and those that remained were being attacked before the dust settled. I looked to see if there was someone, anyone alive that I might be able to save, but the beasts moved through the fields of carnage very quickly.

They were just pouncing, clawing and slicing and biting into anything that moved. There were thousands, no hundreds of thousands of them. Some stood on two feet, while others moved on all fours.

They ranged in color from red to blue, green and purple and looked shiny, slippery. Their size ranged from around four feet to eight or nine feet in length or height. Some tore at the flesh with their teeth, while others used knives and swords, sharpened bone. Each of them was vicious in its own way, gnashing their teeth, growling, and screeching as they ran through the dust cloud. They left nothing alive as they scurried out into the huge blast zone and bit and hacked into what was left of my fallen comrades. I could have flown down and cleaved out a thousand of them, but I felt it more important to try to salvage than to seek my vengeance. I had to stay high enough to be out of their reach, but low enough to look at as many faces as I could. I had no time to land next to each body and check for vital signs, so I had to look for something, anything that would let me know that a spark of life still existed in any of the bodies. The creatures below me were horrific and I wanted to kill them all, but I couldn't stop, not yet. I flew hard and fast. I was desperate to find someone alive. Then I heard a voice. It was faint but echoed in my head. I listened for it again. My heart was pounding out of my chest. I had to get to the source of the voice before the monsters did. Rocks and spears and giant wooden stakes shot past and around me. Dust filled the sky and burned my eyes and my throat. I was looking, searching. There were so many bodies. Then I saw him. He was the only one that I had even seen move. One angel among thousands were still alive. I swooped down and kneeled next to him. I wanted to scroop him up and get him out of there. But he didn't give me the chance. He grabbed me by the armor that surrounded my neck and pulled me in close. Then he whispered to me through his blood-covered lips.

"Joseph, why have you forsaken us?" His eyes opened wide, and he looked to be in an incredible amount of pain. His body tensed up and he gurgled. Blood started to pour out from his mouth, then he went limp, and he died. My head and my heart filled with a mixture of sadness and hatred, and a strong feeling of déjà vu. I had been there, in this scene, before.

"Why have you forsaken us?" I had heard those word before. They echoed in my head. I knew that I knew who this person was. I had seen his face before, on several occasions. He was a warrior, a good one at that. He was one of mine, one of the soldiers, my people. My heart sank when he went limp and expired. I felt the last of his life leave him, and then he just faded away into nothingness in my arms. I knew the monsters were nearly upon me, but I could not look away until he was completely gone. Even then, it took me a couple of seconds for me to move. But when I did, I was possessed. I was going to kill them all. I lowered my face shield of my helmet and drew my sword. I held my shield part way up my forearm so that I still had use of my hand behind it. The blood-rage filled me, poisoned me, blinded me, and I sent a wave of blue energy toward the first wave of the lizard men that approached me, but the blue pulse of radiant energy never made contact with the monsters; instead, it nearly destroyed the practice facility. Winston had pulled me through the vortex just in time to see the light leap out of my sword and completely disintegrate each and every concrete block in the room and almost blast right through the exterior wall of the chamber.

"Stop! Stop!" Winston yelled.

"You'll bring the roof down upon us." I was breathing heavy, my heart pounding. I wanted to kill them all.

"Send me back," I demanded.

"Do you hear me demon? Send me back!" I was furious. Spit came out of my mouth as I spoke.

"Winston, do it or I'll cleave you in half. I swear" I grabbed him by the collar and picked him off the ground.

"I can't. There's no way for me to send you right back to that particular place and time. You did that. You picked that place, and you wouldn't be able to find it again in this state of mind. It would be like finding a needle in a haystack. You could end up in a shadow world again or worse."

"Try," I demanded.

"I couldn't even get you to relax if I wanted to. There's no way to do it. I'm sorry." He was pleading, but I did not want to give it up yet. Then Barnes ran into the room.

"I take it you were successful, "he said as he came in rubbing his hands together. I don't think he was expecting to see Winston dangling in the air.

"Whatever he did, I will take full responsibility for. Please, let him down."

I gritted my teeth and snarled at him, then I just let go. He fell pretty hard onto his butt. He stood there for a minute staring at me. His mouth was hanging open a bit.

"Um, would someone like to tell me why my office just shook so hard, every book that was on my shelves is now on the floor."

"I want you to make him send my back," I demanded.

"Now!" I was seething. Barnes looked at Winston who shook his head slightly. He had the look of fear upon his face. Then the old man smiled a forced smile at me.

"I don't think he can send you back. I don't think you realize where back is. That world that you just visited is something from a different dimension, from a different time, could be the past, could be the future. We don't have a clue. It would be like finding a needle in the haystack, but instead of a stack of hay, you are dealing with a field that stretches on throughout eternity." Then he walked up a little closer.

"What got you so worked up anyway? I thought this was going to be some sort of recon day. You were supposed to get supplies." He looked me over, up and down.

"I see that you got them."

I don't think he was ready to really see me in such a manor. My aura was so bright, it caused him to have to shield his eyes. I was fully clad in my shiny silver and gold armor, and I held a beautiful semi oval shield. It was magnificent and so was I. I could have destroyed the entire compound with a wave of my sword.

"This is what you wanted, is it not Lucious Barnes?" I asked with a condescending tone.

"What would you have me do? What country would you like me to destroy today?" I followed in a joking, but kinda scary serious manner.

"Very good," Barnes quipped back.

"I like your attitude, but I don't want you destroying any countries...not just yet, anyway." He folded his fingers behind his back and started to walk in a big circle around me.

"It puzzles me that you would get this wound up over a dream, a figment of your own imagination, but you can't do it at the thought of your friends and family being devoured by shadows. Do you see what

I am saying here? Why do it take this mind trickery to get you into this state?" He continued to walk and talk.

"Take a couple of deep breaths and calm down. Do you understand? That place you were in is gone. You are back with us, and you have accomplished what you set out to do today." I understood him, and I slowed myself down. I had temporarily lost my mind, but I had accomplished my mission as well. My breathing slowed, and I slowly let down my guard. Even my aura seemed to dim until it was barely visible. When I finally calmed down, it was gone. So was the armor. I stood there for a moment, then I also had to pace around a bit.

"That was crazy. I was in control, yet not in control, if you can understand that" I told the two of them.

"I saw what was happening, but just didn't know how to stop." Barnes stopped pacing and watched me walk around.

"That is what we were looking for. I didn't expect it to be quite so intense but that should only help matters, right?" He looked me over good.

"Walk with me please," he said, offering me his open hand. He slid the hand across my shoulders and guided me toward the far end of the room. He motioned for Winston to join us.

"This is incredible," he said as we neared the place where one of the slabs of concrete used to be. It had been completely obliterated.

"Look here," he said pointing to a crack in the exterior wall of the building.

"I can't believe this," he commented, sticking his finger into the long fissure. He quickly pulled it back out when he realized how hot it was. The edges of the long slice in the wall were still smoldering a bit.

We walked together to the end of the long room. Everything had been destroyed. Nothing was left intact. The rubble from all of the concrete targets lies here in a huge pile of dust and some small rocks.

Some of it was embedded into the far wall, which itself was near cracked loose of the foundation.

"Wow," Barnes said.

"Well, we won't be able to train here anymore." He turned and looked at the entire room, which was now quite unstable.

"I think it's time to start talking strategy. What do we do with all of this power?" I didn't think he was really asking, so I didn't say anything. I expected that he had some kind of plan in mind. He had to be preparing for this since the day he found me and brought me here.

"This is most impressive." He touched a piece of the rebar that was protruding from the wall. He smiled at me.

"You two get cleaned up and meet me at the office in an hour. Let's see what we can come up with, shall we?" he asked with a big smile.

THIRTEEN

One hour later, the three of us were standing in front of a large map of the world. It was presented to us on the screen of the largest television, I had ever seen. I stood next to Winston. It was funny to see him in a suit. He still smelled like crap, but I got a secret laugh knowing how bad he had to be jonesing for a cigarette right about now.

"We have facilities here, here and here," he said, pointing at various points of the map. Two were in Europe and one was in India.

"Now that you two have thoroughly destroyed our training room here, we will have to find a new site. I would like to suggest of course of action for you." I knew that Winston would just follow whatever idea Barnes presented, so basically, he was suggesting a target for me. He put a red dot on the enormous flat panel on the Middle East. I somehow expected that from our prior conversation. The board's image zoomed in on the laser spot to show a close-up view of that region, especially Iran.

"Why would we attack Iran?" I asked. I assumed, hoped this wasn't a side conversation.

"That's a good question. I would rather that we simply cave in the ceiling of the Capital Building in Washington DC with the President and all of Congress inside. We kill off the standing leadership and inject our own. That would be an ideal scenario, but it might not garnish the type of response that we would want. Don't think I haven't turned that over inside my head a few million times, but the timing isn't right. The reason I chose this particular target," he said while motioning toward the map behind him, "is because they are dangerously close to being able to pose a nuclear threat to the rest of the world. Add to that their constant instability and the fact that we are already in a war there, and to me, it makes the perfect target." I did not like the sound of that.

As long as I could remember, it seemed the Middle East was involved in some sort of turmoil. I always felt that if a couple of those countries teamed up, if one of them acquired nuclear weaponry, that they could become quite a problem.

"We can't fix this country with a few dozen nuclear missiles pointed at us, waiting for us to mess up if we give them a chance." He interlaced his fingers behind his back and paced in front of the big screen.

"I would suggest we remove some strategic threats first, then we clean up our own mess." He put the red dot of the laser pointer back on Iran.

"I have located the hidden base right here that is

testing and building a nuclear weapon. It is located three quarters of a mile under the sands right here." The map zoomed in again. It pretty much looked like a barren desert.

"See how it is located midway between this city and these oil fields? This provides cover for easy access without much notice. Employees buses travel this road all day, every day. Two hundred people at various hours of the day depart from this bus, enter this small building here, and are sent via this elevator down into the facility." Each thing he spoke about was illustrated on the screen. A cartoon type of character exited the bus, then entered the elevator and went down into the enormous area below the sand.

"This is an incredible achievement of technology. This is their experiment nuclear reactor," he said, and again the video of the display moved in close to display the reactor. It looked very complex. Then the display moved to show a large water supply and the pipes that brought the water in from the Persian Gulf.

"These pipes bring in sea water from the Gulf into this plant, where water is distributed between this holding facility and this area that cools the nuclear reactor." Each point was illustrated on the board, which I now recognize must have taken a great deal of effort to create. It further confirmed my thoughts that he was not asking me for my input of this target, instead he was telling me what we were going to do.

"This side of the facility provides all of the power that is needed to run this base and to complete their projects." The displayed moved from the illustration of the water holding areas over to a collection of pipes and machinery that seemed to run deep into the earth.

"It's a geothermal energy plant. It creates both heat, electricity, and warm water, all made possible by this tunnel that runs everything down next to the swirling layer of hot magma." Again, the image zoomed in.

"I suggest that you pierce this layer of the earth's crust. Molten hot magma would pour up through the tunnel, flooding the entire base with a liquid rock, destroying and killing everything and everyone." The video showed a small explosion in the tunnel and the lava coning up and filling the entire complex.

"My proposal is that you fly though the mountains, across the desert at a low altitude as to avoid detection, then loop up and then blast your way through the sand into the facility. Most of the hard rock had already been cut out and removed by the Arabians and their Chinese and Russian comrades. You should have time to recover once inside the base, then you can fly down the tunnel and blast a hole through the crust. You should have enough time to get back up into the facility and either blast your way out to the surface or simply fly through the elevator shaft." He seemed pretty pleased with himself.

"Behind you the molten rock would swallow the scientists, their facility and all of the data they have collected." He smiled.

"And since they have no idea that you even exist, it will all be labeled a cataclysmic accident. What other explanation could they come up with? No stealthy weapon like you exists in any country's arsenal."

It seemed like a logical idea. But just like everything else in my life as of late, it just didn't seem real. Lava and secrete hidden bases; it just didn't seem like it could be happening in real life. The illustrations were well made. I saw the display again in my mind's eye. Was this really what I had been training for? Was this my destiny?

"What do you think?" Barnes asked me. I could see that he was pretty proud of his plan, but I knew that it all hinged on me.

"You really expect me to flood our enemy's secret base with lava? It even sounds funny, just coming out of my mouth," I told him with a smile. I could see that he was not happy.

"This is not a joking matter. These people are plotting our country's destruction. They are on the brink of becoming a nuclear power and you find time to jest about it?"

I loved it. The ball was completely in my court. I was no fool. I understood the seriousness of the situation, I did, but for the first time in a very, very long time, I was in command. I ran through the scenario in my mind again, then I looked right at Barnes.

"Did you know that when I lost my phone, I lost all of my phone numbers? I know my parent's number and two other friends by heart, but I haven't been able to talk to any of my friends including Lori in well over a week. I put so much of my energy and mind into this, that I didn't care about anything else. But today, I would like to talk to Lori. I would like to see what she would think of all of this." Barnes looked like I just slapped him.

"That's not possible. She is on assignment, but here is her number. I'm sorry, I didn't know that you no longer had it. Here," he said as he walked to his desk and wrote the digits on a sheet of paper and handed it to me.

"Feel free to call her, but don't be too surprised if she doesn't return your message for up to a week or so."

"Where is she?" I asked, probably sounding a bit pissy.

"I told you, she is on assignment," Barnes chided.

"Now can you keep your head in the game long enough to work up a plan or are we going to fall back into the mindset you had before you had these breakthroughs?"

"My head is right here, sir. This just seems so strange and over the top to me. It doesn't seem possible. A month or so ago, I was installing stereo systems in San Diego, now I'm being tapped to destroy an Iranian nuclear missile base? It just seems stranger than fiction, if you know what I mean."

Barnes smiled at me, then walked over and put his arm on my shoulder. This was the third or fourth time that he did that, and it was widely publicized fact that he did not like to be touched. It was one

thing that people seemed to ask about at least every third time he was interviewed. I've never been much of a fan of being touched either, so this seemed extra awkward to me.

"Son, you were destined for this long before you were born. You've struggled through your past lives, never seeming to get ahead. Well, this is your big chance to fix all of that. If we end the nuclear threat that Iran poses, we would be able to bring a bunch of our troops home from the Middle East. We would be able to relax our military presence all over the area. You would be protecting all of the people in this country as well as all of those in Europe. I know you've never been a very big fan of people in general, but this is the best way for us to wrestle control of the world away from the lunatics that have run things for years. Once the mission is complete in Iran, then you can come home and take care of business here." He finished by given me a big squeeze and big smile. Then he let go of me and walked back toward the big display. I looked at the image on the big screen. It had stopped with the magma flowing in and through the facility. I wondered how many people might be there when I caused the plants'destruction. I had long since given up the idea that Chalmers would return to me to help me figure out what to do. I would have loved to hear his take on all of this. I also had to wonder if I truly even had a choice in the matter. I wasn't a prisoner, but I doubt I would be permitted to simply walk away from all of this. I imagined I would be hunted to the far corners of the planet if I told him no and just left his employment. I had worked so hard to bring my powers to their full potential, that I would never be able to hide them away. I also now had to worry about my friends, my parents and Lori.

I could disappear. It wouldn't be the first time I'd done so, but these people would still be easy targets to use against me. In the end, I almost had to agree with Barnes's proposal. And in a sense, he kind of had me.

"I guess it sounds like a reasonable plan," I said almost sheepishly. That was all Barnes needed to hear to start the congratulations. He grabbed my hand and shook it hard, then he went and did the same with Winston. He was so happy.

"Tonight, we celebrate," he started, "and tomorrow we save the world." He went over and touched a control on his desk and a beautiful woman brought in a nice cask of Amontillado. He cracked it open and poured three glasses. We clinked the glasses together and swallowed the wonderful elixir. It was quite smooth, and I could feel it warming my cold stomach.

"Tomorrow?" I thought half out loud. He was giving me no time to think about things or to change my mind. He had his inch and he was going to take a mile. I handed him the empty glass and he poured another round. His smile was so big, it was almost frightening. We drank the entire cask before I retired.

My head was spinning and at one point when I looked at Barnes, he looked like the Devil laughing at me.

My mind was numb, which was what I needed right now. I needed to feel nothing. Finally, I set my glass down and headed for home. I had barely gotten myself inside the door before I hit the cushions on the couch hard. I was done in.

The next thing I knew I was on the Critterware private jet headed to Barnes's secret training ground in India. It happened that fast. I had tried to call Lori on my way to the airfield to say hi and tell her where I was and what I was doing, but I got her voicemail. I had so hoped to hear from her before I left, but it didn't happen. The ride was extremely cushy and relaxing from the stretch limo to the extravagant private jet. It was the same jet that had brought me to the compound so many weeks prior. I slept through most of the journey. We stopped once to refuel and then in no time we landed in Bombay, India. I really never got to step foot in the city or anything. I went from the plane to the helicopter, which was a totally awesome experience. I had never ridden in a helicopter before, so I was stoked. I had left the crazy, nervous feeling behind somewhere over the Atlantic and now concentrated heavy on the task at hand. The helicopter landed in the middle of the compound, which was set up very similarly, to the one we had left behind in the United States. The difference with this place was that when the car dropped me off at my house, it was a house, not a condo. I had a little duffle bag packed that I carried with me. The whole way, everyone wanted to take my bag for me. I must have told twenty people, "No, I've got it" Everyone knew that I was working directly with Lucious Barnes, so they all wanted to help. I, however, was just looking for one person, and that person was Lori. I had been in the air for at least a full day. I hadn't kept track of the time, but instead marked the time by how many movies I watched.

They have movies that were just arriving in the theaters as well as a good-sized Nautilus machine to work out on, but none of that mattered as much as a phone call from Lori would have. I checked my phone thirty times during the flight and never heard back from her. It was a bit frustrating, but there was really nothing I could do. I wasn't the kind of guy to leave fourteen messages from someone. I was under the impression that one message was always enough. If someone was going to call you back, that was all you really needed. Needless to say, I never received a return call.

I was finally at the front door of my single level home. It was situated relatively close to the edge of the Arabian Sea. I opened the front door and was completely surprised at what I saw. Lori was fluffing a pillow and placed it back onto the couch, but when she saw me, she ran over and jumped into my arms.

"Surprise," she told me and gave me a big kiss. She hugged me tightly and I kissed her back. I didn't want to stop or let go, but eventually I had to ask her why she never called me back.

"Lucious ordered me not to call you. He didn't want me to interfere with any decisions that you had to make. He wanted it to be your choice and your choice alone." I opened my mouth to say something.

"He also told me to run away from you if you started to run your mouth about your upcoming mission.

He also said that if I interfere with anything that I would lose more than just my job." She finished the statement with a smile. I didn't like that last statement, but I didn't let it bother me. I was just happy to see her and hold her.

"So you aren't mad at me?" I asked.

"Why would I be mad? If you weren't who you are, we would have never met. Besides, there is something I need to talk to you about." She stepped back and smiled.

"Do I look any different?" she asked striking a pose. She looked so pretty. I was so relieved. I had worked so hard to push her out of my mind that I had forgotten how much I loved her. I looked her over and did not know what to say. I was just happy to see her that I just stood there looking at her.

"I'm pregnant," she blurted out, with a big bright smile.

"You're going to be a father," she told me.

Wow I wasn't expecting that, I thought.

"I didn't even think that was possible." I told her. Had Chalmers told me that or had I just assumed it? I forced a quick smile, but it quickly changed into a real smile. I rolled the idea around in my head a turn or two.

"How long?" I asked as I stepped up and gave her a big hug.

"I only just took the test a few minutes ago," she told me.

"But I checked, and double checked and the tripled checked. They all say positive"

"We should make an appointment with the doctor then." I couldn't believe it. So much was happening and now this.

"Have you told Mr. Barnes? He gave me a rash of crap about you."

"But it got your head in the game," she cut in.

"Look, I don't' like what happened any more than you do, but he tells me that the end justified the means. I wanted to talk to you so badly, but I couldn't. My presence was interfering with your training but we're together now. I can tell you that I was completely freaked by what you had to say. When I asked Mr. B about it, he explained the whole 'caught between two dimensions' thing. He told me that what I saw, what I fell in love with was human, but that you had the ability to reach into different place and pull strength and power from it.

That all sounds crazy." She looked at me and smiled.

"He wasn't too happy that you told me all of that, but he got over it quick enough when you started producing results." Then her smile got bigger and brighter.

"He said I was to big of a distraction because you couldn't stop thinking about me. That's when he sent me here to get things ready. What do you think?" she asked showing off her work. The place seemed very homey.

"I like it," I told her with a smile. The house was decorated with an eclectic mix of American and Indian culture. There were big pillows everywhere, a nice big couch, beads dangling from the doorways and windows, color, and flare on most of the walls, a big picture of Ganesha, the elephant God, some ceramic camels here and there. Lori opened a small cabinet and pulled out a tall hookah with several long flexible tubes coming out of the top of it.

"This is your special treat," she told me.

"I can't smoke anything with you anymore," she said with a smile, and motioned toward her stomach.

"But here is some really good stuff that I had one of the locals get for me. It is very illegal here, so don't take it off the grounds and don't let anyone know where you got it." Again, she smiled. I so loved seeing her smile. To be honest, I was a bit overwhelmed. I didn't know what to say. What a treat!

"I'm gonna try to slow down a bit too then," I told her. I didn't want to play around and smoke in front of her when she was trying to be good because she was pregnant. She wasn't that big of a smoker anyway. I joked that she was a lightweight and couldn't hold her smoke, especially when we had some really good stuff, and she was able to relax and just let me take care of her. Those were our best, and my favorite nights.

"No, no," she told me.

"You just continue whatever you were doing. I don't want Mr. B getting pissy and asking a bunch of questions or sending me away again."

"You're so good to me," I told her with a smile and a big hug. I was excited to see her I could barely contain myself. She showed me around the house. It was really nice, top of the line. There seemed to be beautiful colored rugs, tapestries and pillows everywhere. It was quite a surprise considering the slums that surrounded us. There were three full, operational bathrooms, and the hallways seemed to stretch on forever. We finally got to the bedroom. The bed was huge, covered with little pillows and a very brightly colored silk comforter. I slipped up behind Lori as she was showing me the fine, intricate woodwork of the nightstand and threw her onto the bed. Then I practically dove on top of her, being careful not to jostle her too much. I loved the feeling of her soft warm flesh in my hands, against my lips.

We kissed and played for what felt like hours and this was only the foreplay.

We were about to get busy when I heard a noise coming from the other room. My new, fancy phone was ringing. Talk about ruining the moment. I looked at the caller ID and saw that it was Winston, so I answered. I had to. He wanted me in the training facility within the hour. I told him that I would be there and then I hung up.

"Ugh," I said out loud. "I should have just let it ring." I turned to my love and kissed her again. It was going to be hard to pull myself away from her, but duty was calling.

"What's up with Winston anyway,"

"He's about as creepy as they come, and what's up with that awful smell?" She laughed so hard she snorted a little.

"I don't' know, but every time I see him, it reminds me why I quit smoking so many years ago."

"What about that body odor?" I asked with a sour puss on my face. She looked at me.

"What do you mean?"

"You don't smell the stank he has pouring off of him?" I asked.

"No. All I smell; all I think about when I see him is an ashtray full of cigarette butts. I saw an invoice once.

It was for a whole crate of cigarettes for him.

Barnes called it a bonus. I couldn't believe it." Then she looked at me.

"What do you smell?"

"He smells like he just swallowed a pile of crap, and when he jumps around, it gets worse."

"Wait," she interrupted, "Jumps around? That old stick of a man actually jumps around. That's hilarious.

I would love to see that, she said with a big smile.

"It is comical," I told her half laughing, then I grabbed her up in my arms and kissed her. I carried her over to the bed and we made out until it was time for me to head over to the new training facility.

They had told me that this was a new facility, but it looked old and ugly to me, nothing special. Then I walked inside and saw that the old building had been retrofitted with the new technology. The foyer looked like a space age command station. There were several people working on computers and flat screens on every wall. I walked toward the double doors that I thought would open to a secured room, but found out that it was instead, an elevator that took me down deep into the earth. We went down, down, down. When the doors finally opened, I saw another set of giant steel doors. Winston was standing in front of the control panel that opened them. He was standing right under a no smoking sign, smoking a cigarette.

"Welcome, my young apprentice," he hissed.

"Today we will practice your entry into the base.

This area is sealed off from the rest of the world just like the one back in the States." The doors slid open to reveal a very big room with a ceiling that was at least seven or eight stories high. The floor was covered in sand with big square concrete blocks scattered throughout the place. There were big steel hoops attached to the concrete and metal walls every here and there.

"I want you to fly through those hoops there, then come down hard toward the ground. Let's see how far down into the sand you can go. You may use your sword and strike out with your energy, or you can try to use your shield to blast a path in front of you. Your choice, but I would like you to try both methods. Try to fly up through the rings, then down through the open air."

It all seemed simple enough.

I took a deep breath and unfurled my wings. I closed my eyes, clenched my fists and thought hard about my armor, shield, and sword. Suddenly I was clad in my shiny suit and armed to the teeth.

"Well, that seemed easy enough. Good job," Winston told me. I didn't want to tell him that I now had something to fight for. I couldn't tell him that I was about to have a family. I had so much to worry about and to fight for now, the trances and the hypnosis would no longer be needed. I had fully given in to the concept of this game plan. I was going to destroy one of our most dangerous adversaries and secure my family's future. I would end this threat of terror quickly and abruptly. For all of their posturing and threats of nuclear proliferation, they would pay. I had trained my brain for a whole life to understand and realize that I wasn't the judge, jury and executioner, but now I was going back on that training. I had accepted my role whole-heartedly and I was going to cast my judgement, my retribution on this land and I was going to do it just the way Barnes described. I bent my knees slightly and then jumped up. I flew up into the air without much effort, up and out into the big room. I zipped around, then down and back up through the big, shiny hoops. I drew my sword, and the blue flame covered the blade as I came

up to the apex of my loop and started down straight, hard and fast. Then I drew in a deep breath and commanded the blue energy to leap from the tip of my sword, down into the dry sand below. I cleaved a pretty good hole, turning the surrounding sand to molten glass. I easily made the three-quarter mile depth that Barnes had mentioned, but when I hit the concrete floor of the facility, I stopped, turned, and back up to the surface. I popped back out into the room and flew high above the giant hole I had just carved into the sand, which was now rimmed with shiny glass. I had no problem with it at all. When Barnes first brought up the idea of flying down through the sand, I had a vision of it getting everywhere, in my eyes, my mouth, but that didn't happen. If I wanted to, I could fly right back down through the glass tunnels that I made without ever touching sand around them again.

"I hit the floor of the facility," I told Winston with a smile.

"No, you hit the concrete barrier I had placed at the bottom of the sand. But that's okay. You did a marvelous job so far today. I was a little worried when Mr. Barnes told me he was re-introducing the women into your life. I was a bit nervous that you would have not have your head on straight today."

"I think he wanted to give me something to fight for," I told him with a wink. I hovered in the air just in front and above him. I didn't even have to focus on the wings' they just flapped slowly behind me on their own. I was becoming a master of my talents.

"Please come with me to the control room. I want to show you something," Winston said as he turned and walked into a small door next to the big ones through which he entered. He pulled up a display on the computer monitor. It was a slide angle view of the chamber. On the screen there was a rectangular box filled halfway to the top of the sand, at the bottom was a concrete box. The walls looked very thick.

Winston tapped the keypad and the image changed to a video of me blasting through the sand right down to the top of the concrete box. It was cool to see things from this angle.

"See how you sliced right through the top layer of sand? How far ahead of yourself could you see?

He asked. He was pointing at the difference between me and the point way below me where the sand was being blasted out of my way, on the view screen. I hadn't really thought about that. I had to think.

"Wow, you know what? I'm not sure. It was as if I could feel the change in density ahead of me. Like I could feel the difference between the sand and the concrete in my mind. I knew it was coming and I backed off."

"That's because the energy you exude is a part of you. It comes from you and is like an extension of you.

How do you feel? Are you tired?"

"Not at all," I told him. I felt great, ready to take on the world. He changed the screen from the bottom of the room, to the top.

"You see how the hoops are different distances away from the wall. They are attached in a manner to provide the perfect pitch and angle of your loop. The bottom one here," he pointed at one of the hoops on the display, "is much further away from the wall than, say one of the middle ones here. Do you see the angle?"

I nodded and even though I did see the angle, he still moved the pointer to show the proper way for my ascent and then descent.

"In front of each set of hoops there is a concrete bunker buried below three quarters of a mile of sand.

You fly up and through, then down, just like you

did a couple of minutes ago. Pause when you reach the bunker, then try to fly back up through the same hole. This would be a time trail for the best-case scenario. Then we will try one where you have to create a new tunnel to escape through the base of this structure."

The rings through which I was to fly through were metallic, round and attached to the walls all over the place. The order that he wanted me to fly through each made sense. It was a practice run for my mission. I would use the same angles to both avoid detection and to give me an optimum flight path. If I were going to do this and do it right, I would have to follow the model laid out for me here. It would keep me under the radar until it was too late, and even then, I would only appear on anyone's sensors and monitors for the briefest of moments. This way there would be no evidence of my existence until it became necessary. The hoops were about ten feet in diameter and made of a bright, shiny metal. They reflected the lights, which covered the ceiling of the great room as well as the blue haze of my aura when I got close to each of them. In order to properly glide through them, I had to try to pass through each one of my wings on a downward stroke. This way they would be angled the best to deflect any impact on the rings and I would be able to glide through unmolested. It wasn't as easy as it looked. I had to avoid both the hoops and the walls and keep my speed up enough to glide through the next one. It was tricky, but I understood why I had to practice this way. We practiced several times, then without warning, Winston came at me with his sword. I quickly deflected his advancements but did not attack.

We swung at each other for five minutes. He was lunging and slashing at me. Then, he just stopped and stepped back and pointed at the set of hoops.

"Go!" he shouted and hit the button on his timer. He had been trying to get me distracted or tired, but I would show him. I flew through the course, blasted into the bunker and got back up to the surface in record time.

"Anything else?" I asked, puffing out my chest. Winston just looked at me and then lit a cigarette.

"Well?" I asked.

"Well, what? I think you are ready. What more do you think we need to do? Do you want to wreck this facility too?"

"Hey Winston, what happens when the lava hits the nuclear reactor? Wouldn't it act like a nuclear bomb? What kind of damage would that do?" Winston looked at me through the smoke.

"Their reactor isn't working. They lack the proper Uranium. Neither China nor Russia has actually fueled the plant as of yet. That's why Mr. Barnes was in such a big hurry to get you trained and ready. We wanted you to attack before their station was fully operational."

For some reason, I just didn't completely believe him; nonetheless our lessons were over for the day.

We got back into the elevator and returned to the surface.

The sun was sliding down out of the sky as I walked down toward my new temporary home. I had taken a picture of Lori with my new cell phone before I left earlier in the day and flipped it open to look at her as I walked. I just couldn't believe there was a possibility of her being pregnant. I wondered if she made

an appointment with the doctor. I also wondered if she told Barnes yet. Just the concept of me being a father, with all of this stuff going on was truly quite an odd one. I never really planned on being a parent and figured that since I wasn't like the normal human male that I wouldn't be able to conceive a child. I did love Lori and I would marry her if she would have me. We already had enough adventures in at least one previous life that I could remember, so I didn't feel like we would be missing out on the fun times a young couple in love would want to experience before we got locked down with children. She seemed pretty happy when she told me the news that I just went along with it. None of the people that I hung out with for the past few years in San Diego had any children. That place seemed more of an adult playground, there were a couple of girls that I knew that were just dying to have kids. I never understood how the desire to have a baby could block a woman from seeing a man's true nature, that only after the child was born did, they find that they were incompatible.

As it stood, when you get to my age, it seemed, there were few single women that didn't have kids. I dated a few of them, but nothing that lasted more than a few months. I was never that big a fan of chasing after someone else's kids or dealing with the ex-baby daddies. It was a lot to think about, but I didn't let it distract me from my mission. That was my primary objective right now. I would be leaving in the next day or so and go from being a once humble, mild-mannered human being to a force that could and would change the course of history. It was a deep concept to consider, one that I was slowly, but surely coming to grips with. I got home and Lori and I went for a walk and talked about the whole pregnancy thing, then we talked about how our child would truly have the best of everything.

"When you told me all of that stuff the other week, I was really scared," she told me.

"I didn't know what to think. I even cried in front of Mr. B. I seriously thought he was going to fire me.

He wanted me to take some time and go visit my parents back home, but I couldn't do that. That would just me more depressed, so he asked me to come here and get this place set up." She stopped walking and looked at me.

"I saw the training facility here," she said, as if she had just dropped some kind of bomb.

"I also tapped into some of Lucious' personal files and saw what you did to the facility back in the US.

Are you going to be cool with all of this? Are we going to be able to live normal life? What if someone steals your parking spot at the mall on one of those famously bad days? Will you be able to keep from turning him into dust?" She took a breath, and before I could answer any of her questions, she continued.

"When you first told me about all of this stuff, I thought you had gone mad. I thought, what have I gotten myself into? But then I verified everything you said, and I almost passed out. I also watched a couple of your training videos on the restricted company website." She paused again.

"I saw you fly." She just looked at me.

"Do you know how freaked out I was? Or how about when I saw you blast the giant concrete blocks with some kind of invisible energy? She looked down at her stomach.

"What do you think this is going to do to our baby?" She finally gave me a chance to answer.

"I don't know what will happen or how much this will affect our baby." What a weird thing to have come out of my mouth. 'Our baby', I thought, 'my baby'. It was so strange. I just never saw myself in the fatherly role. I couldn't imagine it. She was right to wonder about things. I didn't have the answers. I couldn't tell her what I would do if someone got cocky with me. I knew that if someone messed with my family or friends, that I would send them to hell in a bucket. But now with all of these powers unlocking themselves, I would have to be extra careful. I always had been a bit of a hothead. I wondered if I would be able to keep my head about me or if the beast would now be completely out of control. All of the experiments and whatnot were preparing me for a mission. But when happens after the mission? What if someone bumped into me when I was in a pissy mood? I had tried to humble myself and hide myself away my whole life. I prided myself on being able to blend in, to hide in plain sight. Now I was about to destroy an Iranian testing facility. I was about to open a hole in the crust of the planet. How would I be able to contain all of this craziness when the deed was done? How could I not walk around like a God among peasants? There were so many questions.

"I don't know," was all that would come out of my mouth though. We strolled around the compound, stopped and got something to eat, and then went home to relax. It was strange to be in such opulence when surrounding area was filled with poverty, violence, and strife. We were not in a city, but on the outskirts of one. We flew over it in the helicopter and I could not help but notice the slums below, the tightly packed houses and huts. It was sad. And it made me think about the mission on a lighter note.

This was step-one in fixing all of this. When the deed was done, it would put a ball into motion that would repair the damage that the wars, greed, and apathy had done to our world and to our people.

I had noticed a rather large whirlpool tub in the master bathroom of our place. As decadent as it seemed right now, I had decided it was time to use it. My body was not tired, but my mind was. I just wanted to lie in there with her against me and forget about the world, the mission, everything. I ran some warm, almost hot, water into the tub and got in. Lori put her hair up and climbed in. I laid against the cool, sloped back. My wings passed through the porcelain tub and the enclosure as if they weren't there. Lori laid with her back against me. I put some soap in my hands and washed her shoulders. I loved the way she felt. Her body seemed so perfect for me, as if she had been preordained to fit the exact specifications I would have asked for. Or perhaps, I had just pulled those desired measurements and features from a past life with her. I was almost maddening to try to think about such things. It was like looking up at the stars and trying to imagine how far infinity they reached. Understanding that the stars I looked at where a lifetime of travel away, yet the shear depth of space continued on forever. What we saw in the night sky was just the tip of a never-ending iceberg. It was like this when I thought about how many lives I had lived in this dimension as well as the other. I kissed the back of her neck and played with her hair.

"I have some things I need to talk to you about," I told her softly.

"There are some things I would like to get your

input in. Do you remember when I told you about Chalmers? How he said he was going to be able to guide me?"

"How could I forget?" she replied without moving. She had her eyes closed.

"When you told me that, I seriously thought you were insane. I thought, I'm in love with a lunatic." She giggled.

"Has he given you any pearls of wisdom lately?"

"No, nothing lately. That's what's troubled me. It doesn't make sense to me that he would say what he did and act the way he had, and then just disappear, never to be seen again," I told her.

"Well maybe he wasn't who he said he was. Maybe he wasn't a spiritual guide after all."

"Is that what he was supposed to be?"

"I don't know, but it does bother me that he seemed like he was going to be my friend, and then he just poof, disappears. I thought maybe it had something to do with the location of the compound back in the US, but even here, thousands of miles away, I still haven't heard from him. And this mission," I started.

"Don't say it," Lori cut in.

"I don't want to be banished again, especially when I just finally got you back."

That night when I slept, I had a dream of a black menace that attacked our planet. It was similar in shape and emptiness to that of a shadow creature, but this was no shadow. This was a completely different monster. It rose up from the core of the planet like a hand reaching out from hell itself. And this monster killed everything it touched. It slowly reached fingers around to the far corners of the globe.

And as fast as I flew, I just could not outrun it. It had consumed my family and friends, and my heart wept for them. It was a scourge like no other and was rapidly consuming all life of Earth. I tried to stop it. I did everything I could, exhausting every weapon in my angelic arsenal, but I had nothing for it. I threw everything I could at it, and it just laughed at me and continued its onslaught. I desperately tried to find Lori, but she was not where I had thought she would be. I panicked and flew around the globe like a madman. Then when I finally found her, the blackness was nearly upon her. I flew hard and fast, faster than I ever had before. I screamed for her to run, but the blackness absorbed the sound of my voice. It consumed everything, light, sound, life, and it was headed directly for my love and unborn child.

I screamed louder and flew like a bolt of lightning, but I was too late. The blackness had reached out to her and touched her, sucking the life from her body.

By the time I reached her, she was dead and our baby. I held her lifeless body tight against my own and fell on my knees in absolute misery. I sobbed wildly. I laid her body gently onto the ground and looked at her. Mere moments ago, she was full of life, of lives. She did not die alone. My child died with her, inside of her.

I looked up into the heavens and screamed so loud that every being on every world, in every dimension and every plain of existence felt my grief and sadness.

Then I woke up. It was just a dream. I was shaking, breathing heavily. I looked over at my sleeping beauty and remembered how lonely my life had been before her. I had always been one of those that could never seem to get it right, but so many things changed the day I met her. I pulled her tight against me and smelled her hair. I could no longer imagine life without her, and I would kill or die for her in an instant. I held the image of her empty body in my mind.

I had no choice. I couldn't go back to sleep, so I finally had to get out of bed and at least try to call Barnes. He was on the other side of the world, so it had to be near bedtime, since it was just before sunrise here where I was. Luckily for me, he answered.

"Hey, Mr. B," I started. Ugh, that was what Lori called him.

"I mean, hey Mister Barnes. I have a quick question for you." I didn't wait for him to give the okay, I just continued. This topic had just taken on an air of great importance.

"What happens when the lava that I'm going to allow up through the geothermal tunnel hits the reactor core those guys are building? Won't that cause an atomic blast, like a nuclear bomb?"

"A very astute observation," he returned, "but no, the reactor isn't running just yet. All of the simulations prove the same outcome. When the molten rock hits all that water in the facility, it will cool rapidly forming a sort of stopper to plug the hold you created. The entire complex will be filled with solid rock, rendering it completely useless when our mission is fulfilled. Our hope is that there will be no evidence that you had been there, and it will look like there was an issue with the design of the structure. The Chinese and Russian partnership will view this as an epic failure, and hopefully pull back some of the efforts. They will distance themselves from the Iranians and then we can move to our next target.

With this threat ended, our government will have little use for having quite so many troops stationed in that region and will be able to send a lot of our boys' home." He stopped and took a breath. I could tell he wanted to rant about the future plans of our alliance, but he caught himself.

"How are you and Stillwell getting along?"

"Oh perfect," I told him.

"That was a nice surprise."

"Well, I'm not going to beat around the bush here. This is a dangerous mission you will be going on. We can't create a test to see if your powers can protect you should you not be able to outrun the surge of magma that will shoot up through the hole you create. I know that neither of us plan for that to happen, but Winston assured me that it shouldn't be a problem. He said you have the ability to move almost faster than the human eye can comprehend when you put your mind to it." He sounded like a proud papa.

"Look we can do testing to see how much heat your shielding can protect you from, or how much force can be dropped on you before your energy is exasperated. But we don't have time for all of that now.

The situation that you are so worried about is nearing its final phase. The Uranium is being delivered to the facility as we speak. This mission will have to get started today or there will be that risk of failure, that atomic blast that you mentioned, and we sure don't want that. We're supposed to be helping our troops, bringing them home, not surrounding them in a nuclear inferno." He chuckled a little as he finished his last statement. His levity lightened my mood a bit.

"Okay," I told him. There was little chance of backing out of this situation now. I was going to go through with it, no matter what. It just made sense. I would be protecting my family and friends and their way of life, while at the same time giving Iran, Russia and China a big smack down.

"I'm on my jet right now," Barnes told me as I could hear him sip his Crown and Coke.

"I'm heading to Europe to rendezvous with Winston so that we may watch your progress together.

We're going to use the United States spy satellites in the area to watch you, make sure you don't get in any trouble." I could hear him puff on one of his expensive cigars.

"They use my software to power their systems and I, of course, have a back door for everything. I'd be exposing myself to a certain extent, but I think it would be worth it. I could commandeer control of the system, move the units, and watch you for twenty minutes or so. That should give you time enough to complete your mission. When the military got control of their bird back, they will have missed one of the greatest single-handed victories in history. The glory of it all, is that because the damage will be done so far underground, no civilians on our side will ever even know anything happened. The loss suffered by the other guys, however, will be substantial." He had it all planned done to the tee. I was going to be like Harrison Ford and Robert Shaw in Force 10 from Navarone. Just like them, I was going behind enemy lines to blow up the bad guy's property, only instead of a bridge, like in the movie; I was going after the enemy's secret laboratory. It was exciting, and for a brief moment the hairs on the back of my neck stood up.

"Thank you, sir," I told him. I honestly was thankful. He had given me everything I had ever wanted. I had the women of my dreams; we were going to have a family and I was going to be a pivotal player in the changing of the guard. I was actually going to have a say in the ways of the world. Barnes was quiet.

Perhaps he did not know what to say. Or maybe this was the exact situation he wanted. I didn't know, nor did I care. I was truly happy, and I had a purpose again.

"Well thank you too, Joseph. Funny," he started.

"Why do I feel like I'm gaining a new partner but losing my assistant?" he asked with an amused tone.

"She's been my right arm for five years, and now she's over there with you, and I'm here alone. How did that work out? Just kidding my boy. We both thought it would be a good reason to remember who and what you are fighting for. Besides, I want you to have something to want to go home to."

"Again, I want to thank you sir. I won't let you down," I told him, and I meant it. Really, what harm could it do to destroy a place that was a direct threat to my friends and family? I did not want them living through another Cuban Missile Crisis situation. I was going to use my powers to defend who and what I loved. They weren't going to have to live in fear, not if I could help it.

"I know you won't, boy. This is a simple operation. You go in, do your business, and get back out. The next mission might not be so easy," he said swallowing his dark brown drink.

"Oh yeah," I asked with a bit of enthusiasm, "What might that be? Are you gonna have me crush the Capital Building?"

"I love the way you think," he said.

"Winston will be in touch soon. He will have some important instructions and a timetable for you to follow. Be exact. Be precise. Be careful. I will be joining the two of you very soon, and then we will all experience the joys that India has to offer." I liked the sound of that. I hung up my little phone and prepared myself. It was almost my time to shine, I was getting that whole fight or flee feeling beginning to churn in my stomach. I couldn't believe this whole thing was really going to happen. I looked up at the sky and said a prayer that everything would work out just like Mr. Barnes had said. Then I went inside and crawled into bed with Lori. I slid up next to her and snuggled. I relished in the moment as long as I could and wished that it could have lasted forever.

FOURTEEN

I laid in bed next to Lori for about an hour after the conversation with Barnes, then Winston called. He asked me to head to the training facility to meet with him. When I got there, he took me upstairs and showed me the whole scenario on the computer display again. Being the owner of the world's largest software firm allowed for every computer terminal to be hooked up to a large flat screen display. It was both big and colorful and its detail was brilliant.

"You know the plan," he told me as we watched the display together.

"Here is your ticket to Bagdad, a new passport, and this," he said, handing me a small device with a control pad and LCD screen. "It will show you exactly where the target is. It's a GPS navigator. You press the number one here," and he pressed the number one key, "and it will take you straight into Iran and their secret base. Press number two and it will guide you right back here. It's that simple. The rest is up to you. You've practiced the drill, now make it happen." Then he got real close to me.

"We are all counting on you. Please be careful." It was a weird moment between Winston and me. I almost felt as if he cared about me and my safety.

"I will," I told him. I looked over the little device. It seemed easy enough to use.

"Won't I be tracked, if I flew directly back here?"

"Not if you stay well under the five-hundred-foot threshold the entire time. You should be able to clear that easy enough. Stay low and close to the ground until you reach your target. Remember that we will have temporary control of the United States satellites and no one else in the world will be expecting this attack. This base is hidden, so there are no other satellites trained on its location. We have also arranged for a momentary black out of the internet in that region, so that even if you are detected, there will be no way to broadcast anything to their allies. Should you have your photo taken by a surveillance camera, it will not matter because all of the data would soon be buried in an avalanche of molten rock." He seemed so sure of himself. I only wish that I had half of his confidence.

"Winston, why aren't you doing this? You have powers like me. Why didn't they send you in?" I asked him, hoping not to hurt his feelings. He lit a cigarette and proceeded to tell me that he was not nearly as powerful as me and that his hay days were long since over. These days, he had been relegated to trainer. His days of action and adventure were well behind him. There was a sadness in his voice, like he missed the good old days.

"You have so much more power than me, so much more potential. You have to understand," he continued, "you were a general. You were a great leader, hence your abilities are so much more defined and refined than mine." His tone was almost one of a deep admiration, which in itself was a strange thing to hear from this man. Until today, I thought of him as an arrogant fool that enjoyed hurting me.

"I can match you with the sword and whatnot, but only because you are limited by the transitional state you are in, but even in this form, you are fifty times as powerful as me." He smiled and stepped back folding his arms in front of him.

"You destroy the practice facility." He shook his head and chuckled slightly.

"That place was reinforced by what I call 'out-worldy forces', he held up two fingers on each hand, mimicking quotation marks.

"And you knocked the whole building off of it's foundation. Amazing," he finished with a long drag of his cigarette. Wow, I thought. I never knew that Winston even cared. This was quite a moment.

"This world is spinning out of control, and it appears that you have the ability to fix it." He took a drag and let it out.

"I'm happy that I could be of some help to you. Believe it or not, I am proud of you and happy to have been able to help you in this mission."

"Thank you, Winston. That means a lot." And it

did. It really did. He threw his cigarette butt into the ashtray and got back to business. He told me about the adrenaline rush that I would experience when I broke though the concrete ceiling on the facility and how easily I would be able to generate enough power to blast through the earth's crust. I listened to him, but I was still nervous, somewhat unsure of myself as well as the entire situation.

Then he reminded me of an old proverb. "For every act, there is a first time." Truer words could not be spoken, they did little to alleviate my angst.

"You will be fine. You have been trained for eons in your prior life. Remember that you were a general once. You commanded many troops into battle, and not only fought, but strategized, and implemented

that strategy on the fly. This should be a simple task for you," He lit another cigarette, took a drag and blew it out.

"Let yourself go, and you will see that is all comes naturally." The words had barley left his lips when a strange feeling fell upon me.

"Winston, did we meet before? I mean, long before I came to you and Barnes. Did we meet? Did we serve together in corps?"

Winston's eyes twitched. I never liked when I asked someone a question and their eye twitched. It meant that I had caught him off-guard somehow and he was presently cooking up a lie. The words that would come out of his mouth would most likely be a pile of crap or at least a very twisted version of the truth.

"I was once a member of the corps, but I never did as well as you. I acted up a little and was eventually sent here. I wasn't as lucky as you." Hmmm, that was an interesting answer. If he were on my team, I would have recognized him by name and face instantly.

"What did you do to get sent here?" I asked him.

"We are not discussing my transgressions today. We don't have time for that now. Your plane is leaving from the airport in two hours. It will land in Baghdad. You have to make your way to the southwest side of the city and activate your GPS unit. Stay under the five-hundred-foot mark so you won't be seen by radar and get there as fast as you can. We will know if you have been detected and alert you. It is important that you leave here and return here without being seen. If something happens and you cannot come directly home, you get back there and blend in with the crowd. We will find you." He lit up another cigarette and he smile through the smoke.

"When you get back, I will tell you everything, why I am here, how I came to work for this company.

Agreed?"

"Agreed," I said with a smile.

"Your GPS will bring you back to this place, but should you feel unsafe or too fatigued for the journey, then simply return to the airport. We have arranged a back-up transport home for you. Just go over to the ticket window of the airline that you are booked on currently and give them your driver's license.

When the counter person asks if you are flying to whatever city they say, you just smile and nod your head. They will essentially be telling you where you are going. We will clear a path for you to get back home without being noticed. This way will cover your trails and ours. We don't want anyone following you back to our facility here in India or knowing that we are involved in any of this. Our software company is doing great business here and it provides an excellent cover for all of our future Asian activities. This base has direct access to Russian and China, so we don't want to set off any bells or whistles. We're hard-wired in. They can't fart without us knowing about it. So be careful to follow all of your instructions." It all seemed so James Bond, Cloak and Dagger. How could I have gotten myself into this? Why were so many bells and whistles going off inside my head? There was something wrong about the whole situation, but I couldn't quite put my finger on it.

"Do you understand?" he asked me.

"This is not the time for your mind to wander. Get your head into the game and keep it there. You understand that there is no room for error here. I was not a fan of letting you get back together with that woman until this mission is over, but Mr. Barnes disagreed. He thought you needed to be reminded of why you were doing all of this."

"Relax Winston, he was right. I'm okay," I told him. "I'm ready. Will there be an immigration check point in Baghdad for me to go through?"

"Your paperwork has been set so it appears that you are a private consultant for the United States military. You will be streamlined right through. Don't worry about that. Do you have any questions?" I thought about it. It still didn't sit right with me, but I ignored that feeling. I would deal with that when all of this was done and over with.

"No, I'm good," I told him, though I actually had a million questions.

"Well good luck then, my boy. The helicopter will be here within the hour to take you to the airport. He will have a small package of clothes that you may carry so that you don't look suspicious. Just leave it anywhere. You won't need it. I will see you when you get back." He gave me a wicked sort of smile.

"Then we will turn it up a notch with your training." With that Winston extended his hand. I shook it and then he turned and walked away. Step it up a notch, I thought. How was that even possible? It was an intriguing thought. I looked at my ticket and then thumbed through my passport. It had my name and my picture, and there was a special mention of my military consulting job. It had enough stamps that it looked like I had been all over the world twice. I watched Winston walk over to a door, which he opened and went inside. It seemed that the only time I ever saw him was inside of a training facility.

His milky white skin would burn in the sunlight, I joked to myself. I secretly hoped he was going to his room for a shower. "Use some soap," I wanted to yell.

I went home and said good-bye to Lori, then waited for my car to take me to the helipad. When it pulled up, I wanted to laugh. It was a gaudy, bright painted taxicab, a far cry from the luxury vehicles I had been slowly getting used to. I climbed into the back seat where the small duffle bag sat. I dug through it.

There was nothing special, just some jeans and some shirts, and some toiletries and a pair of beat-up sneakers. The ride over to the helipad was uneventful.

As I flew over the destitute city, I marveled at the horrifically snarled traffic below. I was quite happy to be flying over instead of sitting in it. But in no time flat, I was on my plane, in the air, on a short trip to Iraq. I had never been a small, beat-up plane like this. It was rickety and a bit uncomfortable. I had to feel that it was designed for people a great deal shorter than me, but I made do.

The thing that bothered me the most was the smell. It wasn't a Winston-like smell, but rather a nasty stinky, sweaty, deep down disgusting odor that permeated the entire cabin. The plane landed smoothly, and I got off and glided right through the mess that was the customs and immigration desk.

There were soldiers everywhere, both American

and Middle Eastern. They all carried big guns, which made me feel a bit uncomfortable. I knew that in a millisecond, I could pull my shield out from the other dimension and protect myself with it and my electromagnetic force field. But that effort would show my hand and the mission would be exposed. I also knew that I could use my power to blast the entire building into rubble if I had gotten myself into a pickle, but again, I would be showing the world that I was here. I successfully navigated the crowded airport and walked toward the southwestern part of the city. Again, there were heavily armed soldiers everywhere. I just put my head down and walked. Every so often, I would smile and say hello to a passing Marine. It was kind of crazy to turn a street corner and see four or five heavily armed American soldiers walking toward me. It was unnerving, but I just smiled and went about my business. Every so often I was asked to produce my papers. These poor people, I thought. I could not imagine being an inhabitant of this area and having to jump through so many hoops. This city was rife with misery and drama. There were burned out, bombed out structures here and there, but the city still bustled. I walked past children that looked at me like I was a ghost. I had no military escort; nor did I have any sort of protection. I just kept my head down and walked. Every so often, I would see a man, or a group of men look at me and talk among themselves. Sometimes they would stare or start dialing their phones; sometimes they would hastily go inside their homes. I assumed that they were alerting others to my presence, but I didn't care. I wasn't nervous, nor did I pay attention to the people that surrounded me. In another life, in a different time, this kind of behavior might be a bit provocative, but not today, not now. I was not going to endanger my mission, but if some fool felt the need to try to accost me, well I would show him or her that they had chosen the wrong person. I had my mindset and I thought of nothing else. I just walked to the place that Winston had indicated to me on the map and hoped that no one was there that could disrupt things.

The air was hot and arid, and I started to sweat a bit, but nothing was going to deter me today, not the people, not the jets or helicopters that flew over my head every so often, nothing. I could see what appeared to be the edge of the city a couple of blocks away.

Instead of seeing more buildings lined up behind the ones I was passing, it looked like some open space.

I was feeling that wild excited churning in my stomach. Then a couple of guys stepped out in front of me.

I turned to see that there were also a couple of guys behind me as well. One of the men stepped up within about fifteen feet of me. He asked me something in a different language. I didn't know if it was Arabic, Iraqi, or what, but I completely understood him. It was like I had a translator inside my head. He mouthed the words in his native tongue, but my ears heard them in the language that I understood.

"What are you doing here, American?" he asked. I replied to him that I was just passing through, but I was unsure whether he understood me, as I did him. My words sounded like English, but since I could understand him, maybe he could understand me.

"You should not be here alone," he continued. I was in no mood for any crap. Barnes was going to get control of the satellites at any minute. I had to get to my target and accomplish my mission before anyone could see me. If I took longer than the allotted time, there was a good chance that I could be seen and then tracked. I had almost given up the idea of coming back to this place. I knew that I could easily get back to India without being seen. I knew that the adrenaline would be coursing through my body. It would be best for me to use that extra energy to quickly get home. If I came back to this place, that wound up, someone was going to get hurt.

"Step aside," I said and took a couple of steps forward. But the entire group each took a step in toward me. It was like an accordion folding inward around me.

"Please, step back. I don't want to hurt you," I told them, hoping, praying they understood.

"You don't want to hurt us? Look around you. You've already hurt us. You have destroyed out city, our economy, and our homes. We have lost children and are angry and I am going to ask you again. What are you doing here, American?" This man was obviously the leader of the group. He was almost right in my face.

When he reached behind himself, I did not hesitate. I threw out a move like I was going to strike him with the heel of my open palm right in the face. But instead of making contact, a blue bolt of energy jumped from my hand right into his face. He flew back about ten feet and landed in a heap on the ground. The rest of the men looked at each other and quickly backed away. They scrambled and it was like they couldn't clear a path fast enough for me. I walked right past them all. I didn't know if their leader, the big mouth, was dead or alive and at that point, I didn't care.

I finally reached the edge of the city and in front of me were bright, open blue skies and sand, palm trees and burnt-out vehicles. This was it. This was my moment to shine, and I set my mind to it. No longer would I question things or have any doubts. All of that could be saved for a later date. Right now, it was time to fix things. This would be the first step in a long line of projects set to bring this entire world back into the light. This mission would allow for the most of these troops to go home. There would be no need to watch over this wasteland of a region after this. I tossed the little duffle and unfurled my wings.

Then I looked down at my body and thought about the armor, the sword and the headgear and it was there. I was clad in the shiny and gold outfit, ready for whatever came my way. I took a bit of a running start and dove out into the air. I lowered my wicked looking faceplate and drew my sword. I held it out in front of me in an effort to break the wind and I thought of a song I had heard at the beginning of a few football and hocky games. It was Oh Fortuna by Carl Orff. It was both dramatic and exciting.

I left the smell of the burning oil and flesh far behind me. I flew hard and fast across the dry, smoky desert.

Television reports did not do this war justice. There were burned out buildings and dried out human remains rotting in the sun every here and there. There were remnants of tanks and Humvees scattered about, and every now and then, I could hear the sound of gunfire or an explosion off in the distance. The sun was creeping high over the horizon, and it was getting bright. I thought about the hoops and the angles I was to use so that I could generate enough speed, yet only allow myself a couple of seconds above that five-hundred-foot plateau. The sun was so nice and warm. I utilized long even pushes with my wings, stretching them out as far as I could. I had a long way to go and a lot to think about. This was it. If I was going to change the world, then this was going to be my shining moment. I had thought about it at length for some time now. There really was no other way. Barnes had been right about so many things.

He had showed me the way, and now I would be the one to set things right. No longer would this be a world of war, on the brink of darkness. I was going to fix all of that. This was the challenge that I had lobbied for so long for both as a human and as a warrior of light. This would prove my mettle once and for all. The sun felt so warm on my back and across my wingspan. I lapped it up. I could imagine what I would look like to an ordinary human, my helmet glistening, and my shield and sword aglow with a blue flame. I peeked at the ground, not so far below. Small fires dotted the distant landscape. In reality, they were burning oil wells, ignited by radicals. Their smog clogged the skies and people's lung. The dark clouds seemed to go all the way to the horizon. A lot of my friends and family had kids that were approaching the draft age.

There was little chance that the majority of them would be able to avoid the calling if it rang out. Some of those children had already told me that they were going to the wars when they reached the acceptable age. That sucked. There were just too many of our boys and girls being killed and just as many coming back missing limbs and pieces of their brain.

When put against that, what I was about to do was completely justified. If a few lives were lost on this day, then they will have given them for the greater good. For the first time in a very long time, my life had a meaning, a purpose. I had always known that I was meant for so much more and here it was. I was so stoked, but I had to keep my head about me. I knew what I had to do, but there was no way for me to practice such a stunt. I was not going to be a one trick pony, but I really didn't know if I was going to make it back alive. I didn't want to die, but if it meant a chance at possibly ending my punishment and saving the world, then I would have clearly and truly killed two birds with one stone. I was flying really fast now. It was a touch hard to breathe, but I managed. I took a couple of deep breaths and let them out slowly. I was cruising right along when I saw something out of the corner of my eye. I couldn't make out what it was, so I assumed the worst. It could well be a missile or some sort of defense mechanism. I decided that it was now time to make my attack and kick it up a notch. If this were some kind of device sent to stop me, then I had to get on it before it could reach me. I took a last moment to think about all of my friends and family. This was for them – all of them. And if I did not make it, then I will have died for a noble cause. I will have saved them all. I felt the tears welling up in my eyes. My GPS notified me that I was nearly upon my target. It was time for me to bend my back and make the long, tall loop. I beat my wings up and down as hard and as fast as I could. I arched my body and flapped my wings hard. Up, up into the heavens I flew. I felt no stress in my wings or chest. The thing that I had seen headed in my direction was now nowhere to be seen. I looked, but saw nothing, just the clouds and layers of atmosphere going by faster and faster. Whatever it was, I had successfully lost it. I reached the apex of my loop and started hard and fast toward the sandy desert below. I held my sword out in front of me, the blue flames dancing in the wind. I would cleave a path right through the fiery mantle, unleashing the full power of Mother Earth herself.

I was deep in the thought of my mission, flying like a rocket toward the sandy ground when something came up from behind me and hit me. I spun out of control and landed really hard on the desert floor. I then turned to see what had happened, what had hit me, and could barely believe my eyes.

"Bastion?" I asked with a mix of delight and disbelief.

"What are you doing here?" I lifted the faceplate back into my helmet so that I could look at him, and he could see my eyes. I had sand everywhere. He was out of breath and bloodied, possibly from our impact.

"I had," he managed. He gasped for air. "I had to stop you. You don't," he stammered, "you don't know what you are doing." I put my sleeve up over my hand and wiped the blood and strands of long blonde hair out of Bastion's face. It was so good to see him, but why now? He had blood coming from his mouth, nose, and ears.

"Are you okay? My God Bastion, what did you do?" His normally bright blue eyes were glazed over, the brilliance dulled. His breath was still long and deep, but now he was calming down.

"I am alive, but I will not be for long. I have come here against all orders to stop you and to send you home.

"Home?" We're going home, back to the corps, back to where we belong?" I was ecstatic now. It sounded almost too good to be true. Perhaps the thought of doing the deed, the idea of sacrifice was the answer to my test, my punishment. He sounded like he was here to take me back. He coughed up some blood and hacked for a couple more seconds. He was scaring me. I did not want to see my friend like this. He couldn't even speak for a moment due to the loss of breath and blood. Then, after a couple long seconds, he was breathing well enough to speak.

"Now we, you," he gasped. "By coming here, I have condemned myself. I will not be able to return. I will bravely face my punishment just as you have." He wiped the bit of blood from his lip onto his bare arm.

"It was so good to see you again General. It's been a long time." He smiled, then he winced, holding his ribs.

"I wish we would have had more time together."

We were both sitting on the hot sand, bracing ourselves up on our elbows so that we could look each other in the eye. My good friend, my brother, my comrade was dying. He had given his all to get to me, but his words were cryptic.

"What do you mean by that?" I asked. "I'm not going anywhere except straight down into the ground.

Right about there," I said pointing about twenty feet in front of us.

"Yeah, straight down into the darkness," he chided. "General, they tricked you. You are under some sort of spell." He coughed and sputtered out some more blood.

"What?" was all I could muster, as I thought about what he was saying. He must be mistaken.

"I am going to save this world, Bastion. I am going to save my friends and family."

"You are going to kill them all, Joseph." He almost gagged on the fluid that streamed from his lips as he spoke.

"You aren't going to save anyone. You are going to release a gas that will poison this world and hurl it into the darkness forever." He coughed and had to catch his breath again. He was really hurt bad.

"You have been bewitched into believing that you were doing good, but your plan will destroy this world." I looked at him.

He was wrong, "How could this be? If I am who everyone claims that I am, then how could I be tricked like this?" I thought about it hard. How could this be?

"No, Bastion, you are wrong." I felt so bad that he was hurt, but he was mistaken. He gasped for a breath and looked at me.

"You are already lost then" His eyes continued to look me over. "This is truly a sad day." I looked upon this angel of light. He was more than a friend, more than family. We had fought the good fight together for a good part of eternity. He was a great warrior. It was hard to see him all twisted about and hurt. I looked him over good, and the look in his eyes told me that he was not lying. He truly believed that I had been lost.

"Bastion, what are you talking about, old friend." He tried again to fill his lungs with air, but at great effort. He was not going to last much longer, and my heart started to ache for him. We, being the angel corps, were truly gifted, but occasionally one of us died. Those times were far and few in between, but it happened.

Bastion had given everything he had to reach me, and though I knew this, it was still very hard for me to believe that he was right. He gasped, and the blood flowed from his mouth. He stared at me with the strangest look. Then he reached up and grabbed the necklace I wore. When he pulled it from my neck, a part of it stayed in his hand and the rest of it fell into pieces of the sandy desert floor.

"What?" I started to ask, but I was taken back by the amount of craziness that rushed into my mind. My head was swimming. It was as if the floodgates of information had just been opened. I couldn't make heads or tails of any of it. There were colors and blood and wars and carnage. I was dizzy, spinning. I couldn't even hold myself up, and I fell over so that my left ear was in the sand. I could not catch my breath and anxiety started to overtake me. But then, in the middle of all that, I saw him screaming at me. I couldn't quite hear him, or move, but he was there as clear the nose on my face.

"Bloody hell," Chalmers yelled. He stopped yelling and waving his arms and looked hard at me.

"You can see me now, can't you? It took you long enough." I tried to take a breath, to catch myself. It was all too much. There were so many things running around in my head. It reminded me of when I first discovered who I was, back in the old woman's house in the desert of California. I kept my eyes and my mind on Chalmers. Bastion and I laid there on the ground, him bleeding, and me unable to move. I took a long deep breath and let it out. Winston had taught me to control the craziness, and I tried to invoke that technique now.

"What's happening?" I finally asked. "The necklace," Bastion muttered, but could not continue. He still held a piece of it in his hand.

"The bloody necklace. It shielded you somehow," Chalmers told me. "It blocked you from seeing and hearing me, and it kept you from telling right from wrong."

He looked down at Bastion. "This poor bloke broke all the rules to reach you, and now he will pay the ultimate price for trying to save you." I looked at the twisted angel next to me and pulled every bit of my strength for a big push to reach out to him. I got up right next to his body so that I could rest his head on me. I reached my arm around him so as to hug him and keep his windpipe open the best I could. Then this man that had been my friend for so long gasped and gurgled. He breathed his last breath. I felt so sad at that moment that words could not express. Tears streamed down my face and my hands trembled. This was my good friend and he died trying to save me. I pulled my body in close and hugged him. He was dead, and his body began to fade. I sobbed as I held his dead gaze until he shimmered in the golden light of the desert. Then he was gone.

He simply disappeared from my grasp. I looked at Chalmers for answers, but I could see he had none.

So, in a fit of anger and rage, I jumped up and grabbed him.

"Show me the truth." I demanded. "You show me why this had to happen!" In an instant, we were no longer in the middle of the hot desert, but in Lucious Barnes office. He was watching a monitor along with Winston and several other people. I did not recognize any of them. Then a voice seemed to echo throughout the room.

"Something has happened," it bellowed. Barnes turned from the image and looked at Winston, then behind him.

"Nothing has happened. Give him time." He seemed to be talking to no one, yet he was talking to someone or something. It was a strange feeling that I felt many times before, but this was different than all the other times when I moved between the different worlds. I barley loosened my grip on the old man when he grabbed ahold of my hand with his free one.

"Do not let go of me, boy. If you do, we will both be in great danger." I wanted to ask him what was going on, but he motioned for me to be quiet.

"Do not draw attention to us. We are not completely safe here." He looked around cautiously.

"We are in it now, but as long as we are here, then you may as well see that Bastion was right. You have been tricked." I was so angry, but I held his arm tightly and listened. At first, they all just stared at the blue sky that filled their monitor. No one said anything.

"We are waiting," the booming voice bellowed again.

"Please," Barnes pleaded nervously this time.

"Give us a couple of minutes. Our boy will do his job." He turned to Winston again.

"What is he waiting for?" he asked in an angry, but very quiet voice. Winston motioned that he didn't know and then said something to him in an audible whisper.

"I can assure you that everything is just fine. Please relax," Barnes spoke into the air.

"Relax?" the voice chided. "Relax?" it repeated with a sarcastic tone.

"We have a lot at stake here. We cannot

relax until this deed is done, and neither should you Lucious Barnes!"

"Please, please," Barnes begged. "Just give us a few more minutes."

"Whom is he speaking to?" I asked Chalmers, while I looked around for a body to connect to the voice.

"No one we want to meet. Come on, we cannot get caught here," he said, while he gestured with his head. And in an instant, we were back under that same bright blue sky.

"You can let go of me now."

"What is going on? Where are we? I asked as I wiped the sweat from my palm. I had gotten a bit nervous and had been holding him pretty tightly.

"They are waiting for you to complete your mission," he said as he brushed himself off. He gave me a dirty look when he saw the wet spot on his sleeve where I had hold of him.

"Who exactly are they and what was that all about?" I demanded. Chalmers straightened his glasses and smiled at me.

"There are some dark forces waiting for you to complete your mission here, son."

I thought about that voice, and Barnes. I thought about what Bastion had told me and I thought about Lori. She had given me that necklace the first week I moved to the compound. Had she tricked me? Was she a part of this? Had Barnes, her and Winston all conspired to fool me into doing something that would destroy the entire world? "Why?" was all that would come out of my mouth. My mind was reeling, spinning.

"For the same reasons that our friend Bastion had mentioned. They want this planet, and they want you." He continued to straighten out his tunic.

"And do me a favor, don't ever touch me again. You could get us both killed...or worse." My mind drifted between Lori and Bastion and Barnes.

"Believe you, me, son, your boy Bastion really saved you today. That necklace nearly did us in. I tried and tried to get your attention, but eventually I had to sit back and just watch." He bent down and picked up a piece of the necklace that now lay scattered across the sands.

"I thought I had found an opening to get your attention," he started.

"When Winston hypnotized me in the beginning of each lesson," I cut in.

"Exactly, I knew that you saw me. I just didn't know of any other moment to try to reach you. They played you so well. You were completely isolated."

"And I thought that you had abandoned me," I told him solemnly.

"Yes, I heard you say that time and time again. I wanted to tell you what was happening from the very beginning, but I couldn't. That necklace shut you off completely. Having the girl deliver it to you was a genius move on Barnes's part." He looked at me, knowing how well I had been played.

"Do you remember when Winston nearly tore it from your neck? That was all a part of the game. It made you want to wear it, to protect it even more, because it was not only a gift from your girlfriend, but on that day, it was a trophy." I couldn't believe what I was hearing. The last two or three months of my life had been a complete and total lie.

"What about Lori? Is she one of them?" I asked, not sure that I really wanted to know the answer.

"I cannot say," he started, but I cut him off.

"Because you do not want to or because you are not obliged to?" I asked with a sour tone. I was so disgusted by the whole situation now. It sickened my stomach. All of my new friends, my mentor, and my lover had all betrayed me.

"I cannot say because I do not know," he finished without getting ruffled. "I am not omnipotent. I did know that this was going to happen. I did not know that Barnes was an agent of darkness, but rest assured, he will now be dealt with accordingly." He looked around.

"We should get out of here," he told me, and in a moment, we were far, far away from the desert and the war. We were on a warm beach. The beautiful blue ocean was pounding on the soft white sand just a few yards away.

"This is better," he said with a smile. He straightened his sunglasses and ran his left hand through his hair.

"I have seen Bastion in action on more than a

few occasions, and I have to say that he really outdid himself today. I am both surprised and quite proud of him. He was a good friend. This Lori person though, I am still unsure about."

There had been so much going on that I had almost forgot about my friend. I remembered some of the battles that we had fought together. We were as thick as thieves, he and I. We fought the good fight and we bled together on the fields of battle from one end of creation to the other, and I openly wept for him. I actually sobbed very hard for a few moments right there on the beach. This was tough. Chalmers looked at me and couldn't help but feel for me. He knew that I meant well and knew that I was naïve about such matters. These were pros that had done this sort of thing for eons. Their entire job was to promote war and hatred and push a world as close to the brink as possible.

They were like spies that crept in and destroyed a world covertly. He looked at me as he did so many times before and for the first time in all that time, felt pity for me.

'Take hold of my cane," Chalmers offered. He put the tip right to my face. I didn't even think, I just reached up and grabbed hold of it. Instantly I felt that strange sucking, pulling feeling that I had started to become used to. You just got left hanging, and in this case, quite disoriented. You would be in one place one instant, and in another the next. Instantly, we were inside a giant room. Its ceilings had to be at least twenty-five or thirty feet above. The walls had been carved out of some reddish yellow and orange rock and fortified with steel beams and archways. There was a cluster of some enormous pipes running from one end of the room over a small metal abutment, where they disappeared. I walked over and peered over the small barrier to see that the pipes turned down at a sweeping ninety-degree angle and ran down deep into the earth. I knew what this was. This was the geothermal tunnel that I was to blow the bottom out of. It must have run a mile or two into the earth crust. I was inside an Iranian base. The tunnel was similar to what I had expected, but darker and more foreboding now that I was looking at it. The hole was about forty feet in diameter, and it was ringed by a metal lip that was tapered from floor level up about four inches at a forty-five-degree angle. It was about a foot wide, and I figured it was there to ensure that nothing rolled across the concrete floor of the chamber and fell into the abyss. There were four pipes running down into the hole, each about five or six feet in width. They were lined up in a manner around the hole as to allow a fairly good-size channel for me to fly down, and then back up through. I put my hand on the plastic pipe and could feel the cold water surging through it. Then I heard voices. There was someone not twenty feet behind me. I turned and saw Lucious Barnes looking right at me.

"How are things going?" he asked. I was shocked.

I didn't know what to say. I just stood there with my mouth hanging open. Why was he here? How could he be here, I thought.

"Are you on schedule?" he asked me. Again, I just stood there. Then someone walked out from behind him. He was Asian and he was dressed in a green military looking jumpsuit. He spoke and I figured he was speaking in Chinese or Japanese. The funny thing was, I understood him just like I did the guy in Baghdad. I could hear that the words were in a different language, but my brain seemed to be able to interpret them.

"This project is on schedule. We are installing the Uranium that you will bring us tomorrow and will begin nuclear testing in the beginning of August," the smaller Asian fellow told him. What did he just say, I thought? I could not move. I was standing right there in plain sight. Barnes finally stopped staring at me and turned to face the man.

"Excellent," he said as he tapped some commands into the small computer, he carried with him.

"I expect that this should give you the edge that you need to get things in order." The smaller man laughed.

"I would expect so," he said as the two turned and left the room. They had to see me, I thought. They had to. But they acted like I wasn't even there. They had a conversation right in front of me. I had to think about what I had just seen and heard. They had talked about testing the reactor at the beginning of August. It was now the middle of September. That had to mean that Chalmers had sent me into the past. That would also mean that Barnes had lied about the schedule for the Iranians nuclear testing.

I wanted to run after him, but I could not move. I was slipping again, being pulled out of place, sliding into another. It was such a weird feeling, both really good and really bad. I fully expected to appear back on the sandy desert next to Chalmers, but that didn't happen. I slide into Barnes' office. I was there, but not truly there. He stood and looked at the flat screen in his office. He was alone, but not alone. There was another presence there that seemed very familiar. The display went into motion. It was a similar graphic to the one I had seen there a few days earlier. It showed the world, then zoomed in on the Middle East, and then to Iran and to a spot in the desert. It showed the hidden base, then it moved to a slide angle.

Then a projectile appeared on the screen that flew horizontal to the sand, then looped up and blasted down through the sand. Obviously that projectile would be me. It or I flew down into the tunnel, fired off a blast of energy into the crust at its bottom and raced the red magma back up into the base, but the scenario was different. In this one, the magma filled the base and smothered the nuclear reactor and destroyed the water tanks and plant. Then the base exploded in a fury that filled the screen. A huge mushroom cloud leapt up into the sky and the entire region exploded.

"You see," he said, "the nuclear blast is five miles wide and it ignites the oil fields all the way to Bagdad and beyond."

The display showed the magma erupting three miles high into the sky.

"The end results are that most of the Iraqis and Iranians will be destroyed in the initial explosion, the rest will be buried in atomic ash. The resulting volcano will have enough fuel to burn for twenty years."

The display zoomed out to show the entire region.

"Most of that area there," Barnes said, pointing to the Middle East, "will be incinerated instantly. The radioactive cloud of ash and dust will then be spread to the far corners of the globe." A huge black cloud of smoke formed over the whole region and began to grow and move. It drifted across the Arabian Sea and then completely engulfed India.

"Lori!" I wanted to yell out, but I refrained. I had to see the plan through, find out whom he was talking to.

"It appears to be a good plan," a voice told him from the shadows.

"It is the one we plan to implement. The boy is already being trained. I don't think I will have any problems convincing him to do it. The topper is that I will place his girlfriend, Stillwell, right in the line of fire. We will pull the plug on the internet and the satellites surrounding the region so that no one sees what has happened until it is too late. And when the radioactive cloud covers the base in India, no one will survive. With one fail swoop we will cut this world's population in half. Hatred and misery will permeate the planet and this place will be ripe for the picking."

"Are you sure it will work?" the voice asked. I looked into the shadows to try to see who was speaking but could not see no one.

"Of course," Barnes said with confidence.

"Have some faith in me."

"We have shown you considerable faith. We have helped you build an empire and how shown you the way to get into every single computer on this planet, and we helped you get the internet started to further your cause. Please do not insult us by asking for more faith. It is time for you to pay some dividends on our investments." The voice was none too happy with Barnes, and it was evident in its tone. I searched among the shadows for a person or a face, then my heart jumped up into my throat as I realized that there was no person to be found. The voice was coming from the shadow itself. Then I recognized the voice. It sounded like the same shadow creature that I had seen when I grabbed hold of Chalmers out in the desert. I looked back at the image of the black cloud on the screen that spread from the Middle East all the way to the Eastern shores of China, covering Japan and moving toward the United States. The volcano continued to throw rock, magma and burnt oil into the skies. It loomed large on the screen. It was quite visual. I felt the pull on my stomach, and through my legs. I was dizzy, disoriented, drained.

And then I was back again in the sea of sand with Chalmers. We were standing on the spot where Bastion had died. Below was the new functioning nuclear reactor. I felt as though I had just had the wind knocked out of me. I was sprawled out on the sand with a buzzy, dizzy feeling in my head. I felt like I was going to puke. The image of the radioactive cloud falling on my new home in India filled my mind. And I cried in front of Chalmers as I saw her, in my mind's eye, being killed by the thing that I created, her and the unborn baby. I began to shake as I sobbed. I couldn't imagine that I had been played like this, that I was on the brink of killing a billion people. I wept for Bastion and for the angels that were dying all over the universe because of my transgressions. I thought of how I was now trapped in this game. There would be no place for me to hide myself and my family. No matter where I went, they would find me.

The door of the cage had closed on me some time ago. I just didn't know it.

"Once she was dead, you would have blamed yourself. They would have convinced you that you used too much power or that you somehow did something wrong, and that her death was on your hands. You would have no one to turn to. No one would or could believe you. They would have had you in the palm of their hand, and you would have truly been lost," Chalmers told me.

"What do I do? Where can I hide?" I asked. I was starting to freak. I could feel it brewing down inside me. I was losing my mind. I knew there was no place on this world that I would be able to hide from them, not now. Again, I had let my arrogance and lack of insight undo me. I had a dream of saving my friends and family and fixing everything, just like I had once dreamed of pushing back the darkness on a more grandiose scale. I still had not learned my lesson. My heart was filling with toxic mixture of emotions. I gasped for air. I was losing it.

"I can't," I started. "I can't do it. I can't take it anymore help me," I begged.

"I don't want this. I can't." I was stammering, mumbling. "It's too much" I screamed out. I was panicking now. I couldn't catch my breath. My chest was tight, and I thought that I was having a heart attack or a stroke.

"I don't want this! I can't be here! I can't!" Chalmers looked at me, then up to the heavens.

"Get hold of yourself boy. Snap out of it!" he said. And then he slapped me real hard across the face.

Kimi slapped me hard on the face again.

"Joey, wake up Wake up." I opened my eyes but did not see Chalmers. I did not see the sea of golden-brown sand that had just surrounded me either. My heart still raced, and my mind was filled with the agonies of the mess that I had created. But I was in a different place. I had to look around, catch my bearings. I took a deep breath and let it out. Then I rubbed my eyes. The bright sun was no longer shining down upon me. Instead, I was in a room, a familiar room. I looked around, still disoriented.

"Oh man Joey, are you alright?" Kimi asked. She had a worried look in her big brown eyes.

"Where am I? What happened?" I asked as I leaned up a bit, putting my weight on my forearms. I looked around the room at my friends' faces and the nicely decorated red room.

"Dude, are you okay?" Mark asked me. I didn't know how to answer. He reached down and put his hand out to help me up. I looked around and saw that I was back in the old woman's house in the desert. How could this be, I wondered. I scanned the entire scene around wildly. I looked for Chalmers, for my wings, but neither was there. I was as I was before all of this happened.

"She's dead," Karen said, looking over the old women. She was in her chair, arms stretched out across the table to the place where I had been seated. Her head was down on the table, and she made no movement.

"What?!? Are you sure?" Kimi asked.

"I'm sure. She's dead as a rock," Karen told her.

"Oh wow." The words just seemed to roll out of Kimi's lips. Then she looked back at me.

"What the heck just happened?" she was looking to me for an answer, but I didn't have a clue.

"I don't know, you tell me. I'm not really sure exactly where I am, really," I told her.

"You're here with us in El Centro," she told me.

"Remember? We came to get hypnotized. That poor old lady started to put you in a trance, and then she just died. She did a face-plant right there on the table." I shook the cobwebs out of my head and looked around. I was groggy, but coherent. I slowly realized where I was. It was like waking from a dream.

"How long was I out?" I asked.

"Maybe a couple of seconds," Mark told me.

I felt like I had a hangover.

"My head is pounding." I was groggy, disoriented, and for some reason, my body ached like I had just been somewhere else.

"Did anything happen? Did I say anything?"

"No, Joey, but that old lady died holding your hands," Kimi said with a tone that showed that she was weirded out by what had just happened. I looked at the women and felt absolutely horrible.

But at the same time, my head seemed like it was spinning, and my heart ached like I had just lost someone very close to me. This seemed quite odd to me, as I did not know the women that now lay across the table, dead.

"Are you sure I didn't say anything, cause I feel like I was somewhere else. I mean, whatever she did to me; I feel like it worked." I did not want to detract from the fact that there was a dead woman right in front of me, but I just felt so strange. It was like I had just woke up from a crazy dream, but I just couldn't remember any of the details.

"No, nothing," Karen said as she dialed 911. My back felt strange, and my head hurt. I didn't want to piss anyone off or act disrespectful.

"Are you sure you're, okay?" Kimi asked me, rubbing my forehead.

"Yeah, just feeling a little bit off," I told her. Man was I feeling strange. I felt like I was forgetting something, and though it was on the tip of my brain, I just couldn't grasp it. It was a tad bit frustrating.

FIFTEEN

A fire truck, an ambulance and a police car all showed up at the house. The police officer asked us a couple of questions, which we all answered truthfully. He then thanked us, wrote some notes in his pad and left. There was no reason for him to believe any foul play had taken place there.

The EMT had verified that he thought the woman had died from a heart attack, so there was little to worry about. It was just sad to see her being wheeled out with the sheet over her face. Karen and Mark and I watched the squad guys pick up the cart and load her into the truck while Kimi got the personal guided tour of the workings of a fire truck from a good looking, muscular fireman.

Soon enough though we were all alone, standing in the driveway of the woman's home. She had kept the place up very nicely over the years, which made us all realize how sad this day was.

"Now that was weird," Karen said.

"Tell me about it," Kimi replied. Then she looked at me.

"Oh Joey, I can't believe that lady died holding your hands." She shook as though she were shaking something off her back.

"Ha, if only she knew," Chalmers said out loud, though no one would hear him. He rested both hands on his cane and watched us as we got into the car for the long ride home through the desert.

"We narrowly escaped disaster there, didn't we boy?"

I was in no condition to drive, so Mark drove, and I volunteered for the backseat so that Karen could sit next to her husband. I reached into my pocket and pulled out a little bag of pot and set a magazine on my lap as to roll a joint. But the movement stressed my back a little bit. I asked Kimi to give me a rub while I twisted one. She obliged.

"Oooo, you have a big knot back here," she said as she rubbed and kneaded my back muscles. It felt great. I finished rolling and she finished rubbing. I moved my shoulders forward and then back, forward and then back.

"Feels better," I told her, but it still felt strange, like something had hit me there or maybe that's where I landed when I fell off my chair. I gave Kimi the joint and the lighter and let her get it fired up. She took a long drag and passed it forward to Karen. It went to Mark and then to me. I took in a long hit and let it out slowly as we made our approach to the highway. Then it hit me.

"Do you know that feeling that you get like

something big is missing? Like when you come home, down the same street every day and see the same stuff. Then one day, one of your neighbors cut down a big tree out of his front yard. You drive home that day and realize something is different, but you just can't put your finger on it. Then you realize the tree is gone later that day or the next. Well, I'm at that point right now, when I know something is different but can't put my finger on it. It's weird and it's driving me nutty," I told them. Kimi took a big hit.

"Well, maybe you will remember later, and we can talk about it over a drink," she said with all seriousness. Then her look broadened into a smile.

"Come on Joey, snap out of it. You'll figure it out. Just relax and stop thinking about it and when you are least expecting it, all of the answers will come to you."

"I agree," Karen said with a smile.

"Oh, here take this," Mark said, handing the joint to me. He had been listening to the radio quietly as to allow us all to talk, but something caught his attention. He leaned over and turned up the volume.

"...Again, the world's richest man is dead. This is just confirmed. The private jet of the owner and creator of the Critterware operating system, Mr. Lucious Barnes has crashed in the mountains of Washington.

He and his pilot are both confirmed dead, missing and presumed dead is a Mr. Winston and a Miss Lori Stillwell. I repeat Lucious Barnes, and the pilot of his jet are both dead and two of his assistances are unaccounted for and also presumed dead. We will keep you updated as more information comes in"

"Lori!" I thought to myself. But that was an odd thought to have. I didn't know her. Weird that I would feel that way. My stomach even churned a bit. Why would I get like this over someone I never met?

"Wow," Kimi said. "I can't believe it. That's crazy."

"How bout it," Karen added. "Imagine having all of that money and fame and then getting killed in the prime of your life. That sucks."

"Yeah. He was good looking and rich too. What a shame," Kimi commented with a bit of a somber tone.

We all agreed that it was a tragedy, but I was the only one that really felt bad about it. So, I just kept my pie-hole shut. I already felt like an invalid, and I didn't want them to think I was throwing myself a pity party. But something still ate at me. Man, it was frustrating. Kimi could see that I was still feeling troubled, so she gave me a head massage. It felt nice. I was finally beginning to relax a little.

Chalmers stood in the sand. There were a couple of brightly colored flowers near his feet. He watched us drive west through the desert and smiled a big, broad smile. I would not know, could not know, how close we had come to complete and total failure. The world had avoided a long painful death at the hands of the radioactive dust clouds, and I had kept myself out of the darkness for at least another day.

He thought of Bastion and the sacrifice he had made to save his friend. He would put all of that on his report, along with a recommendation for an accommodation for him. It would show bad form to punish someone for sacrificing his own life to save a friend's eternal soul. But his was not the final judgement.

He could only recommend. After all, he was just a Watcher. It was his job to watch things and report back. That was it, nothing more. And though he had overstepped his bounds as of late, he hoped that he would not be judged too harshly. He liked his job. He liked me.

And just like Bastion, he did what he had to do to keep my butt out of the sling. He stood there in the warm desert and watched our car drive out of sight. A calamity had been avoided, an agent of darkness had been exposed and dealt with, and a world had been saved.

"This was a good day," he thought as he took a long deep breath. Then he was gone, but he would never truly be gone. He would always be there. He would always be watching me. Because that was his job. He was a Watcher.

The End

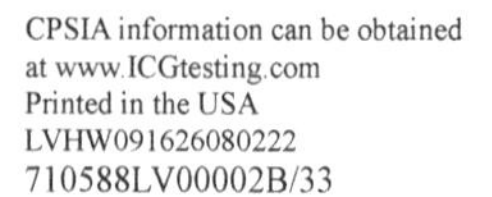
CPSIA information can be obtained
at www.ICGtesting.com
Printed in the USA
LVHW091626080222
710588LV00002B/33

9 781478 778523